ROBAK'S WITCH

ROBAK'S WITCH

Joe L. Hensley

ST. MARTIN'S PRESS
NEW YORK

Design by Nancy Resnick

Library of Congress Cataloging-in-Publication Data

Hensley, Joe L.
    Robak's witch : a Dan Robak mystery / Joe L. Hensley.
       p. cm.
    ISBN 0-312-15642-1
    I. Title.
    PS3558.E55R686 1997
    813'.54—dc21   97-7011
                                             CIP

First Edition: July 1997

10 9 8 7 6 5 4 3 2

For Earl and Carla,
who loaned me Char for a lifetime

There are no cities in Indiana named Bington or Madisonville.

There is a great Bloomington where I was born and went to school.

There is a beautiful Madison where I have been allowed to live and work.

And there are a dozen other Ohio River towns that I have learned to love.

ROBAK'S WITCH

ONE

"We teach our believers all government is bad unless that government is controlled by us."
—Herbert Techni, *Rules for Aryan Citizens,* p. 42

AT TIMES I felt okay.

On this late-summer morning, I awoke and had only occasional pain as I worked out in easy prescribed exercises, twist the neck right, then left, raise the knees, breathe deep. My friend, Dr. Hugo S. Buckner, had told me when he released me from the hospital (where, it was said, I'd tried hard to die) that gunshot wounds in the belly sometimes take a long time to heal.

"You watch yourself," he'd ordered formally. "You be damn careful."

I had watched it. I had been damn careful. It had been six bad months.

Breakfast was black decaf and dry toast at my tiny apartment's kitchen table. I then tried a little oatmeal, a third of a packet, with a smidge of sugar substitute. No orange juice because it burned my insides. No milk because I could no longer tolerate lactose.

1

The breakfast rode well during the fifty-minute drive to Madisonville. The highway had only sparse traffic. To make up for it, there were lots of falling leaves that slickened the pavement, plus many deer. Twice I slowed when I spotted white-tailed deer, first an antlered young buck, then a doe and a fragile fawn. The last four winters had been warm, perhaps from the increasing greenhouse effect. In a weekly feature column, the Bington newspaper estimated that there were likely as many deer now as there had been back in Northwest Territory days. The deer were beautiful, dumb, destructive to crops, and dangerous to travelers, but they'd survived.

I knew Kevin Smalley's Madisonville office address had changed. Two years before, I'd tried a two-week-long personal injury case venued to Madisonville. Smalley had been local counsel in the jury trial and we'd won a substantial verdict. Back then he'd occupied cold, uncomfortable, high-ceilinged offices on the second floor of a decaying building near the courthouse. Now I found his office several blocks removed from courthouse action in a new brick building—Smalley's own.

I was early. I parked and sat for a time, lost in self-pity. I was remembering how it had been when I was last in Madisonville and comparing that time with today. Then, I'd had a wife and son. Now, they'd fled to Chicago and taken up residence with Jo's stunning and, in my opinion, simple-minded sister. Jo had a dissolution of marriage pending against me in Bington, and the waiting period had passed. She'd been resistant to all reasoning so far. She'd filed her action during my hospitalization, then come back to visit only a few times thereafter; a wave, then a word or two when I was no longer in danger.

I'd lost wife number one a long time ago. Now it looked as if I would soon lose wife number two.

One can't change things by wishes. Jo had never liked my legal business or the way I conducted it. Now, when my legal life was about to change radically, she had no trust left for my ways or my explanations of those ways. I was, in her thinking, only going to change the locale from where I viewed crimes and criminals. Bad people would still be after me because trials and sentences were much of what a circuit judge did. Outlaws would still hate and plot against me because I'd be the one who'd send them on to prison. And, mostly, I'd still be a workaholic with not enough time for her or for Joe, our ten-year-old son.

Before Jo left for Chicago, she'd imagined me on the bench: "I know you, Don. You'd question everything!"

It did no good to point out that other lawyers would do the questioning and oral combat. It also did no good to state that I would have more free time because the courthouse opened at eight in the A.M., closed at five in the P.M., and took advantage of every holiday known to man.

Ah, well.

At least I didn't think there was another man for Jo. Yet.

From my parking spot, I could see downhill to the sunny Ohio River, the same river that ran past my town of Bington. Here, in Madisonville, a smaller city of nine thousand or so, piles of flood-water driftwood lay high on the riverbank. I remembered that in Bington you could also see driftwood piled along the river.

The two towns were deadly rivals. Bington High School had special cheers for Madisonville, and last year M-ville officials had bitterly claimed—in a silly and mindless lawsuit, soon dismissed—that Bington had blatantly copied and put to use Madisonville's high-priced historic ordinances. M-ville had also never approved of Bington's having the state university located therein, and Bington was still stiff-necked about M-ville's having a branch of that uni-

3

versity now offering classes at night in an old building downtown.

It had been a rainy spring and a constantly hot summer. My Indiana world, according to some, was now part of a new semitropical zone caused by the decay of the ozone layer. There'd been an unusual end-of-August flood. Now the trees were heavy with red and yellow leaves as summer died late. Rabbits built warrens in residential front yards. Squirrels chattered and played crazy tag in the trees. Maybe each hoped to be the dominant species when man was erased.

I was on the side of the squirrels, but I had nothing personal against the rabbits except that, like man, they multiplied too quickly.

We Bingtonites like to smile superiorly and say we use the Ohio River's water before it gets to Madisonville. That jibe only means the water's not as foul in my town as it is at M-ville. In midsummer, Ohio River water had carried something hot called Bingtonitis: a high fever that appeared and disappeared, aches and pains, loss of weight and energy; it lasted weeks, sometimes recurring, resistant to all antibiotics. The river water was treacherous even when pumped out of deep wells. Eight Bington citizens had died. The scientists at the university were still puzzling over why. Doc Buckner informed me I was lucky not to have contracted it.

"If you had," he'd pointed out jocularly, "you'd likely have been stoking the big fire down under and trying to hold a decent chair for me." He liked that idea. "Yeah, reserving my chair."

Now, in late September, the Ohio was a boater's river, finally at pool, but, for God's sake, don't-eat-the-fish.

I nodded at my own reflection in the mirror and put on a smile.

4

Stop feeling sorry for yourself at the end of summer, Robak.

I partially echoed aloud: "Stop feeling sorry for yourself, Robak."

I climbed out of my smooth, aging LTD and walked to Smalley's building. His outside brass nameplate bore heavy scratches. Someone had tried hard to make his metal name read "Smelly."

The streets were heat deserted, although I'd seen clusters of people gathered under trees in the courthouse yard when I'd driven past.

My newspaper and the Louisville *Courier-Journal* had reported that Smalley was defending a locally unpopular woman who was accused of poisoning a niece and a nephew with nicotine. I'd also read recently that someone had attempted to start a fire at the jail where the woman was detained, willing to burn all the jailees in an attempt to incinerate defendant Bertha Jones. That information came from an irate anonymous letter published in area newspapers, allegedly written by that matchless someone, boldly admitting the arson.

I knew also, from what Smalley had told me on the phone and from what I'd read in the newspapers, that Smalley's client had death penalty problems. That was the main reason I'd come. I was "death penalty qualified." I had tried death penalty cases before. Smalley had not. He'd called me for help.

A second reason, making it easy to help, was that it was now certain that, if I lived, I'd become the new circuit court judge of Mojeff county on January 1. No one had sought election against me for judge, primary or fall. Now it was too late for any opponent to file. I'd filed the day I got out of the hospital and was therefore, before November's balloting, an "electee."

Judge Harner was still recovering from his head wound and it was whispered he'd never again be "right." Pro tem judges sat for him and things had been moving at dead slow speed in Mojeff County.

Jo had questioned me about occupying Harner's "bloody bench."

"Do you really want to be circuit judge after what happened to both Harner and you?" she'd asked. "With lots more crazies around?"

"Why not?"

"Judge Harner got shot by the same man who shot you. I've heard Harner's a vegetable. And you almost died."

"But I didn't die. And nothing's positive about Harner yet."

Had Harner been able to file for circuit judge I wouldn't have filed. He'd been good at the judge business. I wasn't sure how I'd be. I planned to stop by Harner's house, come the weekend, to check on how he was doing.

Our main marital problem might be that Jo was worn out from the years she'd spent worrying about me. She'd said so each time we'd talked since our separation. My wounding (and therefore my death) had been something she'd always expected. The only surprise to her was that my wounding had come in a contested civil matter instead of a criminal case. She'd filed her dissolution with a Bington lawyer who now kept apologizing to me for accepting her case, louder about it now that he was certain I'd be taking the bench, likely worried I'd hold a grudge against him.

In truth I bore the lawyer no malice. An attorney must eat and pay office and family expenses. He (or she) must subscribe to the reporter systems and endless advance sheets to seek holes in laws now grown so complicated that many times they fully embrace silliness.

Jo had taken our ten-year-old son, Joe, along to Chicago. He was now, she explained, attending a private academy recommended by her three-times-divorced sister. And Joe was *safe*.

I was to see Jo this coming weekend. She and I would talk more about visitation and support. I would also spend some time with Joe.

My law partners no longer needed me. If I stubbornly sat in our Bington offices until becoming judge, everything the firm did in those interim months would be suspect on January 1. I'd have to recuse myself from all. We therefore had parted company amiably. They'd bought me out. Not much money, but enough for eating and paying child and wife support. Jo had inherited money and done well with it, but I'd still insisted on paying her reasonable support.

Inside Smalley's air-conditioned office, a late-sixtyish woman sat at her typer-computer and watched me enter.

"You're Robak," she said, smiling through yellowing false teeth. "I remember you from before."

"And I remember you," I answered heartily. I recalled she was a woman who enjoyed her own ill health. "You're Elaine. And how are you?"

"So-so," she said, low voiced. "Arthritis miseries all this past summer and now, with the leaves only part down, fall allergies and heat have got me itchy." She waited for a moment. "He's in the library. I'll tell him you're here. He's been waitin' for you." Her voice had the accents of the region, a river twang in which creeks became cricks but green remained green.

She vanished and I waited.

In a few moments Kevin Smalley appeared. He smiled and examined me critically. It had been a while since I'd last seen him, but he looked about the same. He was a slim, strong man who dressed well. He seemed addicted to muted striped ties and white button-down shirts with French cuffs. He wore a dark blue suit. Neat.

On his left lapel was a small medal, a replica of a Silver Star. It reminded me of an old story told by us enlisted men about military medals. If you saved a general's ass you got the Medal of Honor, a colonel's brought the DSC, and so on. The final line was that if you saved a private's ass, you got your own ass court-martialed. I no longer wore any lapel pin, but I had nothing against someone who did.

He shook my hand carefully. "You've lost a lot of weight. Are you well?"

I remembered Elaine's reply. She was out of earshot. I said, "So-so."

He picked up the small joke and smiled. I could never be sure whether he was laughing with me or at me. He was brighter than I was, and I was willing for it to be that way because I liked him a lot.

"Good old Robak," he said in a mildly sarcastic voice. "You don't change in the head even when you don't look well in the body. Come back to my office. We can sit and talk more easily there."

I followed him back. The office building seemed large for one lawyer. I sat in the soft chair in front of his desk and stretched out my legs.

"You're going to be the judge over there come the first of the year?" he asked.

"Yes."

"Can I expect favors?"

"No, but I'll be courteous when I refuse them."

He smiled, expecting such an answer. "I read some stuff or heard some stuff about you. I guess it was the *Courier-Journal*. They ran a story about someone shooting you in court. Tell me about it."

"Why not? It seemed a routine dissolution. The defendant belonged to one of those legal action groups through a militant country church. There are several Bington-area churches that don't like laws, public schools, or taxes. The biggest one even has its own militia. The wife filed her dissolution through me, and I got her temporary custody of the two kids. Then she refused to arbitrate things with her husband through church arbitrators. I didn't know much about this because she talked to him privately and vice versa. I set the case for trial when she asked me to set it. At the final hearing, he started blasting away with a long-barreled revolver. He shot Judge Harner first. I got in his way when he tried to shoot my client."

"That's not precisely the way I heard it. The paper said you went after the shooter and hit him with a chair before he shot you."

I nodded. "Close enough."

"And he died later?"

"No. He died there in the courtroom."

I'd hit defendant Wilkens twice with my heavy counsel chair. I'd done it with the full intention of killing him. A bully, a child abuser, and wife beater. And, on his last day alive, an attempted assassin, perhaps driven on by his own ideas of what justice should be.

"Now I see you and you've lost thirty or forty pounds. Are you up to helping me in a tough jury case? I mean, you sounded okay when I talked to you on the phone, but I won't hold you to it if you're unwell."

"I'll help you if you want me. If we lose the trial and your client's convicted and sentenced to death, then someone from my old firm, probably Sam King, also death penalty qualified, will carry on and help you with the appeals. Tell me about it."

"No, not that way. I'll walk you to the jail. We'll see my client there. We'll let her do her own telling."

"Wouldn't it be simpler to tell me yourself?"

His face hardened a little and I recalled he was a stubborn man. "Let's do it my way, Don. She's my best selling point."

"Your case. Your call."

I was stubborn too. I didn't have to be involved in his case. Someone else could help him. I could go somewhere, vegetate, and wait. I was assured of six years' employment come the first of next year. I was old enough now to have retired friends re-nested in Florida. Some had built or bought houses near golf courses. Some had moved to where they could witness daily the various moods of old demon sea. Former judge Steinmetz, eightyish, but doing unexpectedly well after quadruple bypass surgery, had retired to a fishing village below Naples. Dr. Hugo S. Buckner owned a condo on the bay side of Siesta Key, near Sarasota, which he never had time to use. He'd offered it to me for what seemed cheap rent until the first of the year.

But first I'd listen. I owed Kevin Smalley that, plus whatever else he wanted of me.

We went out into the heat. Smalley walked medium speed. I struggled to keep up. Once I'd been able to run swiftly for miles. I hoped and believed that one day I'd be able to run again.

We wheeled right, into an alley that bordered the south edge of the courthouse grounds. Half a dozen men stood together in the courthouse yard where we turned. Other men and women sat on benches or stood in the shade of tall trees.

"Here comes Smalley," someone called.

"You going to see your bitch-witch?" a big belly of a man in a red shirt called to Smalley.

Smalley moved on without reply.

"Who are you with, Smalley?" Red Shirt called to me.

"Who are you to ask?" I replied.

Red Shirt's face darkened. "You must be Smalley's new sweetums pie," he yelled in an affected, high-pitched voice that brought laughter.

I counted. There had to be more than thirty hostile people in the courthouse yard, mostly men, a few women.

I walked on.

"Is it like this all the time?" I asked Smalley when we were out of earshot.

"Most times. There are more people when something's scheduled in court. Deputies escort Bertha across for hearings and crowds of people boo and curse her. The sheriff tries to help by surrounding her with deputies. So far it's kept her from being hit with rotten eggs and garbage, but it didn't stop an arsonist from setting fire to the jail."

"I heard about that. Who was Mr. Tub, red shirt, big belly?"

"He lives near Bertha's trailer. I think his name's Tipper or Tinker. He comes here every day, rain or shine." He shook his head. "Might as well not argue with them, Don. It just riles them."

He paused at the metal door to the jail. "You know I came out of the closet three years back."

"I remember you told me about that when I tried that damage case with you. You thought it had gone okay."

He shook his head. "Sometimes now, I wish I hadn't come out. The town took it okay then, but doesn't now. When I spoke my piece, lots were doing it, doctors, lawyers, congressmen. I was a brave gay lawyer. Most of the locals were friendly. They aren't now. Today I'm an old-fart fairy shyster and a damned boy raper. The story around town is that I'm defending Bertha because she sold me sex with the fifteen-year-old nephew she's alleged to have poisoned." He shook his head. "I swear I never knew Bertha Jones or either of the dead kids. Lots say and believe I did. My phone's mostly crank calls, my mail's threatening letters, and someone, or a group of someones, keeps jamming nails and knives into my car tires. My yard at home's a deposit place for junk and bowel movements. The straight young man I took in as an associate gave it up and moved on last month."

I'd known since law school that Smalley was gay. He'd

been top of our class, living happily with a tall German exchange student named Hans. I'd had to work to eat and I'd hovered near the class bottom. I'd survived only because Smalley (and others) lent me their class notes and put me through late-semester question-and-answer until I learned enough to survive.

Smalley, summa cum laude, was my friend. I was heterosexual, but he'd not held that against me in law school or afterward. I'd lived my life believing people had the right to be where they wanted and to do what they wanted as long as it didn't harm others.

In the civil case we'd tried together, I'd learned that, as expected, Smalley was half a dozen times the lawyer I was or would ever be. The only place I outdid him, if there was a place, was in determination. He saw the case around him awarely, knowing both its weaknesses and strengths. I was dumb enough to envision only the ultimate goal of winning, ignoring all else.

The clamor of the mob in the courthouse yard had both angered me and set off my competitive alarm system. I knew then I was going to try to help Smalley and his client if they'd jointly allow it. So no Florida, no swimming in warm seas or sunlit heated pools, and no bad golf.

Back to work, Robak.

The sheriff was out. We talked briefly with a brusque chief deputy. His eyes distrusted both of us. Many enforcement people don't like damn lawyers.

Our client had a cell upstairs in the women's section. A broad-beamed fiftyish jail matron named Anna led us to the cell, bypassing the men's section downstairs by way of steep back steps. When we arrived at the top step, the matron scuttled down again.

"I'll be foot of the steps. You call down when you're done, hear?"

When she had vanished Smalley said softly, "Some of the jail people are afraid of Bert."

"I see," I said, not seeing.

Bertha's cell was more than a cage with bars, it was a kind of room. There was a barred door, but the walls of the room were stucco. There was a toilet, sans lid, in a curtained area, now open. Someplace nearby, an efficient air conditioner hummed, turning the air frigid.

The prisoner could not be called attractive, but she was imposing. She was almost six feet tall, just about my height, but where I weighed a thin one-sixty, down from my usual one-ninety, she couldn't have weighed more than a skeletal hundred and twenty. Her body seemed all long bones draped in pale flesh. She perched on her bed, arms folded, blanket tucked around her white-stockinged feet. She watched her world like an autumn bird no longer able to make it south for the winter, seeing death coming in the soon frozen world. She lifted her eyes to me. They were black and set deep, alive only like coals in the ashes of a banked fire. Her nose was long and curved, a handsome nose. The rest of her features were generous, too big for her face, but not ugly in any way. Overall, she looked as if someone had carved her carelessly out of a whitewood tree, making mistakes but not bad ones.

I guessed her age at forty, then upped it a little. I tried to guess at her ancestry, but no solution came.

I wondered what a jury would think of her, tall, thin, gangly, and accused of two child poisonings. I'd once known a first-class lawyer who dressed his female murder defendants in black and issued them a Bible for reading in the courtroom. He won most of his cases.

Could be.

She observed our arrival without great interest, but she did take a chair and push it next to the bars as we waited.

13

She sat and arranged the blanket around her feet again, as if they were the only part of her affected by the icy air.

"Bert, this is Don Robak from Bington," Smalley said. "I think he's going to help us. Robak, this is Miss Bertha Jones."

The woman nodded. She let me reach through the bars and tentatively shake her hand. I could feel her cool fingers probe my hand searchingly, holding on.

"Why are you come to help me?" she asked, her words sounding of the nearby Kentucky bluegrass rather than the Indiana cornfields.

"Someone has to. In a death penalty trial in Indiana you have to have one lawyer who knows about both trial and procedure."

"And you're that? You done this kind of thing before?"

"Yes."

"You're also sick," she said firmly. "I feel it in your hand. If you don't know you're sick, then you need to know it."

"I know it."

"Someone shot him in the belly a while back," Smalley said.

She nodded, considering the new information. "Yes, that would be it."

Her eyes returned to me and she touched my hand again. "I got some medicine I made up that likely could ease your pain. It's clear liquid in a green bottle, with a label that says Q on it. Herbs, roots, and grasses, no alcohol. The bottle will be on the second shelf, south wall, in the kitchen of my trailer. I made the police leave it when they was using their search warrant. You take a teaspoon or two evenings after you eat. One time a day. You still hurt bad down there, don't you?"

"Yes."

She nodded, encouraging me to tell more.

"My doctor thinks it's from scarring and adhesions."

"He's right. My medicine will grease your intestines, work in between them. You use it, hear?" She loosed my hand, looked up at the ceiling, then back at me. "The man who shot you would have likely killed you if you hadn't done him in. Stop worrying on it."

She could have read the newspapers. I'd been famous for a few days.

"Let's talk about you, ma'am."

"Not yet." She looked at me for another long moment. "Sometimes I see things a little. There are others out there looking for you, aren't there?"

The man I'd killed, Hugh "Big Hubba" Wilkens, had two brute alkie brothers and a potful of in-laws and outlaws, all of them members of a far-out church that desired the right to settle all of humanity's problems. Sheriff Goldie in Bington had told me he believed that members of the family might one day lay in wait for me or, more likely, seek me out.

He'd then lent me a gun. I carried the gun now and then, but not this morning, and not into any jail.

"I killed a man named Hugh Wilkens. He's got lots of kin in and around Bington."

"Would he be a Wilkens come from around Hazard across the river?"

"I don't know."

"All right," she said soothingly. "They's lots of Wilkenses. Some's mean, some's not. I'm even related to Wilkenses a little. There's something else wrong, but I don't feel it clear."

"Where did you hear about me getting shot? On television or in the papers?"

"I don't watch television and I don't read no newspapers."

"Okay." *Someone had told her.*

She waited.

I moved closer to the bars. I left my hand where she

15

could take it. "Tell me about the poisoning. Did you do it?"

She smiled for the first time. Her teeth were uneven, but clean and white. "I think you know I didn't."

"Say it anyway," I said.

"I didn't. I swear it to God."

"What do you remember about it?"

"Have you ever seen an animal die from poison?"

"No."

"I have. I seen dogs and cats. Most I seen died from strychnine. They foam at the mouth and bite and scratch themselves bloody. I knew, when I seen my kids begin to go, that it was some kind of poison, but not strychnine. I made them swallow dishwater and mustard. But they died, and they didn't die easy." She shook her head. "Poor kids."

"They weren't your kids?" I asked, knowing they weren't.

"No, not mine. They was my sister Sara's kids. She died a year ago next month of brain cancer and I took her kids in after that. I was all that was left around here to do it. Some will tell you I mistreated them, but they was bad kids at first. Sara was sick a long time and them two had run street-wild. When I got them we fought about getting things worked out my way. I loved them and maybe they begun to feel for me. Someone put poison in their stew. I'd ate some earlier and it was okay then. Now I'm alive and the kids are gone." She shook her head. "Don't ask me how it got done. I've thought lots on it, but not yet figured it out for sure."

"What day of the week did this happen?"

"A Sunday. They were late home from the survival church on the hill and they'd run themselves hard."

"What else?"

She shrugged. "They died. I got arrested by the sheriff."

I knew the poison that was charged in the indictment: nicotine.

"Have you worked in tobacco?"

"Sure. Everyone except rich people works tobacco around here."

"You know you can get sick just from touching the plants too much?"

She nodded. "You wear gloves."

"Was any of the poison found in your house?"

"No. They looked high and low but ain't found nothing."

"Did they find anything outside your house the poison might have been in, a bottle, a can?"

"No."

"Did you ever get sick from tobacco when you were working in it?"

"Once. And I seen other people sick from it."

I handed her a yellow pad I'd brought. "I want you to write down the name of every person I should talk with, good news, bad news. Add addresses where you can. I'll come back for the list later today. Write anything I ought to check or that you remember after we leave."

She nodded.

Something about her eyes bothered me. "Can you see good?"

"I don't drive no more, not even daytimes."

I looked at Smalley. "Can we get someone to check her eyes?"

He nodded. "Sure."

"I can see okay," she said, perhaps not liking the idea of a doctor checking her.

Smalley answered smoothly, "I'll get an optometrist to look. It won't bother you, Bert, and it won't take more than a few minutes. That can happen while Robak here takes another look at the case against you, questions some of the witnesses again, and picks at all the sores. Then he'll help me try it in court week after next."

"You going to do that?" she asked.

"I'll go back over things. Not all of the things, but enough." I could see the idea pleased her, and that pleased me.

"Take care then. Could be there's someone outside waitin', watchin', and hatin', someone real smart. Maybe it's the one who tried to set fire to this damn jail. Come tell me a name when you can, and if you can."

"All right."

"There's a ton of folks out there in the town and in the county that really hate me."

"Who out there hates you most?"

She shook her head. "Too many to pick and choose a single hater. The neighbors believe I sent them sickness and accidents. Some tell I started trailer fires." She smiled. "I'm a witch."

"Don't say that to anyone," Smalley ordered.

She smiled at him and then stuck out her tongue.

TWO

"You have rights . . . derived from the Great Legislator of the Universe."

BY EXITING ANOTHER door of the jail and walking a block out of the way, we avoided the yard gatherers.

"Who's the organizer of your courthouse mob?" I asked.

"I'm not sure," Smalley answered. "Most likely it's an area preacher named Allwell."

"Someone has to be orchestrating the action. Someone has to find out when things are scheduled, make telephone calls, plan strategies."

He nodded.

"We ought to know for sure," I said.

"Once again, I think it's this preacher named Allwell. The kids used to go to his church."

Later, I sat in Smalley's office while he went through his files and handed me copies of statements and depositions. The pile in front of me soon grew to more than a foot high.

"You've been busy."

"I've never tried a capital case. I know I need to be prepared. I've tried diligently to get that way, mostly by deposing their witnesses. This isn't a good case, Don."

"There's an old Indiana case about poison."

"I know that case. Once upon a time the state had to prove possession of the poison by the defendant. They can't do that in this case, but the law's no longer that way. The old case got overruled by the Supreme Court two dozen years ago."

"Too bad for us. Are there any friendly witnesses?"

"There are a few. There's even one lady deputy sheriff who'll testify for Bert."

"Bert? You've called her that before. Do they call her Bertha or Bert?"

"I call her Bert," he answered coolly. "The newspapers and her detractors don't. They call her the poison witch. To get back to the trial, our lady deputy will testify in court that the trailer was clean, that Bert got someone to call 911 when the kids first complained, and that when she arrived in a patrol car both kids were alive. That was before any emergency vehicles came. She'll say, in her opinion, that Bert was trying to save the kids by forcing emetics down them. There's also the sheriff. He's medium friendly but won't help much. He came on the scene about the same time as the emergency medical crews. He'll say the trailer was clean and that the kids, particularly the boy, hadn't been in trouble for several months. I believe he thinks deep down that Bert's innocent, but he won't say a lot in public because it'd be political suicide. He runs again in November and, like most sheriffs, he wants a second term."

I waited.

"There's also the man who manages the trailer court, and there's a lady who owns a trailer and who's distant cousins with Bert, her only relative left around Madisonville. Bert moved here fifteen or twenty years ago from eastern Kentucky. She worked at the shoe factory until it burned. Some now say she set that fire, but there's no evidence of it and no investigation is pending. She did cleaning and whatever came along afterward. That includes a lot of seasonal work in tobacco fields. The prosecutor knows that and can prove it. He'll also show how easy it is to distill semipure nicotine from raw tobacco."

"How about our Bert and men or women friends?"

"She had men around for a while, but never married. There hasn't been a man for a long time. No women. She's a wild, solitary lady." He shook his head. "She's lost twenty pounds since they put her in jail."

"What else?"

"Bert made the kids pick a church and then attend it. They chose the Church of the Survival on the hill above the trailers, maybe because they could walk up there easily. Some neighbors liked that. But this church preaches against Bert now, so the neighbors' feelings would likely have changed."

"Tell me what a Church of the Survival is."

"There's a local church here in Madisonville where the minister, a Reverend Allwell, who I mentioned to you before, preaches that the world's soon going up in flames. He has a large flock of believers."

"He's the one who may be the head man of the courthouse mob?"

Smalley nodded.

"What else does he preach?"

"Some hate and some love. His church blames gays, Jews, African Americans, Roman Catholics, other churches, doctors, and lawyers for almost everything. But, among themselves, the members share food and clothing, and they pray a lot on Sundays and most nights during the week."

"Any other reason the kids went to that church?"

"Not that I know. Allwell's a man with a loud voice. He has no use for anyone with other opinions. He's Old Testament, lots of blood and revenge. He hates me because of what I am and also because I've no use for him." He nodded. "I remember from somewhere that you and Judge Harner got shot by one religious fanatic. Allwell's another."

"I don't think Hugh Wilkens thought anything in this world was about to go up in flames that day except his wife, Judge Harner, and me."

Smalley shrugged. "Whatever. Allwell now preaches hard against Bert. He keeps the mob excited and likely returning to the courthouse."

"Does this Church of the Survival have any other name? I mean, is it Lutheran, Presbyterian, Baptist?"

He shook his head. "No. None of those. I don't remember any other name for it."

I thought on that. With a church openly against her, Bertha didn't need to be tried by a jury from Madisonville. "Did you file for a change of venue?"

"Sure. What we've got now is an agreed order. We'll pick our jury in another county and then transport them here to hear the case. If we ask it, the jury can also be sequestered."

"Okay with you that way?" I asked.

"Should be. I left the change-of-venue motion pending, and we can see how things go when we start picking a jury. The question and a proper answer are still open."

"Okay," I said. Maybe that procedure would work out. "Tell me what else you know about this Church of the Survival."

"Not a lot. I had Allwell against me in court once in a condemnation case I did alone for the state's attorney general." He smiled. "After we won the case, Allwell threatened to break my nose."

"On the record?"

"No. We were outside the courtroom in the hall. He's a huge man, formidable."

"What did you do?"

"You know me, Don. I do my best to avoid confrontations."

I smiled, remembering law school. What he'd said was not exactly true.

"Has anyone officially inquired into whether one of the children didn't poison the other and then commit suicide?" I asked.

"I have, but of course I'm not an official. The prosecutor never thought it was worth considering. It's a defense we'd have a hard time with. Everything seems to have been normal that day."

"What else?" I asked.

"Allwell wants to be heard in court on any matter a church member gets involved in," Smalley continued. "That includes Bert's trial. And he runs a kind of common-law court out of his church on Friday nights. Prayers and hymns and asking for answers to unsolvable problems."

"People also do such things in Bington. On the day of his dissolution trial, Wilkens brought along some kind of lay minister who wanted to talk with my client before the hearing. My client refused, so I also said no. We then started our hearing." I paused for a moment, then came up with something else. "The church near Bington is called the Church of the New Redeemer and New Saints. Does that name sound familiar to you?"

He shook his head. "It's not the same name as the church here."

"Okay. Tell me then what else you know about the nicotine poison, where it came from, how it supposedly got into the food. Anything."

"Where it came from no one knows. A search turned up nothing. They even dug around and raked the ashes of the fire. As to how it got in the food, there's only the state's theory. When the weather was good Bert constantly cooked stew, soup, or chili in a big pot over an open fire outside her trailer. She did it lots. The kids liked it both before and after they moved in with her."

"Did other people besides the kids eat what Bert cooked?"

"Yes other people sometimes ate her cooking. On the day in question, the first nice day of the spring, Bert cooked some stew. The kids ate it and then died. Earlier, Bert had tasted some of what she was cooking. Nothing happened to her."

"Okay," I said. "If she cooked outside, anyone around could have sneaked poison into the pot."

"Sure. That's our best defense," he said. "The kids ate and died. It wasn't pretty and there are lots of eyewitnesses salivating to testify. The state toxicologist will also appear for the prosecution. He'll say, preliminarily, that a single drop of pure nicotine can kill. He'll testify there was an ounce or more of poison in the stew pot. Nicotine stimulates and then depresses the cells of the peripheral automatic ganglia, particularly the midbrain."

"What did the witnesses see?"

"The kids both began screaming that their stomachs were burning. All present will testify to that. They then became nauseous. The emetics—soapsuds and mustard—made them even more so. Soon they couldn't breathe, and there was unconsciousness. The symptoms followed one another rapidly and by the time the ambulance arrived, maybe twenty or thirty minutes after they ate from the stew pot, and ten minutes after 911 was called, both kids were dead."

"How many eyeball witnesses?" I could, in my mind's eye, see them all in a line, eager to testify.

"More than a dozen. Maybe twenty. Including Reverend Allwell."

"He was there at the scene?"

"He'd come walking down with the kids from his church. A lot of his church members live in the trailer court. He

24

often visited them on Sundays after his service. On that Sunday, he watched the kids die. He wasn't quiet or helpful while it was happening. He called Bertha a witch, then went into a crazed rage. He tried to dig coals out of her cook fire with a shovel and burn her alive, throwing them at her by the shovelful."

"Maybe he was the one who tried fire again after she was in jail."

Smalley nodded. "I've thought on that. They say he's the chief judge and final arbiter in the hearings held at his church. They also say that a trial's already been held on Bertha."

I waited, knowing there was more.

"She's been 'sentenced' to death in absentia. Lots know about it. Allwell's not a quiet man."

"Goody. We'll pick our jury from out of town, and that should screw him and the horse he rode up on."

Smalley smiled.

"What's Bert's ancestry?" I asked.

"When I asked her, she grinned and said she was half Gypsy, half Indian, and half witch. She's likely got some of the first two running in her veins."

"I assume that someone official checked everything else out about the poison and that the state can prove what the kids ingested came from Bertha's stew pot?"

"Right. Bert told me she may have left the pot unattended for a few minutes, but none of the witnesses backs her up on it. The rest of the adult statements say she never left and that she was the only person who ever put anything in the pot. There were some kids around, too, but I guess they'd say what their folks told them to say. Bert's good neighbors will also testify that they kept watch intently because Bert had had a loud row with the kids that morning before church and that sometimes, after she yelled at them, there'd be violence."

25

"What kind of violence?"

"She had a stick she used to spank them. In the autopsy report there's mention of minor bruising, old and new, none of it serious or disabling. Love smacks."

"Keep going."

"The fight that final Sunday morning was about an old .22 rifle the boy carried now and then. She took it away from him." He shook his head. "I thought about asking for our own toxicologist to check things, but it seemed useless. Do you want to ask for one?"

"Maybe. Would the judge go along with us, at this late date, if we asked for a toxicologist and an optometrist, plus maybe a pathologist and a GP?"

"Why a pathologist and a GP?"

"A pathologist to recheck the autopsy. A GP to examine Bert."

"There's an autopsy report on both kids in the stack there. Check it over and see if you want or need more. When I told the judge you were coming to help, he said he'd cooperate in anything we needed. I think he was afraid I'd go to the state public defender. He's also offered us more preparation time before the trial. We'll meet with the judge and the prosecutor tomorrow night at a kind of open house."

I nodded and watched his face change and become a little darker.

"We're not invited guests at this open house," he continued. "We go there for our legal business. I'm a little leery just now of local socializing. The judge was one of the people who warned me about going public three years back, and he likes reminding me about it now." He smiled carefully. "Plus his wife hates me. She made a pass at me once." He nodded. "She really did. Grabbed me right by my pecker. Like to ruptured me."

"No crap?"

"No crap," he answered.

I shook my head and smiled.

"Tell me about your love life, Kevin. Do you have a special someone now, particularly someone local?" I asked. It was not a lot of my business, but we were old friends.

"Not now. Not for a while." He watched me. "And, with the same interest, I'll ask you about Jo. I've heard nothing about her since you arrived, or about your growing super-duper son. Problems?"

"Yes. She's moved from Bington to Chicago. She has a dissolution pending. She took my son along."

"No chance?"

I shrugged. "I don't know. I still have hopes."

He smiled carefully. "There was what you politely call someone for me in Louisville. He died." Smalley shook his head at my raised eyebrows and the unasked question. "No. Not that way. He ran marathons, very dedicated. He ran one in Cleveland, had a heart attack on the course and just died." He looked away from me and then back, and I could tell he was still grieving. "There are places to look in Louisville and Indianapolis. They even say there are some gay men in your town of Bington."

"That's true. I play golf with a guy who teaches chemistry at the university and is out of the closet."

He shook his head. "When Ed died I think something died in me. I haven't tried again. There's too much chance of hurt."

"I don't know for certain that Jo doesn't have someone in Chicago, but I have no one and I'm not looking."

We nodded at each other, two aging men sharing similar problems.

"Another thing for you to know," he said. "When the news got out about how the jury was to be chosen and that it would likely be sequestered, Reverend Allwell didn't like that situation one damn bit. He wrote me a letter about tampering with God's justice."

"Did you keep the letter?"

"Yes, and also my reply."

"What was your reply?"

"I told him he'd be well advised to fuck off, Don. I also told him I'd heard how he'd acted as judge in a nonlegal, asshole, common-law hearing. I wrote I'd try to have him removed from the courtroom if he appeared at the trial other than as a witness. When the state, at first, didn't list him, I put him on my witness list. We'll move for a separation of witnesses so he can't sit in the courtroom."

"Sounds fine to me. What else?"

"I guess that's it for now. Where would you like to work?"

"How about your library?"

"You can use it, and you can use the empty spare office." He held up a hand, stopping my movement.

"I watched you with Bert. You're good with people who are in bad trouble. You already have some special kind of relationship going with her, don't you?"

"I hope so."

"I felt it. She has little use for me. I'm her lawyer and I represent her, so she answers my questions earnestly, but she sits there on her bed and acts like she's about to die of boredom. Maybe she senses or knows I'm gay and that's her reason."

I tried to spell it out for him. "When I met her, I felt as if I'd known her for a long time. I think I can get her to do what I want, and say what we—advise."

"I hope you can."

I remembered something I'd forgotten to ask: "I've assumed without asking that our judge in the case is the local one, Judge Kittaning?"

"Yes. You know him, don't you? He talks like he knows you."

"I know him some. He hears lots of cases in Bington." I

smiled. "He looks like a very fat, old polar bear with a black mustache."

"Good description. He's not a bad judge. How about the prosecutor?"

"I've met him, but not in court. Lemuel Rand, isn't it?"

"Yes. Lem would like to plea-bargain the case. There's an offer made and some broad hints he'd go further."

"That would likely be extremely unpopular with the red-hot locals. Why would he want to do it?"

"The main reason might be that he didn't run again for prosecutor. Over and above that, maybe he knows something I don't."

"Could he?"

Smalley nodded.

"Guess at what?" I asked.

"I wish I could."

I repaired to the library. At noon, I had Elaine pick me up a turkey sandwich on whole wheat, hold the mayo. I ate the sandwich and drank lukewarm tap water. I chewed each bite thoroughly. The sandwich wasn't tough, but it congealed in a lump after I swallowed it and lay on my stomach restlessly all the long, dull afternoon.

Now and then I would hear Kevin through the wall as he talked on the telephone. Not a lot of calls. Sometimes I'd hear him slam the phone down.

I read. I made notes. I skipped the repetitive bits of the depositions and statements, skimmed other passages, and sometimes only read a paragraph or two. I was tired in minutes, but I kept at it doggedly because it was what I did for a living. I wrote out questions and discarded those I found answers to as I read on.

Nothing jumped out at me. The crime wasn't complicated, just a poison murder with a single obvious perpetrator.

I read the indictment half a dozen times. I also read and re-read the toxicologist's report. It was routine. I read the autopsy reports. They were thorough enough. A pathologist had checked the girl, Mary Petrakis, to see if she was pregnant. She was not. He'd entered no opinion as to whether or not she was sexually active, but did state the hymen was no longer present. The girl had no diseases, was well developed and well nourished, and menses had begun.

Thirteen years old?

I didn't know when a girl's menstrual periods began, so I made a note to inquire.

Mary's half brother, James Smitham, was fifteen years old. His autopsy, like hers, was routine, no diseases present, nothing out of the ordinary.

The two had died of acute nicotine poisoning within minutes of each other, her dying first according to both the eyewitness and medical testimonies.

It had, as Smalley had told me, taken them twenty to thirty horrible minutes to die. I read about that, witness after witness.

There was a sheaf of news clips. The reporting of the matter in Madisonville's *Trumpet* had been shrill, angry, and biased. There were front-page articles day after day, plus inflammatory editorials: Why here? Why us? Why kids?

I skimmed the news stories and then put them aside.

Parts of the depositions told me a bit about the lives of the two children. Mary was of normal intelligence according to her school records. She was interested in movies and television, lipstick and boys. She'd played basketball and soccer. She liked to sing.

Jim was bright, a good student in science and reading, nonathletic, and a schemer. His IQ was in the genius range.

Before Bertha had inherited the pair, there were juvenile reports about small thefts of books from the library, food from houses, plus a dozen curfew violations, mostly for

Jim. Once he'd torn down a sign announcing an elementary school play and gotten caught in the act. The report said that Mary had tried out for the play but had not been chosen as a member of the cast. Jim had not tried out. There was no mention of any punishment.

School days.

With the mother dying a little more each day, the two kids might have been very close. Something told me that I'd need to check that out with care. Jim had likely torn down the school play sign to seek revenge for Mary's having been snubbed.

After I finished my first examination of Smalley's files, I sat thinking. I doubted that any jury would take long to convict Bert or long, in the penalty phase of her trial, to recommend the death penalty.

A sure and certain loser?

Outside the library I could hear Smalley moving about in his office. I stacked files and papers together neatly, then looked at my watch, knowing it was after five. I walked into the hall and to his door.

"You want to eat dinner with me tonight?" he asked from his desk.

"No. I'm on a special diet, so I'm a waste at dinner. I'll eat something in my motel room. I packed along a little stuff I can tolerate."

He nodded. "Please don't forget the open house tomorrow night. I'll want and need you there with me. But you should know the good people of this town will see you and that will cause talk. Some of the talk will be like you heard in the courthouse yard earlier today. Can you stay calm if and when that sort of thing happens?"

"It won't bother me," I promised. "I've been called lots of names, lots of times. Might there be some soda crackers and plain water around?"

"Likely." He appraised me again, perhaps doubting my

31

health and stamina. "And, of course, you know why you shouldn't stay at my house?"

"Yes. But I'll stay there if you want."

He shook his head. "It wouldn't help. Do you feel okay right now? You look bad."

"I'm super," I lied. I felt nauseous, but it was a feeling I knew well and I wasn't going to allow myself to give in to it. I'd brought medicine along, but I was stubborn about taking it because it was addictive and affected my ability to reason and understand.

"Can I have the keys to Bertha's trailer?" I asked.

"Sure."

"I'll want to take a look inside. How about the electricity?"

"I think it's still on." He found a key for me in a drawer and then issued instructions about finding the Town Trailer Court. "Edge of town," he finished. "Are you going now or in the morning?"

"I'm not sure. I'll walk to the jail now, pick up Bertha's list, and then decide."

"If you go to the trailer court and are there after dark, be careful. Some of the trailer people hate Bert."

"Did she kill those two kids, Kevin?"

"I don't know. I believe her most of the time when she says she didn't do it. And she won't let me plea-bargain it."

I waited.

He smiled. "She also won't even listen to talk about her taking a lie detector."

"Why?"

"She just won't. You ask her about why. I watched her today. I think she fell a little in love with you."

"Maybe." I wasn't startled at his statement. I'd felt a strong physical attraction toward the woman.

"See you tomorrow," he said.

* * *

32

There'd been some rain while I'd been poring over the files in Smalley's office. Now the skies were whistle clear and the streets were drying in the big sun heat of the Indiana afternoon. There was plenty of daylight left. Madisonville smelled of fish kill, an odor much like that of Bington. Above the Ohio River, I could see a tenuous rainbow of washed colors.

I took the short way to the jail. The rain and the time of day had cleared the hostile crowd from the courthouse yard.

The sheriff was in. I introduced myself. He was a slight, fortyish man with shrewd blue eyes. His uniform hung loosely.

"Sheriff Goldie called me from Bington about you," he said, smiling crookedly. "My name's Debley Hewitt but you're invited to call me Deb."

"Don't believe everything that old horse Goldie says, Deb."

"Never have and never will, but he didn't put you down much. He likes you. He said you was mostly okay for a lawyer and ought to be a good judge. His opinion was that sometimes you could even be trusted. He also said you was mean, but I already knew that from the newspapers." He smiled more widely. "I share a problem with you. I got myself gut-shot about four months ago."

I remembered I'd heard or read something, but it wouldn't come clear for me now, so I waited.

"Someone shot me when I was out hunting squirrels." He watched my eyes. "It was likely an accident, a rifle slug coming wild out of some trees where I guess someone was hid, maybe a someone deer hunting for food out of season. Not exactly like your court shoot-out."

"And maybe a whole lot like it?" I asked, looking at him with increased interest.

He shrugged. "I ain't sure yet. I'm still looking. Goldie, when we talked, he give me descriptions and license numbers for some vehicles from your Mojeff County. He seemed of the opinion that someone might follow behind you over here and give you problems."

"It's possible. The guy who shot up the courtroom in Bington didn't much like our state dissolution laws. He's got a big family there and across the river that believes just like he believed."

"We have people with those beliefs around our neighborhood too," the sheriff said. "Lots of them. A couple of my deputies have been shot at. Maybe some of it comes from members of Allwell's church, maybe it's just some of the other nuts."

"Did you or are you doing anything about it?"

He hesitated and then smiled. "Some of the church members claim we're slow to respond when there's a complaint made by one of them."

"How you doing with the belly wound?"

"It keeps hurting."

"Mine, too. My doctor told me that stomach wounds take a long time to heal."

He nodded. "Same here." He thought for a moment. "I gave my road deputies the license numbers and vehicle descriptions Goldie sent over. They won't stop the vehicles, but we'll let you know if anyone shows up around here and we spot them."

"I appreciate your help, Sheriff."

"You're here to see Bertha Jones?" he asked, returning to business.

"Yes, please."

"Then follow me." He shook his head. "I wish I could get that woman to tolerate me a hair better. It ain't my damn fault the grand jury indicted her. Hell, I kind of like her. She's her own lady. She don't care what the world out there says. And she's neat and clean as a cat."

* * *

Bert smiled out at me as I approached her cell. She looked at the sheriff until he felt the weight of her glance and retreated.

"Here's what I wrote up for you," Bertha said. She handed me the yellow sheets through the bars. "I'll keep the rest of the pad in case I think of something or someone else." Her eyes drank me in and she smiled a good smile for me. When she smiled she was almost pretty.

The sheriff kept watch on us from afar. I winked a secret wink at Bertha as I took the yellow sheets.

"I wrote down lots of names," she said. "Some of them likely don't mean nothin' much. I put stars besides the names of those who might. You need to talk special to Mo Mellish. He runs the trailer park and he's a good man. And he knows the people there and the kids."

"Who else?"

"Talk to my cousin, Virgie, if you can ever catch her at home." She looked around her cell, frustrated at being captive inside it. "Talk to all of them, even the crazy kids who live in the court. I don't think anyone's bothered them yet."

"The sheriff says you don't like him."

"He's a dried up spot of dog spit," she said. "Someone dropped him out their back hole the damn bad day he was born."

I waited, knowing there was more she wanted to say.

Her face softened. "Forget the sheriff, but be on the lookout for my cats when you go to the trailer court. There are two of them that own me. There's a lady in the park supposed to feed them, but she sent in word they'd run off from my trailer."

"What kind of cats?"

"Black cats. Both of them solid black," she said, smiling gently. "And there's one other thing I went and did for you. You wait." She went to her bed and picked up what appeared to be a thick candle. She brought it to the bars and slid it through. I took it and held it up for the sheriff to see. It was just a candle, but one side of it was shaped into a face. It was my face, a decent likeness carved in yellow wax.

"That's very good," I said.

"I do them of people. Keep it somewhere safe. Don't set fire to it. Sun heat won't bother it, but being used as a candle will. It's a good luck candle." She smiled crookedly, the sharp white teeth set. "You may need it."

"Good luck?"

She nodded, now solemn. "Be careful."

I thought of something else. "How well can you see me?"

"You mean now?"

"Yes. Now."

"The light here's poor. But I saw you real good when the sun was bright this morning. You look good. You look like a man who knows how to find things out and who don't give the job up just because someone barks and growls at him."

"I try hard. Thanks for the list and my lucky candle, Bert. Soon we'll send a doctor to check your eyes. Because of your eyes, could you have missed seeing anything the day the kids died?"

"I don't know about that. It was a real nice day, mostly sunny. And I saw better then."

"Sometime soon I want to talk to you about lie detectors."

"No. There ain't no way."

"All we'll do is talk about it. I'll explain how it works and let you ask me questions."

"All right. I'll talk to you about it. Run on now, and be particular careful."

I lingered for another moment. "What's your ancestry?"

She smiled and I saw a hint of fun appear on her face. "My mother was a Kapota Indian witch, my father was a Gypsy warlock. When I was born it rained for fifteen days

before and fifteen nights after, lots of thunder and lightning." She paused and shook her head. "Telling it true ain't
half as good as what I just said to you. You go on now and
think on that."

I gave it up.

THREE

"We are for all citizens except those we don't consider citizens: blacks, Jews, Catholics, and other trash. The list is long, but easy to read by rifle light."
> —From a sign in Mojeff County, Indiana, April 1991

I SAT FOR a time in the LTD reading Bert's jail notes. She'd printed names and addresses in childlike block letters, sometimes with side comments.

There was a whole page on various trailer court kids. She told me who was bright and a leader and who was not so bright and a follower. She estimated or knew ages and sometimes she commented on whether a neighbor child was Jim's friend or Mary's. Most of the kids, male and female, were friends of both.

I went over Bert's list twice. There were maybe three dozen names and I promised myself to memorize them all eventually, but today my memory was ground down from reading through Smalley's files. I'd had enough words and names for one day.

I'd use her list as background, then make up my own. Or, more likely, I'd check out the kids and then compare notes.

I found the Town Trailer Court. It was at the west edge

of town, off Main Street, in the block before the hill highway started north. It had an entrance and an exit on both Main Street and the hill highway.

I drove through the trailer court, looking it over before I parked. There were maybe sixty spaces, about two-thirds of them occupied. Two spaces still held the ruins of trailers gone up in flames. Something I remembered from casual reading in a news magazine informed me that for many years the possibility of fire apparently hadn't concerned those who built the early burn boxes, but new trailers are now built fireproof or fire retardent.

Half a dozen children played on swings and a teeter-totter in a small grassless playground. Some of them looked up when I first drove by. One tiny girl waved, perhaps thinking she recognized me or my car. I waved back.

I turned around at the hill highway entrance-exit and drove back through the court. This time the kids ignored me as old news.

Beyond the playground, on the uphill side of the court, I could see the nearby hills in my rearview mirror. The wide Ohio lay a few blocks south. The incurving hill to the north opened to a pass. The rise was gradual where the hill road intersected the entrance-exit to the trailer park, steeper north. I saw no houses on the hill beyond the highway, but there was what looked like an old railroad cut or a road. If I was right, the Church of the Survival was up that far hill, above and beyond the railroad cut.

A few adults were about. In front of a trailer near the street entrance, a fat man was lounging in a beach chair under a striped sunshade. His trailer, which seemed almost new, was located across the road from the trailer I believed to be Bert's. He was reading a newspaper. His shirt was bright red. I recognized him as one of the courthouse yard mob, the one who'd wanted me to identify myself.

I parked my car and then opened my glove compartment.

Sheriff Goldie's loaner gun was there, a short-barreled .38 Smith & Wesson Chief's Special revolver. Goldie's advice to me, after an hour at the police range trying in vain to teach me to shoot it accurately, had been to quickly fire it empty, throw it, then run like hell.

I took the gun out of the holster and inspected it, holding it low, where no one could see what I was doing. It was loaded with wad cutters. There was an empty chamber under the hammer.

"For my sake, don't shoot yourself," Goldie had instructed me.

I put the gun back into the holster and replaced both in the glove compartment. I couldn't bring myself to carry it in a town where no one had threatened me.

Bertha's candle sat on the front seat. It felt hot when I touched it. In the better light, the carving on it didn't look a lot like me. The eyes were too big and the nose too small. I put the candle down under the driver's seat where the sun wouldn't bother it. I wondered why she'd carved it.

Witch.

And yet, when I thought of her now, I got a warm feeling, as if I'd known and liked her for a very long time.

I locked the LTD doors and walked to Bert's trailer. It was warm in the late sun and still humid from the rain, but my loss of weight had made me almost immune from sweating.

Red Shirt watched me, frowning. He'd discarded his newspaper on the ground beside him and now sat, attention fully directed toward me.

I used Smalley's key to get in, then closed the trailer door behind me and locked it. Through a dusty windowpane I could still see Red Shirt. I watched and waited for a time, but Red Shirt seemed content to sit in his chair and eye Bert's trailer balefully.

The inside of the trailer was hot, and it smelled stale and dusty. No air moved. I found a wall switch and turned on the light. I looked for an air conditioner, but there was none.

I searched the shabby rooms one by one.

There were two bedrooms, each with one bed. Bert's nephew had slept in the smaller of the two bedrooms on a narrow army cot. The two females had slept in the other on a queen-sized bed.

There was a shower-toilet in the back of the trailer with just enough room inside for one person. A tiny medicine cabinet held nothing but toothbrushes and cheap toothpaste.

The biggest and last room was a kind of sitting-dining room up front next to the kitchen. There was a curtained picture window by the dining table. I left the curtain drawn.

In the boy's room I found a double row of schoolbooks on a shelf that was part of the wall. I moved one of the books and several pulled away with it, stuck to one another. Behind the schoolbooks were other books placed low and flat, hidden from casual view. One was a book on knighthood, well used. Another was about Houdini and his magic. There was a copy of Harlan Ellison's *Dangerous Visions,* and of Robert Heinlein's *Stranger in a Strange Land.* There were a couple of pornographic paperbacks, startlingly explicit. Then there was a thick collection of Shakespeare's plays. All the books were well used.

Two superhero dolls, both men in armor, stood on the shelf, guarding the books, ever ready to serve. Their toy swords had been sharpened to needle points.

A small closet held a few cheap clothes, all of them worn but clean.

In the other bedroom was a hodgepodge of schoolbooks, clothes, lipsticks and perfumes, hairbrushes, and a dozen old television and movie magazines. There was also a lone rag doll, one eye gone.

42

Tucked in the frame of a wall mirror was a medium-sized color photograph of a beautiful girl-child sitting alone in front of the trailer, holding the rag doll when it had still owned two eyes. She smiled prettily for the camera and I wondered who'd taken the picture.

The girl in the photo seemed almost a woman, hovering at the brink, tall and well formed. She had huge eyes and dark hair, a fine snub nose, and curved, petulant painted lips.

Thirteen years old?

With her looking like a temptress to die for, living in this poor trailer, I wondered what problems Mary Petrakis had caused in the area. She was lovely enough to stop interstate traffic. Eventually men would see her, want her, and plot to get her. She might be "safe" if her guardian had money and was watchful, but this girl came from nothing. Her face hinted she might have both resented and resisted being watched.

I had new questions for Bert.

In a drawer, I found a picture of Bert standing with the boy, Jim. The resemblance to his half sister was startling. He was thin but already grown tall, his jeans bottoms up near the middle of his white socks. His intelligent eyes looked out of the photo, mocking and challenging the world around him.

And me.

Two lost kids, one now-lost keeper.

I went through all the drawers. There was nothing else of interest. I remembered, from something I'd seen in Smalley's office, that the police had entered the trailer with Bert's permission. I'd want to examine what they'd taken and what of that they'd listed to present as evidence in the murder trial. I wondered if they'd found the porn books and why, if so, they'd left them behind.

Perhaps the police had decided that the porn books would only complicate things for the prosecution in the upcoming simple did-she-or-didn't-she trial.

The kitchen shelves I'd been told about held some canned vegetables, crackers, flour, salt, and sugar. All staples that might draw insects were tightly sealed. I saw no roaches or ants, and no signs that mice lived in the trailer.

The green bottle marked with a Q Bert had prescribed for my aching belly sat, tightly corked, among other medicine bottles on the second shelf. I tugged the cork free and sniffed the contents gingerly. The liquid inside had a sharp odor, something like wood smoke, a bit like green onions, but not the same as either. I could smell no alcohol. Tilting the bottle sent the contents slowly coursing from one side to the other. There were odd shiny flashes through the green glass.

I recorked the bottle and put it in the inner pocket of my suit coat. I'd tell Bert I'd taken her remedy, but I decided not to actually try it. She wasn't a doctor. Instead, she was a woman charged with murdering two children.

But then I got the bottle out of my pocket and looked again, changing my mind as I did. I *would* test the medicine. It came to me that it was a matter of faith in Bert. The woman in jail wouldn't poison me. She liked me. I'd changed her face for the better when I talked to her. She'd discovered a little hope.

I was both sorry and glad about that.

I also believed that Bert would somehow know whether or not I'd taken her nostrum, and also know if I lied to her.

I searched methodically through the trailer once more, looking for anything of interest, something that would answer a question or even make me think of one. There was nothing that gave me reason to pause. It was a place where three humans had existed until two of them had died. Now it was a haunted place.

I asked myself why Bert might have poisoned the two children and, more than that, done so with many neighbors in attendance.

Because she's a witch, stupid. Because she's sick, half blind, bad tempered. Because she hated the troublesome children dumped on her by her dead sister. Because she wanted the children to suffer and die and wanted her trailer enemies to witness their deaths and thereby fear her.

I knew that was the scenario the prosecution would try to present in court.

People had "seen" her do the poisoning job—watched her prepare the stew in the pot, add ingredients to it—then been eyewitnesses to the agonizing deaths of the children.

I wondered about that. According to the sheriff's first report, no one claimed to have seen her poison the pot on the day of the murders. But now many remembered it.

Open and shut, Dumbass Robak. The witch did it.

If the killer wasn't Bert, then why had Bert lived and the children died after all three had eaten from the same stew pot?

There was one obvious answer: Bert lived because the poison hadn't been present in the food when she ate from it. After Bert had eaten, someone else had dropped in the poison, then grinned secretly and waited while Bert, having had her taste, stirred the poisoned pot.

Why?

All attempts to prove Bert innocent began with showing a confused jury, picked from a neutral county, that the poison had been added by a shadowy someone in the minutes after Bert had tasted and before the two children ate.

Was it possible?

I gave up thinking on it for now and walked to the door.

Through the window I could see that Red Shirt was no longer in his chair. I opened the door and exited. I looked around but saw no one. I relocked Bertha's door.

On the north side of the trailer I could see the place where Bert apparently had done her cooking. Someone had piled together yellow bricks to make a crude fireplace. Within it, two heavy metal pieces rose from the ground, each shaped into a Y so that a metal crosspiece could hold something suspended over a fire, but the crosspiece was not now to be seen.

I walked closer. The children had died in the early spring. I remembered from the depositions that it had been a fine warm day, mostly sunny, sixty-plus degrees.

Across the road from the makeshift fireplace were the remains of one of the burned trailers. I walked out and stood in the road, looking that site over. A trailer had burned to its axles. All that was left were some pieces of metal and a few black strips of burned rubber, plus the twisted metal wheels and axles.

My stomach hurt a little. I tried hard to ignore it and, to my surprise, succeeded.

Red Shirt came from somewhere and walked ponderously toward me. "Why you sneakin' around here?" he asked as he drew near. His huge pot belly quivered but his tone was more curious than belligerent. "I know who you are now. You're a shitbird lawyer named Robak from up the river in stinkin' Bington."

"How long ago did this trailer burn?"

He almost visibly thought on my question and finally answered: "A few weeks before the goddamn poison witch killed Hansel and Gretel. Late February or early March maybe. This one and another trailer here both burned within hours of each other. The fire chief never could figure why. The folks living in both of the trailers had testified earlier that same day against the witch for the head lady at Welfare, which was trying to take the kids away. Then a slick lawyer slowed things up and the witch poisoned the kids."

"Was Smalley that lawyer?"

"No. It was another damned local shyster."

"Did you testify?"

"Goddamn right. A bunch of us testified. Then the lawyer for the witch got that empty-headed old-fart judge to take it under advisement for a home report. Hansel and Gretel died before it could get decided." He nodded. "Poor little bastards. That's exactly what they was, poor little bastards. Goddamn you, and those like you, and your stupid laws." He eyed me. "Paper today says you've got yourself appointed to help the witch. How come someone from another county gets sent in here to fuck things up? You wouldn't tell me who you was this morning, but I found out in the *Trumpet,* that shitty local daily disappointment, a rich folks' paper." He looked down and then up. "Ain't nothin' you can do or find that'll save that bitch-witch from burnin' in hell's fire forever."

I waited for his hotness to burn down to coals.

"What do you lawyer shits do when a person ups and tells you they're guilty or maybe gets caught red-handed like the witch done?"

I shrugged. "We represent them in a hearing when they plead guilty."

"You queer?" he asked.

I saw that instead of calming down he was making himself angrier with his own inflammatory questions. His belly shook as his words heated. His eyes were hidden in deep pouches of fat and I couldn't read them. He was a big man, well over six feet tall, weighing perhaps three hundred pounds.

"No. I'm not gay."

" 'Gay' must mean queer to shysters. I think you lie. Smalley likely got you to come here so's the two of you could butt-fuck each other."

"I said I wasn't gay. You got bad ears, fat man?"

The insulting reply stung him. "I think you're queer, damn your eyes. Move out. Get your ass back to stinkin' Bington."

"No."

He took a step toward me. I had to slow him down, so I unbuttoned my suit coat. He watched me do it. I wondered what I'd do if he came after me. I couldn't run.

He slowed down. "That story in the *Trumpet* also said you killed some guy in Bington who shot up the courthouse. It said they tried to call you to ask about that man getting killed, but you never called them back."

"The story's correct and I don't give a damn what your paper here wants from me or reports about me."

I'd either impressed him or scared him. His demeanor went from threatening to ingratiating.

"*Trumpet* also said you was going to be judge over there come first of next year."

I nodded and waited.

"Lots of folks around here ain't got no use for law at all, but I ain't dead set all the way yet." He shook his head, lecturing me now. "You oughtn't to be here. Folks here just general don't have much use for foreign lawyers and particularly Bington lawyers. A man who's going to be a high judge, even in these days, and in stinkin' Bington, oughtn't to let himself get dirtied trying to help a witch and a goddamn queer."

"I don't believe in witches," I answered reasonably. "And people who love people of the same sex are called gay. It's the way some people are. Being that way doesn't make them worse or better than others."

"She could make your toilet back up," he said, retreating to the safe ground of Bertha Jones. "She could sour the milk in your icebox and turn your tap water shit brown. She could start a fire with her eyes and make people sick to death by pointing at them. It ain't no wonder she never got poison sick. Poison won't touch a witch. And they tell all over town how Smalley was hot after that dead boy."

"Did you ever see Mr. Smalley with the boy?"

"Not me. I never even seen him around here until after Hansel and Gretel were dead. But others whisper they seen Jim and Smalley together. I talked to a guy at the union hall who says he seen Smalley patting him real sweet on his bony young ass."

"I doubt that. Smalley never knew Bertha or the two kids before the poisoning. He got appointed by the circuit court judge to defend Bertha Jones. The county pays him for his work. He wasn't hired by her. She's now accused of a double murder and locked tight in jail. The state wants to execute her. If she can do the things you say she can, then why can't she witch her way out of the jail someone tried to burn with her there inside it?"

"Maybe that's different, something she can't do."

"Tell me what's different about it." I smiled at him. "And tell me your name."

"Why do you need to know my name?"

"I think you know lots of things about what happened here," I answered agreeably. I lowered my hand from the jacket. "Maybe, if I find out enough facts, I'll just give it up and we'll plead Bertha guilty. Then I can head home to Bington where I belong."

"It's Tepley Swisher, Mr. Robak. I worked at the damn nail factory thirty some years until they laid me off." He used a big right hand and shifted his semi-independent belly to a more comfortable position, then shook my hand without making it a contest. "Folks around here usually call me Tipper."

"Are you a member of the church up on the hill over there where Bertha's kids went?"

"They weren't her kids," he corrected. "They were her sister's kids. And I don't go up to that hill church much no more. The world ain't about to end." He shook his head, unsure about his final statement.

"You go sometimes?"

"Now and then. My old lady goes every Sunday, but she says the world ain't about to end either. I do most of my business with Reverend Allwell down to the courthouse. He talks and I listen there. He says we're allies against both Satan and his witch. I'm with him on that."

"I'm told he preaches a lot against Bertha."

"Yeah. He used to like her, but now my wife says he preaches part of each Sunday sermon against her. He was here by the fire when the kids died. He saw it just like I did. He tried to burn her right then. And me, I ain't ever going to be the same after watching."

"What else do you know?"

He shook his head.

"Did you watch Bertha cooking the stuff in her pot?"

"Some."

"She says she left the fire and the pot unattended for a time. She also swears to God she didn't poison the kids."

"I never saw her leave." His eyes left mine and I thought he lied. I also thought it would do me no good to show he lied now, so I put away my cross-examination for the courtroom.

"Who else was up close around the fire?"

"I'm not sure."

"Reverend Allwell?"

"I don't know. He must have been up close because he was hot after the witch when the kids was dying."

"You called the kids Hansel and Gretel. Why?"

"Mary was pretty, and I guess if boys are pretty, then so

50

was Jim because they looked alike. At times they ran off into the woods and the witch had to go look for them and she'd be mad as hell, so the kids called them Hansel and Gretel and so did us older folks."

"The kids who live here in the trailers?"

"Them and others."

"What did Bertha do for money?"

"She collected the kids' social security."

"She wouldn't have collected it until she got custody. How'd she get money before then?"

"She'd hike her skinny butt across the highway, cross the creek, and hunt the hills above the old railroad up near the church. She'd pick greens and dig roots and sometimes she'd trap rabbits and squirrels. She cooked and made up medicine inside her trailer in winters, but when it was warm she'd do food and some medicine outside, smelling the whole trailer court up. She'd sell medicine or trade it for food. Sometimes she just gave it away."

"Did you ever eat anything she cooked?"

"A few times. It tasted okay."

"How about the medicines?"

"Not me, but others used them and some even swore by them. Maybe I'd have taken something if it was offered, but me and Bertha was never close friends. Reverend Allwell used to take things she gave him, food and medicine. He'd stand in front of her and preach sweet Jesus plus add a lot of hellfire and damnation in the mix, and the witch would just smile at him. I asked him about it and he thinks now she put a spell on him, but God got him out of it. Now he hates her worse than he hates the damn government."

"County, state, or federal?"

"All of them." He gave me a curious look. "You're telling me it's God's truth that dick-in-the-ass Smalley never knew Bertha or her kids before they was poisoned to death?"

"Right. If Smalley had had any dealings with them, he'd have had to turn down the appointment to defend her."

"And you swear to God you're not queer?"

"I swear on His soul and body that I'm not."

He shook his head, confused by what I was saying. I could read his heartbeat in belly movement.

I said, "I'm now asking you to pass the word to the trailer folks that I was brought here from another town to look into this poisoning. Tell them I don't believe Bertha poisoned the kids and I intend to find out who did. Tell everyone I'll be around the camp for a time looking and that I may stay even after the trial's done. I've looked and found sneak killers before. Those who hide from me and don't give true answers to what I ask will have to go to court."

Tipper smiled. "You better put miles between you and Reverend Allwell, Mr. Judge Robak. He's like to come after you, gun or no gun. If he come after me, big as I am, I'd run and hide. He's a horse and a half."

I smiled.

Tipper nodded. "I'll be happy to remind him of the dead man you left behind in that Bington court. It'll give me pleasure to do it. The reverend ain't always a nice man. One time he got caught reading his Bible with a married lady who lived here in the trailer park. Her hubbie, my blood cousin, was the one caught them. The reverend was maybe praying, but him and my cousin's wife didn't have a single stitch of clothes on. It got so scandal hot in the church that Allwell went on a vacation, but when he got back he beat up my cousin for lyin' and it all quieted down."

"Maybe Reverend Allwell was just angry he got interrupted when he was working a private prayer lesson," I said and watched Tipper grin. Then I thought of something. "How about Mary-Gretel? I know she was pretty. Was anyone fooling, or trying to fool, with her?"

"I never seen anything."

52

"But you heard about something didn't you?"

He shook his head and I saw his eyes again. The subject of sex and Mary-Gretel was something that frightened him. I gave it up for the moment. I knew he wasn't telling me all he knew. I relished the thought of us getting him on cross-examination after he'd testified for the state.

"I'll be back again tomorrow, then maybe again the next day. I'll be around here a lot."

"Will the trial get delayed?"

"Maybe yes, maybe no," I said. "If we don't find out what we need to know, if we don't get answers, then it'll get delayed until we find out what we want to know."

He nodded.

"This church of Reverend Allwell's, is it a regular church?"

"What do you mean?" he asked.

"I mean, do they sing hymns and read from the Bible?"

"Sure. It's good for readin' and singin'. But the church people just don't like a lot of law things that go on now."

"Like what?"

"Like the state taking land, like the taxes that's killing us poor folks, like turning criminals loose."

"Okay. I'll be back tomorrow."

He nodded.

When I got to the LTD, I saw that Tipper had already gathered three neighbors—two women and a man with a crutch. He was talking to them. They watched me. I was far enough away so that I couldn't read their faces.

In the opening next to Bertha's trailer, where the cooking fire had been, two black cats lay in the dust, watching all. They were alley-cat types, thin, but they looked to be in decent shape. I remembered I'd found no sign of mice in the trailer.

I drove to the hill road exit. My belly hurt, and this time thinking on it and willing it to stop hurting didn't work.

53

FOUR

"All statutes which transfer property rights from citizens to states, no matter what the public need, are unconstitutional."
—Speech by Herbert Techni made near the Golden Gate Bridge, San Francisco, March 1994

I CHECKED INTO the motel where I'd made phone reservations. I'd used my private credit card since I'd returned the one that belonged to the law office.

It was an anonymous motel, part of a chain of anonymous motels. The clerk was anonymous, not friendly, not unfriendly. He did his job efficiently with the smallest of smiles. He then abandoned me.

The room was cheap but not bad, a modular unit next to more modular units, thirty in all, built in the shape of a V.

Someday, when things inevitably go bad, I foresee the multitudes of cheap highway motels being used as holding camps or prisons, places for the last rites of the citizenry before mass executions.

The motel had no dining room, but there was a brightly lit Burger King across the road. There'd be nothing for me there. Whoppers were a no-no. Behind the motel, off another road, there was a shopping center. A neon sign above one of the stores there announced RESTAURANT. May I could eat something on its menu, some clear soup, or maybe warm cereal and toast. Not now, but tomorrow. The thought of food made me nauseous.

I carried my bag into the room, dropped it on the bureau top, and after pulling the faded spread back, fell onto the bed. The room smelled of disinfectant. My eyes watered. A window air conditioner moaned softly, switching on, then off. On the far end of the bureau a television sat darkly, and I left it that way.

After resting awhile I felt better. I got up and found my packs of crackers and the aerosol can of cheese. I filled a plastic glass with tepid water from the bathroom sink and, ignoring the cheese, chewed hard and long on the crackers, then sipped the water so I could swallow. I knew I needed more to live on than crackers and water, but I couldn't force myself to think about the cheese or any other food.

My belly continued to ache. Once it had been continual sharp pain, but now it was just a deadly, consuming ache, worse when I was tired. I was still nauseous and I had, periodically, the same contractions and spasms that had plagued me before and after discharge from the hospital. My scarred insides had not yet found a way to fit back together.

But there was no longer blood in my stool, and Doc Buckner seemed still confident I was at the edge of full recovery.

Doc Buckner had also said to return if the pain persisted. His surgeon friends would open me again. I both dreaded and wondered what they'd find.

I got out the medicine Buckner had prescribed and examined the bottle. It was half full. I knew what was in the medicine: morphine. If I took a dose now I'd eventually sleep and not ache much for a while, but tomorrow I'd be only half in the world, and I'd want and need more of the drug.

I put it back in the suitcase.

I promised myself that when Bert's case was done, I'd get my belly opened, if that was what it took.

I took out the green *Q* bottle I'd removed from Bert's trailer. I shook it, sniffed it again, then drank about a teaspoon's worth directly from the bottle. It tasted smoky, like bad Scotch, but with no alcohol bite.

Kill or cure or, more likely, do nothing at all.

I settled back on the bed. Nothing seemed to change inside me. Outside, through the blinds, I sensed the setting of the sun. I heard car motors, grinding truck gears, and the sounds of doors and trunks opening, children shouting, toilets flushing, beds squeaking.

Good old America on the move. Tourists. Lovers. Over-the-road truckers. Business travelers.

Nothing.

When I woke my belly pains had subsided some. A smaller ache inside me came from something I vaguely remembered. I wanted more food.

I went to my window and looked out. Except for the lights of the motel the world was now marked "closed." The shopping center and its restaurant were dark. I'd slept four hours by my watch.

At the far corner of the motel, someone sat in a car smoking a cigarette. I watched the car for a time. I decided it was likely a man whose wife had made him go outside to smoke his stinking cancer sticks. The world's no longer an easy place for smokers or those who produce the smokes.

I ate the rest of the crackers in my bag, squirting cheese on them this time. I drank more water and let that suffice.

I slept once more. A familiar nightmare came: Big Hubba Wilkens aimed his gun toward the front of the courtroom and shot Judge Harner. Harner's bloody head slid down behind the bench. I watched Wilkens roughly push aside his sullen, fat-faced adviser from the Redeemer church and come strutting across the courtroom toward me. The old, unarmed bailiff ran from the courtroom, yelling something I couldn't understand.

I'd known from the papers he'd filed that Wilkens claimed not to believe in the dissolution of marriage (divorce). The adviser he'd brought with him on final hearing morning was a deacon in the big, wild church out in the county where people blew trumpets and sang spirituals and raised hell about the mundane world.

"I don't have and don't want no damn lawyer," Wilkens had announced to Judge Harner before we began.

Harner had politely informed the adviser that he couldn't present any evidence or ask questions for the defendant, but that he could confer with him as needed.

"Die! Die!" Wilkens ordered his wife and the world.

She cowered beside me. I unfroze and got the hundred-plus-pound chair up as he leveled his pistol. His first shot missed. The chair didn't. I felt the steel casters bounce off his forehead and mash into his eyes. I twisted the chair cruelly. The report of the coroner said Wilkens was blind in both eyes by the time he got off his second and last shot. That shot, just as the chair hit him hard again, didn't miss. I fell, taking him down with me.

He died. I lived.

I awoke now in the motel room. There was a thin film of something that had to be sleep sweat on my face and body. The room had grown cold from the air conditioner. I felt clammy but not sick. I arose and turned the air conditioner down low. Outside I could see that all but a few of the motel's outside lights were now dark. The smoker had vanished, car and all.

Maybe I was being watched.

My watch told me it was well past three in the morning. I was hungry, but I knew all the crackers were gone. For a moment I contemplated going up to the motel office to see what I could find in the nibble machine there.

Instead, I slept again.

I was singing in the shower before the sun was fully up. I sang loudly until some damn music lover beat heavily on the wall of the next unit. Chastened, I hummed "The Whiffenpoof Song" to myself softly.

At the shopping center restaurant I had a soft-boiled egg, dry toast, and two cups of decaffeinated coffee. A waitress attended me diligently, then gave me a religious tract along with my bill. She smiled when I left a generous tip.

"Have a good day," she said.

I put her tract in my suit pocket and resisted the urge to tell her I had other plans.

Don't be a wiseass all your life, Robak. After all, you're soon going to be a judge.

I felt good, but I was wary about feeling that way. My belly still ached a little. I'd had good days before. They'd always been followed by hurting days.

I looked the religious tract over. It was from the Church of the Survival, and it seemed innocuous enough: COME AND WORSHIP WITH US.

I drove carefully down the hill and then past the trailer court. A creek trickled from the north and passed through an opening under a highway bridge. I looked to the right and up into the hills that lay on the north and west side of the highway.

I intended to go there today. I wasn't sure exactly why I needed to walk and look where Bert had sometimes walked and looked, in the land where the two dead children had played, but I did need to do it. I wanted to see the hill and perhaps, if I could, look over Reverend Allwell's Church of the Survival.

I drove to Smalley's office and found him agreeable.

"You look better," he said.

"Slept good. Then ate good."

Smalley parked and locked his oversize Buick off the hill road at a wide area of flat grass and gravel. We got out of the car and stood looking over toward the hill. The air at nine in the A.M. was sweltering and there wasn't a hint of a breeze. The sky was a fine and cloudless blue.

"You sure it's okay for you to do uphill walking in this heat? It's already eighty degrees."

"I'm all right. I want to do it."

"Okay, Don, but we'd best leave our coats and ties in the car."

He took off a different suit coat, not the one he'd worn the day before. This fresh black one again sported the bright Silver Star from an almost forgotten war we'd not won. He placed the coat neatly in the backseat of his Buick and then removed his tie and dropped it on the suit coat. He took off his cuff links and rolled up his shirt sleeves.

I did likewise, except my shirt sleeves had buttons, not French cuffs. Somehow he now seemed out of uniform. I didn't. I hated coats and ties. Jo liked to tell close friends I always looked as if I dressed in a hurry and committed many, many errors. Come January I could wear a robe in the courtroom, if I wanted. I could go to the office in a T-shirt and jeans. I knew I wouldn't, but I damn well could.

I reflected on some I knew who wore the robes of the judiciary. Most did fine in them. Others would never be judges no matter what they wore. A fool's a fool in a robe or out of it, male or female. And sometimes the selectors make errors.

I waited for Smalley to lead off.

Smalley wasn't a huge man. He was, however, tall and trim. Muscles rippled in his upper arms, and his forearms looked like Popeye's. When we called him Spinach in law school, he'd smiled gently and tolerated the nickname. I remembered a time when two big football types, plus a crowd of avid helper-watchers, had openly taunted him about his sexual preference. It had happened in a bar near campus. They'd used gutter language and made jokes combining and comparing his sexual equipment with his last name. They'd then moved on him when he failed to be either scared or servile.

Smalley and I were in the company of half a dozen other law students celebrating the last final exam of our freshman year. The size and number of the taunters cowed the rest, but I did some damage and was still standing when the fight was suddenly over. The two main attackers were on the floor and Smalley was standing easily, inquiring if anyone else wanted a little more action. One of the footballers looked like he'd need knee surgery and the other would surely have to see his dentist. Smalley wasn't even winded. His blood was up and he sounded serious about wanting more.

I turned and smiled at the two big ones holding on to me. "Better take your hands off me or there'll be lots more trouble."

They did.

Smalley grinned and nodded at me, then relaxed.

He explained it to me later. "Just because I'm gay doesn't mean I can't or won't fight. I'm not fond of fighting, but I found out long ago I needed to be good at it. So I am."

All through my law school years, I heard many stories about him around campus, mostly about his bravery. He was brave to the point of foolhardiness. Even homophobes found it hard to villify him in their gossip: "Won the Silver Star you know. Damn homo, but he don't take shit from no one. Did you hear about the time he . . ."

I didn't think it unusual to be both gay and brave. I'd known gays in the service and had never noticed a difference in how they acted and reacted in times of danger compared to heterosexuals (except I'd always felt that most of the gays seemed smarter). Warriors don't always appear in familiar uniforms.

"Follow me," the law school legend ordered now.

"Si, Señor Smalley," I answered.

We crossed the road, avoiding the scant traffic, and scrambled down the far side of the embankment and followed the creek bed north until the land began to rise steeply beyond it. We forded the almost-dry creek bed, kicking up yellow dust with our go-to-court black shoes.

"This creek floods at times, if you can believe it, Tonto," Smalley said. "You need a rest yet?"

"No." I was feeling okay.

He looked me over, nodded once, and moved on.

Some of the trees wore gossamer spider webs that pulled away if touched, drifting woods spiders came down on us as we walked beneath the heavy branches. The spiders didn't sting or bite, but the webs tickled.

Mourning doves, many of them in coveys, rose from the grass with sad, whistling noises in flight. A bold rabbit watched us from beside a sweet gum tree, curious but still ready to flee. Squirrels gossiped among themselves and chattered at us from branches.

Interlopers, we climbed and crossed the railroad cut, which was almost indistinguishable from the rest of the hill because of long disuse. Above it were more trees plus thick underbrush.

"How long since trains used this track?"

"Maybe fifty years," Smalley said, wiping his forehead with a handkerchief. "From the looks of the rails it might be even longer than that."

He was sweating from the heat, his white dress shirt sticking to him. I wasn't sweating, because there was nothing left of me to sweat. I was a little short of breath, but my belly seemed okay. I felt I could run, but wasn't sure. Not yet, but maybe soon.

Did you cure me, witch?

Bert's medicine had acted miraculously. I hoped it would last. Several times I'd jarred myself with a misstep during the climb, but my belly remained without significant pain.

We left behind the remains of rusted rails and rotted ties. At the top of the hill the land leveled and the trees thinned out. I could see a cleared spot where there was one impressive large building and several smaller outbuildings built above the ground. There were also a number of tiny chimneys and hatchlike openings in the earth. Old fallout shelters. Here, in the past, people had dug deep in the earth and then covered what lay below with strong roofs. The hilltop was full of them.

Dark clouds had appeared in the sky during our climb and the sun scudded in and out of them like a surfer in a rough sea. The wind had also come up.

"It looks like rain," Smalley said.

I had an old war scar high on my chest that usually foretold wet weather. There was only a minor quivering there, but still I nodded. "Maybe."

No one seemed to be around what I guessed was Reverend Allwell's church."

"Who owns the title to this place?" I asked.

"I'm not sure on title. The fallout shelters were built in the fifties. When I came to town, this place was abandoned. Then a survival group moved in during the early eighties and did some rebuilding. Allwell took over later and has been in charge for six or seven years."

The large building had a naked flagpole in front of it and a thin cross above the roof, a token thing. As we watched and listened, someone inside the church began to play an organ, expertly and with feeling. It was a slow, sad song, but not religious. I recognized it after a moment: "Rainy Day." Suddenly the music stopped.

"Whoever's playing's good at it," I said.

Smalley nodded.

Two skinny black cats sat in front of the church, watching us.

"Those are Bert's cats," I said. "I saw them at her trailer last night."

"I think you're right. They look hungry."

I watched them. Feral cats sometimes do well. These appeared scrawny but strong, like they were eating just enough to survive.

"Maybe the cats are here because they want to be saved," Smalley said. "It's said around town that Jesus Allwell preaches that when the world dies only those inside his camp, or doing his work outside it, will be saved. That means no African Americans, no Jews or Catholics, no gays, and no goddamn lawyers. Cats might be okay, but Allwell hates us lawyers worse than he hates sin and the government."

"You can't fault a man who exhibits good taste," I answered. "Are these grounds the place where Bert's kids and the others from the trailer park hung out?"

"I doubt it. I think there has to be a place on the hill below where they played games. Most of the kids I talked with acted afraid of Allwell. I doubt they'd hang out around his church even if there was no one guarding it."

"Do you think our dead kids might have had a fallout shelter of their own?"

"Maybe, but I know nothing about it and no one I asked questions of mentioned it." He looked up at the sky, now clearing. "Since Bert's kids did come up here for Sunday services, they could have had a shelter, them being part of the saved crowd. I've heard that some of the shelters are crammed with guns, camping gear, and canned food—to be used in the final days to beat off Satan's legions and then be available for whatever and whoever comes afterward. The 'Day' in this camp was once supposed to be when nuclear bombs would fall, but Allwell's preaching has made it a religious terminal time. He screams God's final blackout in his sermons. He's a clever, careful man. He's taken what was already up here and used it for new purposes. I hear he's got more than a thousand believers. Maybe tomorrow he'll have ten thousand or a million." He looked again at the still-troubled sky. "I don't much like the way things go on these days, Don."

"I wonder if he's been careful in all things at all times?"

"What do you mean?"

"I saw a photo of Mary Petrakis in the trailer last night. She was a beautiful thing."

"Yes, she was a pretty child. Do you mean you think that Allwell might have been fooling with her?"

"He followed the kids down the hill on the day they died. He was present when they died, an eyeball witness. What if he'd tinkered with her before, or even on that last day, and thought she might try to make something out of it legally?"

"I like the idea more than you know. Save figuring on it more until after tonight. When I called about your dietary problems, I was informed that Allwell would be at the open house tonight. Be careful while we're there. He has many friends, lots more than I do locally these days." He grinned to show he wasn't seeking sympathy.

"Nice congenial party crowd," I said. "Local outraged citizenry, angry Allwell, the circuit judge, the prosecutor who wants the death penalty, plus us. Very cosmopolitan."

"Small town. And remember we're not social invitees. We just have legal business there."

I shrugged, not caring. "Can we look around now and see if we can find a bomb shelter that's unlocked?"

"All right, but I'm not sure why we'd be doing it."

"No good reason. I was born curious, Kevin. Lock something and I want to open it and see inside. Hide something and I want to find it. Maybe we'll find an open shelter and it'll be the very one that belonged to the dead kids. Kids might not have the money to buy a lock." I shook my head. "I know it sounds crazy, but it's something I suddenly have the urge to check, a hunch maybe."

He nodded, now smiling amiably.

We walked toward the shelters. There were scores of them, marked by metal pipes rising upward from soil-covered roofs, with either a hatch at the top for entry or a dug-out area with a half-concealed door. All we tested were locked.

A flash of light from the woods on the far side of the church touched the edge of my peripheral vision.

"We're being watched," I said in a low voice, not looking at Smalley.

"Where away?"

"Left. There's a thick bunch of evergreen. I saw a flash of light from there. Could there be a caretaker?"

"I don't know. There was an organist." He looked sideways while I stared straight ahead.

"I just saw it," he said.

"Someone watching us through binoculars?" I asked.

"Maybe something other than binoculars," he said, watching openly now. "I've had a bad feeling inside all this sweaty morning."

We waited, both watching.

A tiny red flower of light bloomed on Smalley's chest, then disappeared. A moment later came the sound of a shot, and dust was kicked up near the black cats.

"Let's move out," I said. I looked once more toward the building with the cross. The dust died, the cats vanished. Time to join the flight. "Move," I said.

We turned away and ran toward the crest of the hill. In seconds I was breathing heavily, but I realized I could run.

Whoever had alarmed us didn't openly pursue. I could see occasional flickers as we raced through the evergreens. Once, the red laser-like light touched me and I ducked away, sliding to the ground then rolling backward. My stomach hurt.

But no further shot came. Whoever had sighted us was playing games with us.

We got over the top of the hill and stopped, panting hard.

"Damn," Smalley said, his shirt wringing wet with sweat. "We could have gotten our asses shot off back there. I may need to change my shorts."

"Likewise."

"Listen," he said.

Someone, once again, was playing the organ. This time it was a religious tune I didn't recognize.

Smalley smiled at the melody. I thought he might have enjoyed our moment of fear. He was an odd man and I believed he was better under stress than I was, maybe better than anyone I'd ever known. "Where now, Tonto?" he asked. "Want to sneak around the side of the hill and go back on top? Maybe try a full assault on the organ player?"

"No, but I want to stop at the old railroad tracks. I want to follow the cut up and down some. That's assuming no one comes over the hill after us. I'm damn well not going to be run all the way off this hill just because someone pointed a gun at us."

"I'm game," he said.

We walked and slipped down the hill. There was no sign of pursuit.

I realized the gunner by the church could have shot one or both of us and then either fled or stayed and made believe it was a tragic accident. I thought of Sheriff Deb and remembered he'd been shot. Maybe our gunner had hoped we'd get closer to the church and been surprised when we turned away from the music and toward the fallout shelters.

I was certain the black cats had survived, too.

We found nothing of interest as we nervously searched along the rusty track line, up and down. There were stacks of termite-infested railroad ties, a few moldy sacks, and occasional empty aluminum cans. If there was a place where the trailer-court children played hill games we had yet to locate it.

We moved along smartly, watching and listening. Now and then, from far away, I could hear the organ playing "Rock of Ages."

Eventually we gave it up, headed back across the creek, and climbed up the side to the highway.

I was angry by the time we arrived at Smalley's car. I rested against a fender and surveyed the early-fall world.

"Why would some bastard aim some kind of laser sight at us and run us out of the church camp?" Smalley asked.

"I don't know. It's your town." Now that we were down and safe I was upset.

"We know now we aren't wanted up there. That light touching us gave me the creeps."

"Is there a way to drive a car up to the Survival Church?" I asked.

"Sure. You can drive about three miles up the hill highway and turn left. If you always stay left, an improved road then runs to the camp. It'd take maybe fifteen minutes because of the way the road curves. You want to do that?"

"Could whoever was up there have gotten away by now?"

"Sure again. There are lots of county roads to the west away from the church. That's if you're not heading back into Madisonville. Turn right at any time going up and you'd lose the camp."

I thought of a remedy. "How about you, when you get

back to your office, call the sheriff's office and express a little citizen outrage? Tell Deb Hewitt we were doing some investigating and someone shot at us up by the church. Let him or one of his deputies take a look."

He grinned, liking it. "Good idea. It could cause some excitement. Our sheriff thinks someone shot him on purpose late this spring, and him getting a report about someone shooting near us should stir things up. And give us another thing to do tonight, Don."

I waited.

"We'll ask Reverend Allwell about the someone with a gun."

"Good idea," I said, also liking it.

"We'll also ask the organ player," he said.

"You know who was playing?"

"Maybe. If I'm right, he'll likely be playing at the open house."

"Sounds good."

"Be careful around Allwell, Don," Smalley advised. "He's got a bad temper and he loses it easily. He's been known to hit people without any warning."

"It's your idea. I thought I'd let you do most of the talking with him. I'll be along to play your country bumpkin cousin."

"You'll do well in that role," he said, grinning at me. "For now, do you plan to try to talk to anyone in the trailer court?"

"Yes, but alone. If you're along they'll tell me what they told you, which they'll likely do anyway. I've no intention of talking to all of them anyway. It's useless and would only warn them concerning what we'll try to do to them on cross-examination. They're likely telling a joint lie when they say they saw Bert put poison in the pot. We'll try to break them individually on cross."

FIVE

"Question, challenge, then use deadly force against authority"
—Bumper sticker seen in Chicago, 1997

IT WAS ALMOST eleven in the A.M. when I pulled into the same trailer court parking area where I'd been the evening before. My stomach bothered me only vaguely. After a time I decided it likely wasn't pain. I was hungry again.

The clouds had vanished without leaving behind a drop of rain. It was hot and the air I breathed seemed as thick as a stagnant pond.

A few young girls played in the grassless playground. When I walked near none of them looked at me. I stopped and watched them. They continued to ignore me.

"Which trailer is Mr. Mellish's?" I called to them.

None of the girls replied.

I walked a few steps closer. "Would someone please be kind enough to point out which trailer belongs to Mr. Mellish?"

A thin preteen girl in ragged jeans turned a little toward me and smiled. "We been told by our folks not to talk to you 'cause they say you're bad trouble, Mr. Robak. But the first trailer in the court belongs to the Black King. He's got a sign with his name in the front."

She went back to swinging a younger girl in a rusty swing that squeaked as it flew up and down. The two girls laughed about something they knew and I didn't.

Laughter in the young is mercurial, arriving swiftly, departing in the same fashion. Children laugh at things adults never understand.

"Thank you," I called. "Is the 'Black King' Mr. Mellish?"

The girl swung the swing. "Yes. And you tell the jail witch that Nancy Jane said hello. Us kids don't think she did nothin' to Hansel and Gretel or to anyone else. She's a good lady."

"Could we talk more about that?"

"Not now," the girl said, looking around to see if anyone adult was watching her. "Sometime."

I nodded and walked to the front of the court.

Mellish's trailer seemed almost new and was grand enough to dwarf many of its nearby neighbors. It featured a room off the front that either pulled out from the trailer or had been attached after the trailer was in place. It also had a large awning shading the front door. A fairly new and anonymous dark brown Chevrolet was parked nearby.

A professional-appearing sign in front of the trailer announced: REV. MORRIS M. MELLISH.

Reverend?

There was a doorbell. I rang it and heard interior chimes. After a time a purple gnome of a man opened the door and peered out and up at me. He was not much more than five feet tall, but he spread out vastly below a tiny head. I estimated his weight at two hundred plus. He looked like a weight lifter gone to seed.

"This day has to be hotter than the hinges on the very gates of hell," the purple man said affably. "On Indiana days like this I'm happy to be long on ice and air-conditioning."

"My name's Don Robak," I said. "I'm a lawyer. I represent one of your tenants."

"I know who you are. I visited with my friend Bert up to the jail last night after you'd moved on from there. I heard good things about you. I'll make a bet you ain't heard as much about me as I have about you. As an example, did you expect an African American minister of the glory gospel when I opened my door to you?"

"It wasn't that. I just didn't expect you to be so big."

He smiled engagingly. "You mean big below the top place, where I'm so abominable small?"

"Well, yes."

We smiled together, somehow instant allies.

"Would you have any time available to talk to me now?"

"Sure. I'm a minister deprived of his church by Molotov cocktails. Plus that, me and Miss Bert are buddies. I like her and I know she's innocent. I'll help her against her enemies any way I can because her enemies are also likely my enemies. Tell me what you want me to say and I'll parrot it all on the witness stand, solemn, sworn, and wearing my frayed minister's collar."

"How are her enemies your enemies?"

"I think that a man named Allwell was responsible for burning my church. I think he's done things to other churches and congregations in the area. I believe he's a more likely candidate for murder than Bert. I think he hates the law I believe in. I believe he plans to do more."

"And Bert's your friend?"

"Yes. Not because of my church, although we have prayed together, but because I used to have bad aches and pains in my legs from carrying extra poundage. She gave me some salve and I rubbed it into my legs and now I hobble lots better."

I nodded. "I got shot in the belly early this year. She gave me some medicine yesterday. Now maybe I'm cured. This morning I started to eat again and keep the food down, and I'm not hurting."

"I know about you getting shot from Bert," he said. "And Tipper says you carry a gun in your belt."

"Now and then. I didn't have a gun on me when I talked to Tipper last night."

That amused him. He laughed and shook his head. "Tipper claims you was armed to the teeth and he was only civil to you because he was afraid of getting shot."

"I give you my word on your Bible that I was unarmed when I talked to Tipper."

"I'll accept that word. There are people around this town I don't believe when they swear on a ton of Bibles."

"I hope you're including Reverend Allwell."

"Him first. His flock of believers second. He's a man with a lot of trouble inside him. I used to say prayers and repeat his name in them, but I don't no more."

"You don't believe he can forecast the end of the world?"

"I have doubts when he says the sun will rise." He shook his head. "For the first time in my born-again life, I think I'd like to see a man dead."

"What makes you hate him that much? Your burned church?"

"Yes, but also because he's evil. I know inside me he burned my church or had it burned. I think some of his troops journeyed to Louisville and put a pipe bomb in a synagogue a few weeks back. It didn't go off and I've seen ATF agents here in town, watching and asking questions. I think Allwell plots against the world. He's full of evil and he's the best I've ever heard at mouthing it."

"You've heard him preach?"

"Yes. I never been around his church in the daytime, but

I've been near enough to hear him screaming to his people at night, while I lay hidden in the dark bushes."

I nodded.

"Were you here in the trailer court the day Bert's wards got poisoned?"

"I was around and about. I had a cold, so I was staying close to Bert's pills."

"Then you didn't see the children die?"

"The Lord spared me that. I've got a phone in my trailer and Bert sent someone running to ask me to call 911. She hasn't got a phone in her place and my guess is she didn't trust some of the people living closer to her trailer who did have telephones. I made the call and then I stayed at the window and door and watched."

"Can you tell me what you saw and then tell me also what you know?"

"The two kids were poisoned on the first nice day of spring. That was middle of last March and it happened on a Sunday. I used to preach in my church on Sundays, but now I preach Saturday nights in a loaned Presbyterian meeting hall."

I nodded and waited.

"About everyone in the trailer court except me was out doing something in the warm weather. The sun was out and the robin birds was singing. I watched folks run toward Bert's place after I made the call. I wanted to go with them, but I had a fever. I saw sheriff's cars and emergency vehicles. Tipper—he's the neighborhood scandalmonger—knocked on my door. He said the kids was dead. I saw the emergency vehicles leave with no red lights and no sirens. I saw the sheriff leave after that, taking Miss Bert off to his jail for questioning."

"You never left your trailer?"

"I never left my trailer grounds. I'd open the door and talk with folks when they walked past. A couple of times I went out into the yard just to witness God's sun. The story now is that all the watching neighbors saw Bert drop poison in her pot, but it wasn't that way on the day. It didn't start getting told that way until a couple of days after the kids was dead."

"Someone started telling it and the others chimed in and spread it—is that it?"

"Exactly." He nodded and wiped sweat from his head with a white handkerchief. "Could I ask you please to come inside? I tell you true it's too hot for me to be standing at the door here."

"Are you all right?" I asked, alarmed.

"Doc Schnatter says I got an insufficient heart. That's likely because I'm fat as the butt side of a fifty-dollar mule. Just come on inside here."

I entered his trailer. He closed the door behind me while I glanced around. The trailer was nicely furnished. The walls were covered with photographs and paintings of churches, large ones and small ones.

Mellish walked to a window air conditioner, turned dials, and suddenly there was increased fan noise. He then turned off a talkative scanner.

"Company for the nosy," he said. "Hear about trouble, sheriff's calls, and fires. It's how I learned my own church was burning."

"Insurance?"

"Not near enough to rebuild. Maybe one day."

"Tell me more about when the neighbors began saying Bert dropped the poison in her pot."

"All anyone saw, from what was said the day the kids died, was that she was cooking stew or chili in her pot. Some seen the two kids eating it. Now all the adults say they seen Bert drop poison in the pot." He looked up at me and smiled. "If it was that way, then why didn't someone say it on death day? You have a jury trial and break one of them liars on the witness stand and you'll likely break them all."

I nodded. "We'll try real hard. Why did a small girl named Nancy Jane, up at the playground, call you the Black King?"

He smiled. "Nancy Jane's a sweetie pie. It's a name game Jim started. Hansel and Gretel for him and his half sister Mary, the witch for Bert. There's Attila, Prince Valiant, Merlin. Sometimes Jim and Mary were Romeo and Juliet, sometimes others would be those names and other names, whatever Jim ordered out of his bright mind. It was a continuing thing. Ask the trailer kids. They know. And a dozen of those kids were around the pot on Death Sunday. Talk nice to the kids and they'll tell you true they never saw Miss Bert put anything in her cooking pot but groceries."

"Might Attila be Allwell?"

"He might be, but I'm not sure. I've heard the kids use the name and it came out like it was a 'fear name.' " He beckoned. "Follow me to my kitchen for something to drink?"

"Sure."

I walked behind him to the trailer kitchen, bright with sun from a big picture window that looked out onto the trailer grounds.

"Coffee?"

"Just water with maybe a cube or two of ice in it, please."

He brought me a big glass of ice water and I sipped at it. He poured himself black coffee. He lit a cigarette and I was reminded that the man who might have been watching outside my motel room had been a smoker. And the car in front of Mellish's trailer could have been the watcher's car. I tried to remember what that car had looked like, but could not.

But why would he have been watching?

"Do you own this trailer court?"

"Not me. I run it for the First National. The bank took the trailer court back from the owner when construction work petered out around here and the owner didn't keep up his payments. My lot's rent free plus I get to keep ten percent of the rent I collect. What with social security and the money I put aside, I can preach my messages and do God's work free. All donations go to my church rebuilding fund. I'm big-time rich compared to most of the folks who has to live in this place."

"Tell me more of what you know on Allwell."

"I can only tell you what I see. He claims to be a minister called by God. He preaches hate and death and that the world will soon end, but that his followers will survive. He hates all government, even our local government. He runs a tight church ship. His people do what they're told by him and ignore what others tell or order them. It's rumored he had the sheriff shot. It's also said he's got himself a little band of true believers close to him who'll do whatever he orders, arson, murder, whatever."

"Have you ever talked to him?"

"He don't talk to people my color." He nodded. "He's seen me here in the trailer court and maybe he knows who I am, but he's never spoke a word to me. I think he knows I believe he burned my church, and I also think he'd kill me or order me killed if I got in his way."

"Would you do the same for him?"

He smiled without humor. "I might, Brother Robak. It's something I've thought hard on."

I waited while he struggled with that.

"The Bible says I can't," he said carefully. "Still, I'm thinking on it."

"Okay. Tell me what you hear about the murders now that the trial time is coming?"

"That Bert will get convicted and will be sentenced to death."

"She swears she didn't poison her wards. Assuming she

didn't do it, then someone else did. There has to be a reason those kids were poisoned."

"Yes. The best reason might be Bert's Greek-nosed niece. The reason might also lie in what that girl and her half brother were likely doing."

"What were they doing?"

He smiled suggestively.

"I saw their pictures. She was a little beauty," I said.

"Yes, very pretty. Half this end of town was in love with her. But being pretty isn't being Christian good. Some kids say she was selling snippets of what she was likely giving free to Jim."

"You think she and her half brother were lovers?"

"I believe so. You never saw them together that they didn't have their hands on each other."

"And you believe she was selling herself to others?"

"Not all the way maybe, but a look and a touch of the goodies. A buyer would have to provide the viewing place or take a hike up the hill across the road to a hiding place I'm told Jim and Mary had there. Jim would tag along. He'd hold the money and make sure nothing happened that wasn't paid for. He had an old .22 rifle he carried. I heard the police confiscated it from Bert's trailer."

"How sure are you that the two of them were lovers?"

"I'm dead sure. I never caught them, but then I never tried. They never confessed it to me, but I knew. They sneaked around the camp and on the streets lots of times at night. Hansel and Gretel, Romeo and Juliet. I know they were hiding money because one time they showed up at the hall where where I preached and put a five-dollar bill in my offering. One of the trailer kids told me when there was enough money, the two of them were going to take a bus to Nashville. She was going to be a country singer and make millions, and Jim would share it." He shook his head. "Sweet kid, but she was dumb as creek rock. Jim was smart, real smart. He'd go along with what she said and smile, then get her to go with him into the bushes after dark."

"Did Bert know?"

"No way."

"If she was selling feels and looks at her body then who bought?"

"I don't know."

I took a chance. "Did they ever offer a look to you?"

He smiled, not angry. "Once, after they gave money to my offering, I got invited. Maybe they wanted their forgiveness money back from me. I was tempted, but only by my damnable curiosity. I'm too old a dog to hunt pups. So I turned down the chance to see what some boys described to me as cute, half-grown breasts, and a semihairless mound. She was an astonishing-looking child, a temptress in the making, a harlot-to-be."

"Guess for me about who did buy a look. Someone who did may have been the killer of Hansel-Gretel, Romeo-Juliet, Jim-Mary."

"I don't know. The two kids roamed the Madisonville streets in the warm months. And she got attention, lots of it, male and female. I'd like to have you believe it was Allwell so that you and Smalley can chase him and make his life a bad problem, but I ain't the kind who hears a lot about who is doing what, with which, and to whom. My collar's shaped wrong for that kind of idle gossip. But please remember at all times that Allwell was on the premises with the kids the day they died."

"Tell me more."

"He favored those kids, Robak. They'd go up the hill to his church service most Sundays. Then he'd traipse back down here with them to the trailers. He hated and feared Bert after a time, but that didn't deter him coming down the hill. He never saw me watching because my color made me invisible, but I saw him talking all the time the kids were around him, trying to possess their souls with his crazy visions, add them to his roughneck flock."

I waited.

He shook his head. "Poor little babies. Children with no chance. And something had gone wrong for them before they died. I used to watch and listen close and careful to them. It was songs from her all the time, country-western, with Jim smiling and watching and likely wanting. But, for maybe a month before the poisoning, the singing and the smiling all stopped and there was nothing but the winter cold. Maybe it was just the weather and that they couldn't get out of the trailer at nights without freezing." He shook his head. "Lord, oh Lord, it did get cold in early March. Killed the tree buds, killed the peach crop."

"I'm likely to meet Reverend Allwell tonight," I said.

"Where?" he asked, interested.

"An open house somewhere in town. I'll be going with Smalley. He says Allwell will be there."

"I know where that party is. You step careful," he said. "Allwell has a lot of guards most of the time. Do you know Smalley whipped him up at the courthouse?"

I shook my head.

"I heard it from someone who was present and knows I hate Allwell. There was a land trial. Allwell cussed Smalley out, calling him bad names out in the hall. A man who saw it said Smalley stepped on Allwell's foot and then grabbed him, one hand holding his nose and turning it, the other squeezing his testicles tight. Then a sheriff's deputy got between them. Allwell was screaming loud and hurt." He smiled. "I wish I'd seen it."

I smiled also. When Smalley had told me about the confrontation he'd made me believe nothing had happened.

"I'll ask about that."

* * *

81

A dirty man picked that moment to limp in front of Mellish's kitchen window. He had a scrubby beard and looked like a forced retiree from a coal mine, carrying a burlap bag over his shoulder.

"There's a possible suspect," Mellish said. "He's one of Allwell's favorites. But he's also old as sweet Jesus."

"What's his name?"

"He's jestingly called Cleaner. Last name is Kline."

We watched the ancient man totter on.

"The story's told in the trailers that he used to have sex problems when he was a younger man. Now he's at least eighty and has medical problems instead. He's off on his walking route. He'll move along, mostly by instinct, and pick up everything that's not nailed down. He does alleys. He's a rifler of trash barrels, an invader of unlocked garages. He likes aluminum cans and sells them somewhere. He steals mostly, but he's so sick the cops don't bother him much. Pick him up, take him to jail, and you got to call a doctor for him. I don't see much of him around here these days. Mostly he hangs around up at Allwell's Survival church."

"Tell me more about his sex problems."

"What I've heard is gossip. Nowadays the kids make fun of him. They yell bad names. He watches them like an old hawk with a crippled wing. The kids tell me he used to flash them, but he don't do that now. Maybe he's forgot how."

We watched the old man until he was out of sight.

"Could he have bought a look?"

"Unlikely." He frowned and shook his head. "I think I know why Allwell puts up with him. Cleaner won't talk to anyone who has to do with government. He won't even answer my questions when I go for the rent. He'll tell me he wants a lawyer. I'd move him out, put a padlock on his door, but leaving him here gets the bank his beat-up trailer when he dies."

"Allwell puts up with him only because he causes problems?"

"Sure. So does Allwell. Cleaner causes little problems, Allwell causes big ones."

I decided I could check out Cleaner Kline with the sheriff or Smalley if I heard anything else interesting. I put him out of mind for now.

"Bert had a Virginia Jones on her list she wanted me to talk with."

"She's Bert's cousin. She'd be an okay witness for you and Mr. Smalley. I ain't seen her for a time. She goes to Louisville and stays. She's got a man down there. Her trailer's six down from mine, same side of the road. She's got a blue Plymouth, ten or twelve years old, with the back right fender off. I'll watch for her if you'd like."

I nodded. "I'd like."

I drank some more water and he sipped at the last of his coffee. I looked at my watch. It was noon and my stomach was announcing hunger. I liked the sensation.

"Reverend, could I take you to lunch somewhere and ask some more nosy lawyer questions?"

"You don't have to take me to lunch."

"I'd like to."

He saw I meant it and he nodded, pleased. "I got a place I like. You'll like it also for several reasons. The general menu's okay, but the salads are first-class. They also have an oversize air conditioner. It can make you want to build a fire next to your table."

"I am your man," I said.

We grinned at each other. I wasn't sure why we were friends, but I knew we were. Perhaps we'd known each other in a former existence, a prior life under another flag or an alien pair of blue-white suns.

Something. Sometime.

He looked like a soft pile of jelly, but I knew he was more than that—an angry man trying hard to live in peace.

The restaurant he picked was small and had no flies. The frigid air-conditioning took care of that. A few people, most of them wearing sweaters, were eating. The place smelled good and the menu was Greek American. A large middle-aged waitress wearing a worn apron listened to our order and fought boredom.

I ordered vegetable soup and a cheese sandwich on rye. Mellish sighed over the daily special, but eventually ordered a salad and a diet cola.

"Can't eat a lot," he explained to me and the waitress.

He then stopped her from leaving us by putting out a big black hand.

"If Mr. P's in the kitchen, ask him to come out here. I've got someone he'll want to meet."

"Sure, Reverend," she said, still bored. She waited until his hand went down and then fled.

"Who's Mr. P?"

"Peter Petrakis. He's Mary-Gretel's blood daddy."

Nothing I'd read, heard, or seen had informed me that Mary's father was around and available in Madisonville.

The man who came out of the kitchen wore a sweaty white T-shirt with a Yale University seal. I guessed he was not yet forty years old. He was well built, a couple of inches under six feet, and maybe two hundred pounds. His hair was black and curly and there was a lot of it. He reminded me of both Mary and Jim from the photos I'd seen in Bert's trailer.

"How they hangin', Reverend Mo?"

"Down and dead," Mellish admitted. "I brought along Don Robak. He's Bert's new lawyer."

Peter Petrakis sized me up, grinned, and offered a strong, greasy hand.

I shook with him.

"I read about you in the local paper. You're from over in Bington. A customer told me earlier today about you surviving a courtroom shoot-up there."

I nodded.

"You are Mary's father?" I asked.

"I guess so."

"I saw a photo of her in Bert's trailer and I can see a resemblance."

"Others have said that, Mr. Robak. When she was alive I was never close to Mary. She didn't like me. Now and then she'd come in here if she got hungry enough. I'd feed her. I gave her a few presents from time to time. I gave her mother money when she asked for it. Mary hated me because I didn't marry her mother. We only dated for maybe two or three months, me in a rented room, her sometimes living with Bert, and sometimes in her own trailer near Bert. She never sued me legal to make me pay support for Mary. When she got bad sick I offered to take Mary in, but then Bert and I talked. We decided it was better for Bert to take care of both kids because they needed to be together." He looked down at the floor. "Maybe if I had taken her in she'd still be alive."

"More likely she'd have run off," I said.

"Pretty child," Mellish said, when the silence grew.

Petrakis nodded at both of us.

"Did you ever visit Mary at the trailer court?" I asked.

"No. I went there to visit her mother when she was sick. Mary was around, but when she saw me she took off." He shook his head. "I told Bert I'd give her whatever I could for the girl, but she never asked for anything. Except now and then, at odd hours, when we wasn't busy, she'd bring the kids in and I'd feed them all."

"Were you at the trailer court the day Mary and her brother died?"

"No way. I even stayed away from her funeral. There was talk about Mr. Smalley and the boy, Jim. I didn't want anyone starting something about me and the girl."

"What do you hear in the restaurant about the coming trial?" I asked curiously.

"I hear it strong that Bert poisoned the kids and that the town will get her if the law don't."

"What do you think?"

He shook his head. "I got me this little hole in the wall. All I want to do is stay quiet and hope the town forgets. I called Mr. Smalley one time early on and asked him not to come here to eat because I don't want to get involved in his gossip."

"What did he say?"

"Nothing. But he stopped coming in."

"Is there anything else you can tell me about the poisonings?"

"Maybe one more thing. The father of Mary's half brother got killed in a wreck on the interstate up around Columbus three years ago. He was Greek also, but no relation to me."

"Did you know him?"

"A little. He was a student for years. He played drums and sometimes I'd see him someplace here or in Bington that had live music."

"Did you ever talk to Mary's half brother?"

"No. I fed him when he was brought along."

I could think of nothing more to ask.

When we left Mellish smiled. "See the trouble I saved you?"

"You did good, Mo."

"I'll be looking out for you. Bert told me to do it and I will."

"Sure," I said.

He could have been my watcher the night before.

I dropped him at his trailer. He shook hands strongly and watched my car out of the trailer court.

I then drove back to Smalley's office. He was out somewhere, so I took some depositions I wanted to read more closely and went to my motel.

I was tired but couldn't nap, so I read the depositions for a time. Then I went outside and walked briskly in the motel parking lot for twenty minutes, then did nap for a while. I awoke when Smalley called about picking me up for the open house.

SIX

"When a government fears its citizens, rather than vice versa, you will find liberty in the land."

—Herbert Techni, New York, 1997

THE OPEN HOUSE had already begun by the time we arrived at the white-pillared brick home high on a hill not far past the western city limits of Madisonville. Smalley drove us through open iron gates. The grounds were apparently large enough to park attendees' cars invisibly. We were fifth in line past the gate, but the cars in front of us were whisked away one by one until it was Smalley's turn to surrender his Buick to invisibility.

It was dusk when we arrived and I couldn't see everything clearly, but I could tell the grounds were scoured clean of leaves, the grass cut close, and the wide blacktop road broomed free of mud and rocks.

A teenage boy nodded and grinned insolently at both of us. He gave Smalley a paper slip for a receipt, then gunned the Buick away. We stood for a moment on the entrance road in the half dark. A sweet warm wind blew softly from the northeast, instead of from the Ohio River to the south. The dusky sky was clear of clouds.

We found and walked a brick path lit by sand candles, then climbed broad steps to the columned porch. From there you could still plainly see the wide Ohio River outlined in the lights of Madisonville.

At a corner of the porch a thin, energetic lady behind a table bar dispensed what looked to be both soft and hard drinks. I could hear soft piano music from inside. Some people stood on the lawn in small groups from which came the occasional sound of laughter. Couples walked about or stood watching and admiring the river below.

"I can't remember. Did you tell me whose home this is?"

"Belongs to Judge Kittaning, or actually to his charming wife, Nettie. It's said she's got tons of money."

"Isn't she the lady who made a grab at you?"

He nodded. "She flat out told me a good, experienced woman could cure me, turn me around." He smiled. "She said I was cute and then got a hold on my family jewels. She likes men, lots of men. She doesn't spend a lot of her spare time knitting at home. She's twenty years younger than the judge. She plays golf and tennis. She's also into private, nighttime sports with whoever's single or maritally adventurous."

"How does our trial judge feel about that?"

Smalley smiled. "It's obviously something he doesn't discuss with me."

There was a line waiting for drinks at the porch bar. From the rail along the porch ceiling small pots of flowers swung gently in the slight breeze.

"Let's go on inside," Smalley said. "I've promised myself a drink to help take the outcast taste out of my mouth. I'll do that when we finish with business, but not until then. And you need to know this, Don—we might not even be offered a drink. We're here for a private hearing with the judge, prosecutor in attendance, away from the media, the courthouse, and the nasty crowds who despise our client and therefore us. We're not social guests."

"You already said that and it's okay," I said agreeably. I didn't give a damn.

"My understanding's that we want Bert's eyes checked and we want an MD to give us a report on her general health. We also want a toxicologist. Is that about it?"

"Yes." I wanted a toxicologist and a doctor so I could get answers to some questions I had. I wanted an optometrist to tell us how bad, in lay terms, Bert's eyes were—20/40, 20/100, 20/400, whatever. Something a juror could understand.

"Anything else?"

"Yes. I want someone, either the doctor who did the autopsy or someone else, to give me an opinion on whether the girl Mary was sexually active before and particularly *on* the day she died, if a doctor can give that kind of medical opinion."

He shook his head. "She was only thirteen years old, Don."

"No intact hymen. That's what the autopsy report says. They start young sometimes. I think she did. The man who did the autopsy said she wasn't pregnant, but gave no opinion on what I'd like to know."

"Why the need? The fact that she was into diddling young doesn't mean much to me when I try to connect it with her poisoning."

"Mo Mellish told me that Mary's behavior and demeanor during the last days of her life had changed. She went from being happy to being unhappy, withdrawn, and silent. She was selling sex peeks, look-sees at her body, for dream and runaway money to be used by her and Jim. Jim was helping, usually armed with a .22 rifle, except he didn't have that gun on the last day both of them were alive." I shook my head. "And there was some kind of kid game going on up the hillside across from the trailer camp, a continuing thing. We need to find out where it was being played. We probably also need to find out the rules of the game."

"I never heard about any of this stuff in any of the depositions."

"Mellish told me a few things today. You didn't check out the kids because they weren't on the state's witness list and you figured they'd say what their folks told them to say. Mellish thinks we need to talk to the kids who played the game. Reverend Allwell might also be involved. Remember that he came down the hill from his church with the two kids the day they died. Maybe they stopped someplace along the way and Allwell bought or talked himself into a look, a sniff, or a feel. Or more."

Smalley nodded, suddenly liking what I was saying. "So we want a doctor to give us an opinion as to whether she was sexually active?"

"Only if whoever did the autopsy has no opinion and another autopsy could give us added information."

Smalley smiled. "Good thing she was buried instead of cremated. If we ask for an exhumation that would really blow things sky high in my po' town."

"Can't be helped."

"Yeah." His smile broadened. "It's too damn bad. I wonder, up front, what the local headlines would read if we get Mary's body exhumed."

"Maybe 'Smalley Ponders Dead Girl's Body.' "

He smiled, catching the dark attempt at humor. "Yeah, something like that."

We entered double front doors into a long hall full of portraits, gold- and silver-backed mirrors, and bright candles.

Off to our right was a huge candlelit great room. Inside, people dressed in party clothes stood in little groups, drinking and talking. No one noticed us, or perhaps they chose to ignore us.

In a far corner of the room someone was playing good piano. Old stuff: "The Shadow of Your Smile," then "Stardust."

Smalley said tersely, "Wait right here for me. Don't move."

I watched him lower his head for invisibility and cross the floor of the big room and lean toward the piano player. In a moment Smalley straightened, nodded and smiled, and returned. "We'll now find the judge and the prosecutor," he said.

He paused and held up his hand and stepped back to the wide doors of the great room and looked about inside once more, this time head up. Conversations slowed and I could hear the piano better. One man inside nodded coolly at Smalley and nudged his companion. Smalley acknowledged the nod with a flick of his head, then turned away from the door.

"The piano player in there is the one we heard playing the organ on the hill. We'll try the study. Follow me."

We moved down the hall, walking beneath the portraits of people who appeared to be, judging by their dress, from an earlier time in history. The portraits stared down at us disapprovingly in the flickering candlelight.

I wanted to know more about the piano player, but it seemed a time to wait for answers.

Smalley knocked on a dark wide door. I knew the man who opened the door, but he looked older than I remembered. I'd tried cases before him in his court and in my own county when he'd come special judging. Judge Abraham "Kit" Kittaning. He was a popular judge with the area lawyers, a small fat man with a good sense of humor. Right or wrong, he tried his cases swiftly, bore no grudges, and favored no one.

He gave us a smile, looked outside the door to see if there were observers, then waved us inside.

"Introductions first," he said. "Do you know our prosecutor? No? Don Robak, Lem Rand."

"I know of him, Your Honor." I smiled at an extra-large man. Rand was put together like a college fullback now slightly gone to fat. He smiled back and waved a hand. He was perhaps forty years old, dressed in an ill-fitting suit and a tie that didn't match. He tinkled ice cubes in a dark brown drink at Smalley and they smiled at each other, old acquaintances. Lem's hair was pepper-and-salt, with a prominent bald spot on top.

I remembered twenty years back, in the times when I'd thought attending football games was fun. Lem had been a tailback, fast and strong, second-team All-American, drafted high by the Bengals, soon gone from the pros after he lost a split second to knee surgery.

"You need to know Robak, Lem. He'll take over as Mojeff County circuit judge, replacing Harner, come first of next year." He looked at me. "Lem does a lot of trials, civil and criminal. Don. And he's good at them."

The prosecutor put his drink down on a cloth napkin. He shook my hand easily, a man used to parties.

"Good to meet you," he said, after a while.

"And you. You made a lot of my Saturday afternoons better a few years ago."

"Thank you. It's been a long time since those days. I heard about you getting shot," he said. "And Judge Harner was a special favorite of mine. Smart judge who'd listen. How's he doing?"

"No one's sure yet. I intend to stop past and see him and his wife this weekend."

"Shook everyone up around here bad. We've now got a metal detector you have to go through when you come to court. Lots of angry people out there walking the streets. Some say the cities are real bad."

He was right about that. Almost every day in Louisville, the major city of the area, armed people shot armed or unarmed people in bars, homes, and on the streets. Some of the shootings were planned, some were the result of quick anger, and others were just senseless drive-by slaughters. A mad bomber had recently targeted Louisville parochial schools, trying to explode his pipe bombs when children were present.

After Judge Harner had been shot, many of the area courts had put in metal detectors, a deputy sheriff operating the unit and another deputy or two with riot guns standing watch nearby. It was not yet that way in Bington, county seat of Mojeff County, but I was willing to change it.

"Is there anything we can do for Harner from over here?"

"Hope and pray, then do it some more." I put together what I knew and then told it all because it needed saying. "The bullet hit him a glancing blow. It splintered the left side of his head. It didn't penetrate the brain, no matter what the newspapers and TV reported, but it did fracture his skull in a bunch of places. The doctors had to pick some bone splinters out of his brain. For a time thereafter he was in a coma. It was almost two months before he came up and out of that. His doctor told me that's medically a long time. Now he sleeps a lot. He follows simple commands and sometimes will answer a question with a yes or no. His doctor says he doesn't think there's much pain, but the judge is mostly paralyzed on his right side. He sees and hears." I shook my head. "It's as if someone opened his head and used an eggbeater. He sometimes knows people by name, but mixes them up with other people in what he remembers. When they take him for therapy, his wife says he tries hard. She thinks he's more alert now than he was, say, a month ago. Maybe he'll improve more, maybe not."

"I know you killed the man who shot the two of you," Lem said approvingly.

"Yes. I did that."

"Good for you."

I nodded. "Thanks. Not everyone feels that way. I've got a church I sometimes attend in Bington. Some people there now ignore me, others look at me hard."

"They'll get over it," Judge Kittaning said.

"Please tell Thelma and Judge Harner, if you think he can understand, that we asked after him and send our best," Lem said.

Kittaning nodded his agreement.

"I'll do that, and I thank you both," I said.

"And so you'll take the bench?" Lem asked curiously.

"Yes. There's a chance, if Harner recovers enough to do the job and wants it, that he could do it again. I'd likely go with him to the governor, resign, and let the governor reappoint him, but only if it can work out exactly that way." I doubted that was going to happen because the governor was not of my party nor Harner's. If I resigned, the governor wouldn't appoint Harner—he'd have his own political debts to pay off.

"Can I get either of you gentlemen a drink?" the judge asked, smiling.

"Not yet for me," Smalley said. "These days, because I'm suspected of committing various deviate crimes by lots of good old Madisonville citizens, I don't drink a lot."

Judge Kittaning faced him. "You were the one who shouted out to the whole Madisonville world that you were gay. I'm the one who advised you against it, remember?"

Smalley nodded. "I remember."

"Let's just do our trial talking," the judge said. "We won't worry about bad news, old news, or things we can't change.

If we're going to have ourselves a jury trial week after next, we need to get to planning for it. I'll have to go to South Vernon and do some work with the judge up there." He looked at Smalley again. "How about it, Kevin? Will you and your eminent Bington death-penalty-qualified associate here be ready to start picking an out-of-county jury in South Vernon week after next to hear this case?"

"No, Your Honor. But we likely will be ready to begin voir dire soon after the set time. In order to be ready for trial we need some things you and the prosecutor can help us obtain. Robak wants to go over the evidence, talk to some of the witnesses, including Dr. Willis and whoever assisted him in the autopsy. Then we want the defendant examined by a medical doctor and an optometrist. We want our own toxicologist to retest the contents of the stew pot for possible trace elements and the purity of the nicotine. We want a complete and final list of state's witnesses, and we want to see all the proposed exhibits. We want to have and control all things taken from Bert's trailer that aren't to be introduced by the state, and we want the state to know there may be things from the trailer we will introduce ourselves. We'll divulge exactly what when we decide what. And there's a possibility we may want both bodies exhumed for further tests if the autopsy doctors don't have answers for the questions we intend to ask."

"What questions?" Lem asked.

"The most important one would be whether or not, in the doc's medical opinion, the girl was sexually active," Smalley said. "And, even more important, whether she'd had sex on the morning she died. Then, possibly, we might want to check the boy for the same thing."

"What's that?" the judge asked. "That girl was only thirteen years old, the boy a year or two older."

Smalley turned to me. He winked a tiny wink. "You explain it, Don."

I gave the judge my best and most serious look. "Some things we've learned lead us to believe the girl was selling sexual favors. She was an extremely pretty child and likely old for her age."

"And so? Shit, boys, I see eleven- and twelve-year-olds in juvenile court who give it away for free or charge lollipops for it in the bushes at school. The girls are sometimes worse than the boys. What effect would her being sexually active have in a trial to determine whether or not your client killed her?"

"Diddling kids is a felony, Your Honor. It's a felony to touch them sexually for your fun or theirs. Even if it's consensual, kiddie sex is a felony for the adult involved. If any of the people who were doing sex things with her—and paying her for it—were adults, then they could be in a lot of trouble if caught. Maybe someone got extremely worried. It could be that such a worried person was the one who poisoned the pot." I nodded firmly. "That's also why we want an eye test and a physical examination of our client. We know that Bertha doesn't see well, but we don't know how bad her vision is. Someone dropped the nicotine in the pot and poisoned the kids. The kids then died. That's a fact we'll stipulate. Everyone's willing, even anxious, for the perpetrator to be Bertha Jones. We, of course, aren't."

The judge stood for a moment thinking. Then, finally, he nodded.

"Okay. Sounds okay."

"Anything else?" Lem Rand asked.

"Not now. But what we find out from the various examinations may trigger further questions." I looked at Lem. "You know what I mean."

"Sure," Lem said. "Talk to both doctors, Willis and Gant. Willis did the autopsy on both kids, Gant assisting. You may get what you need from them. If a body, or both bodies, have to be exhumed, there's going to be a lot of local grumbling. But that's no problem as long as we get done with the trial by the end of the year." He smiled, perhaps thinking about the end of the year and his return to private practice. "In fact, there's no problem at all."

"So be it," Judge Kittaning said. "Now boys, I'm going to leave you. I've got the publisher of the local newspaper digging at me for news. He also wants to interview you, Robak, but please don't do that here tonight. With the trial being delayed he may leave you alone for a while. Outside, there's also the owner of the local radio station. He'll also want to talk to you. We'll let them compete for you somewhere else, at some other time. I also have a phone number to call in Louisville. I may or may not call it. There's a lady reporter who's been writing snotty things about our Madisonville justice system in the *Courier-Journal*. She left a message and order with my court reporter that she expected me to call."

"Might be more important for the Louisville paper to examine their Louisville problems," Smalley said.

Judge Kittaning nodded. "True, but they like to consider themselves the area paper and pick on us, too. Can we set another tentative trial date now so I have some hard news to tell them?"

"As long as it's a tentative 'almost sure' date. And we'll use it too, if all goes well and we manage to get our work done," I said. I looked at Smalley and he nodded. "Plus, if you'd like, we could hold a public courtroom pretrial on our old trial date so that we could report publicly how we're doing." I looked over at Smalley and he smiled encouragingly. "Assuming that's agreed to by my esteemed lead defense counsel."

"Agreed," Smalley said.

The judge nodded affably. "All okay with you, Mr. Prosecutor?"

"Sure."

Lemuel Rand looked us over, his face seemingly absent of guile. "I want you two defense gentlemen to understand up front that I will deal this case. I've been assured that our judge here will then recuse himself. That's because he doesn't want to be tarred out of the same pot the locals will use on me if I agree to a plea bargain. We then will pick a judge from far away who'll promise to accept the plea bargain. Do your work and then get back to me. I don't believe your client should get the death penalty despite the fact that the grand jury and most of the town criers think so. Force me to the wall and I'll seek it. Be reasonable and we'll work out a deal."

I watched him and was unsure. There was maybe something he knew that we didn't know.

"Does this Church of the Survival have a branch up around South Vernon?" I asked.

He shrugged and I thought his eyes knew more than his answer. "I'm not sure."

Smalley said, just managing to keep from smiling, "Well, maybe we ought to just skip all this foolishness and burn Bert at the stake in the name of humanity and because she's a witch."

Lem shook his head, "Our evidence will plainly show she's mean and vicious, and a well-known public scold. It'll further prove that she fought with her wards, inflicted many beatings on them, and thereafter poisoned them in the presence of about a score of witnesses. She's a woman who struck mortal fear in the minds of her neighbors and then killed the two children she was supposed to love and care for."

I held up my hand. "I'm going to ask her to reconsider taking a lie detector if the state's offer is still open."

Lem smiled. "She won't take the test, Robak. I think I know why."

"Maybe she might if she could look at the questions before the test."

"No deal on that bullshit," he said. "If she takes a test, then the sky's the limit on questions. And, if she takes it, the results have to be available as evidence for both sides."

"Nevertheless, I'm going to ask her again."

Smalley shook his head, siding with Lem. "She won't take it, Don."

I shrugged at both their answers. "Another thing, which I think you all have already agreed to: we're to pick the jury in South Vernon if that doesn't fall through. When we begin voir dire I'd like the first question to be asked by the court. I want the jury, as a group, to be asked if anyone has contacted them in any way, even in a church sermon, about this case. I want hard questions and straight answers on what the panel knows about this case."

Lem shrugged and then nodded. "I agree."

"You're a suspicious man, Robak," Judge Kittaning said, smiling.

I said, "What we've discussed here isn't all I'm suspicious about," and then decided to say no more.

When an uncomfortable silence grew, Judge Kittaning nodded at the three of us. "Business of the evening is now declared finished." He waited and we waited. "Now, can I bring either of you defense gentlemen something to drink before I sally forth and circulate at my child-bride's party?"

"I'd take a light Scotch and water," Smalley said. "Very little Scotch." He grinned. "I'd not want anyone, male or female, to smell booze on my breath and worry that I was about to molest them."

The judge shook his head. "The town out there will get over its anger at you in time, Kevin. But for now, it might be best for all concerned if you don't mingle here."

"Of course," Smalley said, his voice careful.

"No booze. Water only for me, Judge." I decided to agitate things a bit. "Did you notice if Cardinal Allwell was on the premises?"

"Some call him Bishop Allwell, but I haven't heard him raised to the rank of Cardinal yet, even by himself," the judge answered evenly. "I think he's here. I know he likes to look at the stars and ponder this universe he controls." He smiled, but only a little. "He's been here before as a social guest of my wife, who likes interesting people. I'd imagine you'll find him outside wandering the back lawn or perhaps on our lookout point just below the crest of the east hillside. It's likely he'll be with my wife, or someone else's wife. He has none of his own."

"Where'd he come from, Kit?" I asked softly.

Kittaning looked at me. For a moment I thought he might admonish me for using his nickname, but then he perhaps remembered I'd be joining his robed fraternity come the first of January.

"I've heard it said he miraculously appeared here from the hills of eastern Kentucky just when we needed him to help us survive the Armageddon he predicts. I don't know that to be a fact. He's been around for six or eight years and has done well. That church of his must have close to a thousand members and, collectively and individually, his congregation are problems. Some carry their Bibles into court when called to serve as jurors. Some want to ask their own questions. Many believe the end of the world is near and profess it in open court. I'm told they keep illegal guns in old fallout shelters on church grounds." He shook his head ruefully. "Allwell's a jackass of a man, a bad-tempered shouter of a preacher, and unfortunately a force in my town. He preaches his own law, not yours, not mine. He has no use for the other local ministers, and they have less use for him."

"Someone up near his church aimed a laser-sighted gun at us this morning," I said.

Lem said, "The sheriff said he checked up there and found no one around the church camp when he arrived." He nodded at Smalley. "He called me after you called him."

"Thanks for letting him check it out," Smalley said. "I talked to the judge's piano player when I came in the house tonight. He was playing the organ up there. He told me he didn't know anyone else was around the church this morning except Allwell."

Lem smiled. "Allwell wasn't there when the sheriff's deputy arrived. Deb was glad to check. I'll pass on what the piano player said. Someone shot Deb not too far from that hill church. Let's all remember that I'm not a political candidate. I don't have to kiss anyone's ass or keep any group of voters happy. Me being that way's a knotty problem for Allwell. To add to your store of knowledge, I had state detectives check out Allwell a couple of years back when we started finding it was difficult to use his church members as jurors. When the reverend was younger, he had a church in the eastern Kentucky mountains near the West Virginia line, a little country church in the middle of some bloody coal country. There was trouble in the church concerning Allwell and maybe some members. I think some of the men got together as a mob and ran him out, told him he'd be dead if he stayed or returned. He came to Madisonville then. He started his own church, now preaches his own brand of religion, and apparently isn't fool enough to get caught again with the women."

"Maybe he fools with thirteen-year-old girls instead," I said. "We got crazies around Bington also. The man who shot Judge Harner, and then got me, belonged to some kind of church family there that wants to control the judicial process."

"Everyone has their share of crazies these days," Lem said. "Allwell's the biggest pain around here. He hassles Deb and his deputies. He threatens the court clerk. Some of his people insist on trying to file noncourt judgments with her. When she won't file them, she gets threats. Someone writes demand letters and shows around judgments, not taken in any court of record, against me and against the judge here. They file them with the county recorder in the Miscellaneous Records and inform our recorder she's got to accept them. She does. Things keep building. I think that's why we need to get the trial behind us. I'm willing to go ahead and do it instead of leaving it for the next unfortunate who'll have my office and be under more pressure than I am."

"I run year after next," the judge said. "Allwell's people already have a candidate lined up to run against me. The gentleman has been suspended from practice twice, but now he's a deacon in Allwell's church and so has been forgiven his past sins."

"Any chance he'd beat you?"

"I hope not," Judge Kittaning said. "But who knows?"

"Maybe we ought to do some further clergy study as part of our preparation for the trial," I said.

"What value will that have?" Lem asked.

Smalley held up a hand, silencing my answer. "Don feels the way I feel. I don't like having a gun aimed at me for real or for fun. I feel threatened. I also wonder what the man behind the gun is thinking."

"Allwell's strange," Judge Kittaning said. "Tonight will be about as private as you'll ever find him. Usually he surrounds himself with men holding shotguns and rifles. He lives with guards and behind an electric fence." He nodded at us, obviously on our side. "As I said, you'll surely find him out back."

"Does he send people into your family court hearings—separations, dissolutions, and the like?"

"Sometimes."

"That was part of the background on the day Judge Harner and I got shot. Don't relax your local precautions, Your Honor. Make sure everyone who enters your court-room goes through your metal detector."

He nodded. "You can bet your butt I'll do exactly that."

SEVEN

"Use the jury room in any way you can to start the tide against oppression."

> —Herbert Techni, speech, Madisonville, Indiana, Spring 1997

AFTER MORE HANDSHAKES, Judge Kittaning and the prosecutor left the room for the party. Neither returned. Smalley and I sat in the study alone.

After what seemed a long time, a maid brought us drinks on a tray along with some hors d'oeuvres. The snacks were mostly bite-sized soda crackers spread with deviled ham and cheese. I nibbled one, found it edible, and ate some more while I drank my water and Smalley sipped a drink. I was hungry even though we'd stopped for a sandwich. My appetite had returned. I was buoyed by my own hunger, and, for the first time since I'd been shot, glad to be involved in legal combat.

I knew Smalley felt insulted, perhaps mostly for me, because we hadn't been invited into the general party, but since I couldn't think of a way to lighten the insult, I said nothing about it.

"Want to wander outside?" Smalley asked, putting his almost untouched drink down on an ashtray.

"Yes. Out back. Let's go see if we can locate the good clergyman Allwell."

"If only Allwell and the organ player were on church premises this morning, who do you think zeroed in on us with a laser sight?"

"Could there have been others around?"

"I suppose. But right now I intend to believe that the man having fun with us was Allwell."

We exited the study and soon found our way to a screened back porch where a few diehard smokers nursed cigarettes and sipped drinks. As we passed through, they stared at us silently through their smoke.

After we were outside, Smalley smiled and whispered, "We're in the same class as pariah smokers. If you think it's tough on cigarette smokers, think about someone who's spent an adult lifetime smoking cigars."

"You?"

He nodded. "I'm cured now, but it was a problem for a while."

We walked the rear lawn but found no one other than two aging lovers who sat in a garden swing necking and fondling each other below the neck.

"They're married," Smalley said when we were out of earshot. "But not to each other."

We found Allwell on the lookout point the judge had described. We used the newly risen moon and the lights of the town below to locate him.

Allwell stood on a fenced ledge close to a tall, shapely woman. They were looking together up into the night sky, searching for something, huddled close in the evening heat. Maybe he was pointing out stars, planets, and constellations to her. I heard her laugh. When she spied us looking down, she drew a little away from Allwell and stared up at us.

From another time, long ago, the woman looked familiar. She was fiftyish and comely rather than beautiful. Her perfect teeth flashed in the night and I could see she was angered by our interruption.

Allwell was big. He had a chest that looked a yard wide, His upper legs resembled barrels and his face was about the size of a five-gallon bucket. His hands were big enough to do business with the rest of him. He was dressed all in black except for the white cross he wore around his bull neck. His hair and eyebrows were also black as midnight, shoe-polish black. His features, despite the size of his head, were snub, babyish, almost cute.

I felt the night wind blow up stronger as I examined him.

The woman nodded coldly at Smalley. "Who invited you to my party?"

"Your husband, Judge Kittaning," Smalley answered, voice light. "We earlier had court business with him. We also now have a pressing need to speak to Reverend Allwell before we depart your charming affair."

"It appears I'll need to dictate some rules for my husband to follow about who visits my house," she said. She nodded and started up the fenced path to the top of the hill. She then called back, "Reverend, you're invited into the house once you've finished your trash work. Come alone."

Her words angered me and I thought they might have been spoken for that purpose.

"I'm sure he'll trot right along," I called after her. "Do keep things warm for him."

"I remember you, Don Robak," she said unexpectedly. "I never expected to see you in the company of someone like Smalley."

"I also remember you," I called back, although I didn't.

We waited until she'd vanished and the sound of her footsteps had ceased.

"There has to be some valid reason you two interrupted

my seldom social life, Mr. Smalley," Allwell said. His voice was rich. "Please state that reason. If you seek absolution, I've none to offer you and your sweet new friend here."

"No absolution. If I needed help from God I'd ask elsewhere, not from someone who likely found God about the same time he discovered the Internal Revenue Code. But we could use your help in another way. We were exploring the hill area above where the two children died. Someone inside your camp fired a gun near us and also aimed the same gun at us through what we believe was a laser sight. We want to know who did that illegal act, Reverend."

"Do you now?" Allwell said, smiling, taking charge. "I don't want and don't ask my people to do either illegal or immoral things. But many of my church members are God-fearing people and therefore angry at you, your black-hearted poison witch client, and a system that allows a farce trial. I can't control such feelings. I won't try. Your client committed the greatest of sins in murdering two white children when her own blood is questionable at best. You and your boyfriend here continue to commit your own semiprivate sins against the laws of God. That's also a problem for my flock. Whoever frightened you on my hill may have been any one of the thousand or so of my followers."

Smalley smiled back. "I wonder what your church folk would say if they found out the poisoned thirteen-year-old girl was sexually active? We're informed she sometimes displayed her pretties to older men who paid for the illegal view."

Allwell shook his head, unfazed. "That means nothing to me or mine."

"Slowing down our preparatory work for the trial will also slow down the day there'll be a trial," Smalley continued. "Keep it up and perhaps we'll ask the judge to set a bond and allow Bertha Jones to go free while awaiting the trial that's her constitutional right."

Allwell shook his head, his eyes flashing in the dim light. "All know the witch's trial will begin week after next. I intend to exhort my church members to be present in the courtroom. If you move to delay such trial, then surely a higher court will judge both the murder case and its lawyers."

"The date was always tentative," Smalley said. He turned to me. "Is there any chance we can begin the trial then, Mr. Robak?"

"Not now," I said. "And if great numbers of Mr. Allwell's followers show up in the courtroom the trial will never be held here."

Allwell's eyes moved to me. "I know that you're a Bington criminal lawyer named Donald Robak and that the law firm you're a member of has a black partner in a mostly white community. You're also known around Madisonville as the man who killed a believer from a friendly sister church near Bington. You did this in the Bington courtroom earlier this year. I'm told that man was a good man seeking only the justice that you and your locally owned judge denied him. I can't make myself believe that a man like you will sit on the bench and be the Bington high judge after the first of next year."

"Reverend, you've somehow managed to read my press clippings," I said. "Now know that I intend to read yours. You seem to be some kind of local mystery. I'll do some research here and in eastern Kentucky so that you won't long remain that way."

"Why such interest in me?" Allwell asked.

I saw he was alarmed. "Call it counter interest."

"I'm a simple man of God. What I was before I found God means nothing."

Smalley laughed openly, wounding the big man again. "We think you hide behind a church to cheat the tax people."

I continued, "I like to know everything about those who are my courtroom opponents. And I tell you again that the trial won't be week after next."

Allwell first looked up at the night sky, then back down at the ground, his face full of anger. He shook his head grimly and his voice was cold. "You people. You stupid lawyer people." He lifted his face to the dark again as if listening to a distant voice. "God tires of all of you. There's little time left."

"How much time, Allwell?" Smalley asked. "You pick the pockets of your congregation by predicting endings, but you never set an ending date. That's because any date you set will pass and you'll be exposed as the fraud you are."

Allwell shook his massive head and his voice became almost reasonable. "I know the date, but I will not announce it for a time. You mustn't interfere in what's left of man's existence on this sick earth. The trial of the witch is one of the things that must occur before all proceeds according to the yet unrevealed calendar of God."

He moved a step in my direction as he spoke. For a moment I regretted having left my revolver behind.

Smalley moved in front of me.

Allwell pronounced: "Don't tamper with my church or me. Don't stay what must happen. If you do, you'll pay for it now, and then again at the final time."

Smalley laughed aloud. "No one here fears you. Go shake your cross at the dunces who believe your white-power, ignore-all-law bullshit. Remember that the trial won't begin until we know what we need to know. Don't interfere with us again. You've tested me before without success. Go find your party, your present woman or another one, and use your ears to verify what's been said here."

I added softly, "Please make sure your woman for tonight is full grown."

"Others will try the witch if you delay what the good people of God want," Allwell said firmly.

"Ah, you mean your church court," Smalley said.

I said, "Lots of believers, but I doubt they even own an electric chair."

Allwell muttered something. Whatever it was it contained the words "rope" and "fire." I thought for just a moment that he was going to attack Smalley, but something stopped him. He pushed past us as if we were straw men. He went up the path, walking swiftly.

Smalley then did the unexpected. He took three quick steps after Allwell and kicked him hard in the butt. Allwell screamed, stopped, and turned.

"Want to try me now?" Smalley asked, grinning.

Allwell turned away and went up the path with what dignity he could muster. We waited until he was out of sight.

"I can't believe you got away with that," I said to Smalley.

"He's the one who used the laser sight on his hill. I'd like him to try fighting me again," Smalley said. "But not in a limited space like this. He's stronger than I am, but not as quick."

"You lied to me the other day when you claimed to be a peaceful man, and you also lied to me long ago when you said you didn't like to fight."

"What I said was mostly true."

"Why do you want to fight that piece of dog crap?"

"Because he's evil and because he thinks he's the master of all. He tells his church people that the last time we met outside the courtroom there was an accident. He slipped. I intend to make him slip again. Then, if I can, I'll break some bones, mark him up, damage him enough to make it impossible for him to hide."

"He could kill you. He's strong enough to kill both of us.

And, whether or not he's anything else, he has an elevator that doesn't go to all floors."

"He's crazy only when it suits him."

I shook my head. I found I was still breathing hard.

Smalley suddenly pointed out into the darkness. "See that?" he asked.

"What?"

"Do you see what I see down there?"

I looked where he pointed.

"There, to the left of the river. A little of the way up the church hill, just beyond the old railroad tracks. There's a fire."

I did see it. The fire wasn't large, but it was there.

"You want to hike there now?" he asked, excited.

I shook my head. "I'm dead tired. Maybe we could find that fire in the dark tonight, and maybe not. I want to talk to Bert again in the morning. Then I'm going to drive to Bington. I want to see my sheriff in Bington about some things that happened when I was shot and about any connection between the crazy Redeemer church there and Allwell's church here. I want my former partners to look into other things you and I can't. I'll be back Sunday afternoon. We'll try to find where the fire is then. Okay?"

He nodded. "Okay. And I do believe we've worn out all our welcome here, Don."

"Get Bert's eyes examined this weekend if you can. Have a medical doctor check her health."

"Okay. The judge's wife knew you. From where and when?"

"I don't know. I acted as if I knew, but I don't. Somewhere, sometime. Maybe school. Maybe the service. I think it had to be long ago."

He smiled. "I thought when I watched her that she doesn't hate you like she hates me. She seemed more interested than angry."

114

"I can't remember a thing."

"Memory's the first thing that goes when you get old," he said lightly.

I thought of something else. "A couple of times I tried to link Allwell with our dead girl-child when we were talking. Did you read anything while you watched him?"

He shook his head. "No, but Allwell's a man who's likely been accused before. He never changed expression or blinked when you tried to put him together with Mary. And he was the same way when he built his story that someone other than him was the man with the laser sight."

"Maybe he thinks he's a better debater than a couple of poor country lawyers," I said.

"I'm sure he does," Smalley said.

I left word at the motel office to receive an early wake-up calls, then parked the LTD near my room.

My bag had been moved some and my room looked as if someone had tossed it, but I decided it was likely only the maid putting things into her idea of order.

Before I slept, I went back outside for the .38 from the LTD's glove compartment and put it on the night table by my bed. I flipped open the cylinder and saw it was still loaded.

Just as I was about to climb into bed, the phone in the room rang, startling me.

The voice on the line was that of Nettie Kittaning. "I apologize for ordering you off, but you were with that damnable *man*."

"I appreciate your apology."

"I told Bishop Allwell that you weren't like Smalley."

"Why did you tell him that?"

"Because you're not," she said. "Are you?"

"No. How did you know where I was staying?"

"Allwell knew. He told me." She paused for a long moment. "While you're here I hope we get a chance to see each other and talk over, and maybe even renew, old times. Things are quieter here now at the house. Could you sneak back for a talk?"

"Not tonight, but maybe later." I still didn't remember her and, from what Smalley had said, guessed she was interested in far more than talk.

She said nothing else and we breathed at each other in half excitement until she softly clicked the phone down.

I swallowed a little of Bert's nostrum and slept well, but not without dreams.

Dreams: A huge man in black followed silently behind me as I crossed a hot, sandy desert. I could hear him behind me and, now and again, I would catch a glimpse of him. He kept screaming at me. He was the prosecutor and I'd broken all the rules for defense lawyers.

The man behind me wasn't always Allwell. Sometimes he was just a faceless, angry man, a man who hated the world, all its people, and all its law. A man who cursed churches, accepted welfare, sought divorce, plotted murder, committed rape, and robbed the poor to give to the rich. He wore a crooked white cross around his neck.

I awoke and was afraid in the darkness, not knowing where I was. I listened in the night to nothing at all, found myself, then slept again. This time I dreamed of long-ago college days. I saw my first wife. I hadn't dreamed of her for a long time, but Jo and I had been separated for months now and I remembered the way it had been with wife number one. Once I'd loved my first wife more than anything, so the dream was a vivid, absurdly sexual fantasy of that time.

I awoke again in the early morning just when the light was quickening outside. I thought about the night before, about Kittaning's wife and her late phone call, and suddenly remembered her and when I had known her.

Thirty years.

It had been in my drinking days at the time my first wife left me, then quickly divorced me. That had been the semester I'd almost uncaringly flunked out of college.

I remembered for a while and then tossed myself back to sleep.

In the fullness of morning, under a sunless, mostly gray sky, I jogged wetly three times around the motel, moving slowly, but moving. I watched around me. If anyone was observing me for Allwell or others I didn't spot them. My insides burned more than a little on the final trip around, but after I stopped and had my shower, all seemed well.

On this morning, I sang loud and defiantly. There was no neighboring-room interruption. The motel stood weekend-empty.

I missed Jo and Joe, but I had accepted their leaving me as fact. I was happy again.

I'll get Jo and Joe back. Sure I will.

I walked over to the shopping center restaurant where I'd eaten the day before and had a pair of soft-boiled eggs on top of dry toast. I finished up with a cup of black decaf. The same waitress waited on me. Today she was remote and silent; she offered me no new religious tracts. I wondered if she now knew who I was. It was possible.

I sat for a time after finishing. I thought about the night before and wondered about the laws of chance. Nettie Clelland Kittaning and I had known each other long ago, and now we'd met again. It had been a lot of years since I'd been an undergraduate student. Memories of that time were no longer sharp images. I remembered my first wife, but I no longer could recall exactly what she looked like. I'd loved her then as much as I'd ever loved anyone. I'd met her in Bington at the university. She'd been cute, cuddly, and warm during a cold winter and a better sophomore spring. I was the answer to her dreams, even if I didn't belong to a fraternity. We'd married in heat and haste that sophomore year. We'd believed when we wedded that she was pregnant. When we later found that she wasn't, we'd both been relieved. We'd then fought without rules or reasons until the divorce. She got remarried three weeks later to an insurance salesman who owned both Greek letters and a college degree in business. A big man on campus. They'd had four children before she also found him wanting. Their kids would be grown by now.

When we were married she'd had a friend, a slightly older girl named Annette Clelland who'd belonged to her sorority but who liked the freedom of living outside the sorority house. Annette had lived in a small apartment above ours. The two women had gossipped, shopped, walked, bowled, and traded steamy love novels during the life and times of our short marriage.

Annette had mostly frowns for me at first. That ended when she comforted and then bedded sodden me in her apartment just after my wife's quickie divorce. I remembered she'd whispered to me that we were doing no harm, just having some recreational fun.

It had been okay with me then. The affair had lasted almost two weeks until my rent ran out and I moved on.

I'd also had intimate relationships that year with other young women, two of them also my now ex-wife's sorority sisters.

That was okay too. Maybe I'd pursued her sorority sisters to get even, but I didn't remember it as being that way. One of those girls hadn't even minded that I was an independent barbarian rather than a hotshot fraternity man.

I saw my ex-wife only once after our divorce, at a college reunion. By that time she'd gotten slightly fleshy and was pregnant again. Her eyes became cold when she saw me. I played my part well. I said my hellos with a smile and was both nervous and nonchalant, wearing my best suit of two, sipping Jack Daniels and water, while her insurance-salesman second husband noisily drank beer and told lies with old buddies.

That had been okay also.

Now "old friend" Annette was married to Judge Abraham "Kit" Kittaning and was therefore Mrs. Nettie Kittaning, and anxious to see me again.

Smalley had told me she was the one who had money.

I wondered how she'd come to Madisonville. I wondered where she'd acquired *money*. Maybe inheritance from family or through an earlier husband.

Breakfast completed, contemplation done, I left my waitress her tip and walked back outside to my old LTD. The waitress watched me through the plate-glass window of the restaurant until I was inside my car.

I didn't much like Madisonville this morning. Too many people seemed to both know me and be watching me. All-well knew where I was staying, Kittaning's wife knew my phone number.

The morning remained cloudy. The streets were wet with mist and occasional showers. I wondered whether last night's weather had stayed fine or if it had rained on Nettie's party. Thinking it might have rained made me smile a little.

Too bad.

I had to grind the starter for a while to get the car going, but after that it ran okay.

Bert was up and dressed when I got to the jail. She wore a bright dress and a touch of lipstick. She smiled at me from inside her cell/room.

"You're a lot better," she said, positive of it. "Let me touch your hand again."

I gave it to her and she took it, held it in her cool one, then smiled some more.

"You're going to be full well soon. Do what you want to do. Test yourself. You've been recovering for a long time. My medicine just fixed the last problem."

"I ran a little this morning early. What's in the medicine you gave me?"

"Animals get clawed and bit bad in fights," she answered. "I watched lots of fights and found out what the survivors eat when they get hurt and live through the hurt. I made me up a medicine from the best I learned. It don't always work, but most times it does."

"It's real good."

She was pleased. "You need to be well to help me. Now tell me, what'd you find out?"

"I saw your cats at the trailer. They looked okay."

She nodded and waited.

"The prosecution claims you beat the kids with a stick. Did you do that?"

"Not with a stick. When I was going to switch them I sent them out for the switches. Ask the other kids. The only stick I remember having was one I used to stir the medicines."

"Good. One more: A child named Nancy Jane said to tell you hello and that the kids there know you didn't do anything wrong."

"She's a little sweetie."

I continued to ignore her question about what I'd found out. "Would it upset you if I gave some of the medicine from your bottle to Sheriff Deb Hewitt?"

She thought on it, frowning. "I guess it would. I don't like him. I know he's sure, down deep, that I didn't kill the kids, but I also know he ain't going to help me. I've seen him hobblin' and hurtin' and I've even heard some stories about the why and who of it. Someone shot him. It's said they did it a-purpose because he don't listen when someone important gives orders. I never offered him none of my medicine and I never would give him any. Why is it you want to do that?"

"Because you need to put up with him now. Even more than that, he needs to like you and be beholden to you. If we can get you out of this jail, then you can do what you please. But for now we need him."

She shrugged, not really caring. "If you say it's so, then it's so." She shook her head and muttered something I couldn't decipher. "Just go ahead."

"I thank you. He'll thank you. What kind of dose should he take? You told me to take it at night."

"A spoonful or two, anytime really, but you only need to take it once a day. Taking it more won't hurt or help."

She waited, her original question now seemingly forgotten.

"I have to go back to Bington for the weekend. I'll come back on Sunday. Your trial's been postponed, but not for long. I wanted to see you this morning to tell you some things and ask you some questions."

She nodded.

"It would help if you'd take a lie detector test. You didn't poison those kids. You know it, and Mr. Smalley and I know it. Why not take the test?"

She shook her head stubbornly. "I know I'm telling the truth, but I don't trust machines that makes judgments on my truth. People who hate me may be the ones who read the answers from them machines. And what they read could get in at the trial."

"This reader would be a state police expert."

"There's cops and cops. This one might be part of the enemy."

"Pass the test and you'd likely be out of here."

She shook her head again. "No."

If I could talk Prosecutor Lem into allowing me to control questions, I thought I might, one day, get her to take a lie detector, but I stopped for now.

"All right. There was once a gun, a rifle, in your trailer. Whose gun was it?"

"It was Jim's. A single-shot .22 rifle. He traded some of his junk stuff and books he'd likely stole to another boy for it."

"Did you take the gun from him?"

"No. I just ordered him not to carry it outside no more."

"Was there an argument?"

"Jim always argued hard. He told me he needed the gun bad for a business he and Mary was into. He was a bright boy, Jim was, a figurer. He could read a big book in half an hour and remember it all."

I thought I saw tears in her eyes as she remembered, so I waited for a moment.

"Did he ever tell you what the business was?" I asked after a moment.

"No. He kind of let me think it was ginseng. There's ginseng up above the old railroad tracks. But I never seen him or Mary with any ginseng."

"Okay." I decided to move on before I told her what business Mary and Jim had actually been into. "Your worst enemy outside, talking-wise, is Reverend Allwell."

"I guessed that. One time he begged me to become a part of his church. Now he tells his people I'm a poison witch and that my blood's no good. I'm a Jew and maybe part black. He knew my sister and me weren't the same blood. We was both adopted. He tells people about that over and over. She was good and has gone to heaven, I'm waiting for my seat in hell. I've seen him in the courthouse yard when they take me over that way. He yells and throws things."

"Why does he hate you so much?"

"Other than my dead kids, I ain't for sure. He used to

come by and eat my food and talk sweet with me. He told me I could be a big help to him in the next world that's for sure coming. He said I could see things in the future just like he could. But I knew he was a fake like a thousand other fakes in this world. I smiled at him and stood on my own ground. He was a friend of the kids afterward, not of mine. He went crazy wild the day they died. He hit at me before he threw red-hot coals at me and tired to set me on fire."

"How good a friend was he to the kids?"

"He'd come down with them to the trailer court sometimes after his churching was done on Sundays and be first in line for food.

"Could he have been *interested* in Mary?"

"She was a pretty thing, but she wasn't old enough for that." I thought she blushed.

"I saw a color photo of her in your trailer. She was close to full grown. Your friend Mellish, in the trailers, thinks she was in business, taking off her clothes and selling looks at her body while Jim guarded her with his gun. Smalley and I are trying to find out whether there was more you could buy than just a look, and whether any was bought on the day she died."

"You're joking me."

"No. If the doctors who did the autopsy can't tell us, we may want her body dug up and tested." I nodded firmly. "Believe me Bert, she was old enough."

Tears did come to her eyes then. "I never seen or thought on that sort of thing. She was still a little girl to me, except I knew she was having her periods when she came to live with me. I sleep deep. She could have snuck out nights with or without Jim. And them kids spent lots of their time away from the trailers, over on the hill."

"You believed she was too young, so you didn't guard her," I said soothingly. "Think on it now."

After a time she shook her head. "No. You're still wrong.

I won't believe it. She cried and was scared when her period came."

"If we do need to dig her up we might need you to sign an exhumation petition." I'd never done it and didn't know how, but I knew it could be done.

She shook her head. I thought she was in shock.

"All right," she said.

"Another thing," I said. "Do you recall exactly what the police removed from your trailer? Did they, for example, take the gun Jim carried?"

"I know they took the gun. They carried away other things. I signed some papers for that. They took me with them and I watched while they searched. I let them take samples from the medicine bottles, but I wouldn't let them take the bottles themselves."

"Use the yellow pad and make a list of what you remember. I'll pick it up when I get back from Bington."

She nodded and looked down at the floor. "Let me think on some of these things you've said."

"All right. I'll be back Sunday. And I like that dress."

She smiled girlishly. "Thank you."

Before I left the jail I found the sheriff at a sparse breakfast. He'd dunked his toast in hot water and was eating it in tiny bites. He had a cup of thin tea he drank from now and then. I thought, from its appearance, that it was no more than lukewarm.

I poured him half of Bert's medicine, putting it in a jar he found in the jail's kitchen.

"Take a big spoonful now," I said and then watched until he swallowed it. "This morning I ran three times around the motel. I'm eating real food again. I don't hurt. Bert says I'm well."

He looked me over, perhaps comparing what I looked like now with what he'd seen before.

"Okay. Didn't taste poisonous anyway. And you say she made it up from herbs and stuff?"

"Yes."

"I'm to the place where I'd try something brown I found on the ground if I got told it'd help. Damn, Don, I never had nothing happen to me like this. Some days I'd like to just curl up and die. I sleep a couple of hours a night maybe, and I can't take the stuff the docs give me or I'd sleep all the time."

"I know the feeling."

We looked at each other.

"Can I ask you something?"

He nodded.

"There's a man called Cleaner Kline who lives down in the trailer court. Do you know about him?"

"Sure."

"He's fooled with kids before."

"Yes. That was when he was younger. Now he is, believe it or not, a wino, and eighty-six years old."

"Thanks."

EIGHT

"All present government is stupid. Stupidity is bad, but stupidity in action is terrifying."

—Herbert Techni, Louisville, Kentucky, April 1996

ON THE TENNIS courts in Bington, I found Sam King, one of my erstwhile partners. It was a warm Saturday morning, so the tennis courts were the first place I looked. Had it been Saturday afternoon I'd have looked for him on a golf course or playing pickup basketball in one of Bington's several gyms.

He and three other men stood watching the sky. It was raining hard and all four of the tennis players were wet.

The other three players were white. Sam King was not. He was an African American and he was also a large man who'd once played football for Indiana University. He was smarter than anyone I'd ever known (including Kevin Smalley), and a man I liked and admired both in and out of law. Why Sam had stayed with us in Bington I couldn't fathom, but I was glad he'd stayed.

He was no longer my law partner, but he would always be my friend.

He'd made part of his living before and during law school by being an insurance investigator. Working almost full-time, he'd still managed to graduate from law school summa cum laude.

I don't know where these shining bright ones—black, white, and other colors—are coming from, but I know that in this age of crazies we need them badly.

I tooted my horn and, recognizing the LTD, he came walking to it. He opened the door and got in grinning, nodding his head. He likes to pretend he's a servant and I'm the master.

"Polish her up for you? Clean the windshield?"

I shook my head, smiling.

"Then, what can I do for you, oh supremely powerful judge-to-be?" he asked.

"Can I get you to do one of your insurance-company quick checks on a couple of people for me?"

"For pay or fun?"

"I guess for pay. I can add what I pay you to my bill in Madisonville."

"Go on."

"I need to know what you can find out in a short time about two people." I gave him all the background I had on Allwell and on Annette Clelland Kittaning.

"Can I make some noise while I'm asking?"

"I think that would be just fine," I answered.

He looked out the car window. It was raining hard again.

"Might as well start now. You going to be here for the weekend?"

"Until late tomorrow afternoon."

"Get back to me tomorrow afternoon. I'll be in the office working on an appeal where a judge, lots smarter than you'll ever be, made errors. Stop past. How goes your murder case?"

"Hard to tell. What you find out for me might ease the situation."

I drove from the tennis courts to the office of the sheriff of Mojeff County.

Sheriff Goldie sat in his glassed-in private office watching a deputy operate the radio. He was chewing a doughnut and drinking coffee hot enough to steam his steel-rimmed granny glasses. He was in uniform.

He looked like a big rube, but wasn't.

He saw me enter and waved me on back to his office. I took a seat across from his desk.

"You lookin' real good, boy. They must be treating you better over in Madisonville than they treat most of us nasty Bingtonites."

"The sheriff over there's been friendly. Thanks for calling him for me."

He nodded. "You might need his help. There's still some scurrying going on around here about you, Don. You watch close behind you, sleep with one eye open, and keep your asshole puckered."

"I need to know more about the whys of that. All I did was kill a guy in self-defense. There's a preacher named Allwell over in Madisonville who's doing a lot of shouting about the coming end of the world and also seems to know a lot about what happened the day Judge Harner and I got shot. This preacher's not on my side."

Goldie chuckled. "I've heard of that man. He runs a church over there that's kin to the Redeemer church here. You got yourself caught right in the middle of a power struggle when you originally took on that poor girl's dissolution case. I'll ask you a question you need to think on for your future judicial career: What if we catch a guy here in Bington armed with a rifle and sticking up the Kroger store?"

129

"He'd go to jail and eventually on to prison without passing 'Go.' "

"How about if we catch a clerk in the county treasurer's office with a thieving hand somewhere between the till and the third race at Churchill Downs?"

"Same answer. How much time each'd get would be subject to what the probation officer recommended and what a sentencing hearing disclosed."

He nodded. "Fair enough. One more: What if a guy who goes to the Church of the New Redeemer and New Saints took a secret shot at one of our local preachers, a black one, or maybe a rabbi or a Catholic priest, or maybe even picked out a visiting judge?"

"That's harder, but if he got caught, then the same answer again."

"He won't exactly get caught. If someone witnesses him doing the shooting then five or six members of his 'New' church will swear they were with him at the very moment the gun was fired and testify under oath they were all together saying their joint prayers in the north part of the county. The state's witness will get lots of threats, and so will I. Members of the church, if they're on the jury panel, will answer all the voir dire questions with lies so that they can maybe get chosen to the jury. If the shooter's convicted, then Harner—and now you, as his successor—will get threatened if he gave more than a token sentence."

"What you're telling me is that these people are ignoring the law."

"Thwarting it, fighting it, resisting it. They no longer care about the law because it don't work for them the way they want it to work. It don't stop drive-by shooters, or slow down robberies or assaults. It don't work good and it's riddled with silliness. Put all that together and these people are saying a judge's law and a sheriff's law is nothing but beans and so here's our thumb and here's our nose. I've seen some of their propaganda, like their booklet of instructions to members called for jury duty."

"I can think of some ways to remedy such a situation," I said.

"I'm all ears, learned one, great circuit court judge to be."

"Find out the names of the members of the church. You can do that, can't you?"

"Probably. Most of them, anyway."

"Then furnish those names to both sides. Strike them from jury panels by agreement, or strike them for cause if there is no agreement."

"How about when they file their papers and stuff with the clerk and the recorder?"

"What I can order to be stricken, I'll order to be stricken. What I can't order, I might order anyway and let them take the appeal. If they ask for a change of judge I'll name judges from other counties having similar problems." I thought some more. "If a woman files for a divorce and her husband's a hot 'New' church member, then I'll grant her a temporary custody order for the children. Plus vice versa."

Goldie was beginning to smile. "I look forward to the first of the year. Harner knew all I'm telling you now, but he thought it could and should be handled with gentle diplomacy. More than a year ago I told him he needed a metal detector in front of his courtroom and that all other doors should be locked except the one where the detector was located."

I'd not known that.

I nodded, thinking some more. "I'll call a county bar meeting come first of the year."

"Sounds good." He nodded and smiled. "How about I tell the county commissioners you're dead set on wanting one or two metal detectors plus extra deputies to man them?"

"I do want a metal detector and deputies. How are other judges coping with such?"

"Some still ignore it. They leave what happens in trials up to the lawyers in the case. They try to survive and get re-elected."

I nodded, remembering again why I'd come in.

"Something I want and need to know, Goldie. Is there a branch of the Church of the New Redeemer and New Saints up around South Vernon?"

He nodded. "Yeah. It ain't the same name, but it's about the same. It's big."

I remembered Lem's innocent smile. All lawyers want to win.

No jurors for Bert's trial would come out of South Vernon.

"One more thing. Could you give me the loan of a double-barreled or automatic shotgun and sell me some buckshot shells?"

"You betcha. Twelve-gauge. Loaded and cocked if you like." He grinned impudently. "Even a shooter like you can hit something up close with a twelve-gauge."

The apartment in Bington where I'd moved when Jo and I had separated was situated in a quiet building inhabited mostly by retirees and located near the university.

Jo still owned "our" house. It was in our joint names, but the pleasant home had been mostly bought with her inherited money. I'd made the payments, but they'd been small because Jo's down payment had been large. The house would therefore be hers when the dissolution was granted.

I'd driven past the house a few times. It seemed lonely and unoccupied. I drove past it again. Nothing had much changed. Someone was taking care of the yard and a few flowers grew around the front steps.

I then drove to my apartment. I put my bag in a corner of the spartan bedroom and then inspected myself in the bathroom mirror.

over carefully, not yet angry with me, but working up to it. "You look a lot better. Are you better?"

"Yes."

"That's good."

"Thank you."

"Chicago's quite a city, Don. I've told you that Nance's condo overlooks Lake Michigan. You can stand ten feet back from her big picture window and feel like you're living in a building that's built in the lake."

"How does Joe like it?"

"He likes it fine. I took him to a couple of Cubs games and he liked going. Now that it's fall, Nance says we'll all go to see the Bears play. She's got a good friend who works for the Bears."

I'll bet she does.

The bartender brought the drinks I'd ordered. Hers was bright and frothy, smelling of fruit and gin. Mine was plain water, two ice cubes.

"Fancy that, me drinking, you wagon sitting," she said. She'd never cared for the fact that—before being shot—I drank more, sometimes far more, than she liked me to drink.

I smiled and nodded. *No problems.*

"Can getting our dissolution please wait until I finish up this case?" I asked humbly.

"How long?"

"Not long. A few weeks at most."

"It's another murder, isn't it?"

"Yes. The defendant's a woman. Some crazies over there in Madisonville say she's a witch."

"Is she?"

"Of course not. There are no witches." I decided it was not the proper time to tell her about the medicine or the candle.

"I suppose we can wait a week or two," she said, seemingly disliking it, but not protesting. "I'll trade a delay for an agreement that I get custody except for a month each summer and that your weekend visitation for the rest of this year will be every other weekend in Chicago." She shook her head. "Are you really going to fly to Chicago and visit him that often?"

"Yes. It's cheap to fly from Louisville to Chicago now and not a problem except in the dead of winter." The concession she was asking for in return for not pushing for instant dissolution was one we'd already made anyway. As I remembered that, I felt there was still a chance for us.

She sipped at her drink, watching me. "I'll believe you'll be there when I see you. Don't say you'll come and then not come. That would break his heart."

"I won't be working weekends after the first of the year, and I'm not working them now."

She smiled a nasty, superior smile. "How's the old judge doing?"

"I'm not sure. I plan to stop past and see before I drive back to Madisonville."

"I hear talk that some of the crazies from that nutty church are sorry Judge Harner lived after being shot. I hear also that there are people angry at you for killing the church guy who shot both of you."

I was interested. "Where do you hear that kind of crap?"

"I got my hair done this morning. For some reason I wanted to look good. I heard it there. Just someone yakking, spreading her idea of the local word. I asked her where she'd heard it and she said it was something she'd overheard at Wal-Mart. Then she apologized because she knew me."

I waited to see if there was more and there was.

"She said an old man in Kentucky runs the Wilkens family and that when they hate someone, they hate them forever."

"All I did was protect myself. I didn't have the gun. He did."

"All right. I know." She leaned toward me. "I'd try again if you'd try, Don. I'd want us to make a complete break from Bington. There's plenty of money. That's no problem. Some stocks I bought with my uncle's estate money took off. The dividend from that stock alone is near six figures. Come be with us in Chicago. You'd soon find something to do. There are shows and professional sports and shopping and great food. Nance likes you even if you don't like her."

I shook my head. Nancy, her sister, had been through enough men to staff a Fortune 500 company. She was a spectacular-looking woman with the morals of an eel and the constancy of a ten-cent battery.

"I don't dislike Nancy. I merely like to point out her faults. And no matter what she says to you just now, she doesn't like me."

"Yes she does," she said. "She can tell our son wants us together, and she can see I'm not right without you. I want your time and I want Joe to have it. I don't want to worry that someone out of your past, present, or future will be somewhere in the shadows, under orders from some old man in Kentucky, waiting for the right time to kill you. They say the crazies in Mojeff County are strong and bold and that, sooner or later, they'll run things."

"I doubt it. My getting shot was a fluke. Who worries about getting shot trying a dissolution?"

"It happened, Don." She looked beyond me and smiled at someone who likely was smiling at her in the vagueness. "Bington isn't like it was when we got married. Joe's *safe* in Chicago. There are armed guards at the locked first-floor entrance door to Nance's condo. There are microphones in the elevators. Even if he made it past all the guards, a safe-cracker would have a hard time trying to open Nance's door. A bus picks up Joe for school, takes him to his games, delivers him back to the door. And it's a fine private school, suitable for a bright, athletic ten-year-old."

"I'll think on it, Jo. Would you like to eat here?"

"Like a date?" She smiled at me, the complete charmer, suddenly full of fun, and of herself. Something dormant inside me sprang to life.

"Me and you?" she continued. "Alone?"

"Yep, little girl," I said, snapping invisible galluses and stroking my non-mustache.

"Okay. I can do that. My aunt has Joe tonight. You can pick him up at her place in the morning." She smiled at me. "I'll have one more drink before dinner." She looked away and then back at me for a long moment. "Just don't try to get into my new black bikinis."

I did.

And, in the wee hours, I heard her cry out and then hold on to me in her bad dream, as if both our lives depended on it.

In the morning I took Joe for breakfast while his mother slept in late.

We went to a Bob Evans. The restaurant was near the college campus on a bypass that opened farther on to student housing and fraternity and sorority houses.

"I like Bob Evans," Joe confided to me. He sat solemnly in a chair in front of pancakes and sausage. He worked on the food industriously.

It had been almost a month since I'd seen him, and it seemed he'd grown at least another inch. He had fine features much akin to those of his mother. I could see bits and pieces of me, mostly in his eyes. They were the same color and shape as mine.

He'd picked up the best of both of us in his looks. Many kids seem to do that these days. It's as if they know that becoming more handsome or beautiful is a safeguard as crisis times increase in number.

Maybe Allwell was right about the end of the world. But only an insane, diseased, and impoverished god would use him as a messenger.

I sipped black decaf. My breakfast of eggs and oatmeal was done and I was comfortably full. "How's soccer going?"

"Okay, Dad."

"Is anything wrong?"

Joe leaned closer to me. "Aunt Nancy has different men who come to see her. Some look at mom and talk sweet to her. One's a corporation lawyer. There's another who's an assistant football coach for the Bears. And there's others. Aunt Nancy tries to get Mom to go places, and sometimes Mom will go out for a while with a big crowd. But she hasn't, so far, with one guy." He shook his head, troubled. "I hear her crying lots. I think she's lonely for you."

"I'm lonely for both of you. Your mother wants me to stop being a lawyer and not be judge here in Bington, but be something else up in Chicago."

He nodded. For a moment I thought he might cry, which he hadn't done for a while now. I believed he was smarter than both his mother and his father, trying to figure his own way, aware of the rocks and shoals.

"It's hard," he said. He reached out and touched my hand.

We nodded at each other. I had the urge to take him, hold him, and tell him it would all work out. But that wouldn't be fair to him or to Jo.

I was a lawyer. I was a *Bington* lawyer. I was, come first of the year, going to be a Bington circuit court judge.

I dropped him off at his great-aunt's place after we'd done our regular routines of walking along the Ohio River, searching through a magazine and book store, and shopping for kids' junk at Wal-Mart.

He clung to me at parting, not letting go for a while.

"Try hard to make it up with Mom, Dad."

I nodded. "I promise."

Judge Harner lived in a fine old brick-and-stone home on the south side of Main Street. It had been built before the Civil War and then kept up and kept up. Now, a century and a half later, it still looked grand and beautiful.

I'd been to Harner's house a few times, and Jo had visited there for parties and home tours. She'd also "bridged" with Thelma Harner, the judge's wife.

I parked the LTD down the street and walked back to the house. Thelma Harner sat on her wide porch in a rocking chair. A few other women sat with her, and they rocked and watched the street together.

Thelma smiled at me. "Dr. Buckner stopped past a while ago and is still inside with him, Don." She pointed to an empty chair next to her. "Come sit here beside me. I've got some new things to tell you."

I sat. The other women nodded at me and then went back to fanning themselves and watching Main Street. Watching and seeing were Bington hobbies. Those who didn't have wide porches on Main Street drove past in their cars so as to see and be seen by those who did have porches.

"Judge Kittaning and Lemuel Rand, the prosecutor over in Madisonville, told me to say hello to you. They both wanted to know if there was anything they could do," I said.

She shook her head. "Thank them for me. I had a call yesterday from the Chief Justice. He said Lucas would get full pension the first of the year and that his medical insurance would continue."

"That's good," I said.

"The medical news itself isn't that good. He's better in some ways. He's more alert. Sometimes he knows more than I realize he knows. Sometimes he makes sense when he talks. But Dr. Buckner says things are messed up in his

140

head and that he could die from any one of a number of problems. His heart's not good. All this wore it out." She shook her head again.

"She was a fine, small-boned, pretty woman I'd not known well or liked much until her husband had been shot. The judge's wife—sure of her position in town and proud of it. I liked her a lot now.

I heard the front door behind us open and close. In a few seconds, Dr. Hugo S. Buckner appeared.

He gave me a look of appraisal. "How's your belly now that pregnancy has terminated?"

"Improved. The child's doing well also. When can I expect to see your support checks?"

"For shame. Why pick on me when anyone in town could be the culprit?" He stepped closer and examined me with his eyes. "You really do look a lot better. That's all due to my keen medical abilities," he finished, grinning.

He was a funny man and he'd been my good friend for a lot of years. I decided against telling him anything about the medicine I'd been taking, its source, or the good it had done. I'd save it for another time. He'd then find a valid medical reason the herb-and-root nostrum had worked.

"Can I have a word with you in private?" I asked.

He took my arm and led me to the steps. "Come into my office."

"Let me ask you something I need to know. When, generally, does a girl begin to have menstrual periods?"

"You're doing a book on your odd sexual tastes," he said, deadpan. "Well, for the benefit of your twisted imagination, as early as ten, as late as eighteen."

"Thanks."

"Just pay the bill."

He walked back to the women on the porch and said to Thelma, "I'm going to the hospital for a few hours. Then I'll be home if you should need me."

Thelma walked with him to the top of the porch stairs and stood there for a soft-voiced conference. Both of their faces were serious. Buckner gave her a final shoulder pat and went down to his car.

She returned to me.

"We'll go in now," she announced formally.

I followed behind.

Harner lay in a hospital bed by the big fireplace in the first room inside his house. He was half raised in the bed and he was staring straight ahead at a wall as if there was something there to be observed, but I could tell he perceived us as we walked toward him.

"You remember Don Robak," Thelma said.

He lifted his right hand a fraction.

There was a chair by the side of his bed. I took it and then took his hand. It lay in mine softly, without movement.

I said, "I'm helping Kevin Smalley try a murder case in Madisonville. Judge Kittaning and Lem Rand sent you their regards."

His eyes flickered. The right one winked.

"Ask him how he's doing," his wife said softly.

"Are you doing okay?" I asked obediently.

He smiled an odd smile. One side of his face didn't work well. His hand moved away from mine; the forefinger stuck out and the rest of the hand curled—A gun.

"Cuppa, cuppa," he said clearly.

His wife nodded down at him. "I think he does that because he remembers part of that bad day, Don. I know he remembers you were there because, when I show him the Mojeff County bar picture, he picks you out. Then, each time, he makes his hand into a toy gun and says that."

Harner touched my hand with his now unloaded one. I saw there were tiny tears in his eyes.

"Yes, yes," he said.

"It wasn't fair," his wife said, losing it for just a moment.

"He had so much going and some stinking, damn wife beater . . ."

Harner held up his hand and frowned at her.

"No," he said.

I saw he was crying harder.

Then, as we watched, he slipped into sleep.

His wife took my hand and tiptoed us away.

"He'll sleep for an hour or two now," she said. "I went through the desk in his chambers at the courthouse last week. There were some nasty letters in it, threats, that kind of thing. He'd never mentioned a word to me about them."

"Was there anything there from the man who shot us?"

"Maybe. All of the threatening letters were unsigned. I brought the stuff home and showed it to Lucas. He had me get the bar picture out and then he pointed to you and then at the papers. Then he made that horrible noise. I think he wants you to have the papers. One day soon I'll give them to you."

"Right now might be a good time."

She thought on it and then nodded. "Yes. All right."

I waited while she found them. They were stuffed in an old manila envelope.

We went back out to the front porch and I said my farewells to the women there.

Thelma went down her front steps with me and saw me to the sidewalk.

"He's going to be all right someday," she said.

I nodded confidently. Neither of us believed the other.

I put the manila envelope on the backseat of the LTD when I left.

I had a bite of lunch, still keeping things soft. I felt like I could eat anything, but I remained careful despite what Bert had said.

I drove to my old office. I still had my key because no one

143

had ever asked for it. I'd give it back first of the year. I let myself in and found Sam King in the library.

He handed me two pieces of computer paper.

"Read," he said, and went back to editing his appeal papers, working hard, not seeing me for now. He had an ability to concentrate like no one else I'd ever known.

The two reports had probably come from the joint records of credit companies, insurers, and various other places to which Sam had access. When I'd asked him once to name his sources, he'd just grinned.

The first report concerned Annette Kittaning. It listed her former addresses back to date of birth in Indianapolis. When I read it over, I recognized one early entry: it was the same address where I'd lived with my first wife.

Her mother and father had died in the crash of a commercial airliner a year after I'd known her at school. She and a brother had split the parents' insurance plus a court settlement the report estimated at two million dollars.

She'd been married four times. She divorced husbands one and two, both in the state of Indiana. Property settlements were not listed. She'd then survived husband three when he'd died of an apparent heart attack in North Bend. His gross estate had been six million dollars. He had no children by prior marriage. Except for a few special bequests, she'd inherited all his estate.

Her worth was now estimated to be nine million dollars.

Husband number four was Judge Kittaning. They'd been married eight years.

She'd never been arrested. Her credit records were spotless. She held half a dozen credit cards with no limits listed.

She was fifty-two years old, a year older than me.

Reverend Hoskin Andrew Allwell's report was spottier. He'd been born in West Virginia and was now forty-seven years old. His parents had moved to Whitesburg, Kentucky, when he was three. Thereafter they'd moved around to other towns in coal country while his father worked the mines. His father had died of black lung when Allwell was fourteen, his mother two years later of cancer. Allwell had survived. He'd finished high school and gotten a scholarship to Berea. After graduation, he'd worked construction around Cincinnati while attending Chase Law School at nights. He'd graduated with honors, been a part of a law firm in northern Kentucky for a short time, and then been disbarred for stealing from several clients. After disbarment, and a jail sentence for the theft, he'd moved back to his boyhood area, where he'd been "born again." He'd become a self-styled minister.

He'd never married.

He'd been arrested five other times, all prior to his disbarment. Two of the arrests were for theft charges springing from other difficulties in his law practice in northern Kentucky, across the river from Cincinnati.

One of the other charges was for child abuse, the last two for child molesting and attempted rape, reduced in each case to contributing to the delinquency of a minor.

His law firm had sued him and obtained a large judgment, unsatisfied. Several clients had also sued him and obtained judgments, also unsatisfied.

For the theft causing his disbarment, he'd plea-bargained and served a single year in jail. For the earlier two thefts there'd been suspended sentences. For the crimes with children he'd served ten days for one, and thirty days each for the other two. He'd never appeared for the recommended counseling. There were no current wants or warrants for him.

His credit record was, of course, bad. He had no credit cards and no known bank accounts. There was no estimate of worth.

I folded the reports and put them in my pocket.

And smiled.

NINE

"If you are chosen to a petit jury, then remember from that time on, until you are discharged as a juror, you are the judges of both the law and the facts, and to hell with what the judge and the lawyers try to tell you."

—Advice to jurors in "Asa's Jury Guide," 1947

SAM KING GRACIOUSLY allowed me to use the office phone and call Kevin Smalley before I left Bington. I tried his house first and found him there.

"Don't come to the house," he said. "I'll meet you at the office in an hour or so."

"Is there a problem?"

"Always," he answered laconically.

I hung up and looked at Sam King. "With me gone from the office is there too much work to handle?"

"I remember you and your work habits well, Father Robak. There was already too much to handle when you were still hanging around drinking up our coffee and colas and bothering the secretaries with bad jokes."

"Would you and Jake be interested in another lawyer? First-class trial man."

"Maybe."

I sat down and related all I knew about Kevin Smalley,

finishing up with, "I don't know whether he'd be interested or not."

Sam said, "I'm interested. You ask there and I'll ask Jake, but I'll bet Jake is interested also. We've both been working fifty- and sixty-hour weeks."

I nodded.

I then used the office Xerox machine and made a few copies of the report on Allwell. I didn't bother making extras on Nettie Kittaning. That one had been mostly a product of my own curiosity. I left one of the Allwell reports with Sam. He promised faithfully to check one more thing on it for me. "I'd like the names of the victims in the three cases involving children if you can find them out," I asked.

I put the loaded twelve-gauge pump shotgun on the backseat of the LTD, safety on, sports block removed, five buckshot shells loaded. Goldie then took me past the police range and I fired the shotgun a couple of times. There was substantial recoil. The buckshot pattern spread wide at thirty feet.

"Just the gun for you," Goldie told me. "With it, you can hit everything in about a four-foot circle. What I ought to do is cut about eight inches off the barrel. That would really make you deadly."

"Okay with me," I said stolidly.

"But not okay with our *federales*. Sawed-off shotguns are forbidden. Just remember, you borrowed this shotgun from me to go duck hunting in Canada."

"Right. Duck hunting. What's a duck? And what do you mean by this word 'hunting'?"

He shook his head.

I drove from Bington to Smalley's office and parked on the street. I noticed that someone had smashed the front window of the waiting room and left several paint splotches on

148

the front door. Wet paint had dripped down onto the concrete steps and dried there. Someone had also tried, without much success, to paint messages on the brick walls.

Now, late Sunday afternoon, there was no one around outside the office, but as I got out of my car and locked up, a Madisonville police car drove slowly by. Two officers watched me suspiciously. I avoided the paint, waved and nodded to the gentlemen in the police car, and entered Smalley's damaged front door.

Smalley looked tired and dispirited as he slouched in his office chair.

"You got city police watching things outside," I said. "What's happened?"

He shrugged. "Allwell's people spread the story we were going to have graves dug up. Some people, maybe two or three hundred of them, took offense and came to my house together. Some others obviously visited the office around the same time. I called the police, but it was a while before anyone arrived. I had some damage at home and a lot here."

"Did the police arrest anyone?"

"Not yet. I recognized a few of those who came visiting my house but haven't yet supplied names. Tipper, from the trailers, was one of them." He smiled. "Funny thing is we likely won't need to have Mary dug up. I'm not saying anything about that for now, but I talked to both of the doctors who did the autopsy. Both will testify that the girl appeared to have been sexually active. Both also will testify that they found nothing to show she'd done anything sexually the day she died."

"Neither orally nor anally?"

He nodded. "They checked every cavity known to uncivilized man."

I handed him the reports on Allwell and Nettie Kittaning.

He looked at them both, put Nettie Kittaning's down

after a quick once-over, and began to smile halfway through Allwell's.

"Oh boy," he said. "The lowdown on Allwell. Where'd you dig this up?"

I gave him my Sam King smile.

"Let's make more copies, lots of copies," he said. "For distribution. Warm the Xerox."

I then told him about when and where I'd known Judge Kittaning's wife. He listened without much interest.

We made many copies of the Allwell report and put a stack of them in the trunk of the LTD.

"Where'd you get the shotgun?" he asked.

"I don't think I'm supposed to tell anyone. I thought I might need it to go hunting ducks in Canada."

He eyed me in mock disbelief.

"Honest Injun," I said.

We drove in my car to the pull-off spot near the trailer park. I parked the LTD and waited while a car passed on the highway. It slowed and the driver honked and then lowered his window and gave us the finger.

I returned the favor.

The driver braked and slowed. Fifty yards past us he pulled over on the berm. He opened his door and got out. He was big and young, he was yelling some curses up at us as he walked our way.

I gave him the finger again and he stopped.

"Tough finger, Robak," Smalley said admiringly.

We waited, the angry man waited. After a time I got tired of waiting. I left the .38 in the glove compartment, but got the shotgun out of the trunk. I lifted it, turned my back on the watcher, and sighted the gun up at the sun.

The man in the parked car below decided it was time to dally no more. He started his car and burned rubber, spraying gravel as he spun away.

150

"Even tougher shotgun, Robak," Smalley said.

I put the shotgun back in the trunk and locked it. Then I took the .38 from the glove compartment.

After the other driver was out of sight, we stayed where we were for a time and then crossed the highway. Once across the road we climbed and slid down the side of the embankment. We then waited to see if the driver who'd stopped and watched us would return with reinforcements now that we were gone. Eventually I nodded at Smalley, satisfied. He nodded back.

Time to go.

Our route on the hill this time was at a different angle. We walked forty-five degrees south of where we'd previously climbed the hill. The rise here was much gentler. To the south, between the trees when we were high enough, I could catch glimpses of the muddy Ohio.

I thought on what I should do with the .38. Finally I shoved it into my back right pocket.

After we crossed the railroad cut, the hill continued upward at a gradual rise for the long distance. Then it leveled and opened into an unexpected small valley.

"This is where we saw the fire," Smalley announced.

Below us, in the partly hidden valley, kids from the trailer court were playing some kind of costume game in the Madisonville late Sunday-afternoon sun.

The closest thing to us was what looked to be a watchtower manned by two stripling boys in cutoff jeans and T-shirts plus ancient army-helmet liners painted in bright colors. Both carried garbage-can lid shields decorated with crude designs: a skull and crossbones, a knobbed cross with a snake below it. One boy had a wooden spear that once might have been a small classroom flagpole. The other was armed with a toy-store bow and rubber-tipped arrows.

The boy with the spear lifted a conch shell and blew a

151

loud noise from it. Some of the kids below us stopped play, others ignored the signal. Most of the children, male and female, wore helmet liners in various colors—maybe a special at Wal-Mart. I saw more shields, plastic swords, rubber knives, and one headsman's axe made of stiff cardboard, painted silver and black, with fake red blood on both edges.

The boys in the watchtower awaited us.

"Who approaches?" one of the boys called formally.

I put a warning hand on Kevin Smalley's arm so that I might answer first.

"Friends of the Black King. Friends of the Witch and of the now departed Hansel and Gretel."

The boys in the watchtower whispered to each other. No one seemed afraid of us.

I estimated ages. I thought the youngest of the children was perhaps ten or eleven, the oldest sixteen. I counted twenty children, nine boys, eleven girls. One of the eleven girls was Nancy Jane, who'd directed me to Mo Mellish's trailer. She nodded and smiled at me.

I turned to Smalley and whispered, "I think we've drawn near to Camelot."

He shook his head and smiled. "This keeps getting nuttier and nuttier. I suspect you somehow cause these things, Robak."

"Magic."

Once we passed the watchtower the rest of the kids crowded around us. A thin boy pointed at me excitedly. "One of the lawyers for the Witch has a gun in his back pocket."

I nodded. "That's me. Bad people seem to want to follow behind with the intent to do me harm these days. The gun was given to me by my sheriff. If there's someone among you whom you all trust I'll let him or her hold the gun while we talk. I must have the gun back when we leave this place."

"Let's let Jennie," a small girl said. "After all, she's the oldest."

"Yeah, Jennie," a couple of others chorused. "She's now the rule maker."

No one objected to Jennie.

I took the .38 carefully out of my rear pocket and held it with my thumb and index finger. I snapped open the cylinder and shook the wicked-looking wad cutters into my hand. I put the cartridges in my right front pants pocket and presented the empty gun to a pretty black-haired girl who didn't look old enough to be called the oldest or the rule maker.

"Would you want to look over Shakespeare's Wonderland?" she asked politely, smiling at us, after Nancy Jane whispered to her.

"Who named it that?" Smalley asked.

"Jim. He made up the rules and judged things when we argued. He used some of Shakespeare's plays and some of the books about King Arthur and his knights," she said. "He used lots of other stuff. Jim could read a book in ten minutes and remember it all. It ain't as much fun now with me doing it, but it's still fun and it'll likely last through the fall, playing after school, weekends, and at nights, until the world gets cold. I try to do it like I think Jim would have done it."

"What's the idea of the game? What is it you try to do?" I asked.

"We do quests. We destroy an ogre's castle on the hill, we spy on Attila the Hun, we set traps and snares for fire-breathing dragons, and we build palaces for those we love and honor. We use different rules for each of these quests."

Nancy Jane came up beside me. She nodded and smiled at me. She took my hand, squeezed hard, and then let go. Her small hand was wet with sweat.

"It's fun," she said.

Smalley looked around, openly marveling at the kids and their costumes. "Were any of you kids at the trailer court and watching when Hansel and Gretel, the kids who were also Jim and Mary, died?"

Hands went up. I counted a dozen.

"Did any of you see Bertha Jones—"

"The Witch," Jennie interjected disapprovingly. "It's the rule."

"All right," Smalley said. "Did any of you see the Witch put anything that might have been poison in her cooking pot after she'd eaten from that pot herself?"

A few looked doubtful, but Nancy Jane called in her thin reedy voice: "No. She never done nothin'. I was watching close all the time because I was hungry and what she was cooking smelled real good."

Jennie loftily patted Nancy Jane on her head. "You're always hungry, Lady Jane."

"Did anyone see any person other than the Witch put something in the pot?" Smalley asked.

There was much head shaking, but then a boy's voice said: "Attila was in his black robe and he either blessed the kettle or cursed it. And the Black King was lurking, watching Attila.

Some nodded.

"How did Attila do that?"

"He made a sign over it. He said some words."

"And this Attila, is his regular name Reverend Allwell?"

Several nods, no protests.

Smalley looked at me and smiled triumphantly. His eyes were bright and he no longer appeared tired.

I asked, when the silence began to grow, "Are you all knights and ladies?"

"No. Jim said we could each be who we wanted and he changed the rules to fit," Nancy Jane said. "Sometimes I'm Alice Through the Looking Glass, today I'm Lady Jane. One of the boys is Sherlock Holmes most of the time and Jack the Ripper at others. Sometimes he catches himself by being both. With Jim gone it's harder to play. He remembered all the books and the stories in them and he could fit in whoever you wanted to be and make it work."

"And can you be more than one person at the same time?"

"No, not usually. Not without talking Jim into it," Jennie said. "Sometimes this valley is one place, then another. It's Oz, then a moor in Scotland, a courtyard in old Germany, the arena in Rome, any place, any time. But always it's Shakespeare's Wonderland because Jim liked the Shakespeare plays best, particularly *Romeo and Juliet,* and I guess he combined them with all of the rest he liked. We guard this place against outsiders like Allwell's nosies and the mean East End kids."

"Is Allwell a part of the game?" Smalley asked.

"Sometimes he's an absent player and he's almost always Attila the Hun or the evil Rasputin. Sometimes, if we're keeping watch on him, he becomes the Dark Man like in Stephen King's book. Jim also made a rule that if someone did wrong or cheated in the game then that one had to go spy on the preacher and report back to all of us what he was doing. So Reverend Allwell, he's not always a player in the game, but he's usually a part of it."

"Is he bad?"

"Most times," Jennie said, silencing Nancy Jane. "Sometimes, when the world ends in the game, he's a little good because he rescues us, but then we have to escape from him because he's also very, very bad."

"And you spy on him?"

Jennie nodded solemnly. "Constantly. I didn't cheat, but I spied on him and his church on that last day because I wanted to. It was nice outside and I didn't want to go to Saint Mary's church and take communion. So I watched Reverend Allwell. He likes to come to his church late, when all the people are there and whispering in their places. He likes to make an entrance like he's a king."

"Tell the lawyers what you saw that day, Jennie," Nancy Jane said.

She shrugged. "He went in the wide doors and hallelujahed and prayed up to the skies like he always does. He screamed about black people and Catholics like me. Then he did Jews. He hates laws so much that steam came off him when he yelled about the bad government laws. There must have been a thousand folks in his church that day. Some had to stand outside the double doors." She shook her head. "Then, later, he walked with Jim and Mary down the hill and they stopped at their hiding place. Attila, he was all wet with sweat because of screaming. All three of them went inside the hiding hole. I watched. They were in there for a time and then they came down to where the Witch had her cook fire and pot."

"Can we visit this hiding place?" I asked.

Jennie looked around her crowd of children. Some nodded okay, a few shook their heads, but the vote was in our favor.

"It ain't like it was on that last day. And it's kind of holy to us now," Jennie said. "Jim said if he died he'd come back and haunt it and maybe he will." She smiled. "Someone went in it and caved it part way in right after Jim and Mary was dead. And I guess they took the stuff that was hid there. Whoever it was has never come back."

"Do you think the one who robbed it was Reverend Allwell or someone from his church?" Smalley asked.

"Maybe. Or, more likely, it was kids from the east end of town, the Walnut Street bunch. They steal and they don't play by the rules. They laugh at us. We were going to ask the Witch to put a spell on them, but that was before Jim and Mary died."

"Did the Witch ever visit this hiding place?"

"No. Only the Black King knew about it. Hansel and Gretel wouldn't tell her about it and they never come across the creek if the Witch was across it. When she was hunting stuff in the woods, the rest of us would play tag or hide-and-seek. And we'd wait for Mary and Jim, Hansel and Gretel."

"That's dead true," Nancy Jane said.

Others nodded.

"Did any of you ever see the Witch punish Hansel and Gretel?" I asked.

"Sometimes with a little tiny switch," Nancy Jane said.

"Good. Can we go look now at the hiding place?" I asked.

Jennie and Nancy Jane led us to the hiding place. It was north of Shakespeare's Wonderland, up the rough, steep face of the hill. The climbing to it was difficult.

We hiked along with the kids cavorting, calling out to each other, laughing beside us.

We came to a place on the rough hill where the terrain changed to mostly massive rocks. The kids stopped where two limestone peaks jutted up and held another massive piece of stone caught between them.

"We call this place Hanging Rock," Nancy Jane said. "If you're going up, you can't hardly climb over the rocks above here. If you're coming down, you have to skirt around them. That makes it a good place to hide. Plus someday, in the faraway future, the main rock is going to get loose from the other two."

She climbed near the base of the captured rock and pulled bushes away.

Someone had dug in the ground and then covered the resultant hole with old wet plywood. The excavated dirt had been shoveled back on top of the plywood, and the opening covered with weeds and bushes.

I bent down to try to look inside, but the entrance was clogged by dirt a few feet back.

"There used to be a cave inside that the hiding place opened into. Maybe it also got blown closed," Nancy Jane said.

"Someone set off a bomb inside it," Jennie said. "We heard something boom in the night. You could hear it all the way down in the trailer courts. Next day it was like it is now."

Smalley inspected his dirty and disheveled clothes. "Maybe I could open it up some." He bent and shoveled away dirt by hand. He made little headway, the earth seemingly solid where he dug.

"You'd need men with shovels and maybe even some kind of digger," he said after a while. Then he handed out one thing. "That was in the dirt," he said.

It was a thick paperback book, wet and spongy, the pages bent and crumpled.

I brushed dirt off the cover. Stephen King's *The Stand.*

Smalley moved close to me. "Maybe we ought to bring the sheriff along before we try to do more," he said in a low voice. "Let's go talk to him. Then maybe we can come back later today or tomorrow. Okay?"

I nodded in agreement.

"We go inside by ourselves and someone will say we planted whatever's in there," Smalley finished.

We found Deb Hewitt at his office, eating buttered toast with jelly and drinking steaming hot milk.

I surveyed him. He looked much better. His color was good and he appeared to be enjoying the food.

He shook hands with us. I gave him one of the reports on Allwell I'd gotten from Sam King and watched him as he read it.

"What do you want me to do about this?" he asked carefully.

"Nothing. It's for your information. I've asked someone

out of my old law office to check out one more thing, the dope on the underage victims. If you'd rather say you never saw it, we'll take it back."

He shrugged.

"We spent the afternoon talking to a lot of new witnesses in Bert's case. They saw former child molester Allwell enter a kind of hiding place with the two kids on the day those kids died. The entry may have been for sexual reasons. Those same witnesses later saw Allwell bless Bertha Jones's stew pot by waving his hands over it."

Deb shook his head. "Kids," he said. "Who's going to believe a bunch of kids? Bertha Jones has been indicted for the double homicide you speak on. Soon she'll go to trial. Prosecutor Lem, he'd likely get all pissed off at me, and out of sorts with the world, if I started looking and poking around for new evidence in that damn case."

"You don't believe Bert did it any more than we do," I said.

"What I believe means nothing," he said. "I'm a duly elected sheriff. I will admit privately to you lads that I'm also a curious man and that I got no more use for Allwell than you do. So, good as I feel these days, I might just poke around curiously if the notion comes upon me. But that's tomorrow, Monday, not today. It's too late to do any looking now. It'll be dark in an hour or so. Where's this place?"

Smalley gave him a simple map he'd drawn.

"Her medicine helped you then, Deb?" I asked.

"Lord yes. I feel like a kid again. I got to be careful or I'll bust the gut inside me just from eating too damn much. I got the hot hungries."

We smiled at each other, beneficiaries of a miracle neither of us understood.

"Right now there ain't much I wouldn't do to help the lady who helped me," the sheriff said carefully.

"We'll hold you to that," Smalley said.

The sheriff nodded. "City police will watch both your home and office tonight, Mr. Smalley. Allwell has bunches of people at the cemetery watching the graves of the two kids."

"Let him watch," Smalley said. "If we're going to exhume either or both of the dead kids, it won't be today or tomorrow."

"Okay. I can get the state police to come with us to the cemetery if you get me a court order."

"We won't do anything on that until we talk again," I promised.

"Then you watch your ass, Robak," Deb said to me. "A deputy reported that a car with one of the license numbers your Sheriff Goldie gave us was parked up at Allwell's hill church this morning. It was gone next time someone swung by. Green Chrysler, maybe a '79 or '80."

"Thanks."

In the car I remembered some things I wanted to ask Smalley.

"Did Bert's eyes get checked?"

"Yes. I had Doc Brent—he's a local optometrist and a good one—come look at her. He says that in good light she might see a little, like maybe twenty/two hundred, but if it's dark she won't see hardly anything at all. She's got cataracts. If they were removed she'd likely see good as new."

"And did you get an MD to check her general health?"

"Yes, but I don't have the full report yet. We'll get it tomorrow. He did say there's nothing wrong with her mind and that she doesn't have any medical difficulties that would delay the trial. He said, off the cuff, that she has low blood pressure, incipient diabetes and a minor heart murmur, and is fifteen or twenty pounds underweight."

"We'll call him or depose him, or, more likely, talk Lem into stipulating her medical troubles."

He nodded.

I thought of what Sheriff Goldie had told me. "While I'm remembering things we'll have to pick our jury somewhere other than in South Vernon," I said. "There's a sister church to Allwell's that's strong up there. I think Lem may have known that and, of course, Allwell does too."

"No problem. The matter of venue is still open. Judge Kittaning wants us to be happy and without complaint when we pick the jury. Of course he wants that because he thinks Bert will get convicted."

"My sheriff in Bington says the crazies there stick together, lie, and do anything else they can to screw the legal system up, Kevin. If that's right, then it's likely your Survival church members here will do the same."

He nodded. "The legal system's been around and weathered a lot of bad years. You know it's not perfect. I also know it. But it's better than having things decided by a jackleg minister with kiddie sex problems."

Smalley got out of the car at his office.

"I'm tired," he said. "I'm going home and sleep the sleep of the just. I will see you here at my office bright and early, around nine o'clock." He looked down at me. "And do you know what, Robak, old pal?"

"What?"

"For the first time I feel true hope about our situation. I think maybe we're going to put our dirty fingers in Allwell's eyes, frustrate him and his congregation, and even have a chance to get our client out of jail and back into the herb-and-root medicine business."

"Good for us."

He pointed into my backseat. "What have you got back there?"

"Just some anonymous letters sent to Judge Harner in Bington before he got shot."

"Might be a damn good time for you to go back to your motel, kick up in bed, and read them line by line." He looked around once more, then nodded.

"I think I'll do just that," I said.

I drove the LTD away.

TEN

"Remember, when you look at high school or college text-books on government, that some of the things written therein may sound sensible. Accept my word for it: None are."

—"The Syllabus of Governmental Sins," a pamphlet by Herbert Techni and Allen Dackerty, undated, no copyright notice, autographed by Techni, September 11, 1993

I GOT MYSELF two grilled cheese sandwiches at a drive-in restaurant, took them to the room, and ate them while I drank water with ice from the motel ice machine.

I then sifted through the manila envelope full of letters Thelma Harner had given me. I read them one by one. None of the envelopes had return addresses. Some of the anonymous letters found inside were concerned with Harner's slowness in making judicial decisions. Judging by the handwriting, one frustrated writer wrote him more than half a dozen times, calling him honest but lazy, and threatening him with unspecified punishment if he didn't resign immediately as judge.

Halfway through the stack I found a letter that was more interesting. In it, an aggrieved person informed Harner that his chances for life eternal had been stripped from him in a secret trial and that a dark angel would soon come for him if he didn't leave the bench. The letter was dated less than two months before the courtroom shoot-out.

There followed three other letters that appeared to be by the same angry writer. The written words grew more shrill as the date of the courtroom shooting approached. Each of the letters was stamped with a rubber stamp: "Use the name of the Holy Ghost in your prayers."

I wondered if Big Hubba Wilkens had written them or, perhaps more likely, gotten someone from his church group or family to write them, but there was nothing in them that offered answers to my question.

The only thing the letters revealed was a similar thread about a coming but dateless Armageddon for, at least, both Bington and Madisonville.

I slept, but not well.

In the night, I dreamed again about Big Hubba Wilkens. This time he watched me from behind trees and bushes and called out my whereabouts to a someone I never could see out in the darkness.

I came awake a couple of times. My stomach rumbled a little each time. All else seemed well.

I did push-ups by my bed early in the morning, going at them slowly and easily. I did ten, thought I could do more, but decided against it. Then, just for the hell of it, I changed my mind and did ten more.

I went to my motel room door and opened it, but didn't step out. Outside, for the first time, the weather felt a bit like fall. The sun was up, the sky was blue and beautiful, but I knew fall was coming.

The phone rang at ten past six.

"Are you up?" It was Jo.

"Well, I had to get up to answer the phone," I said and laughed carefully. It was an old joke, clearly never that funny, but we owned and used it jointly.

"Your son and I aren't going back to Nance's today or any

164

other day in the near future. I'm having her package our stuff and UPS it to Bington. I may move back into our house if you approve."

"Fine with me. Is something wrong?"

"Yes. Nance called me late yesterday after you'd left Bington for Madisonville. While we were gone and Nance was sleeping elsewhere with a friend, someone broke into the place next door to Nance's, tortured and killed the two nice old people who lived there, then robbed their place of cash, rare coins, and jewelry. Also Friday night, after Joe and I were already in Bington, someone not yet known set off an old war rocket stolen from a National Guard armory or somewhere like that. They blew up the private-school bus that picks Joe up. They did the job where it sat parked in the school yard, but it could have just as easily been done on the street with the bus loaded with kids. There was a story about it in the *Indianapolis Star* this morning."

"I'm sorry," I said carefully.

"I think I hear 'Told you so' in your damnable tone of voice, Don Robak. Don't you dare say anything about Chicago being more dangerous than Bington. And admit your life is sometimes pretty dangerous."

"I willingly admit it. But I promise it won't stay that way after the first of the year. I had a long talk with Sheriff Goldie over the weekend. I hope and believe there'll be metal detectors and armed deputy sheriffs guarding the Bington courtroom come January. No one will get inside carrying a hidden gun."

"Maybe something like that could help," Jo said, sounding dubious.

"When you say you're moving back into the house, does that mean you and Joe are going to stay there now? All the time?"

"Yes."

"Am I invited?"

165

"Yes."

"To visit or stay?"

"I hoped you'd ask that. It's up to you."

I showered and shaved, grinning at myself fatuously in the mirror. I then dressed with my usual non-care. I found and then ate at a new place, a coffee shop downtown near Smalley's office. My breakfast was a large orange juice, which no longer seemed to burn me, an Egg Beater omelet with a little cheese, plus two slices of toast with butter. And lots of black decaf coffee.

I smiled so much that the counterman almost neglected to tell me to have a good day when I paid the bill and left behind a generous tip.

It still felt like fall with the sun fully up. It was not yet eight in the A.M. and so, feeling like work, I drove to the trailer court before going to Smalley's office. I felt incredibly good. There was no longer any soreness in my abdomen and I had no aches or pains.

I parked and wandered. There was a note on the Black King's door saying he was off to Indianapolis for the day. No one answered the door at Cleaner Kline's dumpy trailer, though I banged hard. The driveway was empty at Virgie Jones's trailer and there was no answer when I knocked. I wondered if she'd ever return from visiting her Louisville boyfriend. We'd likely need her for the trial.

I finally found fat Tepley "Tipper" Swisher sitting in a chair in front of his trailer laboriously reading the Louisville *Courier-Journal.* He had a cup of coffee and two sweet rolls precariously perched on his abundant lap.

"It was reported to me that you were busy Saturday night," I said.

He shook his head questioningly and waited for me to say more, his eyes refusing to meet mine.

"Smalley said he recognized some of the people who

166

came into his yard and thereafter did damage to his house. You were one of them."

"That's wrong," he said stoutly. "I was right here at home watching the Reds and Braves on the television. I can get lots of people to back me up."

"You mean you have lots of liars ready to say whatever Allwell tells them to say, don't you, Tipper? Makes no difference to me," I said. "Smalley says he saw you and I think he'll turn you in unless I just happened to talk to him and he then decided against it. I'm sorry he has to cause you problems, but it's his choice, not mine. You'll need bond money, a lawyer, plus every witness Allwell can suborn. That still may not get you off."

He watched and waited, believing there was more.

There was. I moved at it. "What time does Reverend Allwell usually hold his services at night?"

"There's a church meeting at eight o'clock tonight. Sometimes Allwell's a little late getting there because he's held his big weekly services on Sunday morning and so he sort of takes Monday off to rest. Next time he'll be for sure there will be tomorrow, Tuesday night, at eight, or as soon after that time as Allwell feels like showing up." He shook his head. "I ain't going either time. Like I told you, me and Reverend Allwell, we does our business up to the courthouse. The only time I like to be close to him is when it's bright day and there's lots of witnesses around. You can't tell what he's going to do when it's private. His temperament ain't good these days even up around the courthouse. Some of the church folks lay that onto you and Smalley."

"Maybe Allwell knows the final date for the burning of the world and that's what's worrying him."

He shook his head nervously. "You don't believe that and neither do I."

"Include Allwell as a nonbeliever and I'll vote with you, Tipper," I said.

He smiled and nodded.

"Would you be interested in making yourself a piece of money?"

"How much money?" His hooded eyes narrowed down so I couldn't read them, but I could see the heartbeat in his midsection gain speed.

"A hundred dollars. I'd want you to spread some flyers around Allwell's church. I'll also want it done without you getting seen or caught. Is there a time late this afternoon when you could go to up to the Survival church without the chance of anyone knowing you're there or seeing you? If there is, then we'd want you to spread these papers around, like maybe one paper on every third or fourth church chair?"

He nodded. "Maybe. There usually ain't no one around up there Mondays until it starts to get dark." He nodded to himself. "You'd give me a hundred dollars and also talk Mr. Smalley into not prosecuting me?"

"I'd add that in free. Sure."

"Deal. But I got to see what it is I'd be spreading."

I went to the LTD and, from the trunk, got the copies of the report Sam King had obtained for me on Allwell. I took them back to where Tipper sat. I gave the stack to him and watched while he read the top copy.

When he finished, he smiled thinly up at me and then widened the smile. "He catches me or you or anyone else spreading these papers and he'll crap a thousand pounds all over us. Is what's on these papers true?"

"Yes."

"It ain't no wonder he hates lawyers and judges so damn much what with him having been disbarred."

"And, more than being disbarred, it's the kids, Tipper. Think about the two dead kids. If he did sex things to kids

168

three times before, then he could have done something to Gretel or Hansel after his Sunday church the day they died. He could have done it up on the hill near where the kids play. Some kids saw him stop there with Hansel and Gretel on the day they got poisoned. He could have gotten worried about what he'd done, even if he'd paid money to them to do it, then killed the two kids to keep them from putting him in trouble."

Tipper looked at the stack of papers nervously.

"Dynamite," he said. "He's dog meat."

"Remember, I don't want you to get seen. If someone's around you just save the papers and do it another night. Have we still got us a deal?"

"I'd likely kill the bastard for a hundred dollars. All he ever gives me is five or ten dollars to spread the bad word on the witch and Mr. Smalley. And he don't like me or trust me much on account of my cousin, the one whose wife he diddled."

"I'll give you fifty now and the other fifty after I know you delivered on your part of the deal. If you don't do the job I'll take the first half back."

He smiled and nodded, then spread his hands. "No problem, Mr. Robak."

I gave him fifty dollars.

He smiled and took it. "Is it okay for my cousin to maybe call Allwell, like with a handkerchief stuffed in the phone, and tell him there's a problem and he needs to get to the church tonight?"

I shrugged.

Tipper smiled. "All I got to do is tell Ben that it'll shake Allwell up. He hates him."

"See you later then, Tipper."

"Was you looking for Cleaner Kline?" he asked. I saw you down around near his trailer."

I nodded.

"For a measly twenty bucks more I'll tell you where to find him."

I got out my billfold and handed him a twenty.

"The Cleaner man's up in the hospital in intensive care. He was with me when we went to Mr. Smalley's place. He fell down and passed out when we ran out of the yard. Someone called 911 about him. They come with the siren on and hauled him away. The word I got is he ain't going to make it." He shook his head. "He didn't have nothin' to do with nothin' the day those kids died, Mr. Robak, if that's what you been wantin' to ask him about. I seen him leave the trailer camp about the time the witch started the fire under the poison pot. He never come back until the action was all done."

"Thank you."

At Smalley's office men in white coveralls were replacing the front window and cleaning up the splattered paint.

Smalley sat in his office, smiling.

First I told him about Jo and son Joe, and that widened his smile. I then caught him up on my morning activities. That made him lose the smile and find a severe frown.

"Allwell's dangerous, Don. He's not that dangerous to me because he's afraid of me. I've got the Indian sign on him. If someone's going to pull his chain, then I ought to be that someone."

I shrugged. "I think I can run fast now even if I can't fight."

"Yeah."

"What's done is done. I'm no more afraid of Allwell than you are, Kevin. I mean, as long as I've got you around to protect me."

"Sure, but me around or not, you need to be afraid of him."

"I can go up there and get the flyers back from Tipper if you'd like."

He thought for a moment and then shook his head. "I didn't say I wanted you to do that."

I waited.

"What else do we need to do in the case?" Smalley asked, after a silence.

"The prosecution has the adults, we have the kids. In a fair trial, one that Allwell can't manipulate, we'd possibly win, especially if we could break their adult witnesses who say they saw Bert put the poison in the pot. My feeling is that we should keep things moving along, figure out a new county to pick our jury out of, and go to trial as soon as possible."

"You think Bert's got a real chance?" he asked.

"Sure."

"I guess I agree. Who did the poisoning then? Allwell?"

"Maybe. He could have done it. We've got his hands over the pot, we've got his hate for Bert, we've got the kids stopping in the cave on the way down the hill with him on the day they died. If the sheriff finds anything in that cave, then maybe we've got more."

We looked at each other and Smalley nodded.

"What else do we do?" he asked.

"We sit. We see what happens when and if Allwell sees the report."

"I'm getting a good feeling," he said.

Something ran through my head, leaving only its path behind, some inner feeling that I now stood on the edge of knowing exactly what had happened on Poison Sunday. I felt a chill. I forced myself to ignore it.

"Things are sure to get hotter around here before we get to a trial," I said. "Today, and I do mean today, can you get the word around that we're going to pick our murder jury out of Indianapolis, Marion County? Or maybe make it Evansville, Vanderburgh County?"

"Are we going to do that?"

"I don't know. We'll pick the jury out of the place Allwell dislikes most. You call the prosecutor and the judge and tell them we can't agree on picking the jury from around South Vernon, and tell them why. Then tell them that if we can do an exhumation of both bodies, plus get a quick report on the examination, plus arrange a fair place to pick the jury, we can be ready whenever that's completed. But let's do whatever we do publicly so that all the newspapers, television stations, and radio stations find it out. I want everyone to hear about it."

"What do you need the exhumation for? The autopsy doctors said what you wanted them to say, didn't they?"

"Maybe. Maybe we'll only want one exhumation. I've got a telephone call coming that'll likely help us decide."

"What call is that?"

"Sam King, in Bington. I asked him to check something out for me about Allwell's child victims."

He shrugged. "Exhumations do make Allwell nervous for some reason."

"Yes. At the same time you're doing your chores, I'm going over to the jail and talk to Bert one more time. I'm going to ask her to please take a lie detector test."

"She won't do that," he said.

"I'll bet she will if I talk to her just right. I'm going to try to get Lem to promise not to ask questions in one single area."

"He won't do it. He told you that."

"Maybe he will when I tell him what the area is I want him to stay away from."

"What exact area are you talking about?"

"I'm going to ask him not to ask any questions concern-

172

ing who Bert thinks poisoned her kids. That's assuming Bert tests clean and pure on did-she-or-didn't-she."

"You act like she knows something she hasn't told us."

"No. She really doesn't know anything, but maybe she thinks she does. I bet she'll take the lie detector if 'Who else done it?' Isn't a part of the questioning."

"So go try." He gave me a wise look. "I wonder if you're thinking about the same possibility I've thought on some since the poisonings."

"Maybe."

"How about me calling Lem and then you do the talking to him?" Smalley asked.

"Okay. Want to go to the jail first with me?"

"Not yet for me. I happen to know something you don't know, Don. The sheriff and some of his deputies are up on the hill digging around in the kids' hideaway cave just about now. I want to be at the jail when they return."

"I'll go on over alone then."

"Yeah, go see your lady friend."

I smiled at him.

"What are you going to tell her?"

"Not a lot. She's sat for a lot of months inside her cell and never gotten used to the idea of being caged. I don't want to build a lot of false hopes." I thought more on that and then nodded at Smalley.

"I may hint a little."

"Get out of here," he said, smiling. "You're a badass." He picked up a heavy book and acted as if he was about to throw it.

I escaped.

I walked to the jail and went through the ritual of getting in to see Bert. The sheriff was, of course, absent. In a while I stood outside her cell, holding her hand.

"Listen to me," I said carefully. "If I could get the state to agree that they won't ask you anything about anyone else who might have poisoned your wards, would you then take a lie detector test?"

She started to shake her head, but then stopped.

She pulled at the blanket around her feet and shuffled it closer to the bars. Then she put her hand back through and I gave her my hand to hold again.

"Is this place too cold for you?"

"No. Unless I think on it, I don't feel the cold. My feet feel it, but I don't."

I waited.

"How would you get them to do that?" she asked.

"They'd promise in writing, Bert. If they reneged on the promise then you'd just not answer their questions. But if they promise, they'll keep the promise."

"And they'd ask me only if I poisoned the kids?"

"About that, yes. They could ask you other questions about where the poison came from and why you gave the poison to the kids."

"I might fail the test. I gave them the stew. Maybe, when I was putting things in the pot, I put in something that was poison without knowing it."

"Did you?"

"No. I do things mostly by feel and smell. But that day it was bright and I could see pretty good and I know I never put nothing in that pot that oughtn't to have been there."

"You've got bad cataracts on both eyes," I said. "Most times they can peel things like that off and then you'd see fine. You could likely drive again if you want."

"If I pass the lie test and they let me go, I'm going back across the river to the high hills."

"Whatever you'd want to do."

"Would you come see me there?"

"Maybe. I'd try."

She shook her head. "No, you likely never will. Most of what was wrong inside you is gone. There's still someone out there looking for you, but you're well and getting strong. I feel whoever's out there is the one who needs to be careful. You had wife trouble when you first came here to see me, didn't you?"

"Some. She'd left me and gone to Chicago. Now she's come home, along with my ten-year-old boy."

"Did their coming home make you happy?"

"Yes."

"Maybe she'll stay with you now. I can't tell one way or the other. Up to you, up to her. How about you promise me nice that you'll come over the river and see me if she leaves you again?"

"I would do that."

She smiled at me and the smile made her desirable. I was used to her face and body and I somehow knew there was a lot of woman in her.

"I'm going to get out of this place soon, ain't I? People are going to quit hating me and instead go to hating someone else about the poison. I feel it."

I held her hand for a little while.

"How does Mr. Smalley feel about this?" she asked.

"Like I do. We hope and believe that you'll soon be out of here."

"He's so sad. When I touch him nothing comes through to me but the sadness."

"Maybe he'll do better when this is over," I said, hoping he would.

I left her and went back downstairs to the sheriff's office. The sheriff and his helpers had not yet returned, so I sat for a time, waiting. After a while I heard them call in on the radio. A deputy at the desk called Smalley. He came and both of us waited.

* * *

Sheriff Deb sat at his kitchen table.

"We dug back through the dirt and it finally opened up to a kind of cave. We found a lot of books and some clothes. There was an old purse that maybe had once had some money in it. There were some pictures. There was a book that the two kids were likely writing together." He shook his head. "There was nothing of interest in it. There was one page torn out and stuffed back in."

He handed me a piece of paper. It read: "We promise by the moon to stop." Both kids had signed it below, the signatures now faded brown.

Smalley nodded when I handed the note on to him. His eyes found mine and I knew we were thinking the same thing.

"We found something else that might be of much more interest." Deb held up a mason jar. It seemed empty. "Did either of you ever see this jar before?"

"Not me," Smalley said.

I shook my head.

"Promise me," Deb said grimly.

"I swear," Smalley said.

"Me too," I said.

"There's residue of something inside. I smelled it, but I couldn't tell much from smelling. I've got the state police coming to take it to the lab. I ain't sure, but I think maybe that nicotine was once in that jar. I believe that's where the poison come from."

"Our kids will tell you that Bert never was in that cave."

"Well, we pretty well know she wasn't there on the day the kids died," Deb said.

"Allwell was," I said.

Deb nodded at me. "One of your former partners called Goldie, when he couldn't reach you, and had Goldie call me.

176

He gave me the names of the three kids that Allwell assaulted years ago in Kentucky."

I waited.

"You may be a little surprised," he said.

"Probably not."

He read the three names from a scribbled sheet.

I wasn't surprised.

Smalley wasn't either.

ELEVEN

"As to elected and appointed officials each of you should do all you can to make their lives dangerous."

—Herbert Techni in an unsigned letter to various militia groups, dated April 10, 1995

I WATCHED THE rearview mirror on my way back to the motel. No one followed. By now, anyone equipped with half a working brain would know where I'd stayed in Madisonville before and likely was staying again. It was, after all, a small town. A watcher wouldn't need to follow behind me all the time. He'd have seen my car at the motel both the week before and the night before.

Things were moving fast for Bert. Sheriff Deb was helping move them. I thought it was likely that, with luck, she could be out of jail by tomorrow. It had been a big day for the defense.

Smalley and I had been interviewed by a steadily increasing crowd of newspeople as the day wore on, Smalley doing most of the talking.

"All we want," we repeatedly told the reporters, "is a fair trial." That could be accomplished by picking a jury out of a big city where there was not the same kind of hate found

179

in the Bington, Madisonville, and South Vernon areas. It could also be helped by a second medical examination of an exhumed body.

The location where the possible poison jar had been found became known to the media in the early afternoon. A full examination of the contents was scheduled for the morrow at the state police lab, but the state police were already presuming, through an unnamed spokesman, that it was in fact the previously undiscovered poison jar. The outside of the jar had been wiped clean of all but smudged prints.

When we were asked, we spread the word that, if it was the long-sought poison jar, then Bertha Jones could have had no access to it on the day her two wards had died and, more telling, no way of placing it in the cave after their deaths.

In the afternoon we were front page, top right, of the Madisonville paper. By evening, area television and radio stations carried the stories, top of the news. A few commentators even grudgingly admitted that "someone else" might have been responsible for poisoning Bert's wards.

We finally quit answering questions when deadlines passed and the groups of reporters slipped away. I was tired and so was Smalley. We went our separate ways.

I drove alone to the restaurant in the shopping center, going there more because I was familiar with the place than because of the promise of good food. I parked in front and entered. There were a few other diners.

A new waitress led me to a small table. She smiled commercially and I smiled back. She wore a little white thing on top of her head, a kerchief, something like what Amish women wear. She also wore a St. Christopher's medal on a chain around her neck.

Under my coffee saucer was a religious tract. I picked it up and looked it over after I'd ordered the baked meat loaf special. The cover page read: "Big Attraction Coming Soon. RU Ready?" The tract was not from Allwell's Survival church. I reflected that most Christian churches believe in the Second Coming. As a Christian, I too presumably believe in it, but not in anyone who says they know when it will be.

Outside the sun set and the sky became dark.

I ate slowly, chewing up each bite of my first full meat dish in six months, relishing the dinner. I ate the potatoes, the green beans, and the bread. Everything seemed to sit well in my stomach.

Allwell and three of his guardsmen entered the restaurant as I was finishing. They walked to my table, smiling at me. Allwell nodded. His men stood at attention behind him like soldiers on duty.

"I owe you an apology, Robak," he said in his deep fine voice. "I talked a long time with Mrs. Kittaning Friday night after you'd left her party. She says you're not a non-man and I believe her. I should not have insulted you by implying you were gay."

"I wasn't insulted," I said.

"Well, you certainly should have been."

I almost told him his statement was odd for a man who'd had his own earlier sexual troubles with juveniles, but it didn't seem wise. There were four of them, one of me.

"Have you been watching or listening to the local news?" I asked carefully.

"I've been resting. I rest from God's work on Mondays. I seldom watch television, listen to the radio, or read newspapers."

We watched each other for a long moment. His eyes remained unreadable, but he smiled again. "I do apologize," he said.

I nodded and waited. There was to be nothing more.

Allwell wheeled away from me and walked back toward

the door. His men followed behind. A tough-looking young one, wearing boots, turned and grinned narrowly at me. I thought he was trying to memorize my face.

I called out when Allwell was at the door, "Thank you, Hoskin." I used his first name from the report Sam King had supplied me. "Maybe you should turn on your car radio to hear about the new evidence."

He stopped and looked back at me. Then he shook his head and exited. He and his men got into a black Lincoln Town Car, almost new, and drove away.

I looked at my watch. It was almost eight o'clock. Soon Allwell would or could arrive and make entrance at his church.

I thought about what he might find in the church if Tipper had gotten the delivery job done and those present for the night meeting had done their reading.

I also thought some more on the many things that could go wrong in my personal world. I got up, took care of the bill and tip, and drove the short distance to the motel. I parked the LTD away from the front of my room.

My room this week wasn't the same room as last week, but it had the same general layout. I sat on the bed and called Smalley's home number. I let the phone ring a dozen times. There was no answer.

I went back outside, having again forgotten something that now seemed important to me. I pondered taking my major armament but decided to leave it in the trunk of the LTD. I did take the revolver from the glove compartment. I carried it into the room, keeping it hidden in my back pocket, suit coat buttoned.

I sat on my bed again and thought some more, then called Sheriff Deb Hewitt. He was in.

"I just had a meal in the shopping center restaurant behind my motel, Deb," I said. "I had a meat loaf dinner with mashed potatoes and green beans, plus bread and butter. I ate every beautiful bite."

"Goody for you. I'll likely try my first really solid stuff to-morrow. I'm looking forward to greaseburgers and fries by the end of the week, lots of pickles, mustard, and ketchup."

"Sounds nutritious. When I was finishing up my meat loaf, I was visited by Allwell and three of his storm troopers, maybe to identify me to them."

"Problems?"

"No. He was polite. He said he'd heard no news when I inquired. I invited him to turn on his car radio when he left. There may be problems when Allwell sees the same report we gave you. That could be tonight. Allwell apologized to me for something he'd said to me. What I keep wondering about is why he bothered. Can you keep a special eye on Smalley tonight?"

"We're watching his house and office. He's out now, but I know where he's eating and I have a car there."

"Watch close. If something bad happens tonight, Allwell now has me available as a witness for the defense as to his civility. He was a lawyer before he got disbarred. He's still court-smart enough to line up an extra witness."

"Watch your own ass," he said. "He also might have been friendly in public because he's set up some big nighttime plans for *you.*"

I hadn't thought much on that. If he didn't have such plans now, he'd likely be considering them after he heard or read the news and saw a copy of the Sam King report.

"Thanks." I hung up.

The picture-window curtain near the entrance to my motel room stood drawn. I closed it. That done, I inspected the room. The door was flimsy. A good kick or shove would surely open it. I had two queen-sized beds, a bureau, a cur-tained closet, a bathroom with toilet and shower, a couple of tables, two chairs, and a television. Except for not being penned in by steel bars, I had about the same arrangement that Bertha had in jail, with one bed added. A fine place to get trapped in and die.

I was dog tired.

Allwell could be at his church by now if he'd taken the bait. He'd surely have been curious enough to turn on his car radio and that might also have sent him to his church.

He was there.

There was perhaps a little time. I turned on the television and watched an old war movie for a few minutes. Everyone died heroically.

The television control had a mute button. I hardly watch TV these days without mute button protection. The commercials grow more shrill and mindless by the day.

Buy this. You've got to buy this, OR ELSE you'll lose all your friends and your sex appeal.

My antacid, my pain reliever, my deodorant, is better than theirs. So's my car, my television, and the food on my table.

Soon our people will be at your door to present you with twenty million dollars.

Liar's poker.

I turned it off and napped, but only for a moment.

My bathroom had a high window opening to the outside. I laboriously worked the window open and removed the inner screen in case I needed a quick exit. I turned off my room lights and surveyed a bit of the parking lot through a slit I made in the bottom of the picture-window curtain. I could see no one outside.

But I felt someone.

The phone rang. I picked it up. I identified the voice as that of Reverend Mo Mellish.

"Get out now. Don't use the front door if there's another way."

184

I hung up the phone and moved to the bathroom again. I took off my shoes, climbed onto the toilet seat, then snaked myself out the narrow window. Once outside, I put my shoes back on and slipped the .38 from my back pocket into my belt and snugged it there.

The motel was built in a V shape. I walked in darkness to the end away from the office. I moved out a few feet from the end and found a place where I could observe the motel parking lot and still be partly hidden behind ornamental trees and shrubs.

Someone sat smoking a cigarette in an almost-new black Lincoln Town Car. The car was parked with its rear end toward me. I couldn't tell for sure if it was Allwell's, but it looked to be the same car. I memorized the license number. I could identify the watcher only as a man. He seemed intent on staring at the motel units on my side of the V. I stayed outside the motel lot in the shrubs and trees. After a time I moved out a little more. I was in dim light but probably visible. Had the watcher turned my way, he'd likely have seen me.

He didn't.

The smoker in the car flipped a cigarette onto the pavement and opened his door. He walked directly to the door of my motel room. He wore black or dark blue pants, a gray shirt, and a dark Yankees baseball cap that hooded his face.

I was alarmed, but stayed where I was.

He stood there, then stepped to one side of my room door and pointed emphatically at the knob. He was facing the other end of the motel.

I craned, trying to see who he was communicating with. Whoever it was was just outside my line of vision at the front of the motel on the far end of the V. That wasn't all bad, as I was out of his line of sight also.

My watcher walked swiftly back to the Lincoln and got inside. He started up, put the car in gear, and drove slowly out of the motel lot. In a short time I could no longer hear the sound of the motor.

Gone.

I moved back to the rear of the motel and ran until I came to the office corner. From there I could see what I believed to be the second watcher. This one was driving an old green Chrysler, the car I'd heard Sheriff Deb describe. As I watched, he started the car, then drove it, motor missing some, into the motel lot. He took the same spot where the Lincoln had been parked.

I ran across the driveway of the motel, trying to avoid light from the office. On the far side of the drive there were more trees and bushes, some of them grown large. I walked swiftly, using the trees and bushes for cover, sometimes stooping or crawling.

I was breathing hard. I looked for Mo Mellish's car but didn't see it. He had to be watching from somewhere in order to have warned me.

A few cars were parked at the edge of the shopping center lot, possibly the vehicles of cleanup crew members working inside the shopping mall. I used those for further concealment and moved on toward the old green Chrysler, I watched the occupant of the car, afraid he'd discover me.

But the Chrysler driver remained intent on his own project. I heard the driver's window being rolled down. A rifle barrel projected through it. A tiny red flower of light bloomed on my room window.

Laser sight.

I stepped from behind the last shielding car.

The man in the car began to fire at and through the picture window, spacing and moving his shots around, first right, then left, then high, then low. The rifle made odd noises, *spang, spang, spang*. The motel clerk must have either heard the noises or the breaking glass. All the lights in the motel office went off.

186

I waited until I believed the rifle was empty and until I saw it being withdrawn through the Chrysler's window for stowing or reloading. I then ran toward the shooter's car. My stomach burned and I was afraid. I arrived helter-skelter, skidding a little.

By the time the shooter heard me coming, it was too late. I put the .38 barrel against his left ear.

He was a strong young man, likely in his early twenties. His face was tough looking, with a thin shadow above his mouth where he'd tried, without success, to grow a mustache, and a receding hairline. I'd seen him earlier in the evening.

"Don't do anything except what I tell you to do."

He was the man in the boots who'd visited me, along with Allwell, in the restaurant, the one who'd narrowly smiled back when he'd departed.

He didn't smile now.

He moved an inch too much and I turned the gun away from his head and fired a single shot through his windshield. It starred the glass badly. The sound of the shot froze all his motion and I thought the powder from the gunshot had likely burned him.

"I can and will kill you. The next shot will make you a third ear. Open your car door and get out. Keep your body close up to the door and open it slowly and carefully. Don't jostle my hand and don't alarm me or you'll never live to see the sun."

He waited.

"Leave the rifle where it is and get out of the car. Now!"

He came out of the car in exactly the way I'd ordered. I moved the gun a little away from his head, and let him read my eyes.

"Lie on the ground, face down, and put your nose flat against the pavement. Stick your arms straight out from your body and, after that, don't move."

He did.

From far away I could hear sirens.

We waited together.

"You'll be fuckin' sorry," he said angrily.

"Shut up. I want bad to kill you now. I don't give a damn who you are and I don't even give a damn why you shot into my motel room. Bug me a fraction and I'll shoot you in the balls for fun, then in the head when I get tired of laughing."

"You killed my blood cousin in the Bington courtroom," he said. "My family will have you dead."

I bent over and put the gun to the back of his head. I pulled the hammer back and listened to it click. So did he. I put my finger on the trigger and he saw the motion and closed his eyes tight.

"Jesus," he said. "Don't."

"How about we make the score Robak, two, and Wilkenses, zero?"

As he imagined the bad things that might happen to him, I saw his young face change. He sniffled. By the time both a police car and a sheriff's car arrived and cuffed him he was bawling.

Smalley came with a sheriff's deputy in a marked car. His suit coat was off and his shirt was open at the collar, but he was still wearing his gold cufflinks.

"I was at my office. The sheriff had the deputy come get me, maybe to identify your body."

"Thanks."

From a far corner of the shopping center lot I saw lights come on and blink twice. A car moved there. I thought it was a brown Chevrolet. I gave the driver a tiny unseen wave.

We promised the two police officers and the sheriff's deputy that we'd be along to the sheriff's office within the hour.

"If Deb wants to know where we went, tell him we're driving up to the Survival church. Maybe he might want to meet us there in a bit," Smalley told the deputy.

He nodded dubiously. "You ought to follow me to the jail now."

Smalley shook his head. "Not yet."

None of the officers asked for the .38

"Are we really going up there?"

"Sure," Smalley said.

I knew that if Jo was with me right now, she'd never let me through the door of our house again. But I was angry, ready, and Jo was in Bington.

"Okay," I said. We got my LTD.

There were still a few cars at Allwell's church.

One of them was a black Lincoln Town Car, almost new.

I looked around carefully. At the far edge of the church, almost in the trees, I thought I also saw a brown Chevrolet.

Maybe, maybe not.

"No problems," I said to Smalley, deciding not to mention Mellish's call or car for now. "I don't want to shoot anybody."

"Sure. I don't want problems either. I had a good talk with myself earlier tonight. You know why I wanted to come here?"

"I think so. It's likely for the same reason I was willing to come along. We both want to shake up Allwell some more, then see what he'll do. If he runs, then Bert's likely off the hook. If he doesn't, then the case against her still might have some life to it."

He nodded.

"Another thing," Smalley said. "Let's tell him that we're

going to withdraw the motion for change of venue from the county and try Bert's case here."

I thought about it and then nodded.

We got out of the LTD and walked toward the double doors. Outside, in the light, four men stood talking. One of the men held a piece of paper I recognized.

"I ain't believing someone like the man described in this paper can tell me what God's planning to do," he said loudly. "And I ain't going to burn no jail and courthouse just because that man's screaming in his church for it."

Two of the men nodded, but the last one, a man with a gray beard, raised his own voice.

"Allwell says this paper's a lie and it's that black-hearted poison witch that's spreading foul rumors with the law helping. He says she needs to burn."

"If it's going to be that way then where is everybody?" the first speaker answered. "Ain't enough people left around here to start a fire in a barbeque pit."

Smalley stepped out from the darkness. "The paper you're holding was my doing. And it's the truth."

The four men watched us.

"You, with the beard. Go inside the church and tell Allwell that Kevin Smalley's out here to see him."

"Why the hell should I?" the man blustered.

"Because if you don't, I think I'll break your damn nose, smart mouth."

Gray Beard thought about it, measured Smalley, perhaps remembered stories, and then turned.

"Okay. I don't need his troubles. I'll tell him. But that's all. I'm out of here for good."

We waited.

In a bit Allwell emerged from his church. Two men came with him, neither with a beard. One was the man who had parked the Lincoln in front of my motel room. I recognized his clothes and his Yankee cap. The other man carried a shotgun. I was sorry I hadn't exchanged the .38 for the shotgun in the LTD's trunk. Now I was outgunned.

Smalley said, "I bet you just lectured your church people about how evil I am, Allwell?"

Allwell nodded. He touched the man beside him who held the shotgun.

"Easy with that, Ned." He looked around carefully, perhaps trying to to see if there were witnesses.

"I came up here to report how things are going for you, Reverend Asshole," Smalley said. "The sheriff's right behind. In fact, a few of his men may already be watching from the bushes."

"Bullshit," Allwell said. "You got nothing and no one." He walked on until he was only a foot or so away from Smalley. "You surprised me a couple of times, fairy. You're quick and strong, but then coal black sin always is. I won't be surprised again tonight. I want to warn you in the presence of these men, and any other witnesses out in the dark, that I once killed a man with my fists. I want all those watching to realize I'm on my home ground and you're the challenger in this, not me."

"I'm not looking to fight, but I will if you want," Smalley said reasonably. "Robak and I came to tell you we know a few more things about you that aren't mentioned in the copies that were distributed. The kids described in that report, weren't girls. They were boys. One was thirteen, the other two were fourteen. We're not going to exhume the girl's body now, but we will be exhuming the boy's, even if it takes the state police and the National Guard to get that job done. And then we want you to know we're dropping the motion for change of venue from the county. When the state tries Bertha, we'll try you."

Allwell's facial expression never changed until the last words. He shook his head, a fighter who'd suffered a heavy blow.

"You need to die, Smalley," he said, recovering.

Smalley nodded. "Here I am."

Allwell took a swift step forward and hit at Smalley's body with huge hands. I heard the sounds those hands made, like chops of a sharp axe against a hardwood tree. For a moment I was certain Smalley was horribly hurt.

Instead, Smalley, unslowed, stepped away and looped a fist between Allwell's arms, striking the bigger man hard in the neck.

Allwell screamed angrily. "Goddamn your eyes, queer. Stand still and fight me fair."

Smalley feinted and struck again, this time a hard blow to Allwell's nose. I heard bone break.

Allwell lunged forward, still screaming, all gutter words now. Smalley rained blows in return, then caught the huge man over a hip and flung him away, using Allwell's strength along with his own. The big man thumped down hard, skidding in the dirt and gravel.

As he came up and pushed himself to his feet, I could hear his breath rattle.

"Run, Allwell," Smalley said. "By tomorrow there'll be warrants out for you. There's two poisoned kids."

"I never did anything bad to those kids. All I did was touch the boy a little until that little bitch got mad. The witch killed them."

"There's a man they just took down to the jail. Earlier tonight, he tried to shoot Robak. You likely sent him. This time you won't get off with a few months. You'll get big time, disbarred lawyer. And you'll do your time where the inmates hate 'short eyes,' people who trail after and abuse little boys and girls."

I thought that Allwell might renew the fight, but he didn't. He stood and watched his night world, breathing hard. His hands opened and closed, but only on air.

His guard with the shotgun nodded at me.

"I ain't taking this up," he said. He carefully put the shotgun down on the pavement and walked away.

"Me either," I called after him. I looked at the other guard. "You look familiar," I said.

"Saw you at the restaurant," he answered, smiling the good smile.

"And I saw you later too. I watched you point out which door in the motel was mine. I'll bet the young man with the laser rifle might be mentioning your name down at the jail about now."

"Not me," he said. "You're mistaken."

He turned away from me and walked swiftly toward the Lincoln. When I did nothing to stop him, he moved more quickly. He got into the big car and looked back once at Allwell. He then started the car and drove away.

The license number was the one I'd memorized.

I could hear sirens again.

Allwell looked down at the shotgun. I thought I saw the desire to reach for it in his eyes.

"I'm a dead shot," I lied. "I'll bet, on your Bible, I can put four bullets in your head and heart before you can reach that gun."

He turned away. By the time Sheriff Deb arrived, Allwell had vanished into the night. Smalley and I had made no attempt to stop him.

When we drove back down the hill I saw that Reverend Mo Mellish's car was still parked near the edge of the parking lot. I didn't see Mellish, just the car and the two black cats sitting on the hood.

We were most of the rest of the night at the sheriff's office. Many and varied police came and took my statement. They then called and asked a state police detective to come to the jail. He came, then asked lots of the same questions plus a few of his own.

193

Lem came and did likewise.

"Damn it, Robak," he said. "I hope you're less of a problem as a judge than you are as a lawyer."

Newspeople returned, at first one or two, then a crowd. The sheriff's office soon looked like a mob scene.

I told my motel story, minus any mention of Reverend Mo Mellish or his call, several times. Then Smalley and I told the state police detective, who'd not heard the story, about last week when someone had put a laser sight on us several times near the Survival church.

No one asked us exactly what had taken place at Allwell's church. Smalley had already mentioned that action to Sheriff Deb Hewitt, lessening the fight into a couple of pushes by each man. Most people exaggerate fights, but Smalley was a perpetual trivializer.

The motel operator appeared and made a statement about the shot-out picture window and the resulting damage to the motel room. He eyed me several times, morosely.

"Could you please move out in the morning?" he asked at a quiet time.

"Not me." I smiled at him. "I like your place. It's nice, clean, and homey."

He looked horrified and said, "I went in your room. It's shot to pieces. Why didn't you stop that man before he did all that crazy shooting? He ruined the whole damn room." He was distressed. "The owners will kill me."

"I had good reason not to try to stop him when he was doing his shooting. That was when we both had loaded guns."

Lem and Smalley shushed the motel man, smiled at him, shook his hand, told him he was a hero for calling the law, and finally sent him on his way, somewhat appeased by soft talk and advice concerning insurance.

* * *

In the early morning, the final four of us—Lem and Deb, Smalley and me—had bacon, eggs, buttered toast, and decaf coffee together in the sheriff's kitchen.

"My deputies and the Madisonville city boys looked for Allwell all night. He has to be running hard," Deb said. "I got a first-class statement from the shooter, Robak. He'd completely caved in by the time the deputy got him here. He said Allwell gave him the rifle and loaned him one of his elite guards to show exactly where you were staying. He also said the Reverend gave him fifty dollars and said he could keep the rifle when the job was done." He shook his head. "You must have scared him bad. He kept saying, over and over, that he thought he was dead when you had your gun in his ear."

"Have you got the slug from the time you were shot from ambush?" I asked him.

"Yeah."

"To satisfy my curiosity, try ballistics comparison with the slugs you find in my room."

Deb nodded. "I'll do just that."

"What am I supposed to do?" Lem asked.

"What we'd like you to do is release Bertha Jones," Smalley said.

"I don't know about that. Give me more reasons."

"She didn't kill her wards," I said. "She will even take a lie detector test now, with the exclusion you were thinking about granting before."

Smalley said, "Also those people outside the church led us to believe that Allwell tried to raise a mob tonight to come here to the jail and burn both it and the courthouse. You don't owe someone like him any leeway."

Deb smiled. "Kevin and Lem know this, but you don't, Robak: the main problem we have with the women's section of this jail is that Bertha Jones's cell and the other two

195

in that section are infested with termites. One day the floor will fall clean through. Bertha could escape just by clawing the outside wall, but she's never tried, no matter how much she hates being behind bars."

Lem nodded at Deb, smiling a little at the termite story. I could tell he was tired.

"How did Reverend Allwell, or whoever, get the poison from the cave to the kettle in the trailer court?" he asked.

Smalley answered, "It had to be moved in something combustible. Put the poison into the stew pot and then maybe drop the plastic carrying bottle in the coals to get rid of it. Plus scatter the coals by trying to set Bert on fire."

"If I talked the judge into letting your client go free on her own recognizance, do you think you guys could get her to go somewhere else, like Kentucky, for a while until things cool down some?"

Smalley and I both nodded.

"Let me call Kit."

196

TWELVE

"All's well that ends well, 'well' meaning when us good people win out over the governmental forces of chaos and oppression."

—Herbert Techni to the press in Montana, May 1996

"WHY DON'T YOU try practicing in both Madisonville and Bington?" I said to Smalley late the next afternoon after we'd both had sufficient sleep. "Spend what time you need to spend here in Madisonville and the rest in Bington working with my former partners."

He shook his head, but not adamantly.

"They have an interesting practice, Kevin. A little of this, a little of that, and a lot of the rest. They make good money most years. And they're swamped and need someone."

"Madisonville people just don't get along with Bington people," he said.

"So what? That problem's not your problem. You'd like life in Bington better than here in Madisonville. Here, you're a lonely man. You're openly gay and you've got this insular town polarized against you. It may remain that way a long time. It won't easily forget its own self-inflicted distrust of you. Plus, you'd make new friends in Bington."

"Gay friends, you mean?"

"All kinds of friends, gay and straight. The university's there with lots of bright and amiable people. There are shows and plays and concerts at the university auditorium. There's a local symphony orchestra that big-city critics say is first-class."

"All gays aren't lovers of the arts, Robak. When we used to kick around at law school what did I like?"

"Drinking cold beer, eating peanuts, and bashing offensive linebackers."

"Close enough. Substitute Scotch for beer and you have Kevin Smalley in his fifties. I have a tin ear, and I find plays boring. The only place I'm good with language is in a legal brief."

I ignored him. "It would be a chance for a new life, Kevin." I nodded encouragingly. "Try it for a while. My former partners truly would like you to do that. They could use you."

"If I came to Bington you'd try to introduce me around to friends of yours who are gay, wouldn't you?"

"Not unless you asked me," I said, lying gently.

"I wouldn't want you wandering around trying to create romance for me."

"I'd never do that," I protested. "I'd not interfere in your life. I'll remind you, however, that there are two gay bars and several first-class restaurants, all serving single malt, that cater to gays in Bington. I'd write the names down for you, is all. Bington would truly be a far easier town for you to live in than Madisonville."

"And you believe your partners would accept me?"

"Yes. They want to meet with you and work it out. I've told you who and what they are and I've told them you're gay."

He shook his head, but he was smiling. "A non-Christian, an African American, and a gay as the three partners in a

Bington hotshot law firm. Jesus, Don, how would we all get along? And with such a mix almost any client would find a way to be prejudiced against one or more of us."

"That's not the way things occur in Bington. No client automatically hates ability."

"How about that Wilkens guy who shot you in court? Did he inquire into your ability? How about the people in his church?"

"All towns have problems. That crazy church is out in the Mojeff County boondocks. I'd heard of them, but not a lot. I heard more only after that guy tried to kill me."

He shut his eyes and thought for a moment. "I'll promise you, I'll talk to your former partners, but that's all," he said, smiling.

I smiled back.

"Now, can you and I go over a few final things about Bert and her case before you head out?" he asked.

"Of course," I answered carefully. "Let's confine such discussion to whether or not we think that Bert could be convicted once Allwell's caught."

He smiled and nodded, careful also. "Yes, only that."

I waited.

He said, "You're the one who took Bert home from jail and did the last talking with her. After they let her out of jail this morning, and I'd said goodbye to her, did she say more about having to go back to Kentucky?"

"She was willing. She'll visit her family there for a time. Maybe she'll come back here, maybe not. Lem talked Kittaning into releasing her from jail on her own recognizance. I doubt we'll hear more about this case. There's enough doubt in Lem's mind to allow him to promise to dismiss the grand jury indictment against her before the end of his final year in office. The next prosecutor would have to be a fool to revive it. Lem even decided not to make Bert take the lie detector test."

I smiled, remembering: Lem had kept saying sorrowfully, "No use. No way."

I'd escorted Bert out of the jail. She and Smalley had then said goodbye to each other, both of them stiff but smiling.

Then I'd helped Bert put her few things into my LTD and driven her to the trailer court. Eventually I'd left her with Mo Mellish at her trailer. Her cats were waiting for her, licking themselves clean by the old fireplace, looking hungry. They'd twined themselves in and out of both my feet and hers when we'd appeared. She'd petted them and made over them and so had I.

Black cats. Black as midnight.

I'd shaken Mo Mellish's hand and said my thanks to him for his call and for watching over me.

"I want to talk to you soon," I said.

He gave me a solemn nod. "Call."

Later than that Smalley asked, "Are they really looking for Allwell for the murders?

"Maybe. You know as much as I do. I think the wording Deb gave the media was that they were looking for Allwell to charge him with other offenses and question him about the murders. Allwell could have dropped the poison in the pot. He could have feared what would happen if Jim lived out the day and started talking about being attacked in the cave. Thereafter he could have forgotten the poison jar or he could have sent an incompetent back to the cave to remove or destroy the jar it was carried in."

"True," Smalley said.

"The main thing is that there's a provable big-time charge against Allwell for conspiracy, attempted murder, and some assorted other offenses based on what they got out of Bobby Joe Wilkens, the rifleman at my motel. Lem's made a deal with my pot shooter for a reduced charge and sentence. I agreed to go along. Wilkens signed a statement for Deb and has agreed to testify that Allwell lent him one of his bodyguards to point out my motel room."

Deb had described the kid pouring the story out in a flood of words after listening to his Mirandas.

I added, "Allwell shook the kid's hand, blessed him, and handed him a fifty-dollar bill and the laser-sighted rifle."

"Well," Smalley said, grinning, "You never were worth a hell of a lot. Fifty dollars seems a sufficient price to pay for your already perforated hide."

"True."

He waited for more, but I decided against saying more for now.

I said seriously, "Let's talk again after things quiet down. For now, our client's out of jail and likely will remain that way. Our legal job's done."

"Yes," he said. He gave me a careful smile. "Our client is free. But we will talk of this again?"

I smiled in return. "Of course."

"You hated Allwell almost as much as I did," he said. "Why was that?"

"He was against us in the case. My hate was case hate. Yours wasn't. You hated him because you knew he was evil, and that he believed he could do and get away with whatever he wanted. He was therefore your enemy."

"Yes," he said. "I refuse to say I hated him because I'm gay and he was a perversion of what I am. It wasn't that. It was that every time I saw the man he tried to shame me for something I believe is my right. I wanted to hurt him for that." He shook his head. "It started the first time I saw him, Don."

"And also the first time he saw you. He couldn't be what he was and lead his church. He couldn't have problems and be a manipulator of this town and area. He couldn't be as he was and burn and bomb churches and order people killed. He had to be a superior man, a gay basher, an agitator, a hater-bomber-killer. Not only of gays, but of all minorities, different colors, different churches."

"You think Lem knew about the Allwell type church in South Vernon?" Smalley asked.

"Maybe. He might also, from something he learned from being prosecutor, have known things about Allwell that we only learned when we saw the Sam King report. That might be one of the reasons he was willing to plea-bargain Bert's case. Or he may have seen that Bert was almost blind. Maybe one of us will find out what it was up the line. But he goes out of office on the first of January, so maybe not."

"You'll be judge in one of his cases someday. Ask him."

I nodded. "Or you'll be his local counsel or he'll be yours, should you come up river to Bington. You ask."

And so we left it like that on my last day in Madisonville on Bert's case.

I sought out and paid a grinning Tipper his fifty dollars and then went home to Bington and to the house that Jo and I had lived in for almost a dozen years. We smiled a lot at each other, tried harder, spent more time together, determined to make the marriage work. And son Joe was happy because we were happy.

The marriage worked better mostly because there was time for me and Jo, me and Joe, and me and Jo and Joe. Lots of time.

I took the rest of the year off. I went to soccer games, I went to football practice, I drove the LTD with loads of boys to indoor swimming practice and soccer games when the weather got cold. I fished the muddy river and the clear ponds with Joe on fine days. I drove to Cincy and watched the Reds and then the Bengals with Joe and Jo.

My stomach problems became a thing I remembered, but not well. I quickly got into running again. Long distances after a while.

Two months after I was back, the phone rang late. I was reading and thereby avoiding Jo's late-night television in the bedroom. Because I was now well and still not drinking alcohol I was able to stay up late and rise early. I lived easily on five or six hours of sleep and was alert to all the sounds around me.

Someone might still come for me and mine in the night.

I had both the guns I'd had in Madisonville. They were hidden, but hidden where I could get to them quickly.

The voice at the other end sounded both old and courtly: "This is Raymond John Wilkens and I'm calling long distance from over in Kentucky. Is this Mr. Robak, the Bington lawyer?"

"Yes. I'm Don Robak and I'm a lawyer."

"Now, please don't get yourself angry at some questions I need to ask. Listen to me all the way through and don't hang up on me. I need to make sure of things. Are you the same lawyer who had a courtroom fight with one of my nephews and then later catched my favorite grandson, Bobby Joe, when he come to Madisonville to tree and shoot you?"

"Yes."

"Mr. Robak, I called to tell you that the fighting war between you and the Wilkens family is now over as far as we're concerned. You took my nephew's life by beating him to death with some kind of cruel lawyer's chair in your courtroom. That upset both me and my family and we had a meeting about it."

"Wait a minute. Your nephew came after me with a gun in the courtroom," I replied. "I was unarmed. I hit him with the chair I was sitting in."

"Yes, I know about that, but hate ain't always logical or right, and that chair was a mean weapon. I offered to hire him a lawyer for that divorce case, because I knew he was upset and drinking heavy, brooding over it. But he was a stubborn man always and wouldn't hear of it. He loved his wife and kids, but I now believe the loving of them maybe got mixed up in some bad things, things where he thought he was the king and they was his hand servants and was to do as he ordered."

"All I did was act as his wife's lawyer in a hearing until he came across the courtroom shooting his gun."

"I understand. But blood is blood, and so my family met and a lot wanted blood back. Then my grandson, Bobby Joe, he told us from the jail that you could have took his life with your revolver, that you had it to his head with the hammer pulled back and he could read death in your eyes. But you didn't shoot him and you later let him get off light in court. That made it so you kind of gave us back a life for the one you took."

I waited.

"Us folks in the Wilkens family ain't likely to fall in love with you, Mr. Robak, but I promise on the Bible that no one else from this family, from this time forward, will come to seek you out. We had us another meeting and there was an agreement that we was now even. That's instead of it being Robak two and us nothing, like you said to my favorite grandson when he was on the pavement."

"I appreciate that."

He was silent for a moment.

"Could I now ask a kind of favor that you don't need to grant?"

"Go ahead."

"I'm ninety years old and it's hard for me to travel. Someone has to drive me and help me. Could you come meet me somewhere? I want to ask some questions of you about that church near Bington, the one all of my family there belongs to. Things they tell me about it don't sit well with me and I think there's trouble coming from it. They got a bunch of my family in their church militia."

"Sure. I'll talk with you. You can call and name the place and time as long as it's before the first of the year. After that I'll be the one who has to set the time."

"Thank you," he said. "I'll call you again and real soon. I know Goldie, the sheriff there in your county. I already called him and said to him what I've said to you. He'll tell you I can be believed. And, when I come see you, I'll bring along a cousin of mine who talked to me about you. She was all on your side. Her name's Bertha Jones."

"Yes, sir. I'll look forward to seeing her again and meeting you. Is Bert well?"

"She's put on twenty pounds since she got back here and she's slick as a summer catfish. She said to tell you her black cats that liked you and led you to that bad church are well also. A doctor in Lexington cut the cataracts off both her eyes and she sees better than most now. She'll be doing my driving."

"That's good."

"She doctors me some."

"She did that for me too."

"Yes, I know about that. We sure could use a lawyer in this crazy old family," he said softly. "You think hard on that."

"Yes, sir. I'll do that and thank you for calling," I said.

I heard a click at the other end.

I hung up the receiver. Beside the phone sat my carved-face candle. I'd had it encased in glass by a good local artisan. The glass was fashioned so it couldn't be opened so the candle inside could never be burned. Sometimes, in the light of day from the window, my eyes in the candle look back at me, watching each move I make.

I went to bed. Jo had just turned her television off and lay beside me, awake.

"What was the call?" she asked.

"Just some good news concerning an old problem that's

now solved. Nothing to worry your sweet head about. And I promise I'll sleep better now. Plus I'll soon take the two guns in the house, the ones you worry about because of Joe, back to Sheriff Goldie."

"That's nice," she said, snuggling, a thing she does very, very well.

The next spring, after I was sworn in as judge, Smalley sold his office building and apportioned out most of the practice he owned in Madisonville. He moved to Bington as a full-time partner in my old firm. He told me that business in Madisonville had remained slack, that the town still resented him, mostly for being both right and gay. Someone made him a decent offer for his building, intending to turn it into a medical office.

He reported that Allwell's church was still operating, but at a reduced speed, and that the new lay minister was the lawyer who planned to run against Judge Kittaning next year.

I met Raymond John Wilkens in a restaurant near Lexington, Kentucky, and we talked at some length. Wilkens seemed a fine man. We complained together about taxes, government law, and rules. He was driven and accompanied by Bert Jones. She held my hand throughout the meeting and pronounced me hale and hearty when it was done.

Bert had left her black cats back in the hills, so I didn't see them.

The Redeemer church near Bington soon lost all the Wilkens family.

There came a time near the end of the year when I invited all the bar to our house and got Smalley to help me serve drinks. He treated me with great courtesy, and we never talked about Bert Jones.

I also saw him at parties and area bar functions. I left him alone mostly, knowing if I did anything he might resent it.

For a time he was alone, but by spring he had a new companion, an English professor at the university. The professor was a little younger than Smalley, a gentleman who dressed well and was an expert on both good books and fine wines.

Happily, I had never known the man until Smalley introduced us.

Sheriff Deb called Sheriff Goldie and had him report to me that the ballistics tests on the laser-sighted rifle slugs and the slug that had torn through Deb were identical.

I made a special trip to Madisonville before the end of the year to see Mo Mellish, having purposely let substantial time pass. We went to lunch at the Greek's place and found a quiet corner. Through lunch Mellish told me stories about old times when he'd been a circus strong man and I told him stories about going to law school with Smalley.

But we were uneasy with each other.

Allwell's name was not, at first, mentioned. I brought it up when we were down to coffee.

"I think Smalley firmly believes that the two kids committed suicide," I said.

"I guess they did," he said, not looking directly at me.

"Let me tell you a few things that mean little or nothing to me. Remember, while you listen, that I'm done with Bert's case, and satisfied with how it ended. Remember also that I'm not a peace or police officer."

"I'm glad of that."

"Then give me a penny now and hire me to be your lawyer."

He smiled at me and offered one single penny. I took it from him and pocketed it.

"I am now your lawyer. Tell me first, do you hear anything from Bert?"

"She's called. I'm invited to visit. I may do that soon."

"She doesn't blame you in any way for the kids?"

"No. Why should she?"

"She must know you poisoned the pot?"

"I know nothing about what you're saying."

I said, "You told me you never got away from your trailer the day her kids were poisoned."

"I guess I said that to you. Maybe I remembered wrong. You was hot on Allwell's track and I didn't want or need you sidetracked."

"The trailer kids, when we tracked them to their play area over the highway, told me you were around the pot. They said you also knew where the cave was."

His face never changed expression. "Go on."

"I think you likely added the poison to the pot. Before you did it you likely also told Bert's kids not to eat from it. The poison was for Allwell because you thought he'd eat the first bowl."

He waited for a moment longer and then said, "By eating time I was in my trailer."

"Allwell molested Jim in the cave that morning and so Jim and his half-sister, when they got around the fire, did eat. Maybe the trauma of the molestation made Jim and Mary forget what you said or maybe they just wanted their lives to end. Allwell lived and they died. I thought, for a long time, that Bert wouldn't take a lie detector because she didn't want it to appear as if her kids had committed suicide. But maybe it was also because of you."

"Bert and me are forever friends. And she knows I would never willingly hurt a child, any child."

"You're a good man, Mo. I know that."

"Thank you."

"Where's Allwell then, Mo?"

He shook his head and smiled widely. "I don't know. And

I suppose you've shared these crazy theories with Smalley?"

"No. I never have or will. I'll never share them with any-one other than you. And you are now my client and our communications are privileged."

"That's good."

"Where's Allwell," I asked again.

"Maybe deep," he said, smiling a little. "I now say a prayer for him 'most every night." He smiled. "That's only if you believe what I'm saying to you just now and never will say to anyone again. I have promises to keep, places to go, and work to do."

I believed.

We shook hands when we parted.

Nettie Kittaning continued to cohabit with Judge Kit in her big house above the river. She called my office and I talked with her after I was judge. I got the distinct impression she had the roaming hots to work under another judge. I ex-plained to her that such was impossible because Jo, who I claimed I'd have to ask, wasn't agreeable to that kind of be-havior.

I didn't hear from her again, but I did see her at judicial functions, her eyes hungrily roaming the crowd.

Sheriff Deb sent me a later note saying that one of the East End Walnut Street kids had confessed to dropping a single stick of construction-site-stolen dynamite into the hiding cave of Hansel and Gretel. Nothing more, no ques-tions for me, no other answers.

Judge Harner, after a long new sleep of oblivion, died in March. His funeral attracted judges and lawyers from all over the state. He'd been "good at the business."

Thelma told me, when I visited frequently, that he never got any better than he'd been on the day I saw him, just be-fore I finally returned to Madisonville, and that he'd stopped coming up from sleep that same night I left. She said Doc Buckner had called what happened that night a small, kind stroke.

No one, now two years later, has ever arrested Reverend Allwell. Sometimes I fantasize that I'm wrong about Mo Mellish and maybe Allwell now leads a cult in some remote part of the world where all believe in him and he neither hates nor is hated.

I sent Mo Mellish some money for his church building fund, the day after I got paid for Bert's case by Madison County. He wrote a thank you and said he'd heard that some of the fanatics at the Survival church on the hill believe Allwell went to the river and that he's there now, under the dark water, waiting for the final day. It was as if our conversation in the Greek restaurant had never happened and that was all right with me.

Somehow also, Smalley and I have never gotten around to talking about a logical answer to the poisonings of Jim-Mary, Hansel-Gretel, Romeo-Juliet. Maybe one day we will, but so far, no. There has been no need. Our client is free and unsought. Our job is done. And I will never tell him about Mellish.

Lawyers are detectives only for their clients. Bert's out of jail and Mellish is my client.

Beside, anyone could have killed the kids. Mo Mellish could have been just making dark fun and it could have been other kids with poison, or a shadowy adult from the town or trailer camp. It could have been Bert or Tipper or Reverend Allwell.

I thought that Smalley likely believed that one of the two dead kids, almost positively Jim, had dropped the poison in the stew pot on that bright, spring day. One child murdered the other child, and also committed suicide himself or herself.

Bert was what she was. She was fair and bright and fine.

She would not accuse one of her kids of murdering the other, even to save her own life. In her mind it couldn't be and yet she'd likely figured it *was*. Nor could she accuse Mo Mellish because she knew he was a good man and her close friend.

I thought there was about a ninety-nine point nine percent chance that Jim and Mary had remembered about the poison and still taken it.

I remembered the joint pledge note found in their hiding place. I believed what they'd promised each other by signing it was that they'd stop sex. I never heard it confirmed by Sheriff Deb, but I believed they'd signed the note in their own blood.

And then, before they could sweetly or sadly renege, when they were both in mourning and depression for what they'd lost singly and jointly, Poison Sunday had arrived.

I thought Jim-Romeo had been shamed by whatever Reverend Allwell had savagely forced on him as they tarried in the cave before coming down the hill on the last morning.

So Allwell, in a way, had killed both kids.

And I thought both Jim and Mary-Juliet had recognized that their conduct in selling small pieces of Mary while Jim watched, made them less than the true lovers Jim idealized in his games on the hill and in the books he/they read. I felt both of them had been driven downward by what they'd allowed to happen, or been forced into, in their new sexual world. Allwell had been the final blow.

Sometimes I wondered why Mo Mellish had not destroyed the evidence jar of nicotine, but I never asked him although I saw him now and then.

I never could bring myself to believe that any of us, Smalley, Mellish, or me, had been unfair to Allwell.

The two dead children had owned only themselves. No one to talk with, no one to seek advice from. If they'd talked to Bert then she'd have done something to separate them.

I thought they'd once gone to Mo Mellish's church meeting to seek something, perhaps advice and help, but then had not completed the task.

Sad because the sex had ended, but unwilling, yet, to take it up again. Depressed, sick of themselves, sick of what they'd both become, and finally, dead sick.

Children, genius and not genius, commit suicide because the world and its inhabitants become too much for them. Romeo and Juliet, finding their own ending to their own play.

Sometimes, when I think on them now, I wish I could have discovered them when they were alive. Or that Smalley could have done the same. Or that Allwell had left them alone and gone to an earlier glory from nicotine poisoning through the first bowl.

A final thing: In the summer of my second year on the bench I appointed Smalley to represent poor Hiram Winkler when Winkler was charged by the rich and angry Gingle family with felony murder and arson. Most people now say that that was the craziest criminal jury trial ever seen or heard in a courtroom in southern Indiana. It was the case that justly made Smalley and Sam King famous. But it also is another story.

Santa Clara County Free Library System

Libraries located at:

Alum Rock	Milpitas-(Calaveras) (Civic Center)
Burbank	Morgan Hill
Campbell	Mt. Hamilton
Cupertino	Saratoga-(Village) (Quito)
Los Altos	Union-Cambrian Park

Central Research Library

at

Headquarters

A GUIDEBOOK TO THE SUNSET RANGES
OF SOUTHERN CALIFORNIA

*From the stacked boulders off the Black Mountain Road
in the San Jacinto Mountains there are many fine views
into the rugged back country of the range.*

TO

THE SUNSET RANGES

OF SOUTHERN

CALIFORNIA

Including the San Jacinto Mountains, the Santa Ana
Mountains, the Palomar country, the
Julian-Cuyamaca country and the Laguna Mountains

BY RUSS LEADABRAND

THE   WARD   RITCHIE   PRESS   ·   LOS   ANGELES

TO MARYLINN, MIKE
AND LAURIE . . .
WHO FINALLY GOT
TIRED OF TRAVELING

Cover photo by Jim Stevens
Maps by Cas Duchow

DISTRIBUTED EXCLUSIVELY BY LANE BOOK COMPANY
MENLO PARK, CALIFORNIA

CONTENTS

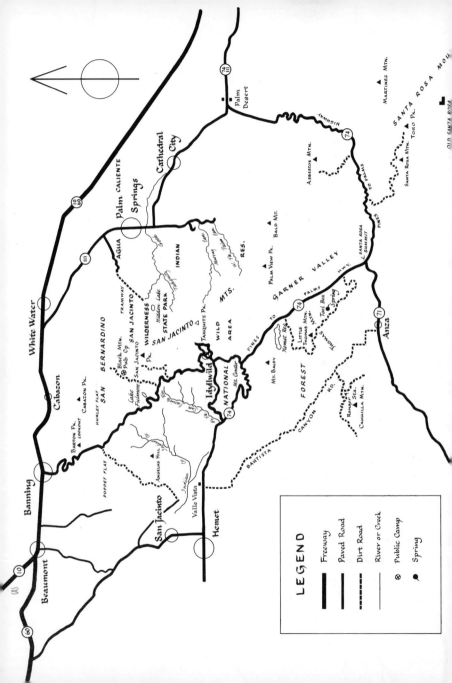

LEGEND

Freeway

Paved Road

Dirt Road

River or Creek

⊗ Public Camp

● Spring

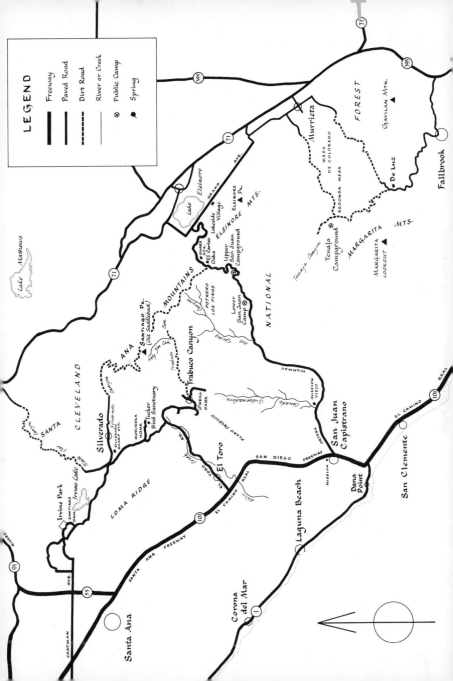

LEGEND

Freeway
Paved Road
Dirt Road
River or Creek
⊗ Public Camp
• Spring

PREFACE

This is the third book in what has somehow grown into a series about the mountains of Southern California.

In 1963 I wrote a GUIDEBOOK TO THE SAN GABRIEL MOUNTAINS. In 1964 there was the GUIDEBOOK TO THE SAN BERNARDINO MOUNTAINS. It was only logical to continue the explorations, to cover the San Jacinto Mountains of Riverside County and to look, then, on toward the southernmost corner of the state.

In the prefaces of the two earlier books I have said the same thing: given enough time and a bigger book format I could have built a much larger volume here. Instead I have condensed and boiled and pruned. I have used only a few of the fine legends and folk stories that I have uncovered in my research. There are good pickings here for the patient digger. It is fascinating work, this excavating into the mountains of yesterday.

I stress this point for I wish no lover of the San Jacintos to feel that his range has been slighted. I do not want the Santa Ana Mountains' fan to think that I have callously tried to condense into a few pages the local history of this place when it took Terry Stephenson a plump volume merely to touch on some of the tales. My contribution is, I acknowledge, limited and brief.

But these books are designed to be guides, not definitive works.

Still it took many hours and many people to help build this small guidebook. In the first instance I wish to thank the gentlemen of the U. S. Forest Service for their assistance. Most of the country that I have covered lies within the boundaries of either the San Bernardino National Forest or the Cleveland National Forest.

For their support on a Regional level I thank Charles Connaughton and Grant Morse. Don Bauer, supervisor of the San Bernardino National Forest; and Stanley Stevenson of the Cleveland National Forest, aided me.

It was people like Vern Smith, district ranger on the San Jacinto District of the San Bernardino, who made the book more fun. I made several trips into the field with Smith and his fund of fact and his good humor made the days pleasant. For similar trips into their districts I wish to nod to Clifford Stevens, district ranger of the Trabuco District of the Cleveland; Russell Engle, district ranger of the Palomar District of the Cleveland; and John Benediktson, district ranger of the Descanso District of the Cleveland.

I wish to acknowledge, too, the many Forest Service personnel who helped with a word or a date; the lookouts in the many towers that I visited; the patrolmen.

At Mt. San Jacinto State Park I talked with Keith Caldwell. At Cuyamaca I had help from Frank Davies.

Old friends, as well, helped me along this path. Harry James, at Lolomi Lodge, briefed me on the history of his end of the San Jacintos; Ernest Maxwell, at Idyllwild, provided historical facts and loaned me pictures.

In Santa Ana I spent pleasant hours with Don Meadows, fellow Westerner and historian.

Frank Haggarty, in the Office of Indian Affairs in Riverside, helped untangle me from a web of reservation facts and fiction.

Letters from Jack Garner, of the Garner Cattle Co.; Second Lieutenant Gale B. Lawson, Marine Corps Air Station, El Toro; Ethel Fischer, at the Idyllwild Arts Foundation, were helpful.

Pearl M. Lyng, at the Title Insurance and Trust Co. in San Diego, dug out some old photographs to brighten the pages of the book. Jim Stevens made a special hike into the San Jacinto Wild Area to get the excellent photograph for the cover of the book.

My thanks go, as well, to Miss Patrice Manahan, editor of *Westways* magazine, for letting me use some bits and pieces from my "Let's Explore a Byways" articles on this same country. My thanks, too, to Miss Manahan for being a good friend and a guide, for she has steered me through many of the pesky thickets that bumbling travel writers frequently wander into.

I wish to thank Arnold Huss, managing editor of the Pasadena *Independent Star-News,* for giving me time and encouragement to write. Don Porter, friend and consultant, has stood by me when the going got rough and helped to push. Ray Duncan assumed many of my newspapering chores when I had to get into the field.

I thank Virginia Alexander for her fine typing assistance. Barbara Leadabrand suffered through this as did I and I bless her for her patience.

For their wisdom and support, their guidance and their prodding I thank the gentlemen of the Ward Ritchie Press: Ward Ritchie, Dick Lewis and Joe Simon. Somehow, thanks to them, it got done.

I would, in all seriousness, like to thank, too the disc jockeys on a half dozen radio stations in the Los Angeles area, whose conversation and music kept me awake on my many, many early morning and late evening lonely drives from home to the various mountain outposts and back. Few people realize all the private hells of writing a book. Early morning freeway boredom was one of the worst.

This has been a satisfying book to write, brief as it is, because now, in three volumes, there is a kind of continuity of fact and fiction about the most heavily visited mountains of Southern California.

There are many more pieces of mountains to write about out there: the Topatopas, the San Miguels, the San Felipe, the lower Santa Rosas, the many mountain sprawls that are entirely within desert boundaries. Maybe, someday, a book could be fashioned dealing with all of these. Because many of these mountain areas are essentially roadless, it would have to be a book of history and legend, one of essay and contemplation. I am not a horseman so

I could not write books such as those of yesterday by J. Smeaton Chase and Charles Francis Saunders. I am not the poet like Judy Van der Veer. But it would be fun to try my hand at such a work, whatever its flavor.

While writing this has been tedious at times, frustrating at times, even maddening at times, it has been, in general, pleasant. It was sort of like scratching a place that persistently itched. It was a book I had to do, once I had written the San Gabriel and San Bernardino volumes.

I thank all the many people who made the itching stop.

I INTRODUCTION

The Sunset Ranges are made up of the attractive mountain regions of the San Jacintos, the Santa Anas, the Palomar country and the Julian-Cuyamaca-Laguna Mountains area.

A GOOD PORTION of Southern California is crammed with mountains. Start with the San Gabriels and the San Bernardinos and explore to the south. Minor range after range stands in the way. There is a break where the Salton Sink interrupts, but then the mountains start to march again in the desert country: small ranges, interesting ranges, mountains without end.

This book is an effort to look at some of these minor mountain ranges—and they may be called minor only in respect to their shorter length and breadth and height. For surely here is some of the finest scenery that the Southland has to offer. No, the word minor is not one of deprecation. I have too much affection for these high places, these canyons with their secrets, these tree-overgrown roads that see little travel, the sweet springs of water, the incredible views.

Taking a bit of poetic fancy we have called these the Sunset Ranges of Southern California. It is a title with a strong link with yesterday. In the boom era of Southern California there was a great use of the word Sunset. California was the land where the sun edged down into the western sea.

The book encompasses the San Jacinto Mountains of Riverside County; the Santa Ana Mountains of Riverside, Orange and San Diego Counties; and some of the mountain country of deeper San Diego County, notably the Palomar region, and the Volcan-Julian-Cuyamaca-Lagunas complex.

1

*These mountains know many gentle little roads
where exploring is both pleasant and stimulating.*

All these uplifts have history—some of it runs all the way back to the first white men in the state, the explorers and the mission fathers. Before that the Indians had names for the high places.

There are legends and folk tales connected with these mountains; stories pleasant and profane. Mining has taken place in a hundred places and in most cases the despair of bust has followed in the footsteps of sudden boom. California's mining history is filled with a thousand such tales.

The mountains have known roads for more than a hundred years. The Palomars were invaded by mission workmen who wanted the straight and true cedar beams for the *asistencia* at Pala. Logging drew the first people into the San Jacintos. The lure of gold pulled the pioneers into the Julian area. There was silver in the Santa Anas. And so it goes.

You will discover fine roads reach into all these mountain areas today: good, high-gear highways. You will find pleasant camping facilities, spots to put up a tent, to park a camper or trailer, places to picnic, to sit on a rock and admire a tall tree, paths to walk, places to go to get away from the press of home life and its problems.

For these places in the mountains, in the woods, we must be grateful to the U. S. Forest Service, to the California State Park system, to the park and recreation departments of the various counties concerned.

No one man knows all of these mountains of our Sunset Ranges. It is an endless sort of territory embroidered with small meandering dirt roads and trails and laced with history of a dozen different periods. Yet many men know small corners of these mountains and take great—and understandable—pride in their knowledge.

Happily it is possible for even the casual visitor to learn to know the land here—to learn it and to enjoy it.

It is best to start by studying a map of the area. Then drive the

3

many paved roads. Learn the colorful place names such as Wild Horse Peak, Sourdough Spring, Monkey Hill, Chariot Mountain, Tragedy Spring, Holy Jim Canyon, Eagle Crag, Dark Canyon and Hidden Lake.

Then walk the land. Venture outside of the campground area. Know the trees by their shape, their scent, their drop of leaves. Become familiar with the comings and goings of small birds and small animals. Learn the sounds: a falling acorn, the racket of the squirrel and jay, the call of the hawk out hunting. Observe the workings of the wind; the pattern of clouds and the pattern of cloud shadows.

It will take time, but after a day and another day, after a week, a season, you will find yourself at home in this mountain kingdom. You will have learned the smaller secrets, and the high hills, familiar now, will seem a bright and friendly land. Hopefully, this small book will help you toward that understanding.

II INTRODUCTION TO THE SAN JACINTO COUNTRY

The San Jacinto Mountains of Riverside County elbow boldly out into the Colorado Desert, yet there are 10,000-foot peaks here and winter snows can be heavy.

FOR THE PURPOSES of this guidebook the term San Jacinto Mountains is an expanded one, made to include not only the San Jacinto Mountains proper, but the Desert Divide country, Cahuilla Mountain, Thomas Mountain and a portion of the Santa Rosa Mountains—an area generally encompassed by the San Jacinto District of the San Bernardino National Forest.

This mountain mass is completely separated from other major mountain areas by low passes, valleys, and the desert area. The elevation ranges from 1300 feet in the Snow Creek drainage, up to 10,831 feet at the summit of Mt. San Jacinto. The area is bounded by the historic San Gorgonio Pass on the north, by the Coachella Valley arm of the Colorado Desert on the east, the Anza-Borrego Desert State Park and adjoining mountain ridges on the south, and the San Jacinto Valley on the west.

A peninsula into the desert country, the San Jacinto Mountains provide some of the most dramatic geographic contrasts in the state. High enough to support several peaks taller than 10,000 feet, lodgepole and limber pine, the San Jacinto also knows cactus and palms along its many lower slopes. Ringed by Indian reservations, the pile of mountains is sprinkled with legends and the strange stories of history.

Cattle graze here, and here, too, the patient watcher can see the furtive bighorn sheep that make the desert-facing ridges their home. Mountain lions range across this reach of sometimes

5

Trails lead back into the San Jacinto Wild Area,
offer spectacular vistas.

6

wooded, sometimes barren, ridges. There are icy springs in improbable places and the water is not only sweet and restoring, but it makes a territorial convert out of the drinker. For those who live here and know the land, few places can present a fairer face most of the twelve months.

From the top of Santa Rosa Mountain, when the weather is right, it is possible to see the jeweled skirt of the Pacific; down into Mexico; north toward the Sierra; and to the east, it is possible to count the layers of purpled silhouettes that stand like cutouts, the desert ranges that march off toward the Colorado River. Once, it has been written in a time when haze was less, peak climbers have thought they saw the snowy cones of the San Francisco Peaks near Flagstaff in Arizona. Such views are no longer offered.

Still from the top of Santa Rosa Mountain there is an incredible view down into Borrego Valley and the Anza-Borrego Desert State Park. The dome of Palomar is close at hand. Out there, not too far, are the misty Lagunas of San Diego County. Closer at hand is the table of land where the flat hand of geologic change has impressed the Anza, Terwilliger and Cahuilla Valleys.

History. It was across the Cahuilla Valley country that the first white man into the area walked and looked, close at hand, at the San Jacintos. (The name Jacinto, according to Erwin G. Gudde, honors the Silesian-born Dominican, Hyacinth, whose feast day is August 16.)

Pedro Fages, in 1772, is said to have passed this way. Two years later, in the winter of 1774, Spanish Army Captain Juan Bautista de Anza, and a party of 34, came up out of Mexico headed for Monterey, California. They walked the Anza-Borrego desert region, escaped from that valley via Coyote Canyon which flanks the long arm of the Santa Rosa Mountains and nearer-at-hand Coyote Mountain. Into the Cahuilla Valley they walked in March

7

that year, crossed under the shadow of the bulk of the San Jacintos and headed on northwest through what is now called Bautista Canyon into the San Jacinto Valley.

Bautista Canyon now holds an unpaved county road—there are rumors of its being improved into a paved highway. It is open all year to the public. The Coyote Canyon passage into the state park is suitable only for jeeps.

The Indians were here first, of course. The several Indian reservations around the edge of the mountain country make this clear. There are many places in the mountains where you can find old house rings, rock shelters, pictographs and bedrock mortars. There is a delightful Soboba legend about the rocky peak of Tahquitz. The top of Toro Peak is supposed to be tabooed country to the Santa Rosa people.

The signs of Indian trails were common in the mountain country. In an account by historian Margaret Boynton an old Indian chief is quoted as reporting:

"The trails of the Indians were everywhere. They led up all the canyons. They were hunting trails for the men, and used by the women to gather the seeds, nuts, plums and acorns, so many things. They led from the land of one tribe to another. All the Indians did their part to keep the trails clear. The trails were sacred to the Indians.

"A trail led from Chino Canyon up to the San Jacinto Peak. Another went from Chino [Canyon] across the hills to Snow Creek at the foot of San Jacinto. . .

"There were two trails from Snow Creek to the San Jacinto Peak. . . From Dry Falls a trail crosses to Chino Canyon. From Little Tacheva a trail goes to Lincoln Peak. This is a hunting trail and leads into the trail going to Hidden Lake and the San Jacinto Peak from Tahquitz Canyon. Another trail goes up Andreas Canyon to the San Jacinto Peak."

8

White men put their first mark on the land in the San Gorgonio Pass area. Paulino Weaver—an American born in Tennessee—lived with the Indians in this area in the 1840's and logged in the San Gorgonio country. Lt. R. H. Williamson of the U.S. Topographic Corps, ran his railroad survey through the Pass country in the early 1850's.

It was in 1876 that the Southern Pacific started construction of the railroad through the San Gorgonio Pass. A construction camp called Hall's Siding, after Colonel M. S. Hall, grading contractor, was born in the Pass. Here was a labor camp, store, sawmill, hotel, saloon, blacksmith shop, a dance hall. It ghosted within a year. The first railroad station here was called San Jacinto or Jacinto and this name was later changed to Cabazon.

According to historians, including DeBoyd Leon Smith, there might even have been a monumental confusion in the names of the two tallest mountains here: San Jacinto and San Gorgonio. There is some evidence to support the theory that San Jacinto was once called San Gorgonio, and vice versa.

During the railroad construction labors in 1876 there was much scrambling for timber and wood in the San Jacintos. Part of this effort was spent in Snow Creek facing the San Gorgonio Pass.

The year before, in 1875, Joseph Crawford, a homesteader at Oak Cliff, on the San Jacinto Valley side, ground out the first toll road into the mountains. From Oak Cliff, up from Valle Vista, the road ran to Strawberry Valley where, in 1899, the Post Office Department gave the nod for a new community name to Mrs. Laura Rutledge's selection of Idyllwild. The toll road was a hand-built little horror, not wide enough in places, too steep in places, often too rough. Comments of the day went like this: "Steep? Why in places it leans over backwards"; and "It climbs seven feet to the rod!" There was a stop with water at Halfway House Spring, where men and animals usually collapsed. Incidentally, water still bubbles up here, even in the dry season. Higher up the old toll road would skirt Alvin Meadow and would reach on into the Strawberry Valley area.

With the advent of the automobile this route, somewhat improved, would become a control road. Today it stands as a fire road, a Forest Service truck trail, and is closed in the summer months because of the fire hazard. It is driveable by passengers—much better down than up for there are still some rough steep pitches—and while it is still bumpy and narrow and dusty, it is an interesting old road to drive.

The first men into the mountains, aside from the meat hunters, were the wood gatherers. Harry James, who lives at Lolomi Lodge behind Lake Fulmor, and is a good and patient explorer of the range, reports finding old seasonal shake camps in several places in the high country. Here the valley men would come for a summer with a pack string—later wagons—and would haul out as much as they could of cedar and sugar pine shakes, posts, stakes.

Later the loggers came and there were several mills in the Strawberry Valley area—and all that country from Strawberry Valley through Fern Valley was probably logged over—and to the north. An old mill, possibly one of Fuller's earlier ventures, sat near Lake Fulmor. Fuller's regular mill was on the ridge between Dark Canyon and Black Mountain. Some of these mills can still be traced—others have completely vanished, even the old sawdust piles are gone. Such a logging camp was old Rayneta in the Strawberry Creek area. A mill stood next door to the present headquarters of the state park in Idyllwild. There was a mill at Dutch Flat.

After the logging boom, which saw its biggest days between 1880 and 1910, the mountain country was noted as a health resort. A sanitarium was built in Strawberry Valley and tuberculosis patients were hauled up the toll road to the site, the belief

10

*By winter deep snow visits the high country
in the San Jacintos.*

11

being that the high mountain air would cure the disease. It helped but it didn't cure, and after a few years of this the settlers here decided that the Strawberry Valley country was really awfully nice as a summer resort and the area realized its permanent destiny. The first Idyllwild Inn was built on the site of the sanitarium. It burn in 1945 and was rebuilt.

In the early 1900s there was some gold mining activity at a place called Kenworthy in the Garner Valley area. It was likely little more than a stock promotion camp with salted mines, but the town flourished enough to have a two-story hotel and a school that was moved around from place to place for several years. There has been considerable prospecting through all the area ever since but history argues against the prospector—nothing big has ever been found. At last count there were 89 mining claims on the district, none of them in operation. There are two private dolomite mines on private land in the Pinyon Flats area.

Gemstones, precious ones, including tourmaline, have been found in the Thomas Mountain country. The first find was made in 1872; among them were some rare green crystals with red centers. These were purchased by Harvard University. Other gemstones from Cahuilla Mountain are on display at the American Museum of Natural History in New York City.

One of the first men into the south side of the mountains was Charles Thomas, who came into the Garner Valley—it was unnamed then—as a friend of the Indians from the rancheria in Cahuilla-Anza Valley country with his Spanish wife. Thomas bought a great spread of land from Juan Antonio, a famous Mountain Cahuilla Indian, for—depending on your source—seven head of cattle or 200 head of cattle. In time the place would be known as Thomas' Valley; later, when the San Jacinto Valley people started studying the possibility of pulling irrigation water down the South Fork of the San Jacinto River, the place would be called

12

Hemet Valley after Lake Hemet, the reservoir in the mountain area. Later still, when the Garner family bought the 7000-acre spread from Thomas, the place would get the name Garner Valley.

Thomas was tied in solidly with the Ramona story-legend. Juan Diego sheared sheep for Thomas at one time and Ramona is supposed to have worked in the house and kitchen. (A hired hand by the name of Herkey or Hurkey died after being mauled by a grizzly. The creek and campground here bears this name—Hurkey Creek and Hurkey Creek Campground.)

The water seekers here built the dam, 135 feet tall and out of rude masonry, between 1890 and 1895 at a cost of $183,000. Lake Hemet stands behind the dam and water is still taken from the site.

Finally the roads came, first the Indian trail that Thomas fashioned into a road up out of Anza into the Garner Valley; then Crawford's toll road. Hall built a kind of road into the north shoulder of the San Jacintos and in time, following a similar route, the Banning to Idyllwild Highway would evolve. The road from Hemet up to Mountain Center would be fashioned in the 1930s, and shortly thereafter the other end of it, the Pines to Palms Highway, would climb down through pronounced life zones to the desert.

The Indians. Six Indian Reservations roughly border the San Jacinto Mountains. Starting on the west, situated just outside of the community of San Jacinto, is the Soboba Indian Reservation. All tribal land; seventy-one families live on the 5056-acre tract. The land is used mostly for grazing.

In the Cahuilla Valley is the Cahuilla Indian Reservation. Its church and cemetery may be seen right beside Highway 71 as it runs through the region. The Cahuilla Indian Reservation consists of 18,272 acres of tribal land. Twelve families live on the land and use it for grazing and agricultural purposes.

13

To the north of the Cahuilla Reservation a short distance is the smaller Ramona Indian Reservation; 560 acres of tribal land with no residents. The land is used for grazing.

The Santa Rosa Indian Reservation lies off the Pines to Palms Highway against the southeast corner of the San Jacinto country. Here there are 11,093 acres of tribal lands with two families living on the Reservation. The land is used primarily for grazing.

The Agua Caliente (or Palm Springs) Indian Reservation is a mixture of allotted lands and tribal lands. The mountain sections of Indian Reservation land are mainly tribal lands. About sixteen sections are thus involved. No one lives on these mountain lands nor are they used. The Agua Caliente people also have extensive holdings in Palm Springs.

The Morongo Indian Reservation is located on the north side of the San Jacinto Mountains in and around Banning. Some 30,927 acres are involved, used for grazing and for homesites. Some of the lands are allotted. Sixty families live on the Reservation.

While there is understandable curiosity among the uninformed about the California Indians, or all Indians for that matter, I'd like to quench such curiosity somewhat. Indian Reservation lands are private property and should be treated as such. Unless you have personal friends among the Indians who have invited you, do not drive onto Reservation lands. Most of these Indian people are hard-working farmers. They have last names now much like your own. They are friendly folks, as all the farmers and ranchers in this area. Respect their fences and their boundaries. Indian Reservations are not public lands. The considerate thing is to stay out.

As for the old days, Ernest Maxwell, Idyllwild newspaperman and historian of the San Jacinto country, has chronicled the legend of Tahquitz. Maxwell's version tells how the leader of the Soboba Indians—named variously as Tahquitz, Tah-Quish, Tauquish, Tauquitch—was much loved by his people. One day his pleasant manner changed. Some argued that an evil spirit had taken possession of the Soboba chief. Sinister events took place. Maidens and small children vanished from the tribal area—all such happenings were traced to Tahquitz.

The bad chief was tried, convicted and burned. But his spirit escaped. He made his home on Tahquitz Peak high in the San Jacintos and continued to bedevil the Sobobas. In a subsequent battle between Tahquitz and a good chief, Algoot, the evil spirit turned itself into a serpent, was killed, and the body burned. Again the spirit escaped to Tahquitz Peak, where it lived on to haunt other tribes of the area.

Whenever thunder and lightning or strange rumblings visit the peaks of the San Jacintos, the faithful claim that it is Tahquitz expressing one of his violent moods.

Another version of the Tahquitz legend, offered originally by Elmer Wallace Homes in a history of Riverside County and written in the Riverside *Press-Enterprise* by George Ringwald, goes something like this.

Tahquitz was an Indian living in the San Jacinto Valley. He had a great fondness for an Indian maiden by the name of Amutat. Several other young Indians had a similar fondness. To circumvent competition Tahquitz kidnaped Amutat one day and with her headed up into the Strawberry Valley country.

It wasn't long before the girl was missed, there was a chase and Tahquitz was cornered in the mountains. Tahquitz killed the girl and tried to escape. But the Indians from Soboba surrounded the kidnaper and clubbed him to death.

While the Soboba tribesmen were chanting over the event the body of Tahquitz began to glow like fire. The body rose into the air and settled on Tahquitz Rock—and disappeared. And a loud rumbling shook the ground.

15

This story holds that Tahquitz is still there, with a rattlesnake and a condor for company. And they say that when the mountain shakes and rumbles, it is not an earthquake, only mountain-dwelling Tahquitz up to his evil tricks.

The San Jacinto District of the San Bernardino National Forest. Most of the San Jacinto Mountain country lies within the irregular boundary of the San Jacinto District of the San Bernardino National Forest. There are 248,476 acres within the district boundary; of these 172,708 are Federal land. The San Jacinto Wild Area, created in 1931, consists of 21,942 acres of this Forest Service land.

The area has had a curious history under the aegis of the Forest Service. Created February 22, 1897, as the San Jacinto Forest Reserve, the original tract was an enormous one, extending from San Gorgonio Pass all the way to the Mexican border. It ran from the Colorado Desert westward to the major valley area seaward of Palomar and the Lagunas.

Bit by bit the borders were altered as the years went by. The Homestead Act saw the withdrawal of many acres of flatland from the forest domain.

The year 1907 saw the change of the name of the territories so administered from Forest Reserves to National Forests and the following year, 1908, the San Jacinto was combined with the smaller Trabuco to create the Cleveland National Forest. It was a gigantic region and at the same time the old San Bernardino Forest Reserve was coupled with the San Gabriel Forest Reserve to form the monumental Angeles National Forest.

It was probably the bad fire year of 1924 that caused the administrators to take another look at the big tracts of federal lands. The following year the San Bernardino and the Angeles were sawed apart again and the San Jacinto district was lopped off the

Cleveland and attached to the San Bernardino National Forest. It has been administered this way since.

The San Bernardino National Forest, under the U.S. Department of Agriculture, is charged with the management of the land under the general dictum "the greatest good to the greatest number in the long run." As a result the Forest Service here is in the recreation business, in the logging business, it deals with miners and stockmen, it is concerned with game management and insect control. Its main sphere of activity comes with managing the watershed, flood control and of course with fire control. And since fire control is the business that the Forest Service is in whenever newspaper headlines flash, the two terms—Forest Service and fire control—have become almost synonymous. Running a National Forest is an endless job.

The supervisor's office of the San Bernardino National Forest is located in San Bernardino in the Civic Center Building, 175 West Fifth Street.

The headquarters for the San Jacinto ranger district is located in Idyllwild; address: Idyllwild, California.

There are smaller ranger stations located at Cranston, on Highway 74 just east of Valle Vista; the Vista Grande ranger station is located on the Banning to Idyllwild highway about three miles south of the Forest boundary sign; the Alandale station is situated near the Dark Canyon road turnoff from the Banning to Idyllwild highway; the Kenworthy station is in Garner Valley; the Keenwild station is just south of Idyllwild. There is a small, rather isolated station at Tripp Flat off the Bautista Canyon road near Anza Valley. Older stations at Thomas Mountain and Keen Camp are not manned now. Active Forest Service lookouts in the district are located at Black Mountain, Tahquitz Peak and Red Mountain. The old 60-foot metal lookout tower atop Thomas Mountain is used only during emergencies.

17

Within the San Jacinto District of the San Bernardino National Forest there are 763 miles of road and 237 miles of trail. Not all the roads are open to the public. Many are in or across private land or Indian reservations and thus are barred from public entrance. Many of the roads—unpaved generally—are within the seasonal fire closure and are closed to the public much of the year.

The trails—and the roads—are all coded by the Forest Service. A section on trails appears elsewhere in this book. For primary information on roads, trails, campgrounds, landmarks, scenic areas, etc., within the district, the visitor should obtain one of the free recreation maps offered by the Forest Service. Such a map can be obtained at the district headquarters in Idyllwild, at the various ranger stations, or at the San Bernardino National Forest headquarters in San Bernardino.

Because of the high fire hazard in the Forest, particularly along the west and south edges of the district, a fire closure is enforced each year. It begins, generally, in June or July, and extends through the year and until the first appreciable rainfall. Such areas are posted and the map issued by the Forest Service plainly shows the closed area's boundaries. It is against the law to enter such closed areas.

While there are deer and game bird hunting seasons in the mountain country, certain areas are within a game preserve. This area is also outlined in the Forest Service map. There are no bear now in the San Jacinto Mountains although 26 were introduced into the area from Northern California in 1933. The last grizzly bear was killed in the mountains here around 1890. Reports of bear sightings still crop up—1957 was the last one—but these are largely discounted. Game wardens, rangers and fire lookout people —reliable observers—have not seen any wild bear in the country.

Bighorn sheep inhabit the desert side of the mountains, can be seen sometimes around the middle altitude by the tramway, range out onto Martinez Mountain. They are scrupulously protected by law.

While the San Jacinto Mountains have few streams that run all year long, some are vigorous enough to support fishing in the spring and early summer. These are stocked at times. Two spots offer all-year fishing: Lake Fulmor on the Banning to Idyllwild highway, and Lake Hemet in the Garner Valley area.

During the season from May 1 to December 15 it is unlawful to smoke in the National Forest area except at campgrounds, resorts or designated smoking spots along the highway.

While the Forest Service maps show most of the features of the land and the special boundaries, it is wise for anyone who would study the land in greater detail to acquire a set of topographical maps issued by the U.S. Geological Survey. These show the mountain region in particular detail. They are not available from the Forest Service.

Overnight camping is allowed in the district only in places designated as campgrounds. Fires are permitted in campgrounds and picnic areas where stoves are provided and when the user has a fire permit. Such permits are available from Forest Service stations and from most Forest Service personnel on patrol. A special fire permit is required for the San Jacinto Wild Area and the Mt. San Jacinto Wilderness State Park. An open fire is allowed in the Wild Area under such permit. Open fires are permitted at campgrounds where fire rings exist.

There are Forest Service campgrounds at Black Mountain, Dark Canyon, Fern Basin, Fuller Mill Creek, Marion Mountain, Pine Flat, Thomas Mountain, Pinyon Flat and Santa Rosa Spring. Lake Fulmor and Dos Palmas are picnic areas. There are other, smaller, unimproved campgrounds—used as hunter camps—in the Forest. In the San Jacinto Wild Area there are improved campsites at Tahquitz Valley, Little Tahquitz Valley and Skunk Cabbage.

The San Jacinto Wild Area. One of the most delightful features of the San Jacinto Mountains is the unspoiled 21,942-acre Wild Area. Set aside with the idea that it would always remain roadless and unimproved, the region was created on April 21, 1931, by the Chief of the Forest Service. The only improvements are trails, necessary signs, and minimum sanitary facilities. Camping areas are left undeveloped and contain some stoves and no tables.

Tahquitz Peak is the dominant feature of this attractive high country region and it lifts to a stony 8828 feet. Nearby is Lily Rock, better known as Tahquitz Rock, which is the delight of rock climbers of Southern California. Some fifty to sixty routes up the sheer stone face have been climbed by the piton and carabinder fraternity.

There are several trails into the Wild Area and in addition to the more improved campgrounds listed above there are sites at Caramba, Laws, Willow Creek.

The jumpoff place into the Wild Area is from the end of the road and parking area at Humber Park, a timbered area named after a former Idyllwild area developer, Rollin Humber.

The lookout atop Tahquitz Peak is serviced by trail—no road crosses the Wild Area. Bounding the Wild Area on the north side is Mt. San Jacinto Wilderness State Park.

Today this mountain country knows many improvements and enjoys almost a daily development. There are paved streets in the residential areas where many people live in comfort throughout the year. There is a fire department, supermarkets, schools, specialty shops, restaurants, many resorts, even a motion picture theater. In the summer even more attractions are offered: riding stables are busy, there is a golf course, youth groups flock to the score of organization camps in the area and hike and commune with nature.

The region has highways into its high country on three sides and on the most precipitous an aerial tramway makes the ascent.

Blessed with distinct seasons, these San Jacintos each year dye the leaves of the black oak and the sycamore, the cottonwood and the poison oak in salute to fall. And each year the innocents gleefully pick to take home armsful of the scarlet-leaved poison oak, and when you find them doing this unhappy thing it is too late to give them warning. Winters here can be cruel or merely coolly comfortable. Ice thick enough to support skaters has formed on Lake Fulmor and snow has stood six feet deep on the level in the high reaches.

Spring sings a light song here; wildflowers appear and the springs run as though they would never stop. Summers are long—sometimes seemingly endless—and in time they become dusty and pregnant with the threat of forest fire. But even by summer the top of Thomas Mountain and Santa Rosa Mountain and Black Mountain and Tahquitz are cool places to visit. Sometimes by summer angry storms—perhaps brewed by the Soboba's evil ex-chief—call on the forest and great slashes of lightning rake down. It is then that the lookouts on Black Mountain and Tahquitz and Red Mountain are extra alert. Often the dazzling display of lightning is accompanied by a more soothing drenching of heavy rain. Then, with the duff damped, even wet, with the great trees adrip with water, with a fresh smell and a brand new breeze walking the mountains, it is a delightful place.

And when the Santa Ana (or Santana, if you will) winds blow, from the high viewpoints you can get unchecked views for miles and miles.

Ripe with history, sewn with legend, blessed with scenery, the San Jacinto Mountains of Riverside County offer some of the best there is in Southern California.

III THE BANNING TO IDYLLWILD HIGHWAY

Following the course of old logging roads, this byway offers a scenic route into the Idyllwild country.

IT IS COLONEL M. S. HALL, grading contractor for the Southern Pacific which built its line through the San Gorgonio Pass around 1876, who is credited with scratching the first tracks into the San Jacinto Mountains along its north edge.

Hall was undoubtedly looking for timber and firewood; timber for ties for the railroad; firewood for the locomotives that were coming along behind. He worked into the area of Indian Creek where, above Lake Fulmor today, stands Hall Creek. He moved a sawmill around and, according to Historian Tom Hughes, ended up with the mill in Snow Creek, with the supply of logs supposed to come down a steep skidway. The operation was not a success although some patient searchers can still find traces of the old skidway.

Hall's wanderings around in the mountain country here were marked by wagon roads he built. In time these would be improved by shake cutters and post trimmers until the time stood when you could get into the timber country above Vista Grande on a kind of a road.

As late as World War Two this was still a pretty crude avenue, unpaved, steep in places, fording streams and narrow most of the way. It wasn't until the years after the war that the road became a reality.

The road was opened in August of 1948. In October, 1950, the new 26-mile road was formally dedicated, the realization "of a 20 year dream," to quote the newspapers of the day.

Surveyed by County Surveyor Alex Fulmor, the first route of the high gear road was mapped in 1933 and 1934. Construction started in June 1935 at the Idyllwild end. Prison labor did much of the work, there was some WPA labor, and the rest was on contract.

On that bright day in 1950 motion picture actress Jane Powell cut the ribbon, the Banning High School band played, and the road was opened to the public.

The Highway. Starting in Banning San Gorgonio Avenue runs south toward the mountains, finds the first hill and slants away to the east, climbing briskly. While the drive is a high gear road all the way to Idyllwild, the road makes no fuss about climbing.

In a series of long switchbacks the road conquers the San Gorgonio Pass-facing hill. There are few turnouts along this section of road, and this is unfortunate. Few places in Southern California provide a vista of a valley below that is so similar to a view from a low flying airplane.

This is all chaparral country that the road climbs at the beginning. The 3000-foot elevation sign is passed. On the left is the entrance to the Twin Pines Ranch. In a dense thicket of oaks is the Vali-Hi Park and campground. Further on the dirt road leading to the west and down into the Poppet Flat country is passed. Then the road enters the San Bernardino National Forest and soon the first pines appear. There is the turnoff into the ranching area of Hurley Valley.

Here is the Vista Grande ranger station, a government site dating back at least to CCC days.

There are various pieces of private land on either side of the highway and the entrance to private land is marked.

Mist partially obscures the beauty of Lake Fulmor,
snow-fringed and ice-decorated.

—Photo by Harry Jar

The drinking fountain at Bay Tree Spring is signed. This little spring, which struggles valiantly to bubble even in the dry season, gives up some of the most delicious mountain spring water I've yet tasted. Good idea to stop here and fill your canteen or thermos.

You'll find a place or two along the highway here where viewpoint turnouts are provided. You can see deep out across the Angelus Hill area into the San Jacinto Valley. The Cinco Poses trail, which climbs to the brow of Black Mountain, takes off from the left here.

Lake Fulmor takes its name from the county surveyor who laid out the Banning to Idyllwild route. There is a Forest Service park here on Forest Service land, a park that offers fishing all year long, and picnicking as well. No camping is allowed. There are bedrock mortars in some of the big rocks around the edge of the lake, and on the side hill on the south side of the lake the patient explorer can find old Indian shelter caves.

Beyond Lake Fulmor the road rounds a curve and faces the Fuller Mill Creek drainage. To the left the road takes off up the hill through an area called Metate Flat onto Black Mountain.

Side road to Black Mountain and the Black Mountain scenic area. One of the Forest Service's most attractive campgrounds lies near the summit of this unpaved road up the side of Black Mountain. It is a four-mile drive up this dusty and sometimes bumpy dirt road to the lookout turnoff and eight miles to the gate at the far end. But it is well worth the drive. Part way up, on the right, there is a side road that leads back to the private homes in the Pine Wood area. The road is gated here. But back in the Pine Wood area is the site of the old Fuller sawmill, one of the earlier lumbering operations in the mountains.

Three miles up from pavement there is a turnout on the west side. Park here and walk for a short distance to the south to a giant boulder set among the pines. The sign here will explain that this is a famous old Cahuilla Indian ceremonial site—note the pictographs on the rock. Nearby is an Indian ceremonial cave.

Four miles from pavement is the side road up to the Black Mountain lookout. It is open to the public from nine to five daily. You'll find all Forest Service lookouts most friendly and helpful. They'll be happy to point out the landmarks in the region and will point the way to high country trails. The lookout is their home, remember, and behave yourself as you would in any stranger's home.

Beyond the side road to the lookout tower the Black Mountain road climbs to the campground site. This is a most pleasant off-the-highway camping area and is busy all the year except when weather closes the road.

Beyond the campground the road runs on north to a couple of spectacular viewpoints. It then drops down the back side of Black Mountain to a locked gate at the entrance of an organizational camp.

Resume Banning to Idyllwild Highway. Here is the Fuller Mill Campground. You must park in the parking area and walk down to the stream to the camping area, but the trees here are magnificent.

Lawler Park, an organization camp operated by Riverside County, occupies a historic spot in the mountains, and beyond is the Forest Service's Alandale station.

To the left the road takes off into the Dark Canyon country.

Side road into the Dark Canyon area. The road to the left here quickly reaches a series of first rate Forest Service campgrounds. Those nearest the highway are kept open later in the year. Those furthest back are closed with the slackening of the press of campers and with the advent of bad weather.

Here, in the order, you will find the Pine Flat Campground. On a spur road there is Fern Basin and higher on the same spur, Marion Mountain Campgrounds. On the main Dark Canyon road, and in a couple of more miles, along the Dark Canyon stream itself, is an attractive site, the Dark Canyon Campground.

The road continues on up the far side of the canyon now to an organizational camp, and on a northward spur, toward Pine Wood. This latter avenue is gated.

Resume Banning to Idyllwild Highway. There are typical mountain resort features here now, like places where you can trout fish in a private pond without a license. The Pine Cove general store and gas station are passed. Here is the elegant Tirol restaurant. Here is a golf course (on the site of an old logging mill) and finally, at a stop sign, Idyllwild is gained.

In Idyllwild you'll find the headquarters for both the San Jacinto District of the San Bernardino National Forest, and the Mt. Jacinto Wilderness State Park. For any hiking forays into the mountain country, consult these people for information and permits.

Idyllwild is a modern resort community with a year-round population of 2700 and a summertime population many times that. People-counters have estimated that during certain three-day summer holidays the casual population has ballooned as high as 50,000.

There are all the conveniences a visitor could ask at Idyllwild. There are specialty shops, supermarkets, lumber yards and bakeries. Here are schools, churches, motels and restaurants. There are some beautiful mountain homes in the area—and these can be traced by their age from the Strawberry Valley area south of Idyllwild through Idyllwild and north into the Fern Valley region.

The Forest Service lookout tower atop Black Mountain.

There is picnicking and camping in Idyllwild at the State Park facility, at Humber Park, and at Idyllwild County Park—the latter the largest with more than 100 units.

In the area commonly thought of as old Strawberry Valley is the famed Idyllwild Arts Foundation, affiliated with the University of Southern California.

The Idyllwild Arts Foundation was founded as a non-profit educational institute in 1946. It sits on the side of Strawberry Creek in an attractive wooded region. In 1962 the Foundation became an official campus of the University of Southern California.

Here a complete adult program is offered in music education, ceramics, graphic arts, photography, folk music, folk dance, contemporary dance, sculpture, crafts. There is a children's campus; a junior high age program in orchestra and choir; a resident drama group. Concerts are frequently presented to the public.

Off on the side road that leads back to the Arts Foundation is the entrance to the Alvin Meadow country—a CCC camp once stood here and now the Forest Service has a corral and pasture on the site. Beyond is the beginning of the old toll-control road down the mountain to Oak Cliff on State Highway 74.

The highway runs on south from Idyllwild, past the county dump—and there are plans to move this site—past Keenwild ranger station and on to Mountain Center and State Highway 74. Mountain Center is a relatively new community, coming up generally since the fire and the demise of Keen Camp.

Here this byway ends.

For purists, the new official name of this highway is now simply the Idyllwild Road. Before it had gained the longer name of the Banning-Idyllwild Panoramic Highway. The change, the shortening, was made by the San Bernardino County Board of Supervisors in 1964 who ruled that although the longer name had an attractive sound, it was impractical.

IV THE HEMET TO MOUNTAIN CENTER ROAD

This high gear road up out of the San Jacinto Valley into the mountain country was the first paved and improved avenue into the region.

RUNNING EAST out of Hemet through Valle Vista into the San Jacinto Mountain country following at first, at least, the drainage of the San Jacinto River, is State Highway 74.

At the community of Valle Vista, on the southward pointing Fairview Avenue, we turn right.

Side road into Bautista Canyon. This is a paved road until it reaches the low hills to the south. Then the road curves briefly to the east and enters Bautista Canyon proper. The road draws its name from Spanish explorer Juan Bautista de Anza who marched through this country in 1774 on his historic passage from Mexico to Monterey. While the lands on either side of the road are closed during the fire season, the county road is open all year.

This byway climbs slowly, passes stands of cottonwood and willow in the stream bottom. Water appears here infrequently.

The old Bautista guard station of the San Bernardino National Forest is abandoned but the old spring here still supplies water for a quail guzzler and for a Forest Service water tank. There are future plans to improve the area into some sort of a recreation facility.

The dirt road continues to climb, the site for a state prison camp in the Horse Creek crossing area is passed. There is a foot trail—Alessandro Trail—from a point here up toward Little Cahuilla Mountain. Here is Alessandro Spring.

At a road fork the right hand course leads back to the Forest Service's station at Tripp Flat. Beyond, on a locked road, is Juan Diego Flat on the north side of the Cahuilla Mountain. The left hand truck trail climbs into the Thomas Mountain country. The Bautista Canyon road continues through the Hidden Valley property and gains State Highway 71 just west of Anza.

Resume State Highway 74. Beyond Valle Vista State Highway 74 continues east, enters the mouth of the San Jacinto River, passes into the National Forest boundary and comes to Cranston ranger station.

This station is named after Leon J. Cranston, district ranger of the San Jacinto District of the San Bernardino National Forest in the late 1920s.

Just beyond Cranston station the North Fork of the San Jacinto River bends away to the northwest. Turkeys are raised in the area. At Oak Cliff, just beyond, the old Crawford toll road—later control road—starts its crooked climb up to Strawberry Valley following most of the time along the west side of Strawberry Creek. Built in 1875, the toll road was one of the first avenues into the mountains. Closed during the fire season, the old toll road can be driven by motorists in passenger cars today although it is an easier trip down hill than up. There is a small water source at Halfway House Spring part way up the mountain. The road is used primarily today as a fire road by the Forest Service.

Above Oak Cliff the highway continues along the South Fork of the San Jacinto River, climbs as the river turns away to the south, executes White Post Turn—there is a passing lane here—and with conifers making more of a showing now, comes into Mountain Center and the junction of the side road leading back to Idyllwild, 4.7 miles to the north.

*Lake Hemet is stocked with fish and is open
to public fishing all year long.*

V THE PINES TO PALMS HIGHWAY

This spectacular road shows clearly the changes in life zones from the forested country in the San Jacinto Mountains down to the desert zone near Palm Desert.

THERE ARE two explanations due the reader from the outset. First, this highway is simply a continuation of State Highway 74 east from Mountain Center and down the hill into the Colorado Desert. The name, Pines to Palms Highway, has frequently been used to refer to the entire run of State Highway 74 from Hemet to Palm Desert. Actually, it should only apply to the section from Mountain Center to Palm Desert. Or vice versa.

Second, there are two camps here as far as the name of the highway is concerned. Some call it Pines to Palms Highway. Some call it the Palms to Pines Highway. You will find it both ways on reliable maps. Even the natives will argue and experts claim that they have heard it used both ways for a long time and see no objection to a little confusion.

In an effort to be technically correct, we will here call the route the Pines to Palms Highway, and will follow it the 36 descending miles from Mountain Center to Palm Desert, a difference in elevation from 4444 feet down to 223 feet.

Starting then at Mountain Center we drive east, and climb gently as we reach toward Keen Camp, an older mountain resort that had electricity before Idyllwild and was the scene of many Western motion pictures that were filmed in the rugged mountain setting. The Keen Camp lodge burned in 1943 and since then the camp has been less active. The old ranger station at Keen Camp is not manned now, and the old resort facilities are used

33

by an organizational camp. During the depression years there was a CCC facility at Keen Camp.

Just beyond is a side road to the right which leads up into the Baldy Mountain country. The peak is 5500 feet high. Closed to the public, the road crosses private land. But at several spots on Baldy Mountain there are areas of Forest Service lands that recreation experts feel would be excellent for picnic and camping sites.

On either sides of the road here reach areas of the sprawling Garner Cattle Ranch, a historic land holding dating back to 1904 when the Garner family bought the old 7000-acre Thomas Ranch.

A road running back to the left toward May Valley along the Keen Ridge is open to the public even though it is gated. It dead-ends back at the edge of private property. A good view of the higher Desert Divide country can be had from the Keen Ridge road.

At Keen Camp Summit, 4917 feet, the road tops out and starts its descent toward Palm Desert. Views of the attractive sprawling Garner Valley open up. At the bottom of the hill the road crosses Hurkey Creek and here, on the left, is the Riverside County site of Hurkey Creek Camp. There is a small use charge. The campground is open all year and is quite popular with campers. Hurkey, or Herkey, was an early-day workman on the old Thomas Ranch in the area and was mauled to death by a grizzly bear.

To the right now is the public road back into an area above the Lake Hemet Municipal Water Co. land where a trio of ramada-shaded picnic grounds stand. The area has been developed by Riverside County. The land belongs to the Forest Service.

There is year-around fishing at Lake Hemet and fish are planted here regularly by the State Department of Fish and Game. For those who wish to camp nearby, or park a trailer, a second road,

34

The old 60-foot metal lookout tower atop
Thomas Mountain is only used during emergencies.

The church back on the Santa Rosa Indian Reservation.

on private land, leads to these accommodations—where a small fee is charged—and on to the lake. This latter road leads all the way back to the tall masonry dam, built in the 1890s of blocks of hewn native stone. The water level of Lake Hemet has been extremely low in recent years but plans are being drafted for possible recreational improvements in the area.

There are some attractive fringe area stands of Jeffrey and Coulter pine in this portion of the Garner Valley. An earlier name for this flatland region was Hemet Valley and before that, after the pioneer rancher, Thomas' Valley.

Just beyond on the left is the private road back to the Garner Cattle Co. ranch headquarters—once the headquarters of the Thomas Ranch. Some of the original buildings still stand.

On the right, a short distance farther, is another side road. This one climbs Thomas Mountain.

Side road to Thomas Mountain. This road is signed Little Thomas Mountain Road, but it is the beginning of a network of mountain dirt roads through this country. The road climbs quickly to the top of the great ridge that runs from the northwest to the southeast. To the west of this access road the mountain country is all within the fire closure. To the east, the country is open by summer, and is one of the favorite places for deer hunters in season.

There is a road junction up on the shoulder of the ridge. There is an unpaved truck trail running west along Horse Creek Ridge (in the closure), and to the east toward Thomas Mountain. (Another dirt road runs straight ahead and then drops down into the Ramona Indian Reservation country and Cahuilla Valley.)

Following the Thomas Mountain road we pass out of scattered pines into a denser forest of conifers. Little Thomas Mountain lies off the north. Here is the attractive Thomas Mountain Forest

Service campground, small and not greatly improved. Beyond a spur road angles up to the summit of Thomas Mountain, 6811 feet, where there is an old Forest Service outpost and a spectacular 60-foot-tall metal lookout tower. This tower is only used in the case of emergency on the Forest now.

Beyond the summit site the road passes the Tool Box campground and descends, again through chaparral, to the Pines to Palms Highway.

Resume Pines to Palms Highway at Little Thomas Mountain Road turnoff. Through Garner Valley Highway 74 runs on toward the southeast now. On the left is the marked turnoff back to the Forest Service's Kenworthy ranger station—again the site of an old CCC camp. Kenworthy is the name of a vanished gold mining camp that existed probably between 1896 and 1901 in the Pine Meadow area a couple of miles east of the ranger station. A school and other buildings stood here briefly. Some say a fire destroyed the site.

Kenworthy, his first name lost in the years, was supposed to have been a miner and speculator. Sam Chilson built a small stamp mill at the site. The mines were probably salted. The camp is all gone now, even the state mining records are vague on the subject. A careful search of the area today turns up little more than some old soldered-bottom tin cans, indelible proof of the age of the settlement, but not much more. The site is on private property.

To the right on the highway here is the settlement of Thomas Mountain. Beyond, the road from Thomas Mountain comes back to the highway.

Garner Valley ends near the junction of State Highway 74 and State Highway 71 coming in from the Anza area. This side road runs through the Anza, Terwilliger and Cahuilla Valleys, passes the colorful Bergman Museum and reaches all the way down to Aguanga on State Highway 79. This route, first an Indian trail—later a wagon road—from the Indian rancheria at Anza, was the first route into the San Jacinto Mountain country.

The area summit is reached and the road continues its descent, dropping through the life zones from Canadian to Transition, to Upper Sonoran and down to Lower Sonoran at the desert's edge.

The turnoff into the Santa Rosa Indian Reservation is passed. There is an interesting church and cemetery on Indian land here, but get written permission before visiting the area. It is private property. Two families live on the lands. Other Santa Rosa Indian families in the area use the lands for grazing.

Just beyond the Santa Rosa Indian Reservation, in an area where red shank, or ribbonwood, grows luxuriantly, is the side road to Santa Rosa Mountain and Toro Peak.

Side road to Santa Rosa Mountain and Toro Peak. (See Chapter VI.)

Past Ribbonwood now the Pines to Palms Highway descends. The promontory to the north is Asbestos Mountain, 5265 feet. The Pinyon Flat Forest Service campground is reached. There is a subdivision development here in land now spotted with agave instead of pine, yucca instead of cedar; cholla and beavertail cactus even show here.

The road continues to drop. It bends to the north. The first of the desert vistas appear. At a spot called Seven Level Hill all manner of views of the desert country ahead can be had as the road switchbacks lower and lower. There are few turnouts here.

Then, at last, the road is down off the mountains, runs through desert subdivisions to the Palm Desert junction with State Highway 111. To the north, along State Highway 111, Palm Springs is only 13 miles away.

VI THE SANTA ROSAS

This desert edge mountain country is just about the most fascinating in the San Jacinto area. The views from the tallest peaks are without compare.

ABOUT SEVENTEEN MILES east of Mountain Center on the Pines to Palms Highway (State Highway 74) is the unpaved turnoff to the south onto Santa Rosa Mountain.

There is a small confusion of place names here. Santa Rosa Mountain and Toro Peak lie out along this arm of mountain, but then on the south, separating Coyote Canyon's defile from Coachella Valley is a greater mass called the Santa Rosa *Mountains*. In this guide we are concerned more with the former.

The rough dirt road up to Santa Rosa Mountain and Toro Peak is dusty—that's about the worst thing that can be said about it. Rough and dusty. Still it permits passage of passenger cars all the way to the uppermost gates. And it is a splendid mountain country to explore.

The road tops a ridge, drops down past a mining claim, then starts an assault on the west face of the mountain. After about eight miles the first pines are reached; the passage until then has been through mature chaparral. Queen Creek is crossed and the road works industriously at climbing.

There is a three-unit Forest Service campground at Santa Rosa Spring and—as elsewhere in the mountain region here—delicious spring water.

All of this country gets heavy use during deer season in the fall. In deep winter it is closed by bad weather frequently. But in the spring, and in the winter before the first big storm, it is a delightful region.

39

A short distance beyond you'll see the first sign painted on a roadside boulder by Desert Steve Ragsdale—who owns the section of land encompassing Santa Rosa Mountain's summit—warning of forest fire. Trees here carry similar warnings—some of them rhyme, like: "To man and tree, I say to thee, beware of fire, it's killing me."

At a saddle, just short of the summit, a spur road scrambles up the last few hundred yards to the top of Santa Rosa Mountain, elevation 8046 feet, where Ragsdale built a roomy log cabin with a giant man-sized fireplace.

In the top of a nearby 40-foot Jeffrey pine Ragsdale put up a log and hewn-timber lookout tower. Even the steps up are chopped logs. And from the top of this lookout the view is magnificent.

Ragsdale once wrote of the view from the mountain top thus:

"From my windows, yard and stairway lookout . . . I plainly see the mountains in Old Mexico, nearby San Jacinto, San Gorgonio, Baldy and Wilson, the Panamints near Death Valley to the north, the Chocolates, Chuckawallas, Cottonwoods, Palens, Granites, Santa Marias and Muir Mountains to the east, even as far as the San Franciscos and the mountains between Flagstaff and the Grand Canyon when snow capped with the sun's rays flashing on them.

"I can see . . . Lake Henshaw, Hemet Lake, Lake Elsinore, Railroad Lake, and the Salton Sea at my feet. I can see several cities . . . Niland, Brawley, Yuma, El Centro, Julian, San Diego . . . Riverside, San Bernardino and Pasadena . . .

"I can see clearly 20 airway beacons, thousands of automobile lights . . ."

The above was written in 1938 and viewing experts claim that haze accumulations in the desert area prevent such long range viewing as that of the San Francisco Peaks today. But even so, this is one of the most spectacular viewpoints in Southern Cali-

*This log lookout tower built in the top of a pine tree
was fashioned by Desert Steve Ragsdale
on the summit of Santa Rosa Mountain.*

fornia. Ragsdale had the world at his feet from his tower in the Santa Rosas, and, happily, he knew it.

Closer at hand, from the peak, it is possible to look down into Santa Rosa Indian Reservation land, and hidden down here, almost forgotten, are the ruins of Old Santa Rosa, where the yesterday people of the reservation once made their home.

In the 1920s Charles Francis Saunders in *The Southern Sierras of California* wrote of a visit to the spot in his usual poetic style:

". . . of an ancient life once active here there were abundant vestiges—ruins of rock houses, a parched and broken reservoir, rotted fences and basket granaries, broken pottery, mortar and rubbing stones, arrow-straighteners and what-not. At the back a trail wound around the mountain to a spring gushing out from between two huge alders—a lovely, green peaceful spot, where we may imagine the Santa Rosa damsels of long ago coming to fill their water-jars and gossip, glad of escape, if it were summer, from the persistent sunshine of their treeless village."

It would appear that by driving south and then east—across closed Indian reservation land to be sure—it would be possible to drop down to the Coachella Valley area. Not so. It can be managed on foot or on horseback, but no jeep trail makes the crossing. The Santa Rosa people run cattle on much of their reservation lands and do not welcome strangers, particularly careless hunters who shoot cattle by mistake, or jeep explorers who beat down the sparse feed with their vehicles.

To the east, from the viewpoint atop Ragsdale's log lookout, the Salton Sea shines like a pane of brass. Closer at hand stands Toro Peak. The road runs on from the spur side road up to Ragsdale's mountain toward this promontory.

There is a legend that the local Indians regard the top of Toro Peak a tabooed area. It is still on Santa Rosa Indian Reservation lands—Indian land encompasses the entire section that holds the

42

peak. But from the brow of Santa Rosa Peak, past the green spot called Stump Spring, past Cedar Spring, the gently climbing forest road invades stands of pine and cedar. There are hints of great vistas off to the north. Some of the desert country to the east is glimpsed. If you travel this route by summer you have climbed from a little over 4500 feet at the highway to an elevation of over 8000 feet. The air is markedly cooler, and even though there was no wind on the Pines to Palms Highway, a bright cool breeze can be dancing through the tall conifers here.

Finally you will come to a fork in the road. You are near the end of the distance you can travel. Take the upper road, for you will find the lower road gated. It is an old logging road. The upper road, too, will be gated in a short distance and from here, if you would persevere, it is a stiff hike on up the road to the peak.

The U. S. Marine Corps has installations just shy of the top of Toro Peak and again on the summit. The Marine Corps uses Toro Peak during training exercises which require radio communications between Marine Air Stations at El Toro; Yuma, Arizona; the Marine Corps base at Twentynine Palms and Camp Pendleton. Their radio relay equipment is located on the desert peak. The Marines have a lease agreement with the Santa Rosa Indians for the installation. There is also a micro-wave TV signal retransmission outpost here which services such spots as El Centro, Borrego and Yuma. A helicopter landing field has been built atop the 8716-foot peak.

From Toro Peak it is again possible to look to the south and see the arm of the Santa Rosa *Mountains* running down into the Anza-Borrego Desert State Park. The highest peak in the desert range is Rabbit Peak, 6627 feet. There is a fold in the mountains almost due south that deceptively looks as if it would provide at least a jeep access up from Borrego Valley into the Old Santa Rosa country. I have heard accounts of people driving out the ridges onto the Santa Rosa Mountains from the Toro Peak area, but not all of these attempts have been happy ones. Recently a caravan of seven jeeps attempted such a back country outing, ran into such difficult up and down country that all seven vehicles were stranded and help had to be summoned from Indio.

To the east now is the timberless dome of Martinez Mountain, 6582 feet, within the range of the bighorn sheep of the San Jacinto Mountains complex. The sheep wander from Martinez Mountain north, across the Pines to Palms Highway and onto the Desert Divide country; further still, beyond the tramway, they explore and feed along the north face of the San Jacintos.

This, then, is the Santa Rosa Mountain-Toro Peak country. Like Thomas Mountain, it is surprising with its thick pine forests along the higher elevations. Hikers along its random slopes are apt to find hints of old-day logging operations, the marks left behind by early-day miners. Indian house rings and bits of broken pottery can be found under pines and cedars by the most patient searchers. The region, reached only by a slow-traveling dirt road, is completely unspoiled. While subdivisions have scarred the forest of red shank on the Pines to Palms Highway below, this attractive country is not much changed from fifty, one hundred years ago. Jets make a mark in the sky now but the trees nod to the same persuasion of wind and winter that they did when Old Santa Rosa knew the comings and goings of its patient people.

44

VII THE PALM SPRINGS AERIAL TRAMWAY

From Chino Canyon near Palm Springs an aerial tramway carries passengers to a high crag atop the San Jacinto Mountains.

ON THE NORTHEAST shoulder of the bulk of the San Jacinto Mountains is Chino Canyon. Its wide mouth is within the Palm Springs city limits. Part way up the canyon is a cienega, green in season with wild grape. Up this canyon from the valley floor runs the access road to the Valley Station of the Palm Springs Aerial Tramway. From here, suspended on stout steel cables, a pair of 80-passenger cars daily haul visitors to Mountain Station, a luxurious outpost within the San Jacinto Wilderness State Park. There is nothing like the tramway in the West, probably nothing like it in the world.

In the 1930s, when the state park here was being born, the idea for some sort of a lift, a ride, a tramway, up from Palm Springs into the high mountain country was first discussed.

During the war years—though it was fought constantly by conservationists who thought that a wilderness region like the San Jacinto Wilderness State Park should not be defiled with a mechanical contrivance such as a tramway—legislation was first offered on the tramway proposal. It was in 1945 that the Mt. San Jacinto Winter Park Authority was created by law. The storms of protest continued to rage but in 1961 construction started on the project. The tramway started operation in September of 1963.

From Valley Station, at an elevation of 2643 feet, it meant that a straightline route for the tramway had to be picked from country that was almost vertical. The erection of the five towers that sup-

*The Palm Springs Aerial Tramway offers
an exciting ride from the desert side of the
San Jacinto Mountains up into the State Park.*

port the cable and the tram on its climb up the 5873 feet it lifts to Mountain Station would have been impossible but for the assistance of helicopters. Men and material were flown to artificial perches on the steep face of the mountain.

There are five of these towers along the 13,200-foot ride. The first, 214 feet high, is located 1175 feet up from Valley Station at an elevation of 2820 feet. Tower Number Two is 158 feet tall, is 3280 feet further up the mountain. It is located at an elevation of 4100 feet. The third tower is 144 feet tall, the span to it is 3223 feet. The elevation here is 5755 feet. Tower Number Four is only 57½ feet tall. The span to it is 3455 feet. The elevation here is 7576 feet. The last tower is 63½ feet tall, the span is 969 feet and its elevation is 8102 feet. Mountain Station is at an elevation of 8516 feet, 714 feet from the final tower. It is a steep and breathtaking rise.

There are two gondolas here. One moves up as the other moves down. Counterbalanced, they meet, naturally, at midpoint along the run of cable. Depending on the speed chosen by the operators—usually based on the visitor load—the tram makes the trip in from 11 to 18 minutes.

Most of the 80 passengers in the gondola must stand. There are four small jump seats. There are convenient handholds within the cab.

While veteran airplane pilots have been known to pale at the prospect of riding the tramway, it is actually not a scary excursion. There is a pleasant sensation of ascent or descent, depending on your direction. The awesome up and down craggy scenery passes close at hand and is instantly hypnotic. In windy weather a water-hauling tank on the bottom of the gondola is filled, providing adequate ballast against side sway.

In its first year of operation the Palm Springs Aerial Tramway hauled 300,000 people. The busiest day saw 5000 people make

47

the trip. During summer months, when Palm Springs temperatures top out over a hundred degrees, traffic is frequently light. The Valley Station, an attractive big building housing offices and souvenir stand and snack bar, is air conditioned.

The road up from State Highway 111 just north of Palm Springs up Chino Canyon is steep and in the summertime your car may boil making the trip to the parking area. Drive accordingly. There are signs along the way suggesting that motorists turn off their air conditioning; radiator water is offered. From the lower parking lots a bus provides transportation up to the Valley Station. There is a charge for parking.

Mountain Station, cliff-perched and filled with windows, embraces the natural contours of the crag it commands. Also a modern and attractive building, it encloses a bar, dining room, souvenir shop, many outdoor decks for viewing. And the viewing is spectacular.

From here it is possible to see the bald dome of San Gorgonio to the north. The Little San Bernardinos stretch out to the east. The Palm Springs area and the Coachella Valley unfolds. On crisp and clear days some unusual photographs can be taken from the site.

From Mountain Station a trail switchbacks down into the Long Valley state park campground. Nearby is a state park ranger station. It is a delightful mountain country, craggy and pine-shaded. Remember that the difference in temperature between Valley Station and Mountain Station is roughly 40 degrees. If you show up on a shirtsleeves day of 70 degrees in Palm Springs you are apt to find it below freezing at Mountain Station. Dress accordingly.

From Long Valley trails branch out into the various corners of the state park. For those who wish to hike down out of the mountain country, across the state park, in the direction of Idyllwild, there are 10½ miles of good trail from Mountain Station

48

to Humber Park—the end of pavement in the Idyllwild area. If you consider hiking down the route of the tramway, forget it. Even mountain sheep refuse to make the trek. There is a rugged trail that descends from Mountain Station to Palm Springs—not to Valley Station—but it is not recommended for novice hikers. From Mountain Station it is possible to hike to Mt. San Jacinto, at an elevation of 10,831 feet, the tallest spot in the San Jacinto Mountains. Some trails run through the state park into the San Jacinto Wild Area of the San Bernardino National Forest to the south and thence return to the Idyllwild area.

The Palm Springs Aerial Tramway smacks of high adventure like other transportation engineering feats in the West: the old Mt. Lowe Railway above Pasadena, the Pike's Peak cog railroad. While it is now operated by the Mt. San Jacinto Winter Park Authority, under present plans one day it may be an adjunct of the state park system itself.

The tramway operates daily from 8 a.m. until 10 p.m., except for the third Tuesday in each month when it shuts down for maintenance work.

By summer, with Palm Springs and the Coachella Valley shimmering in 100 degrees plus temperatures, the Mountain Station frequently offers 60-degree weather. By winter, with snow crowning the Mountain Station country, it has been known to cool to 8 degrees at the top of the lift. But either way the ride is spectacular, the views are impressive, the entire outing is a pleasant adventure.

49

VIII MT. SAN JACINTO WILDERNESS STATE PARK

Established in 1937, the Mt. San Jacinto Wilderness State Park is a wilderness-type island within the San Jacinto Mountain country

ON SATURDAY, June 19, 1937, there was a gala celebration at Idyllwild in the San Jacinto Mountains. There was band music, a boxing exhibition, contests and games. There was a demonstration of trick and fancy horseback riding and a potato race. All this was icing on the cake. The cake was the new 12,687-acre Mt. San Jacinto State Park which was dedicated that day and among those who made speeches were State Park Commission Chairman J. R. Knowland, and W. C. Moore, Honorary Chairman of the Riverside County Board of Supervisors.

The idea for a state park atop the high country of the San Jacinto Mountains was not a new one, not even in 1937. Mountain men and conservationists had talked about the scheme as early as 1928 when just getting up on the mountain was difficult.

In a period that roughly stretched from 1930 through 1935 the land atop the range was acquired by the state. In 1937 the dedication of the park was staged. Parcels of land have been added to the park since. The name was changed to the Mt. San Jacinto *Wilderness* State Park in 1963.

In addition to the block of high country there is a 14-acre tract right in Idyllwild that consists of the park headquarters and ranger's residence, and a small campground.

More recently the state park acquired 800 acres that joins the southwest corner of the existing park. This land, along Stone Creek drainage, will be developed into a new campground area

50

with, in time, perhaps as many as 300 units. The park headquarters will be moved to this new area.

The original high country section of Mt. San Jacinto Wilderness State Park lies beyond the end of roads. Only trails—and the Palm Springs Aerial Tramway—invade the wilderness-like region. It is heavily used by hikers, mostly those with youth groups. Upwards of 15,000 hikers a year use its trails and campgrounds, many make the trek all the way up to the summit of Mt. San Jacinto, 10,831 feet, one of the three tallest mountains in the Southern California region (the others being Mt. San Gorgonio, 11,502 feet; and Mt. San Antonio, 10,064 feet).

There are 26 miles of primary trail in the state park and 30 miles of secondary trail. Jump off places are Humber Park, just outside of Idyllwild under the brow of Tahquitz Peak; Mountain Station on the Tramway; Idyllwild; and Pine Wood up the Dark Canyon road.

Mt. San Jacinto Wilderness State Park is bordered on three sides by National Forest Lands. On the east private and Indian Reservation lands touch the edge of the park.

There are camp sites in the state park at Round Valley, 9100 feet; Long Valley, 8600 feet; Little Round Valley, 9300 feet; Deer Springs, 8800 feet. There is a shelter atop Mt. San Jacinto. All the campgrounds—except the peak—have toilets and stoves. There is limited water at Little Round Valley and Long Valley. There is no water at the peak.

A special campfire permit is required of all who use these facilities. State park people suggest that users of the state park—engaged in more than a casual one-day hike-in-and-out adventure—check in at state park headquarters in Idyllwild before they leave. The park is open to hikers all year but in the wintertime deep snow and storms frequently preclude use of the park. It is well patrolled. There are two state park ranger outposts in the reserve.

51

This is the stone hut atop San Jacinto Peak.
Hikers frequently spend the night here.

Several peaks in the state park are in the 10,000-feet family: Mt. San Jacinto, Jean Peak, Marion Mountain, Folly Peak, Miller Peak. From Mountain Station off the tramway winter sports enthusiasts get in some snow fun in the state park.

There have been tragic accidents in the area; almost always such are the result of not abiding by the practical set of rules that the park people here have drafted and which they issue visitors to the high country park. In a "things to remember" leaflet the state park issues, the following reminders are offered:

1. Dress properly. Choose the right shoes.
2. Never go alone; a party of four is best.
3. Keep together. Don't cut switchbacks.
4. Carry a good pocket knife, wooden matches in a waterproof case, a compass and a reliable watch.
5. Tell family or friends exactly where you are going and when you expect to return.
6. If lost, stay in a protected place. Take it easy.
7. In snow areas use goggles and sunburn cream. Don't climb during storms.

Principal trails into the Mt. San Jacinto Wilderness State Park are: the Devil's Slide Trail which jumps off from Humber Park and crosses the San Jacinto Wild Area and forks at Saddle Junction. Into the state park via the Wellman Cienega Trail it is seven miles to the peak of San Jacinto. It is five miles to the Round Valley Campground. From Saddle Junction it is five miles to Long Valley Campground and Mountain Station via the Willow Creek Trail across the upper edge of the Wild Area and into the State Park.

The Deer Springs Trail starts at Idyllwild and runs up the west side of the mountains seven and a half miles to Deer Springs Campground. It is another two and a half miles from Deer Springs

53

to Little Round Valley Camp. It is another mile to the summit of Mt. San Jacinto.

According to the Sierra Club, the rugged north face of Mt. San Jacinto—one of the most precipitous escarpments in the nation, dropping over 10,000 feet in six miles—makes an interesting climb for experts.

The north face was first climbed by Sierra Clubbers in 1932— via Snow Creek in ten exhausting hours. Since then, and at this writing, some 40 ascents of the north face have been made. It is not a Sunday afternoon scramble for amateurs—it is very rugged, very difficult, very dangerous. That is unless you are an old hand Sierra Club rock climber . . . .

There are other trails in the State Park and a free map will be issued to you at the park headquarters in Idyllwild. Such maps are also available at Mountain Station and at the Long Valley ranger station.

Tahquitz Rock by winter with snow on the ground.

—Photo by Dwight Metcalf, courtesy
Idyllwild Town Crier

IX THE TRAILS

There are several hundred miles of trails in the San Jacinto Mountains and these run from the desert to the tall timber country.

ACCORDING to latest measurement there are 237 miles of maintained trails in the U. S. Forest section of the San Jacinto Mountains. Add to that the 26 miles of major trails and the 30 miles of secondary trails within the Mt. San Jacinto Wilderness State Park, and there are plenty of places to walk in these mountains.

Some of the major trails are listed here.

Cinco Poses Trail. This three and a half mile popular trail runs from the spur road near the lookout turnoff off the Black Mountain road, down to the Banning to Idyllwild Highway. There is a cutoff that leaves the main Cinco Poses Trail and angles for a mile and a third to the Banning to Idyllwild Highway nearer Vista Grande.

Seven Pines Trail. This trail runs for better than three miles from the Pine Wood area—between the Dark Canyon and Black Mountain roads—over into the State Park and the Deer Springs Trail.

Marion Mountain Trail. A lesser trail runs from Marion Mountain Campground east to the Deer Springs Trail within the State Park.

Alessandro Trail. This popular trail runs from the Bautista Canyon county road southwest for four and a half miles to the Cahuilla Mountain Road above Juan Diego Flat.

Cahuilla Trail. A two miles long trail that runs from Cahuilla Saddle up to the summit of Cahuilla Peak. Rated by many to be an exceptional nature trail.

Caramba Trail. Within the San Jacinto Wild Area, this trail runs from Laws Camp to Caramba Camp.

Devil's Slide Trail. One of the main courses out of Humber Park into the Wild Area and into the State Park.

South Ridge Trail. Ten miles long, this one runs from the Devil's Slide Trail and over Tahquitz Peak southwest to a junction with the old road running through Keen Camp.

Thomas Mountain Trail. This one runs from the Thomas Mountain Campground down four miles into Garner Valley.

Strawberry Cienega Trail. Another one of those courses on the edge of the Wild Area. This one connects the Deer Springs Trail with the Wellman Cienega Trail. Distance two and a half miles.

Deer Springs Trail. One of the principal trails in the mountain country, it runs from Idyllwild, near the State Park headquarters, up to Deer Springs in the State Park. Eight miles long.

Desert Divide Trail. This trail runs along the Desert Divide country from Spitler Peak south to Bull Canyon in some rough and rocky country. Distance thirteen and a half miles.

Ramona Trail. This one runs up from the Garner Valley into the Thomas Mountain country, runs through Tool Box Spring and then drops down the far side onto a dirt road that runs into the Anza area. Six miles.

Hikers on the Wellman Cienega Trail into the San Jacinto Mountains back country.

—Photo by Ernest Maxwell

Palm Canyon Trail. A trail almost twenty miles long reaches back Palm Canyon from the end of the Palm Canyon road on Indian Reservation property south all the way to the Pines to Palms Highway west of Ribbonwood.

Fobes Trail. This one marches from the Fobes Ranch in Garner Valley up Fobes Canyon to the Desert Divide. Two miles.

Live Oak Trail. From the Desert Divide Trail near Bull Canyon this one runs east down into Live Oak Canyon and finally hits the Palm Canyon Trail. Nine and a half miles.

Cactus Springs Trail. Far out on the east end of the mountains, this one runs from the Pinyon Flats area down through the foothills on the north side of Martinez Mountain to Martinez Canyon. Fifteen miles. It reaches southeast on into the desert country.

Horsemen also use many of the trails in the San Jacinto Mountains.

X AN INTRODUCTION TO THE SANTA ANA MOUNTAINS

The Portola expedition in 1769 gave the name to these attractive coastal-facing mountains.

THERE was a great mining excitement in the Santa Ana Mountains in the 1870's and 1880's. The mines have long since been inactive, the tunnel mouths are choked with brush, the old machineries are rusted and the plats are faded.

Still there are residents here who are firmly convinced that a mining change will visit the Santa Anas, that lodes like the Blue Light will once again be active, that the zinc-lead-silver ore will come down out of the canyon on its way to the smelter at Salt Lake City and that Silverado will be a boom camp again.

This is the dream.

It might be a good thing, but the Santa Anas now hold such a flavor of peacefulness and rustic charm that it seems almost a pity to spoil it with boom.

Silverado and Modjeska and Trabuco Canyons are among the fairest in the city-facing hills, but in time, to be sure, they will change with "progress." Still they remain a pleasant link with the older, gentler days of the mountain country.

The Indians were the first people in the Santa Anas and by name they would be known as the Juaneños and the Gabrielinos. These were people who lived both on the coastal plain and the mountains and in the Santa Anas their rancherias could be found in places like Hidden Ranch, up Black Star Canyon; in the Los Pinos country; at the mouth of Gubernador Canyon. Indian trails lined over the mountains following Black Star Canyon into the Corona country; the Horsethief Trail ran from Trabuco to Los

Pinos and down into the Elsinore region; the San Juan Canyon generally followed the design of the Ortega Highway but made a more direct descent into the Elsinore basin.

In 1769 Don Gaspar de Portola, together with such notables as Fathers Juan Crespi and Francisco Gomez, Lieutenant Pedro Fages, and a small expedition started from San Diego on an overland journey to Monterey. They passed through the edge of the Santa Ana Mountains in the latter part of July that year.

The first baptism of Indians in California took place at the edge of the Santa Ana Mountains, at a stream-side rancheria on what was to be named Cristianitos Canyon, near the San Mateo Canyon. Here two dying Indian children were baptized by Fr. Crespi.

Portola's camps through the Santa Ana foothills were made at the Plano Trabuco, at Tomato Springs behind El Toro, on Santiago Creek and then on to the Santa Ana River.

The Portola party handed the area some of its first place names: Santiago Creek; Trabuco (the Spanish word means "blunderbuss," the Portola soldiers lost such a weapon here); Santa Ana River (the padres called it *el dulcisimo nombre de Jesus de los Temblores* because of the earthquake they felt at the camp).

The mountains here, themselves, would not only be known as the Santa Anas. Font called them the Sierra del Trabuco; an early map labeled the ranges as the Sierra de Santiago.

The mountain country had won its present name by 1860, however, and no arguments have been presented since the 1861 survey.

Still there were other place name disagreements. The tallest mountain peak here, Santiago, or Santiago Peak, has been labeled variously. Most affectionately it is called Old Saddleback—not Saddleback, mind you, but *Old* Saddleback. The geographical term of course applies to the saddle that exists between Santiago

Santiago Peak, tallest mountain in the Santa Ana range, is frequently dusted with snow in the winter.

Peak, 5691 feet, and Modjeska Peak, 5470 feet. From some angles the saddle is most pronounced. From other spots in the range it almost vanishes. Historian Terry E. Stephenson perpetuated the colorful name with his fine regional book *Shadows of Old Saddleback*.

Josiah Dwight Whitney, state geologist, climbed the mountain in the early days and stuck the name Mt. Downey on the prominence. It was a name that didn't take, however. A more persistent name, usually given by the folks on "the other side," or the east side of the range, is Temescal Mountain.

In spite of repeated stories to the effect, there were never two mission sites for Mission San Juan Capistrano. However it was founded twice. The first time, in 1775, Father Fermin Lausen set up a cross, hung some bells and dedicated the ground. Word came of the Indian uprising in San Diego. Father Lausen ordered the bells buried, hurried to San Diego. It was more than a year later, on November 1, 1776, that Fr. Serra came back, had the bells exhumed, and recited the founding service.

The confusion comes from the plot of land referred to as the Mision Vieja or Mission Viejo where a small sub-*asistencia* was built. There were never two mission sites.

Mission Viejo lands run into the edge of the Santa Ana Mountains. The rancho was granted to Augustin Olvera in 1845; it went to John Forster who patented the 46,433 acres in 1866.

In time the Spanish ranchos blossomed. In addition to the Mission Viejo, there were the Santiago de Santa Ana, the Cañada de los Alisos, the Lomas de Santiago, the Potrero Los Pinos and the Trabuco.

One of the largest land holdings in Southern California, the Irvine Ranch, evolved from two of these: Rancho Lomas de Santiago and Rancho San Joaquin. Title of the Irvine Ranch was contested by the railroad and by homesteaders, but the property, which was said to have consisted of 115,000 acres at one time, remained intact.

There are stories of bear hunts (the last grizzly was killed here in 1907) and deer hunts in the mountains in the Spanish-Mexican period. The Mexicans—and perhaps even the Indians—mined placer gold from Lucas Canyon very early but it must have been a shallow lode. Recent prospecting there has yielded nothing.

Shortly after California became a state in the union of states the Santa Ana mountain country knew a wave of outlawry. According to documents, Don Juan (John) Forster was particularly plagued by the badmen in 1852.

One of the worst of these ruffians was Juan Flores and in 1855 he was captured and packed off to prison for ten years. Yet two years later he was out of jail and was back in the Santa Ana country, terrorizing the countryside. He led a gang of outlaws and they raided into San Juan Capistrano one day. Here they killed a storekeeper, vandalized shops, stole horses, shot up the town and headed for the Santa Anas.

In time word of the outrage got to Los Angeles and from there Sheriff John Barton, with six deputies, rode south.

Flores and his gang met Barton in the foothills of the San Joaquin. It was a clever ambush. Barton and three deputies were killed. The other lawmen rode for twelve miles before they found sanctuary.

The people of the Southland were stunned at the easy comings and goings of the badman. A large "get Flores" posse was organized. Don Andrea Pico, along with picked lancers, Indian scouts, tough Californians, went after Flores. They captured him in a cave in the Santa Ana Mountains, hauled him and his confederates to Rancho San Joaquin. That night Flores, along with several of his men, slipped away. Pico, back in the Santa Anas looking for the rest of the gang, promptly hanged the Flores men who

The Irvine Park area is heavily grown with giant oak trees.

were still being held prisoner, started looking for the outlaw again.

Flores was finally captured miles away from the Santa Anas, all the way out in the San Fernando Valley. He was taken to Los Angeles and was executed in a public hanging.

There were other outlaws who met their end suddenly at the end of a rope in the Santa Ana Mountains, but history has touched on them lightly. Left behind is a hanging tree of doubtful authenticity, several "robbers' roosts" and stories of buried bandit treasure.

In counting the early pioneers you must list J. E. Pleasants and Samuel Shrewsbury. Their lands included the oak- and alder-grown canyons and the fresh-running streams along the western face of the Santa Anas. One of their favorite creek bottoms was the place known as *Cañada de la Madera* (the canyon of the timber) and it was here on a fall day in 1877 that Hank Smith and William Curry of Santa Ana found the translucent blue and white quartz ore that carried an unmistakable hint of silver.

Smith and Curry had the quartz assayed: $60 a ton was what it ran. They filed on one mine; then, finding more of the translucent, stained quartz, filed on another. Word leaked out. The country was still filled with all manner of prospectors—there had been a flood of them into California since 1848. These prospectors began to file down into the Santa Anas and seek out Cañada de la Madera. In a few days 500 claims were staked and the silver boom camp with the fitting name of Silverado was born.

Coal, of all things, was also found in the canyon at about the same time, and this had commercial value. Miners at the coal strike wanted to have their own town and they called the camp Harrisburg in honor of their mine superintendent. The post office people shook their heads. There was already another Harrisburg in California. So the name Carbondale was suggested, accepted, and Silverado Canyon had a pair of boom camps.

Two stages ran daily from Silverado to Los Angeles and three stages made the trek into nearer Santa Ana. Newly arrived miners who found no hotel to greet them in the canyon slept on the ground under the oaks and sycamores and alders and the population in the canyon inched up to 1500.

Neither of the boom camps was destined to be a bonanza. By 1881 the excitement was over. The stages had stopped running and the stores and saloons had closed. Carbondale went down without a trace and by 1883 even the die-hard post office shuttered its doors. By the end of the year the canyon was deserted.

Old-timers can remember camping up in the Silverado Canyon area in 1910, and they report that they remember its being deserted then. "You had to take an axe with you to get through. New growth had come up in the old wagon road. It was hard even then to get in there with a team." But by World War I the canyon knew inhabitants again. Some of these first returnees were living in the old boom camp shacks. Some were raising bees. Since then the canyon has known nothing but growth. There is a pleasant community here now; there is a post office again, modern homes, paved road, even piped water.

Trabuco Canyon, with its unusual place name, has a stranger tributary. Holy Jim Canyon takes off from the upper end of the Trabuco and runs toward Santiago Peak.

This attractive canyon, now dotted with pleasant cabins in its lower reaches, and blessed with a fine trail up the middle region, was named in honor of "Cussin' Jim" Smith, the early-day beekeeper in the area. Because so much of Smith's language was punctuated with colorful profanity, he easily earned the name Cussin' Jim, and the name soon became attached to the canyon where he lived. But in 1900 when the government map makers were putting down on paper the place names on the streams and mountains, they vetoed Cussin' Jim in favor of Holy Jim. It

*West of the Santiago Canyon Road unfolds
some beautiful foothill country.*

doesn't mean the same thing at all and purists among the historians have lamented the fact ever since. But Holy Jim it has remained.

In the middle Trabuco another mining venture dozes. This is the Tin Mine, or Tin Mines property, once called the Old Borden Mine, where tin was actually dug for in the old days. Tin was also sought on the Temescal Valley—or east—side of the mountains. There is a Tin Mine Canyon, too, just south of Corona in the Santa Anas.

It was a strange Russian emigrant, a recluse who called himself "William Williams of Williams Canyon," who is credited with first inviting Madame Helena Modjeska, the famed actress, into the Santa Ana Mountains' foothills for a look at the fair land.

Madame Modjeska came, fell in love with the place, named the wooded site "The Forest of Arden" after a famous Shakespearean scene. She built a home here which was "elegantly furnished with antique furniture made of mahogany and other rare woods; the floors were covered with rugs of intricate pattern and skins of wild beasts; and every nook and cranny was filled with expensive articles of vertu, curios, ornaments and various kinds of relics." The home is on private property today and is closed to the public.

Trabuco District of the Cleveland National Forest. Most of the Santa Ana Mountains lie within the boundaries of the Trabuco District of the Cleveland National Forest. The Trabuco Forest Reserve was created in 1892, was first tacked on to the San Jacinto Forest Reserve to form the Cleveland National Forest in 1908 and later stayed with the southern Forest when the San Jacinto country was separated from the Cleveland National Forest in 1925.

There are 163,244 gross acres in the Trabuco District of the

Cleveland National Forest inside a linear boundary of 88.5 miles. There are 124,473 acres of Forest Service land within the area: they lie in Orange County, Riverside County and San Diego County.

Like all Southern California units of the Forest Service, the main job of the agency here is to manage the watershed.

The district office is located at 2045 North Broadway in Santa Ana.

Other ranger stations on the district are located at Corona, Silverado Canyon, Temescal, El Cariso, San Juan, Tenaja and Trabuco.

There are improved Forest Service campgrounds at Upper Trabuco, Lower Trabuco, El Cariso, Upper San Juan, Lower San Juan, and Tenaja. There are separate picnic facilities at Trabuco and El Cariso with smaller, less improved camps at Fisherman's Camp, near Tenaja; Morrell Potrero; Los Pinos Potrero; and Oak Flats.

The north half of the district is within the annual fire closure, which runs from about June to the first appreciable rainfall. The south half of the district is open all year but supports fewer roads. Hunting, in season, is allowed in the south half. Many of the Forest Service truck trails cross private land and are hence gated all year and closed to public entry.

In comparison with the other mountains of Southern California the Santa Ana Mountains are not nearly as tall. Santiago Peak only lifts to a shade over 5000 feet, about half the height of San Antonio, San Gorgonio and San Jacinto. As a result, most of the mountain country is covered with the 100-odd elfin varieties of flora that make up the chaparral. In some places there are stands of sturdy manzanita. In the stream bottoms maples, sycamores, oaks, alders and bay put on a show. There are comparatively few areas of conifers on the district—but here you'll find big cone spruce (a cousin to the Douglas fir) and the Coulter pine.

69

There is a complex of electronic installations an
Forest Service lookout tower atop Santiago Pe

West of O'Neill Park, on the way to El Toro, the
fields can be loaded with spring wildflowers.

Visitors to the Santa Anas will find the mountains cooler than the valley lands, but not the sharp contrast they might find at Chilao in the San Gabriels, or at Idyllwild in the San Jacintos. In summer fire hazards are great.

Still one of the best viewing spots to be found in all of Southern California is that from Santiago Peak, where the Forest Service has one of its two Trabuco District fire lookouts (the other is on Margarita Peak south of the Ortega Highway).

From Santiago Peak there are 360 degrees of delightful viewing. To the north the community of Corona stands plain, and beyond, past other valley cities, is the blue-purple wall of the San Gabriels. This runs, like a barrier, to the east, making its familiar dip at the Cajon Pass, then, as the San Bernardino range, runs on east until it crests at Mt. San Gorgonio.

To the east is the separate mass of the San Jacintos; to the southeast, the Palomar Country and the Lagunas.

To the west, through the haze and fog, the tops of the Channel Islands are frequently visible.

In the Trabuco District of the Cleveland National Forest only a couple of streams are full enough in the spring to allow fish planting: the Trabuco, the Silverado and the San Mateo. Deer are numerous in the mile-high mountains and old-timers and ranchers still claim they see tracks of mountain lions. (During the Silverado boom days a hunter by the name of Cash Harvey killed 120 deer in a single season to supply meat for the hungry mining camp.)

Bobcat are frequently spotted in the mountain by hikers and patrolmen. There are coyotes, foxes, raccoons, skunks and possums.

At one time—it is said—condors nested in the Santa Anas. On the road to Trabuco there is a strange geographical landmark called Vulture Crags.

A fire permit is required for picnickers or campers using the stoves in the Forest Service campgrounds. Such a permit can be obtained at any ranger station and from most Forest Service personnel on patrol.

And students of the district map, that the Forest Service will give you without charge, will note that there are many *potreros* in the district. In your Spanish dictionary you'll find that *potrero* means pasture lands. There are many such on the southern half of Trabuco District: Morrell Potrero, Verdugo Potrero, Los Pinos Potrero, Indian Potrero, etc. These are flatlands, usually, where the trees and chaparral have receded, offering perfect grazing lands—and this is how they are utilized. Most of the *potreros* lie on private lands within the National Forest boundaries.

Many of the names on the land on the east side salute the early day settlers: Leach Canyon, Morrell Canyon, Decker Canyon, McVicker Canyon, Rice Canyon, Mayhew Canyon, Anderson Canyon, Bixby Canyon, Brown Canyon, Bedford Canyon, Mabey Canyon, etc.

Many of the place names on the west side of the range bear Spanish names, reflecting the flavor of the early-day settlement: San Mateo, San Juan, Trabuco, Santiago, Verdugo Canyon, etc.

The well-traveled Black Star Canyon was once called Cañada de los Indios—Indian Canyon—and there was at least one rancheria site up its run.

Stephenson, in his excellent book, writes of events and landmarks in Peters Canyon, the fascinating Canyon de la Horca, Limestone Canyon, Black Star, Cañada de la Campana—and all his accounts make delightful reading.

XI THE SANTIAGO CANYON COUNTRY

An assortment of roads reach back into the Santa Ana Mountains and touch on many historic sites.

FROM the coastal plain of Orange County the Santa Ana Mountains loom close at hand, pleasant and inviting. They look taller than they are but less wild than the experts know them to be. There are all manner of roads here, good paved highways along the edges, a trio of paved roads piercing deep into the range, and one major highway crossing the mountains right through its middle. There are unpaved roads, some dating back to old wagon track days, others built by the CCC's in the depression days. Some lead back to private land, one—the Main Divide Truck Trail — walks the wooded spine of the Santa Anas from one end to the other. Not all of these dirt roads are open to the public; some are closed only in fire season, others are gated because they cross private property. Still this is an interesting mountain region to explore by road—paved and unpaved.

From the extension of Chapman Avenue east out of Orange, the first main mountain area road begins.

Labeled S18, it runs to Irvine Park, a major area recreation center.

This 180-acre county park was the gift to the county by the Irvine Ranch; it lies along the Santiago Creek drainage and is shaded by sycamores and California live oaks.

Irvine Park offers picnicking, boating, bike rentals, baseball, and the charm of a tree-shaded out-of-doors with room enough. There is a small zoo here.

Irvine Park can be surprisingly cool when the rest of Orange County bakes under the summer sun.

73

Just outside the park there are private riding stables and a five-and-one-half-mile riding trail.

Past Irvine Park, the Santiago Canyon Road, as it is called here, reaches toward the southeast. It climbs, runs past private Irvine Lake, where boating and fishing are offered in season, comes to a four-way intersection.

Black Star Canyon Road. From this intersection the Black Star Canyon Road runs to the northeast. It is only paved for a short distance. The road is closed in the fire season mainly by county ordinance. In the winter and early spring it is open to the public and is a most pleasant drive. It climbs past Hidden Ranch—the site of an old Indian rancheria. Remember the canyon was once called Cañada de los Indios. Hidden off the road is a spectacular deep gorge.

The road climbs in a businesslike manner and timid flatland drivers should stay off. At the summit there is a collection of electronic equipment—you'll find this on several peaks in the Santa Anas—and then offers a straight down the hill shot on the far side into Corona. This latter is called Skyline Drive and is ungated. Other side roads leading down the mountain are likely to lead you to a locked gate at the bottom. You may drive south, along the Main Divide Truck Trail, all the way to Santiago Peak, and once here you can leave the mountain country via the road down Silverado Canyon.

Resume Intersection. The road east from our four-way intersection leads up Silverado Canyon, past a fantastic modern church, past the site of vanished Carbondale, into the summer home and cabin community of Silverado. The mouth of the canyon that holds most of the old silver mines is not marked, but you'll find an historic marker at the end of the pavement. It reads:

74

SILVERADO

Located in Cañada de la Madera (Timber Canyon) Silverado was a mining boom town founded in 1878 when silver was discovered nearby. During the colorful life of the boom, 1878-1881, miners, flocking to the area, established a thriving community, served daily by stage from Los Angeles and Santa Ana.

Here, at the end of the pavement, is a gate. During the fire season the Forest Service keeps it locked. In the winter it is open and it is possible for visitors to drive the eight miles on up to the peak of Santiago.

This is an enjoyable drive, ranging through the sycamores, maples and oaks of the stream bottom, past springs, up through the healthy chaparral into areas of almost pure manzanita, and higher, into the region of big cone spruce and Coulter pine. The road is rough and dusty in places—all unpaved—but never really spooky and hundreds make the drive each winter, weather permitting, to the top of Santiago.

As the road nears the summit it passes Modjeska Peak with a small scattering of electronic devices, crosses the saddle of Old Saddleback that lies between the two major peaks here, and then climbs via a post-CCC road onto Santiago.

Here there is a jungle of electronic towers, radio relays, power and telephone company installations. By count more than 125 separate operators have business on the summit of Santiago. Atop it all, perched on the roof of a telephone company building, is the tall Forest Service's lookout tower, all metal and glass.

This tower, like others of the Forest Service, is open to the public from 9 a.m. to 5 p.m. daily. Like other such towers it also serves as the lookout's home—act accordingly.

There is a commanding view of much of the Southland from

75

The Tucker Bird Sanctuary—open to the public—is located at the end of the Modjeska Canyon Road.

here and the lookouts, between their duties, will be happy to point out the various landmarks to you. You'll recognize Mt. San Antonio (Old Baldy) in the San Gabriel range, Mt. San Gorgonio and Mt. San Jacinto. Without too much trouble you'll sort out the Palomar Mountains from the Lagunas. You can see deep into San Diego County along the coast. At sea, there is the island world of San Clemente. Northwest the whole Los Angeles basin unfolds.

The road runs on past Santiago Peak along the Main Divide Truck Trail toward the Ortega Highway, but it is gated at the far end—private land. Still this avenue leads back to historic Bear Springs, the jumpoff down onto the Holy Jim Trail, and past the gate, onto Los Pinos Potrero. It finally reaches the Ortega Highway just west of El Cariso Station. The road is signed at this northern end: "Main Divide Truck Trail."

On the back side, the east side, two or three roads drop down into the Temescal Valley or into the Elsinore area. These all cross private property and are gated.

Resume Intersection. The road to the south here follows along Santiago Creek toward Modjeska Canyon.

There is some attractive creek-bottom land here, outside the National Forest, then the side road centers into Modjeska Canyon, runs past the Modjeska homesite, a collection of houses, and back, just at the end of the pavement, to the Tucker Bird Sanctuary.

The Dorothy Mae Tucker Bird Sanctuary was originated by Long Beach banker B. F. Tucker who gave the property to the California Audubon Society following the death of his wife.

A year-round parade of hummingbirds to the site is the big attraction here, though bird watchers have listed 140 different California birds that have been seen in the canyon, including six

There is a small lake at Irvine Park.

hummingbird species. The bird sanctuary is open daily without charge. An attendant is on hand to help with bird identification. Many youth and school groups call here.

Past Modjeska Canyon the highway points on to the south, climbs Modjeska Grade, runs through oaks and alders to Cook's Corners. Here we turn inland, to the east, back along Live Oak Canyon, to O'Neill Park.

This park was a gift to the county in June of 1950 from the sprawling O'Neill Ranch. There are 270 acres here of alder, sycamore, and oak-shaded hill and flatlands. Camping is allowed here—it is not at Irvine Park—but campers are advised to bring their own firewood and furniture. Trailers are allowed. Picnicking is free but a fee is charged for camping.

O'Neill Park has an incredible use—people have visited the site from all fifty states and from foreign countries in recent years.

From O'Neill Park the road runs on east, comes to the store and post office at Trabuco Canyon. A brief spur road runs back to the north into a residential area. The right hand road leads into Trabuco Canyon.

Almost immediately the pavement stops. Wise canyon dwellers shudder when they think of the press of visitors attractive shaded Trabuco Canyon would get if the road was paved all the way to the end. The rough, dusty dirt road keeps out many would-be visitors. It may be a blessing of sorts.

The road bumps along Trabuco Canyon—always pretty much a flatland drive—finally enters an area of great stream-bottom shade trees and comes to Lower Trabuco Forest Service campground. In the late winter and spring there is a busy stream here. Up above the Fish and Game people dump trout into the watercourse and spring finds anglers on every rock. By late summer and fall the fish have all been caught and the stream has dried up. Sere grass stands under the alders and crisp leaves carpet the ground. But even then the wooded canyon has great charm. It suffers greatly from too many people—but it is so attractive that it is understandable.

There are about 55 cabins in Trabuco Canyon and tributary Holy Jim Canyon—some of them quite striking, but most of them old and dated in their appearance. There is a volunteer fire department here, but a Forest Service guard station is situated in the canyon and these patrolmen keep an eye on the dangers of fire.

There is another campground, Upper Trabuco, above the fork in the road into Holy Jim Canyon. A trail runs from the end of Holy Jim Canyon up to Bear Springs on the Main Divide Truck Trail.

Resume Highway. Back at Cook's Corners our southward-trending highway crosses farmland, passes small ranches and curves to the west toward El Toro and the Santa Ana Freeway. It ceases to be of interest to us at this point.

*From one of the turnouts along the Ortega Highway
you can look down at the lake and
community of Elsinore.*

XII THE ORTEGA HIGHWAY

The Ortega Highway, named after one of Portola's soldiers, crosses the waist of the Santa Ana Mountains.

From San Juan Capistrano State Highway 74 climbs over the waist of the Santa Ana Mountains, affording high-gear automobile travel to Elsinore. It is called the Ortega Highway locally after Jose Francisco Ortega, a sergeant in the Portola expedition into the area in 1769.

Out of San Juan Capistrano it first runs through farmland and a growing residential area, past grazing lands, some of it belonging to the Mission Viejo—Mision Vieja—and finally enters the Trabuco District of the Cleveland National Forest at the Forest's San Juan Station. Nearby is the historic hot springs, now on private land, where heated water bubbles from the rocks of the Santa Ana Mountains.

This is the foothill country of the Santa Anas and the road climbs steadily. The Forest Service campgrounds of Lower San Juan and Upper San Juan—the latter recently modernized—are passed.

Still climbing, the Ortega Highway passes the side road to the Main Divide Truck Trail—a route back to Santiago Peak. The road is gated, however, since it crosses private land.

Near the top of the rise here is the El Cariso complex. There is a ranger station, a modern Forest Service campground, a delightful nature walk (it will take you about an hour to make the guided tour, a brochure is available; groups may arrange for the guide services of a ranger).

The nearby highway summit—2,666 feet—explains why there

81

are no conifers along this highest stretch of the Ortega Highway. But canyon live oaks are plentiful.

Before the Ortega Highway was built the area was used mainly for mining—the old Dominion Mine with many shafts and tunnels is nearby—and was reached by the old Perry Road which crawled up steeply from Elsinore.

There are a couple of fine view points of the Elsinore country on the Ortega Highway as it starts its descent: Jameson Point and Ortega Terrace are a pair of them. Nearby you"ll notice that the canyons are named and signed. Slater Canyon, Guthrie Canyon, Edwards Canyon, Harlan Canyon, Brooks Canyon—all named after Forest Service fire fighters who were killed in the Decker Fire of 1959.

The view of Elsinore and its sometimes lake is impressive all the way to the bottom of the grade.

XIII THE EAST SIDE OF THE SANTA ANAS

The Tenaja ranger station has few visitors but by spring and by fall this is delightful country.

FOR THE most part there are not any through ungated roads into the Santa Anas from Corona south to Murrieta with two exceptions which have been noted elsewhere. The Skyline Drive, a dirt road, reaches up out of Corona toward the north end of the mountains. This area is usually closed in the summer. Then the Ortega Highway, paved State Highway 74, crosses the middle of the Santa Ana range.

But it is not until you get down to Murrieta that you find an open road into the Forest Service land. Much of the approach is across private land, but this county road is kept open.

From Murrieta turn off Palomar Avenue running south from Elsinore (it becomes Washington Avenue) on San Mateo Road. Turn right, toward the rim of mountains not far distant. Paved for only the first half mile after the turnoff, the San Mateo Road passes alfalfa fields, horse ranches, rural dwellings, and reaches the chaparraled Elsinore Mountains (the southward running arm of the Santa Anas).

The climb up this edge of mountains is neither overly steep nor winding. The first summit is quickly gained and the first of the attractive *potreros* appear.

This is all cattle land, part of the Santa Rosa Ranch of the Vail Company, here a 47,000-acre holding. While our access byway is a county road and county maintained, the land to either side is private property; trespassing and hunting are prohibited.

*An attractive road runs through the potrero country
from Murrieta to the Tenaja area.*

*Great oaks decorated the land near the
Tenaja ranger station.*

Along this stretch the road runs level, climbs and dips only slightly on its run to Tenaja. This is oak country and there are fourteen different varieties in the area. But the canyon live oak here assumes heroic size, casting a long shadow, shading the road, dotting the pale green meadowland with its deep olive-green bulk. Kingly sycamores also grow in the *potrero* region.

It is approximately 12 miles from the turnoff in Murrieta to a road junction near Tenaja. From the road junction the ranger station lies off to the right about half a mile. We are in the Trabuco District of the Cleveland National Forest now. There is a small campground behind the Tenaja station, situated among the streamside boulders. There is evidence of previous Indian occupation at this site—several bedrock mortars are visible. The Indians who lived here—Luiseño or Juaneño—made a good living from the acorns and the game in the area. Arrowheads have been found nearby.

From Tenaja station a dirt road runs northwest for about five miles to the San Mateo Creek bottom and a small streamside campground called Fisherman's Camp. Best to check at the Tenaja ranger station about the condition of this byway before you start your descent to the San Mateo—the track is sometimes in sad shape.

There is a wonderful but spooky dirt road that runs from Tenaja south into the De Luz region. It is not advised for those who come unglued on a narrow mountain road with a sheer dropoff on one side. But for old hands at back country exploring, this is among the best.

From the road junction just shy of the Tenaja Station drive on west. About a mile farther on, near the Johnson Ranch which sits off to the right with some eucalyptus trees shading the old buildings, there is another junction. Take a hard left here, along the road marked "Margarita Peak Lookout." A few yards down

85

*There is a spooky mountain road that runs from
Tenaja down into the De Luz region.*

*Between De Luz and Murrieta there are several places
where oaks hang over the good dirt road.*

this road, at another fork, turn left again, this time onto the De Luz Road. De Luz, by the sign, is seven miles away.

There is a brief stretch of *potrero* country here, some private ranches hidden behind coppices of oak and chaparral.

Then the road pinches in slightly, the turns are sharper, the grades are steeper. There is a corner to duck around, with a steep dropoff on the left and a great pale overhanging rock on the right.

Though it's downhill all the way to De Luz, it is a fairly gradual descent. There are some fine overlooks into De Luz-Gavilan Mountain country to the south. You'll not find that you have a traffic problem.

This is Cottonwood Creek we are bordering, and when the canyon bottom is reached the thickets of oak close in over the top of the road.

There is water, even a pond where frogs make a racket in their marshy hideout. Pavement resumes.

Here is a junction, with a sign pointing east to Murrieta, twelve miles away. Just beyond is a large, two-story white house and on its mailbox the sign "De Luz." That's all there is to the foothill community. A post office was established here in the 1800's but has not been active for many years.

There is a pleasant return to Murrieta along De Luz Creek. Turn east past the De Luz school, leave the pavement again, run through some attractive stretches where oaks hang over the byway.

There are many pleasant vistas here: an abandoned farm with a patiently working windmill still standing sentry in a weed-grown field; a great windrow of white-barked eucalyptus; an old orange orchard; deep thickets of oak where the road ducks and hides.

Finally the byway climbs out of De Luz Creek, enters chaparral country, and in such a setting regains Murrieta.

If you were to follow the paved road south from De Luz you would come into the ranching area of Fallbrook.

East of De Luz there are some beautiful windrows of white-barked eucalyptus trees.

XIV THE TRAILS

Several trails scramble up through the chaparral and pines of the Santa Ana Mountains.

WHILE there are 102 miles of trail on the Trabuco District of the Cleveland National Forest, not more than 25 miles are regularly maintained.

The principal trails, then, are the following:

The Holy Jim Trail. The most heavily used trail is the one from Holy Jim Canyon, which lies up the Trabuco Canyon road, up the hill to Bear Springs.

From the end of the road in Holy Jim Canyon, at the end of the cabin area, there is a wide "side-by-side" path carved out of the canyon bottom for about nine-tenths of a mile. In the spring, particularly, when the stream is running full, this walk has exceptional charm. Many youth groups use this first stretch of the Holy Jim trail as a nature walk.

Beyond the wider portion of the trail, the course leaves Holy Jim Canyon curving to the northwest slightly and works at climbing. The distance of the trail is about two miles. Bear Springs, at the top, is on the Main Divide Truck Trail that runs from Santiago Peak south down to the Ortega Highway.

Cold Springs Trail. From the end of the Cold Springs road—this trail in the southwest corner of the District reaches back into the San Mateo River drainage and on through to Indian Potrero.

Hot Springs Canyon Trail. A trail runs from Hot Springs Canyon near the San Juan ranger station on the Ortega Highway, north to Los Pinos Potrero on the Main Divide Truck Trail.

To make your hiking outing more successful and more fun, obtain first a copy of the district map from the Forest Service. And check with a local ranger on the condition of the trails you plan to hike. He can tell you if there are any bad spots you should watch or avoid. Many older trails in the mountains have not been maintained since the 1930's.

XV INTRODUCTION TO THE PALOMAR COUNTRY

The land of the giant 200-inch telescope also supports a deep wooded region, pleasant mountain valleys and a curious Primitive Area.

THE LARGEST telescope in the world stands here, a mute thing; a great dome of silver that moves only when the shadows are long and whose skyward-pointing doors, like the mouth of a great beast, yawn at sunset.

The largest telescope in the world stands here on this sudden mountain flatland and around it is some of the fairest mountain country in Southern California: quiet country where, by autumn, the drop of an acorn makes a racket; tall cedar country, up and down country grown with Coulter pine and black oak and chaparral.

The Indians knew this land and their game trails ran over the mountain mass. There are places where the knowledgeable can find bedrock mortar holes in the granite rocks of the mountain; arrowheads have been found. The Indians had a name for the place: they called it "Paauw," and the word meant mountain.

When the Spanish came to the mountain country and walked it and made their crude notes they saw the flocks of band-tailed pigeons that roost here and eat the acorns and the Spanish called the place "Palomar," meaning pigeon roost.

After the gringos came there was a time when the mountain was called Smith Mountain for Joseph Smith who had built a cabin in the hills. Smith was murdered in the 1880's but the mountain carried his name until 1901, when, in response to the petition cf residents, the U. S. Geographical Board returned the name Palomar to the mountain.

Here we will call the transverse range that starts at the San Diego County-Riverside County border and slants southeast to Lake Henshaw, the Palomar Mountains. It is actually made up of at least three different mountain uplifts, the Agua Tibia, the Aguanga, the Palomar itself. But as a place, the whole range can be called the Palomar Mountains.

The tallest peak in the expanse of high country is unimaginatively called High Point. The knob here is 6140 feet high and atop it is a new 67-foot metal Forest Service lookout tower.

Much of these Palomar Mountains are within the jurisdiction of the Palomar District of the Cleveland National Forest. But the 1900-acre Palomar State Park is here, as well. There is a county park, and much private land. Some of the latter dates back to homestead days and is still within the ownership of the original families.

There is a small net of paved road across the top of the mountains, plus a wide assortment of unpaved byways. Most of these latter are Forest Service fire access roads, and many of them are closed to the public; this is due partly to the seasonal fire closure and partly to the fact that the side roads cross private land.

Actually the first road into the mountains was etched in the Indian-Spanish period when an ox trail was chiseled out onto timbered Palomar to get cedar beams for the old Pala *asistencia*. This was virtually a one-time road, however, and it took pioneer Joseph Smith to fashion the first regularly used route up the hill. This course had some incredibly steep pitches, some of them 30-degree grades. Drivers, coming down the incline, were forced to strap metal plates on the bottom of their wagon wheels to prevent runaways. The Smith byway was all but abandoned when the county built a road into the Palomar country at a point fur-

*View of the Palomar observatory site showing the
200-inch, 48-inch and 18-inch domes.*

ther south. Mail riders continued to use the old road for a while but even these tough horsemen dismounted and walked up the steep pitches.

About 1900, when demands grew for a better road into the scenic mountain country, a seven-mile road was built up along the mountain's northwest flank. This was the famous Nate Harrison Grade and its pays homage to a former Negro slave by the name of Nathan Harrison who lived in a cabin part way up the incline. A plaque marks the site of his home.

This road has been greatly maligned. It has been called hazardous, and horribly steep and narrow, while today it is none of these things. It is much better to drive it down than up, but the old sharp switchbacks are gone. There are some hair-raising drop-offs, but the road is wide enough to allow cars to pass almost all the way along its run. It is actually an interesting old avenue to explore. It is being paved at the Pauma Valley end.

The Highway to the Stars, the present road up to Palomar, was started in 1935, before work began on the big observatory project.

It was earlier than this, however, that the idea for the State Park was born. As far back as 1932 the state of California started buying up parcels of land. The park today is 1900 acres, and includes some of the most attractive mountain country in the area.

There are three camping sites in the park: Cedar Grove, Palomar Mountain and Doane Valley. There is a fee for use of the facilities. There is a small lake here that is stocked by the state for public fishing. There are several school and organizational camps in the vicinity.

The main tourist attraction on the hill, of course, is the great observatory.

The site was dedicated in 1948; before that day there were years of preparation as the 200-inch mirror was poured and polished, and as the great dome and its precision machineries were

94

*The 200-inch Hale telescope pointing to zenith. Interior
of dome is not open to the general public.*

fashioned. Since its first year the Palomar telescope has peered
into the far corners of the universe.

Actually there are three telescope domes on the mountains and
there are plans to build a fourth. In addition to the giant Hale
telescope, there are two smaller Schmidt instruments.

The road to the observatory ends at a large parking lot. Nearby is a small museum where illuminated photographs of the telescope and other interesting objects are displayed. Entrance into
the interior of the great Hale dome is not permitted. Visitors may
enter an interior viewing post and through a heavy glass window
look in at the workings of the world's largest telescope.

The Palomar District of the Cleveland National Forest. The Palomar District of the Cleveland National Forest includes not only

the Palomar Mountains, but an area of high country between State Highway 79, the Anza-Borrego Desert State Park, and the Los Coyotes Indian Reservation. Also within the Palomar District is the mountain area between Palomar and Ramona; and some of the National Forest land around Julian.

The Palomar area proper is within the Forest Service's seasonal fire closure. However, the region frequently gets more than 35 inches of rainfall in a season.

One of the features of the Palomar District is the Agua Tibia Primitive Area. On maps—even Forest Service maps—you will find this identified as the Agua Tibia Wilderness Area, the Agua Tibia Wild Area. Both are incorrect. It is the Agua Tibia Primitive Area and it was established by the Chief of the Forest Service in 1931.

There are 37,234 acres in the Agua Tibia Primitive Area, of this 27,608 acres are National Forest lands, 1284 acres are private land, and 8324 acres make up a "Mission Indian Reserve" under a *temporary* Indian withdrawal that dates back to 1903.

This latter "reserve" is a curious establishment. It is not assigned to any particular Indian tribe in the San Diego County area although not far away, in the Pauma Valley country, are the Pala Indians, the Rincon Indian Reservation, the La Jolla Indian Reservation, the Yuima Indian Reservation, the Pechanga Indian Reservation and the Pauma Indian Reservation. In spite of repeated attempts this anomoly has not been resolved. Indians use the land in a limited way—mostly they like to come here in December and chop Christmas trees. This is a privilege allowed no one else (unless they own mountain land). The Indians also hunt and do some limited logging in the area. The Mission Indian Reserve (or Mission Indian Reservation, as it appears on some maps, and neither is technically correct—it is a withdrawal) is beautiful mountain country heavily grown with white fir, incense

96

cedar, big cone spruce, Coulter and Jeffrey pine. The black oak grow to magnificent heights here. Wild azaleas shoulder out from damp banks and the bracken fern is thick.

Unlike all other wilderness, wild and primitive areas within the Forest Service here in California that I know of, this one is pierced by a maintained dirt road. This, as the existence of the strange withdrawal, has caused concern among conservationists and foresters alike. One of the features of the primitive area here is that there is a stand of chaparral that has not been burned over for at least 100 years. Some of the species are 14 feet tall.

The road that runs into the primitive area, across Morgan Hill and out to Agua Tibia Mountain and beyond, down to Highway 79 is closed to the public. It has been left there as a fire access road. Some of the canyons on the northwest shoulder of the district are very precipitous. Fire here, in virgin chaparral, is a terrible thing to contemplate.

Improved Forest Service campgrounds are located at Dripping Springs, on the far north edge of the mountains; at Palomar Observatory, just south of the observatory atop the mountain; at Oak Grove, on State Highway 79 on the east side of the range; at Crestline, at the top of the Highway to the Stars; and San Luis Rey, on State Highway 76 on the southwest side of the Palomars.

There are picnic grounds at Crestline (San Diego County has a small picnic-campground nearby). There are several hunters' camps in the back country.

Ranger stations, where you can obtain a fire permit or a Forest Service district map of the area, are located at Dripping Springs, Oak Grove, Lake Henshaw, and Palomar.

Address for the district headquarters is 732 N. Broadway, Escondido, California.

Forest Service lookouts are located at High Point in the Palomar country, and at Hot Springs, to the east in the Los Coyotes

Indian Reservation. There is a state lookout at Boucher Hill west of the state park.

Indian Reservations. There are five Indian Reservations in the Palomar area. These are:

The Pechanga Indian Reservation is located at the northwest corner of the mountains here. It lies in Riverside County at the north end of the Agua Tibia Mountains. Some of the lands are alloted here, with a total of 4125 acres. Population on the Pechanga is only 10 and the lands are used primarily for grazing.

The historic Pala Indian Reservation lies south of the Pechanga, still on the west side of the Palomar Mountains. There are 7800 acres here and a population of 180. The lands are used partly for grazing and in addition some of the Reservation contains irrigated lands suitable for crops.

The Pauma Indian Reservation, in the Pauma Valley, contains but 250 acres. Forty people live here and the excellent land is used for crops and orchards.

The Yuima Indian Reservation is part of the Pauma.

In the Rincon Indian Reservation, again along the west side of the Palomars, there are 3700 acres. The population is 110 and the land is used for grazing and orchard crops.

The La Jolla Indian Reservation on the west side of the mountains again, has 8280 acres, supports 50 people whose land is suitable for various crops and walnut orchards.

XVI THE ROADS AROUND PALOMAR

Good paved roads run into and circle this delightful mountain country. Even the unpaved roads are inviting.

Pala to Lake Henshaw. State Highway 76 runs southwest from the Indian Reservation community of Pala down along the edge of the Palomar Mountains, to Lake Henshaw and junction with State Highway 79—Moretti's Corner—beyond Monkey Hill.

Pala is the site of an *asistencia* of the Mission San Luis Rey at Oceanside. It was Father Antonio Peyri in 1816 who fashioned the sub-mission. The name Pala was taken from the local Indian word for water. The site was generously supplied.

It was for the *asistencia* here that the Indians and Spanish invaded the Palomar mountains with their oxen to haul down cedar logs.

Following secularization the condition of the Indians at Pala was reported by travelers as "heart-breaking and pitiful." The mission lands passed into private hands. The mission outpost became a ruin, visited by flood and earthquake and the gnawings of time.

In May, 1903, the Cupeño Indians were evicted from their tribal lands at Warner's Hot Springs and they made their historic and sad trek to Pala. Housing was not ready for them. Their first winter at Pala was a distressing one.

The Landmarks Club started the work of restoring the *asistencia*. In 1948 the Verona Fathers took over the outpost and have tastefully restored this little-known site along the Franciscan mission chain.

From Pala State Highway 76 runs southeast through the fertile Pauma Valley. Here are orange groves and ranches. A country club and golf course has been built.

The junction at Rincon is passed and the State Highway climbs the foothill country toward the junction with the Highway to the Stars. Beyond, along the San Luis Rey River the grade is punctuated with curves as it ascends through stands of chaparral and black oak. Here stands the Forest Service's San Luis Rey campground. Then the road drops down toward Lake Henshaw. There is a junction with the road coming down from the high ridges of Palomar. Lake Henshaw, a popular fishing and duck hunting site is passed. The dirt road on the right leads up into the Mesa Grande Indian Reservation.

The State Highway ends when it runs into State Highway 79 at Moretti's Corner at the foot of Volcan Mountain.

The Highway to the Stars. From State Highway 76 above Rincon Springs this byway built in 1935 commences a crooked route up toward Palomar's summit. There are many curves in this climb and at one such bend there is a spring where the public can stop for a drink. This spring generally runs all year and the water from it is famous. I have seen flatlanders loading up with drinking water here for it is greatly superior to the chemically-treated water we drink in our Southland cities.

Above the spring a ways is an intersection and a small village. This is called Crestline—the post office here is Palomar Mountain—and nearby, across the road, is the Forest Service's new Crestline picnic ground.

In the vicinity, in an area known locally as Bailey's, there are roughly a dozen cabins. Nearby Birch Hill supports a population of about 150 cabins. All these are on private land.

The side road to Palomar Mountain State Park takes off to-

The bell tower of the historic sub-mission at Pala.

Looking down from the Mesa Grande road toward Lake Henshaw. State Highway 76 is in the foreground.

ward the northwest from the post office site and is about three miles long. At the State Park there are three camping areas: Doane Valley, Palomar Mountain and Cedar Grove. From a lookout point back here the Nate Harrison road descends back down into the Pauma Valley.

On a side road in the area is the State Division of Forestry's Boucher Hill lookout, a tower with a view of the west edge of the Palomar Mountains and the valley country beyond.

An unpaved road runs north, past the last of the State Park units, into a beautifully unspoiled region of oak, cedars and pine. This road is gated after a short distance and there is no suitable turnaround. But it can be a pleasant hike on a cool fall or winter day, scuffing through the leaves and fallen acorns.

From the site of Crestline the road running to the north is the one to the new Forest Service campground labeled Palomar Observatory. A nature trail is planned here along the Fry Creek drainage. It is 11 miles back to the end of pavement at the actual observatory parking area. Adjacent is the Forest Service's Palomar station. An unpaved road, three miles long, leads back to the lookout at High Point. This road is gated but provides the path for an interesting hike.

The High Point lookout is quite an adventure in itself. It is 67 feet tall, and access is via a series of steep metal steps. It is frightening to many, and is apt to make you huff and puff climbing the metal tower, but the view is spectacular. The lookout is open to the public from 9 a.m. to 5 p.m. daily and there is a guest register for visitors to sign.

As with other vantage points in the Sunset Ranges, the view from this spot is noteworthy. The lookout here reported that during the big 1964 mountain fire at Santa Barbara the flames were clearly visible from High Point lookout—easily a distance of a hundred miles.

103

Looking south along attractive French Valley it is
possible to see still the great dome of the
200-inch Hale telescope.

The several private land valleys of the area are plainly discernible from here: Mendenhall Valley, Will Valley, Dyche Valley—tree-fringed and fine for grazing. The depression of Barker Valley yawns to the south marking the course of the West Fork of the San Luis Rey River as it runs southeast on its meandering course toward the sea. From here, likewise, the viewer can see the distinct mountain masses that go together here: Agua Tibia Mountain (or Mountains), the Palomar, and Aguanga Mountain being the principal landmarks.

From the Forest Service station at Palomar Mountain the dirt road runs north across private land and the picturesque French Valley area, back, across other parcels of private land, to the curious Mission Indian Reserve—actually a land withdrawal—and beyond, into the Agua Tibia Primitive Area. Eagle Crag stands here, a dramatic punctuation mark in dramatic country.

South from Crestline the mountain highway here runs past the Forest Service's Crestline campground, borders Dyche Valley—there are Indian mortars in the rocks here—runs through to Will Valley and then drops down to the junction with State Highway 76 near Lake Henshaw.

State Highway 71 and State Highway 79. Starting at the road junction southeast of Temecula, off U. S. Highway 395, Highway 71 runs east past the Forest Service's outpost at Dripping Springs —ranger station and campground—and comes to Radec. Here we pick up State Highway 79. At Aguanga, a short distance beyond, we lose State Highway 71 which curves north into the Anza, Cahuilla country.

On State Highway 79 we follow southeast now to Oak Grove, another Forest Service complex with station and campground. Oak Grove is an historic old Butterfield stage station. Always to the west lift the Aguanga-Palomar Mountains.

105

The Forest Service lookout tower on High Point is 67 feet tall.

A view of Eagle Crag in the Aqua Tibia Primitive Area.

At the turnout into Puerta La Cruz is the access into the Forest Service Hot Springs lookout high in the Los Coyotes Indian Reservation.

Equally historic is Warner Springs, way station since the days of the early Spanish explorers and on the Butterfield route. Just south of Warner's State Highway 79 bends to the southwest. We follow it on until it junctions with State Highway 76 at Moretti's Corner.

The Mesa Grande Country. Near Santa Ysabel, an *asistencia* of the parent mission at San Diego, a paved road runs northwest from State Highway 79 into the Mesa Grande Indian Reservation. The road travels through farm land and chaparral. There is a small store at Mesa Grande and beyond it the pavement curves to the northeast, providing an exceptional view of the Lake Henshaw area below. Pavement ceases after a portion of the descent, but the dirt road is a good one. The descending road is overgrown with oaks and is most attractive.

This side road ends when its gains State Highway 76 just below Lake Henshaw.

There are other unpaved roads in the Mesa Grande Indian Reservation; in fact, a small mission church lies back on one of these. But without express permission to use these side roads it is more polite to stay out.

XVII TRAILS

There are not a lot of trails in the Palomar country but the ones that are available offer hikes through some picturesque areas.

THE PRINCIPAL mountained trails in the Palomar country seem to be anchored mainly in the Agua Tibia Primitive Area. There are others. These are listed by the Forest Service:

The Magee Trail. This trail runs for about seven miles from the end of the road on Agua Tibia southwest to the Magee Ranch behind Pala. The descent is through conifers and oaks into the chaparral region. To get to the jumping off place it would be necessary to walk out to the end of the Agua Tibia Primitive Area road, a distance of about 12 miles from the end of the pavement at the Palomar ranger station.

The Mission Trail. This course takes off from a point about a mile into the Mission Indian Reserve along the Agua Tibia road. It climbs the ridge and then descends to the west to a junction with State Highway 76 north of the Pauma Valley complex. It is roughly 12 miles in length.

The Gomez Trail. Roughly parallel to the Mission Trail, above, this trail starts at the same spot but seeks a course a little to the south of the Mission Trail through the Reserve. It, too, ends at Highway 76 near Pauma Valley. Distance: nine miles.

The Section 16 Trail. This one runs from a point on the Palomar Divide Forest Service road west of the Palomar Station down to the Cutca Valley road. It is about two miles long.

The Aguanga Trail. This trail connects the Cutca Valley road with the dirt road that runs into the foothills south of Aguanga. Length: six miles.

There is a trail that starts on a point east of High Point on the Palomar Divide road and runs east across the upper end of Barker Valley into Mendenhall Valley. It ends on private land. About four miles is the distance.

The most practical way to tackle any hiking project here, of course, is to obtain a Forest Service map of the district and to talk with a ranger about the latest condition of the trail. For more detailed map information it is suggested that topographic maps issued by the U. S. Geological Survey be obtained.

XVIII INTRODUCTION TO THE JULIAN COUNTRY

Here it was the discovery of gold that brought the first pioneers into the mountain country.

FROM LAKE HENSHAW in San Diego County south to U. S. Highway 80 stretches a great arm of mountains. On the north end there is an uplift called the Volcan Mountains. A big bite is taken out of this mass by the Santa Ysabel Indian Reservation.

South from Julian the Cuyamaca Mountains march in a series of peaks. The first, North Peak, is 6000 feet high. To the south from this promontory are: Middle Peak, 5883 feet; Stonewall Peak, 5370 feet; Cuyamaca Peak, 6512 feet; Japacha Peak, 5825 feet.

Southeast of Julian runs a high ridge called the Laguna Mountains.

Scarred with many fires, this is still some of the most heavily forested mountain country in the Southland. Oaks and pines grow side by side up the green and rocky slopes. Deer are common residents in this attractive region and all the year long it is a rewarding place to visit.

The Julian area mountains, if we may call them thus, sit on the edge of history. On the desert side is the famed Carrizo Corridor, where Spanish explorers starting with Pedro Fages pushed north and west starting in 1782.

General Stephen Watts Kearny brought his Dragoons to California this way in 1846. Colonel P. St. George Cooke, with the Mormon Battalion, used the Carrizo Corridor in 1847 and when gold was discovered in California the "argonauts" came to Cali-

A view of the mountain community of Julian,
taken around 1912.

fornia by the thousands through the desert route into Warner Springs. The Butterfield Overland Mail made this southern crossing of the desert country and the passengers could look from the rocking, jouncing stages at the timbered Lagunas and Volcans to the west as the pushed up through the Corridor into the San Felipe Valley toward Warner's. The Jackass Mail used some of this country, but it actually left the Carrizo Corridor and climbed into the Lagunas on a run to San Diego. E. I. Edwards has written an exciting account of this desert area entitled *Lost Oases Along the Carrizo*.

On the west side of the mountain the early history centered around the Indians and the coming of the missionaries. From the mother mission at San Diego came priests who established the *asistencia* at Santa Ysabel in 1818 to handle the many Indians who lived on the mountain rancherias. Following secularization and the coming of the gringo the missions and *asistencias* all over the state fell into disuse. By 1850 the Santa Ysabel outpost was a ruin. The striking new chapel was erected by Fr. Edmond La Pointe in 1924. Today the Verona Fathers of Santa Ysabel serve the Indians of the reservations, Mesa Grande, Los Coyotes, Inaja, Barona, Manzanita, Sycuan and Campo.

A delightful mystery concerns the old bells of the Santa Ysabel chapel. For years after the chapel had fallen into ruins the old bells hung on a crossbar near the roadside ramada which served as a church. The local Indians held the bells in high esteem. They had bought them in the nineteenth century from the old Rosario Mission in Baja California at the cost of six burro loads of wheat and barley. These two bells at Santa Ysabel were considered the oldest in California. One was dated 1723; the other, 1767.

In 1926 the bells disappeared.

The Indians maintained the white men stole them—collectors or simply out-and-out vandals.

*Bells of Santa Ysabel—picture taken prior to bells'
disappearance in 1926. Bells were oldest of any
in California missions.*

White men in the area opined that the Indians had hauled the bells away to a more secret meeting place. I have talked with one old-timer who reports that one day while exploring an Indian cave in the Santa Rosas he discovered a large old metal bell. It was too heavy for him to move. When he went back with help years later he could not find the cave site.

But the history of this region is most firmly rooted in gold.

It was gold that opened up the mountain country, that gave birth to Julian, that started another one of those periodic mining booms that dotted the map of California after the Mother Lode strikes.

The first miners who wandered up onto the timbered walls of the Volcan Mountains shrugged and said: "This country is too beautiful to contain gold." But these men were wrong.

It was in January of 1869 when Elza Wood and a man named A. H. Coleman found traces of placer gold in a stream that won the name of Coleman Creek. Placer gold in the stream meant only one thing to these Mother Lode-wise prospectors. Something better probably lay upstream. Upstream they went that winter. Others joined the search. There are many accounts of what happened next in this bright saga. One study holds that a youngster by the name of Billy Gorman was gathering firewood in the mountains here on February 21, 1870. He found a bit of white quartz flecked with gold. The following day was George Washington's birthday and when the Gormans staked their claim they called the mine The Washington.

The first two tons of quartz ore from the Washington Mine were hauled down to San Diego and from there shipped north to the smelter in San Francisco. Some of the more spectacular bits of ore were displayed in store windows in San Diego. That was all the advertisement the country needed. The gold rush started that day.

114

*The mountain community of Julian today. Peaceful,
pleasant, a pleasure to visit.*

Miners funneled into the area from all over the West. That was the order of the day. Whenever anyone struck it rich anywhere in the country, the floating population picked up and moved. Boom camps and ghost towns came about just that way.

Drury Bailey and Mike Julian laid out a townsite in the pines and called it Julian. The prospectors searched every inch of the land, staked out claims as they crawled over the country. Some of the mines were worthless. Some would make a fortune for their owners.

Mines bearing the names of San Diego, Hayden, Owen, High Peak, Helvetia and California opened. Down the hill from Julian toward the desert, along a rough road called the Banner Grade, the Antelope, the Madden, Kentucky and Shaparell claims were filed. The Golden Chariot group, one of the Banner area's big producers, put up a stamp mill.

All kinds of characters moved into the raw camp. Saloons were built. There was hard drinking and hard words. There was gunplay, a couple of murders, a quick hanging. But Julian was never a bad town.

It was a black day however when owners of the nearby Cuyamaca land grant claimed that the golden gopherings were getting onto rancho property. Some of the miners swore they'd never pay a share to the Cuyama's owners. They pulled out. Others hired lawyers and put all their profits to fight the claim. The north end of the rancho had never been mapped. After repeated surveys of the area it was decided that the rancho ended short of the mines, a few miles south of Julian.

The boom continued in a dizzying fashion.

In a few short years the mines that sprawled from Julian north into the Wynola country and down to the east toward Banner, produced $2,500,000 in gold. The figures multiplied. One mine, the Stonewall Jackson (whose name would be changed to the

Our Lady's Grotto at Santa Ysabel Indian mission.

Fascinating historical museum at Julian is open daily during the summer months.

Stonewall later due to political feelings), was on Cuyamaca Rancho land, and was discovered by William Skidmore in 1870.

According to historian F. Harold Weber, Jr., "In 1886 Robert W. Waterman, Governor of California 1887 to 1897, purchased the Stonewall Mine . . . and from 1888 to 1891, this mine yielded gold valued at nearly $1,000,000."

Other accounts put the Stonewall's production at $2,000,000 and at $3,600,000. Later there was some reclamation of gold from tailings.

The total gold produced by the mines of the Julian area have ranged all the way from $7,500,000 by the *Julian Sentinel* in 1880, to "between $4,000,000 and $5,000,000" by more conservative accounts.

And then, almost overnight, the boom ended. When Tombstone, Arizona, had its 1880 boom, the migratory rainbow-seekers at Julian packed up again and moved east.

"When Tombstone came up, Julian went down like a punctured balloon," one historian wrote of the event.

It was not the end of the area as an attraction, however. When gold came out of the ground, settlers found that grass grew heavy and cattle could graze. Apples and pears did well here and orchards were planted.

The old mines still yawn and some owners fuss around with a little production once in a while, but the big gold mining days for Julian are behind her. Today it is a sleepy mountain community, populated by friendly people who have found that mountain living is better, somehow, and prefer the hill. Julian has the flavor of a Mother Lode town and each year it celebrates an apple festival in October and a spring wildflower event.

The Sunrise Highway down into the Laguna Mountains from Julian all the way to Highway 80 was opened prior to World War II. It gave San Diego County folks an opportunity to visit a re-

Looking east at Julian, town that once rivaled San Diego in population. Julian fought to have the county seat moved to mountain community.

gion that could know snow by winter, and the valley's snow bunnies were pleased.

Cuyamaca Rancho State Park was created in 1933. It is one of the most attractive state parks in Southern California.

From Santa Ysabel's legends, up the State Highway 78-79 into Julian, through the Wynola country, out the Banner Grade, down into the Lagunas via the Sunrise Highway or down into the Cuyamaca Rancho State Park, this is exceptionally fair mountain country.

Much of the region is managed by the U. S. Forest Service.

The Descanso District of the Cleveland National Forest. This southernmost district of California's southernmost National Forest reaches down to within seven miles of the Mexican border.

Here we are concerned with the mountain region from Julian south to U. S. Highway 80. While a small portion of this country lies within the jurisdiction of the Palomar District of the Cleveland, most of this is within the Descanso District's boundaries.

The district headquarters are located at Descanso. The office here is open seven days a week. It is to this office that you must apply for permits to use the many reservation type campgrounds —for horsemen, trailer users, organizational camps and family groups—in the Laguna Mountains. This office can also supply you with a free district map, which shows the boundaries of National Forest and State Park lands, of private and Indian Reservation lands, of the fire closures, landmarks, etc. The district ranger station, as do the smaller stations and many patrolmen, issues fire permits.

All the camping areas along the Sunrise Highway through the Laguna are on National Forest lands. Here you will find the following recreation areas:

Pioneer Mail Trail Picnic Area; Laguna Mountain Camp-

121

ground; Horse Heaven Meadow group camping area; Burnt Rancheria Campground, the Wooded Hill recreation area.

There are ranger stations in the area at Camp Ole and at Laguna Mountain.

Most of the hiking in the area is done in the Noble Canyon area. Here there is considerable cross-country hiking. There are few maintained trails in the area.

Cuyamaca Rancho State Park. See Chapter XXI.

Indian Reservations. At least four Indian Reservations touch the Julian mountain area. These include:

The Santa Ysabel Indian Reservation, which is divided into three pieces. Two of these comprise the Mesa Grande Indian Reservation. The third is the Santa Ysabel. There is a total of 15,527 acres here. Approximately 106 Indians live on the reservation lands which are used mainly for grazing.

The Inaja Indian Reservation consists of 880 acres; while the population is about 15, most of the land is made up of homesites. There is some grazing.

The Los Coyotes Indian Reservation off to the east of the Palomar Country and to the north of the Volcan Mountains, is a big region: 25,050 acres of mountain and grazing lands. Thirty people live on the Reservation. This is the original home of the Indians that were moved from Warner Springs to Pala.

The Cuyapaipe Indian Reservation is located at the southeast corner of the Laguna, mostly mountain country. There are 4100 acres in the tract but no Indians live on the reservation.

Anyone wishing to communicate with members of any of the Indian Reservations should write to the Area Field Representative, Bureau of Indian Affairs, 6848 Magnolia Ave., Riverside, Calif. This representative will put you in touch with the tribal spokesman.

XIX THE ROADS AROUND THE JULIAN COUNTRY

The San Diego County back country community of Julian has all the charm of a Mother Lode town.

STARTING at the intersection of Santa Ysabel—the rebuilt *asistencia* lies three miles to the north along State Highway 79—we pick up State Highway 78 coming up from Ramona and head up the hill.

This is the west side of Volcan Mountains here, and much of the land close at hand is within the Santa Ysabel Indian Reservation.

Ours is a wide and high-gear road. Past the Inaja Memorial Park and the site for a planned nature walk, the road climbs the side hill, curves along Coleman Creek, where that first gold was found in these mountains, and approaches another intersection community—this one is called Wynola. Nearby is a picturesque Christmas tree farm. Back on the side road—Wynola Road—here are some fine apple ranches.

The road has entered the pine area now and the change in temperature as you drive up the hill from Santa Ysabel is pronounced.

Here is the side road to the right into the Pine Hills area and beyond down into the Boulder Creek or Engineers Road region. The State Highways 78-79 enters Julian from the south, passes the Julian museum, open Saturdays and Sundays and holidays. You'll find an interesting assortment of Julian area memorabilia here.

The community, as we have said elsewhere, is strongly reminiscent of a Mother Lode town. The people are quiet and friendly.

123

*A fairly recent picture of the new chapel at the site
of the old asistencia at Santa Ysabel.*

There are grocery stores, a drug store, several small restaurants and gasoline stations.

From the main intersection a road runs to the west.

Farmer Road. This side road runs west, past the hilltop Julian cemetery, along a canyon and past some ranches. There is a large apple ranch back here, a sawmill and some smaller orchards. Wynola Road comes in from the west. Farmer Road jogs. The spur of Wynola Road that runs on to the east connects with the Banner Grade. The jog of Farmer Road that runs to the north deadends at an organizational camp.

From Julian the twin state highways run east and fork. State Highway 78 runs down the Banner Grade, a gradually steepening road that follows the side of Banner Canyon, passes some old gold mines and prospect holes, finally gets to the floor of the valley. Here is the store-gasoline station outpost of Banner and the Banner Queen Guest Ranch. This road runs on east through the San Felipe Valley, past Scissors Crossing into the Anza-Borrego Desert State Park area.

From the fork at the edge of town State Highway 79 runs south into the Cuyumaca Rancho State Park. (See Chapter XXI.)

XX THE LAGUNA MOUNTAINS

A long ridge of pine-covered mountains stands as barrier along the western edge of the Colorado Desert.

LAGUNA is a Spanish word meaning lake. How then did a desert-bordering mountain range deep in San Diego County gain the name Laguna?

The answer is simple. Once there were a pair of small lakes here atop the mountain country. The Laguna Lakes—Little Laguna Lake and Big Laguna Lake—appear on some maps today but for most of the year, particularly during these cyclic years of drought, the little lakes are dry.

Still they were landmarks in the 1870's when the mountains were named.

Mountains like the Lagunas are not uncommon in California and yet, because of their contrasts, they are surprising. There are pines atop the Death Valley-edging Panamints; the Santa Rosa Mountain-Toro Peak complex sticks out into the Colorado Desert, and again here can be found tall pines. So it is in the Lagunas. From vista points here it is possible to see deep into the Anza-Borrego Desert State Park wilderness—the rawest kind of desert country. Still there are pines here, snow whitens the land by winter, rainfall runs as high as 40 inches a season.

Because of the lofty contrasts this has become an enormously popular recreation region—particularly by summer. And the Forest Service has gone to great lengths to make the mountain country attractive. There are viewpoints, picnic areas, campgrounds,

126

campgrounds for organizational groups, campgrounds for trailer campers.

There is good reason for the popularity of the Laguna Mountain area.

Let us start our exploration of the area at the north end, at the fork in the roads at Cuyamaca Reservoir, where State Highway 79 angles to the right and runs through the State Park, and where the Sunrise Highway bends away to the southeast.

The Sunrise Highway. This byway runs through private land and some Bureau of Land Management lands on its course now. Here is grazing land and some unimproved chaparral country. There are glimpses of the desert country off to the east. On crystal clear days, such as those during or just following a Santa Ana windstorm, the Salton Sea can be spotted from this area.

Garnet Mountain, elevation 5665 feet, stands off of the highway on the desert side and below is Oriflamme Canyon, one of the reputed routes for those who came up from the Vallecito country seeking the hills of San Diego.

The entrance into National Forest land is spectacular. The road rounds a bluff where the highway has dramatically been chiseled from rock. Just within the boundary is the Pioneer Mail Trail Picnic Area, a small but pleasant site in a stand of trees. The name pays homage to the crossing here of the 1857 Jackass Mail on its way to San Diego.

Beyond is Garnet Peak, 5909 feet, and a ridiculous and confusing choice of place names: Garnet Mountain and Garnet Peak side by side.

Off to the left is one of the mining areas in the district. Here are some tungsten prospects—the Sundown Mine. A jeep road leads back into Indian Creek.

This marker honoring the "Jackass Mail" stands alongside the Sunrise Highway. Route in 1857 was one of the first via which mail from the east came to San Diego.

128

The motor scooter type of conveyance is allowed in the area—it must have an approved spark arrester—but the unlicensed variety is prohibited in the campgrounds. Best check with a ranger for where you can and where you can't go with your Tote Gote or Honda.

To the left here is a Penny Pines plantation—the Penny Pines idea originated in San Diego County.

That small forest of aerials off to the right is the Air Force's GATR installation.

Here is another fine overlook into the desert region. Beyond a ways we come to the Sierra Club's mountaintop outpost—Guymon Lodge.

On the right now is one of the Forest Service's finest new campgrounds; this one is named the Laguna Campground and within its area, but on private land, are the small lakes that gave the region is unusual title.

This is a charge campground and it is closed in winter. Here you'll find the Meadow Trailer Loop, the El Prado Cabin camping area, the El Prado group camp area, the Big Sage group camp area, the Shady Loop camping area, the Sunny Loop camping area, the Roadside Loop picnic area.

The group camps are available by reservation only.

Here is a rustic log seat amphitheatre where on Saturday nights during the summer months a ranger-naturalist conducts evening lecture programs. Frequently the merchants of the Laguna Mountains area donate marshmallows so that youngsters in the lecture audience can have a pre-lecture marshmallow roast over the friendly fire ring.

You will notice many private cabins on your drive through the Laguna area. Some of these are on private land, some are on special use permit with the Forest Service.

Part of the radar complex at the Air Force's installation at Mt. Laguna.

Horse Heaven Meadow is a group camp and for use of this attractive site it is necessary to make reservations with the Forest Service at the Descanso Ranger Station in advance. This is also a charge camp, and there are fire rings for each of the camps. No horses are allowed in Horse Heaven—that local place name pixie at work again.

Camp Ole is the major Forest Service station and work area in the region.

On the opposite side of the road, out on the side of Mt. Laguna, is the Mt. Laguna Air Force Station—a radar site. The peak to the north here, also with a cluster of electronics on top, is Monument Peak. Mt. Laguna's other name is Stephenson Peak.

About four or five week ends out of the winter season the Laguna Mountains have snow on the ground. This is the beginning of the snow area.

On a spur up behind the Air Force installation—you'll see the sign on the highway pointing to it—is Desert View Point (or Vista) and the Desert View Picnic Area.

Now we pass the Laguna ranger station, manned on week ends in the summer as an information post, and then come to the Laguna Mountain Lodge, the post office of Mt. Laguna, a store, etc. Toboggans are rented here in the winter, and while there is no regularly developed snow play area in the mountain region, snow bunnies find many places to slide down small hills. The elevation here is roughly 6000 feet.

There are other businesses here in the community of Mt. Laguna —store, restaurants, riding stables (open only in the summer), etc.

Then, on the left, is the Burnt Rancheria Campground, another Forest Service installation. Also a charge campground, Burnt Rancheria, offers trailer camping and conventional camping. The Cuyapaipe Indian Reservation lies off to the desert side of the mountains here.

The Sunrise Highway curves toward the west and we come to the Wooded Hill recreational complex. Here is the Forest Service's Wooded Hill Nature Trail, the Agua Dulce walk-in campground for both small organizational groups and for families. The walk-in idea is new on this National Forest. The camper leaves his car in a parking area, carries his dunnage for a walk of about 15 minutes to a camping area. There are toilets, stove, tables and water in the camping area. It has proved quite successful with visitors here.

All the facilities here are on a reservation basis—contact the Descanso station.

This ends the recreational facilities of the Lagunas.

The road descends toward U. S. Highway 80, runs out of pines in chaparral, offers a view of the old road in Scove Canyon below to the west. Then Laguna Junction and State Highway 80 is gained and the Sunrise Highway has run its course.

Statistics indicate that most of the users of the Laguna Mountains come from San Diego and the Imperial Valley areas.

Highway 80. If you would explore on south on U. S. Highway 80 you'll find the road drops sharply, passes a couple of older—no charge—campgrounds at Glencliff and Boulder Oaks. There is a rest area on the left, where the weary traveler coming in from the desert will find shade, water, picnic tables, toilets, etc., and a graphic explanation of a vast and dramatic land conversion project being undertaken by the Forest Service. Here, in Cameron Valley, the brush has been cleared in an effort to create a barrier against fire, grass has been planted and the entire complexion of the land has been altered. The main aim: good fire prevention.

To the west of Laguna Junction U. S. Highway 80 runs through the inviting, modern, well-kept and attractive community of Pine Valley, to Guatay and on to a junction with State Highway 79 coming down through Cuyamaca Rancho State Park.

This stretch of U. S. Highway 80 will be replaced by a freeway within the next few years.

A dead pine tree stands on guard in Cuyamaca Rancho State Park.

XXI THE CUYAMACA RANCHO STATE PARK

A gold mine, a battle of a boundary, Indian names give color to this mountain region.

YOU CAN find evidences of Indians in countless places in this mountain region. Bedrock mortars have been found in boulders. Arrowheads have been discovered here—beautiful works of the arrowmakers' skill. Indian names are on the land.

The word Cuyamaca is an Indian word meaning, probably, "rain above" or something very similar. It is pronounced by the old-timers as "Queermack," which sounds as much like the spelling of the old Indian word for the place as the present spelling.

Don Augustin Olvera filed for petition for the lands here in 1845. He asked for 35,501 acres and proposed to call the rancho the Cuyamaca. Rejected in 1845 the petition was granted in 1858 by district court. When gold was discovered in the Julian district a dispute arose as to whether the diggings were on rancho land. As the boundaries of the rancho had never been painstakingly mapped, it took prolonged legal jousting and surveying to find out that the Cuyamaca Rancho ended seven miles south of the mines.

Gold ore was discovered on rancho property in 1870 by William Skidmore and the name Stonewall Jackson was tacked onto the claim. But it wasn't until California's Governor Robert Whitney Waterman acquired title to the rancho that the mine was operated.

A big mill was built on the site and between 1888 and 1891 the Stonewall was a good producer.

135

*An 1890 photograph of the old Stonewall Mine
on the Cuyamaca Rancho. Mine produced
gold ore that totaled into the millions.*

*Team-drawn scrapers used to help reclaim tailings
line up in front of the Stonewall Mine on
Cuyamaca Rancho in this photograph
taken around 1900.*

—Photo courtesy Title Insurance and Trust Co., San Diego

When the Jackass Mail from San Antonio ran through to San Diego, California, in 1857, it was up from the desert and across a section of this land that the track followed. One of the way stations was the Lassator Ranch stop, a stone outpost near the present Indian Exhibit building on state park property.

Governor Waterman, who owned all the rancho after the gold boom, died in 1892. The Stonewall Mine became the property of the Sather Banking Co. of San Francisco. In 1918 it was sold to Colonel A. G. Gassen, who died in 1920. In 1923 the estate was purchased by Mr. and Mrs. Ralph M. Dyar who spent $75,000 on improvements on the property—including the building of an attractive home—during the following ten years. In March, 1933, they sold the 20,000-acre rancho to the state of California at about half of the land's appraised value. The State Park was thus created.

Today there are 166 individual campsites in the park, 145 picnic units, 50 miles of riding and hiking trails.

The Cuyamaca Rancho State Park lies essentially in a wooded mountain area with several tall peaks. It is a region of chaparral in the lower elevations, of several types of oaks including the beautiful black oak. Among the conifers are sugar pine, ponderosa pine, Coulter and Jeffrey pines. Here, too, are cedars and the white fir.

Along stream bottoms will be found willows, alders, sycamores.

In 1950 a great fire exploded across the old rancho. Before control the conflagration had burned 10,000 acres. Scars of the fire and the snags of the burned trees can be seen from State Highway 79, which threads through the Park, near the north end on Middle Peak and Cuyamaca Peak.

The Forest Service maintains a lookout in a 35-foot tower atop Cuyamaca Peak. A great region of land to the west of the tower is within the administration of the Forest Service.

Starting at Julian and driving out to the fork in the road where State Highways 78 and 79 separate, we follow the latter south

The old Dyar home has been made into an Indian exhibit hall in Cuyamaca Rancho State Park.

through pleasant rural country where there are small homesites, some grazing, some chaparral. On the west the densely forested bulk of North Peak stands close at hand.

There is a side road on the right into Harrison Park, a small collection of private residences.

There is a fork of the road here. The Sunrise Highway bears off to the left and runs down through the Laguna Mountains and through a developed Forest Service recreation area on to U. S. Highway 80. (See Chapter XX.)

The road to the right curves around North Peak. The meadowland straight ahead is the bed of the Cuyamaca Reservoir, created when an earthen dam was fashioned here in 1886. Before the site had been known as Cuyamaca Lake—the Indians admitted that it only had water in it "sometimes." The Spanish term for the site was *la laguna que de seco*—the lake that dries up.

The San Diego Flume Co. in 1886 built 31 miles of wooden flume down from the newly dammed reservoir to San Diego via the El Cajon Valley. The reservoir is owned now by the Helix Irrigation System, and the lake seldom has much water in it.

The road makes a curve here. On the right is paved road leading to the west side of North Peak.

Engineers Road. The first short distance of the side road is paved. Mostly it is unpaved as it runs through private property but some very attractive woodlands through to Pine Hills ranger station on the Boulder Creek Road. From this point this dirt road runs north, through the edge of the fashionable Pine Hills residential area, on to State Highway 78-79 just west of Julian.

Past the turnoff into Engineers Road State Highway 79 runs south now, enters the enormously attractive Cuyamaca Rancho State Park.

Almost from the beginning you'll notice a difference here. No

*Ruins of some of the old mining equipment
at the Stonewall Mine in
Cuyamaca Rancho State Park.*

signs, no billboards, in most places even the telephone lines are routed away from the road.

You pass through pleasant meadowland. The Los Caballos Camp and the park's horseman's group camp lie off to the east here. Both of these camps for horsemen are considered fine examples of how such recreational facilities should be designed. There are individual corrals for horses, tie racks, loading ramps. For the campers there are stoves, toilets, piped water. There is a small charge. Reservations are required.

That rock-topped mountain off to the southeast now is Stonewall Peak which is named after the old Stonewall Mine. A spur road runs back to the mine site.

There is a gentle trail from the park headquarters site up to the top of "Old Stony," as the peak is called.

At the park headquarters you can obtain a free information brochure with a good map of the park. At hand is the Paso Pichacho Campground. There is a use charge. Also from this area the truck trail takes off for the climb up to the lookout tower atop Cuyamaca Peak. Many make the hike up the three-mile road but it is steep. The lookout tower, open to the public from 9 a.m. to 5 p.m., offers an impressive view of much of Southern California.

South still on State Highway 79 we come to the site of the old Dyar home, which has been converted into an exhibition hall for various Indian artifacts found in the area. The home is made of native stone, some of the old rocks coming from the Lassator Jackass Mail depot that stood nearby. The beams are native oak.

There are three organizational camps within the park.

On south, still on State Highway 79, we reach the park's other major campground. This one, named Green Valley, offers both camping and picnicking. There is a small charge for either.

A trail leaves from this site to the Green Valley Falls. No swimming is allowed in the park.

South of the Green Valley area State Highway 79 runs south, leaves the park, follows through chaparral and oakgrown canyon areas to the Descanso area.

Cuyamaca Rancho State Park is a well-tended, woodsy wonderland for the half million people who pass through or use the facilities each year. The region gets as much as 40 inches of rain during wet winters, and snow stands here briefly.

Deer roam freely in the park and exotics such as ring-tailed cats have been seen in addition to the more common wildlife varieties such as coyotes, mountain lion, foxes, raccoons, possums, gray squirrels, etc. Beaver have been introduced to the park and are thriving. The hawks here are fat and bold. Rattlesnakes are found in the park in the summer months. The park is noted for its varieties of wildflowers.

In wetter seasons portions of the Sweetwater River are stocked with fish.

For inquiries about use of the park facilities, including organizational camps, write the Superintendent, Cuyamaca Rancho State Park, P. O. Box 338, Julian, Calif.

BIBLIOGRAPHY

Cowan, Robert G., *Ranchos of California,* Fresno, California, Academy Library Guild, 1956.

Cunningham, Glenn, editor, *Day Tours, Geographical Journeys in the Los Angeles Area,* Palo Alto, Pacific Books, 1964.

Desert Magazine articles, various.

Edwards, E. I., *Lost Oases Along the Carrizo,* Los Angeles, Westernlore Press, 1961.

Gudde, Erwin G., *California Place Names,* Berkeley, University of California Press, 1960.

Hanna, Phil Townsend, *California Through Four Centuries,* New York, Farrar and Rinehart, 1935.

Hughes, Tom, *History of Banning and the San Gorgonio Pass,* Banning, Calif., Banning *Record,* n.d.

James, Harry C., *The Cahuilla Indians,* Los Angeles, Westernlore Press, 1960.

Layne, J. Gregg, *Western Wayfaring,* Los Angeles, Automobile Club of Southern California, 1954.

Leadabrand, Russ, *Westways,* Los Angeles, various articles.

Robinson, W. W., *The Story of Riverside County,* Los Angeles, Title Insurance and Trust Co., 1957.

Ruby, Jay W., *Aboriginal Uses of Mt. San Jacinto State Park,* Archaeological Survey, Annual Report, Department of Anthropology and Sociology, University of California, Los Angeles, 1962.

San Bernardino National Forest Multiple Use Management Plan, San Jacinto Ranger District, San Bernardino, U. S. Forest Service, 1961.

Saunders, Charles Francis, *The Southern Sierras of California,* New York, Houghton Mifflin Co., 1923.

Stephenson, Terry E., *Shadows of Old Saddleback,* Santa Ana, Calif., Santa Ana High School and Junior College, 1931.

Weber, F. Harold Jr., *Mines and Mineral Resources of San Diego County, California,* San Francisco, California Division of Mines and Geology, 1963 (paper).

Wilson, Neill C., and Taylor, Frank J., *Southern Pacific,* New York, McGraw-Hill Book Co., 1951.

Wilts, Chuck, *A Climber's Guide of Tahquitz Rock,* Glendale, Calif., La Siesta Press, 1962.